D1130701

PACIFIC GLORY

**Center Point
Large Print**

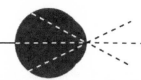

**This Large Print Book carries the
Seal of Approval of N.A.V.H.**

PACIFIC GLORY

P. T. DEUTERMANN

CENTER POINT PUBLISHING
THORNDIKE, MAINE

This Center Point Large Print edition
is published in the year 2011 by arrangement with
St. Martin's Press.

The text of this Large Print edition is unabridged.
In other aspects, this book may vary
from the original edition.
Printed in the United States of America
on permanent paper.
Set in 16-point Times New Roman type.

ISBN: 978-1-61173-062-3

Library of Congress Cataloging-in-Publication Data

Deutermann, Peter T., 1941–
Pacific glory / P. T. Deutermann.
p. cm.
ISBN 978-1-61173-062-3 (library binding : alk. paper)
1. United States. Navy—Fiction.
2. World War, 1939–1945—Naval operations, American—Fiction.
3. Large type books. I. Title.
PS3554.E887P33 2011b
813'.54—dc22

2011000394

To Vice Admiral Edward S. Briggs,
U.S. Navy (Ret.),
once a prince, always a prince

ACKNOWLEDGMENTS

I want to thank my editor, George Witte, and my copy editor, India Cooper, for their substantial help in scrubbing the manuscript. As always, they make me look better than I am at this business. My father, Vice Admiral H. T. Deutermann, is long gone, but he felt passionately about what happened off Samar in October 1944, and this was the spark, I think, that ultimately led to this book.

Pearl Harbor, Hawaii

My son who wasn't really my son steered the boat around the western edge of Ford Island, bringing into view the distant naval shipyard, its dock cranes festooned in blinking red aircraft-warning lights.

He was such a handsome young man, both hands on the wheel, big, tall, and spread-legged at the console, every inch the successful lawyer, husband, and father, confidently enjoying yet another of Oahu's perpetually perfect evenings.

"Anywhere along here," I called up to him from the drinking deck.

He put the thirty-six-footer into neutral, then reverse, and let her idle down to a stop about two hundred yards off the rusting, gull-splattered battleship moorings. A moment later, as she gathered bare sternway, he hit the button to drop the anchor, then shut down the engines. He went forward, checked the anchor, and joined me back aft. He topped up my Scotch and then his.

"I gave her full scope," he said. "Deep here."

"Good idea," I said. "People forget—Pearl Harbor's a drowned crater."

He sat back in his deck chair, tipped his glass in a casual salud, and enjoyed my single malt. I tipped my claw in his direction and did the same. He frowned at my stainless steel appendage.

"They make such good prostheses these days," he said. "I can't believe you want to keep that thing."

I smiled in the growing darkness. "Koa wood peg leg, surgical steel claw? Aa-a-r-r, matey. All I need is an eye patch, an insolent parrot, and a bit more hair. Make all the pretty girls shiver their timbers—and other things."

He laughed. "Used to make us kids shiver, too," he said, "but for different reasons." He sipped some more Scotch, then put down his glass.

"So," he said. "You've flown all the way out from the East Coast. Great to see you, as always, but what's the occasion?"

"I need to give you some news and tell you a story," I said.

He frowned again. Being a lawyer, he probably did that a lot. People rarely brought good news to a lawyer. "You're okay?" he asked. "Mom? Health issues?"

"We're fine," I said. "Nothing like that. No, this goes back to the war, and even a few years before. First the news."

"Okay," he said expectantly.

I took a deep breath. "I need to make a confession of sorts, and to tell you a very personal story."

"A confession?" he asked, frowning. He was a

corporate law guy, and for just a second, he'd dropped back into professional character.

"Yeah," I said, "but not about a crime. Like I said, this goes back to the war."

He looked away for a moment, staring off across the dark reaches of the harbor, toward the reed swamps of the Waipio Peninsula and the baleful sodium vapor lights of the naval ammunition depot.

"Am I going to like this story?"

"You need to hear it. I'll let you decide how you feel about it. Is there more of that Scotch in the locker?"

"The world's supply," he said, settling into his chair.

The world's supply, I thought. His father used to say that.

ONE

Guadalcanal, August 1942

"Mister Marshall Vincent, I'm ready to relieve you, sir."

"Mister John O'Connor. I'm so *very* glad you're here, sir."

"I'll bet you are," Jack said. "Still, the midwatch is no lovely prospect, either. What've we got?"

They were standing on the port side of the

pilothouse, turning over the Officer of the Deck watch of the heavy cruiser USS *Winston.* Two more officers were doing the same thing a few feet away, turning over the junior OOD watch. Across the darkened pilothouse, the captain was dozing in his chair, which meant that all the watch standers were keeping their voices down. You didn't wake sleeping dogs, and you sure as hell didn't wake Captain Archibald Corley McClain III, not if you could help it.

Marsh recited the tactical situation. "Steaming in column formation, with *Vincennes* ahead and *Astoria* astern, two thousand yards interval. Darkened ship, battle condition II, modified material condition Zebra. Course three one zero, speed ten. *Quincy* is guide, and OTC is CO *Chicago.*"

"*Chicago?*" Jack said. "I thought the officer in tactical command was the Brit admiral in HMS *Australia.*"

"He and *Australia* apparently went to Tulagi for some kind of conference. That left *Chicago* as senior ship. There's another group of cruisers south of us, but nobody's told us where or who's in charge."

"Wonderful," Jack said. "Any night orders from *Chicago?*"

"Nope," Marsh said. "We haven't heard a word from them."

"Hearing from *anybody?*"

"Hourly radio checks, but just routine. We've got troops on the beach at Tulagi and over on Guadalcanal proper. That's all we know right now."

"Okay," Jack said, shaking his head. "What else you got for me?"

Marsh knew it was a pretty thin turnover, but the troops had just gone in a few days before, and it looked to them that the top brass were playing it by ear until the Japs responded in force to the landings. They'd sent one air strike already the previous afternoon, and one of the big transports was still burning to the south, the fire reflecting off the low overcast hugging the sound.

"The nearest hazard to navigation is Savo Island, bearing two five zero, eight miles. Visibility is darker than a well-digger's ass, and, so far, no Japs."

"That we know of," Jack said.

"That we know of," Marsh agreed. "And if they come, let us pray that they come in daylight."

They'd been briefed at an all-officers meeting earlier that a Jap task force had been spotted the day before, headed down from Rabaul toward the Slot, a narrow body of water running the length of the Solomon Islands. That could well put them off Guadalcanal sometime soon. As everyone knew, Jap cruisers tended to go fast.

"If they do come tonight, hopefully our two radar-equipped tin cans will see 'em."

"Amen to that," Jack said. "Picket stations?"

"*Blue* is out there somewhere to the northwest, above Savo. *Ralph Talbot* is northeast of Savo. They both have radar. We had one TBS check with *Blue* an hour ago. Lousy comms, but nothing to report."

They then reviewed the status of the main battery guns and the engineering plant. Nothing had changed since supper. "Okay, Beauty," he said. "I've got it. See you in six."

"I stand relieved," Marsh said and handed over the heavy 7 × 50 Bausch & Lomb binoculars. Then he turned toward the dark figures behind the helm and lee helm consoles. "Attention in the pilothouse: Mister O'Connor has the deck," he announced as quietly as he could.

There was a chorus of equally quiet aye-aye-sirs from the rest of the bridge watch. Marsh checked to make sure the captain was still asleep and then made his way aft to the door leading into the charthouse. The night was warm and muggy, and the darkness was absolute, with only the dimmed red lights from the companionway below showing as he went through the door. He hadn't been kidding about a night encounter with Jap cruisers. As assistant gunnery officer, he knew *Winston*'s gun director optics were no match for the comparable Japanese equipment, not to mention that their cruisers were faster and better armed than the Americans.

He smiled as he went below. Jack had called him Beauty. He'd acquired that nickname during plebe year at the Naval Academy, back in 1928. Marsh was not a handsome man. In fact, "homely" would probably be the kindest description of his facial features. He was not quite six feet tall and had large ears and a long face with a bit of a lantern jaw, topped by an unruly shock of black hair that ended in a widow's peak between friendly farm-boy blue eyes. The day the brigade of upperclassmen returned to Bancroft Hall after their summer cruise, a firstie slammed into their plebe room, looked the fresh meat over while they stood at rigid, sweaty attention, focused on Marsh, and said, "Aren't you a regular beauty." There it was, forever and ever.

He got down to the main interior passageway and slipped awkwardly through the scuttle in the armored hatch. His eyes were heavy, and he made his way to his stateroom like a zombie. See you in six, Jack had said. With the ship at battle condition II, everyone aboard was standing port and starboard watches now, six hours on, six off. That routine had Marsh dragging his ass. Right now he had the slightly better deal, with the 0600 to noon watch in the morning, six hours off, then the eighteen to midnight. That sequence roughly lined up with his normal circadian rhythms. Jack had the noon to eighteen and then the dreaded midwatch, midnight to six in the morning, extended until the ship stood down from dawn general quarters. Still, they both had it better than the poor bastard Marines who were clinging to Henderson Field as hordes of insane Jap infantry gathered to probe their strength.

Winston's main battery of eight-inchers was manned up, with the gun crews permitted to "rest" on station in the gun turrets, handling rooms, and magazines. The ship was mostly buttoned up, with only certain scuttles open in the otherwise dogged-down armored hatches belowdecks. It was like an oven down below in officers' country with all the big hatches locked down, especially since their ventilators were running on low speed so that the big enlisted berthing compartments farther forward got more air.

Marsh made a pit stop at the forward officers' head to off-load six hours' worth of coffee and then went to his so-called stateroom. He kicked off his sea boots and dropped into the lower rack fully clothed. He and Jack O'Connor were roommates. The stateroom, which was eight feet long and five feet wide down on the second deck, was just aft and starboard of turret two's barbette. It actually had a porthole, but that, too, was dogged down. Marsh thought about opening it anyway to relieve the awful, sweaty South Pacific heat but settled for locking back the stateroom door and pulling the privacy curtain across. Then he fell back into his rack.

He was a long way from San Diego, both in time and distance. His mother still lived there; his father had passed on after a heart attack three years ago. Marsh had been born and raised there in the north county, in the village of Escondido, and had gone off to the academy in 1928, courtesy of an appointment from his father's law partner, now a congressman. Since graduation in '32 he'd been at sea on various ships in the Pacific Fleet, keeping his head down from the ravages of what they were calling the Great Depression. Many of his classmates had been forced out of the service because of the Navy's budget problems, and those who'd been retained had had their pay cut. He felt that it was fortunate he hadn't married, and often wondered how the guys who did get married made ends meet.

He'd only been in *Winston* for three months when the battle fleet was moved to Pearl. They'd just finished a shipyard overhaul and didn't come out until right after the attack on December 7. Now they were boring holes in the ocean in the steaming darkness around the island of Guadalcanal, a word none of them had even heard until a few months ago. Marsh didn't know which Navy headquarters genius had picked this hellhole to make a stand, but he fervently wished whoever it was could be sent out here to enjoy some six on, six off watches with the rest of them. He could smell the sweat that had his khaki uniform stuck to 90 percent of his body. One of the ship's two freshwater evaporators was on the blink, so the whole crew was on water-hours, which meant one shower was allowed every three days. That was a Navy shower: Water on, water off. Soap down. Water on, water off. Out you get. He thought about sneaking down to the head to get a quick rinse and then was instantly asleep.

He dreamed that he was flying and then woke up with the sudden pain of crashing onto the steel deck next to his bed, the echoes of a huge explosion compressing his eardrums while the ship heeled over to starboard and then rolled back upright, covering him in personal gear, loose paperwork, and upset chairs. A fine acrid and oily mist suffused the air. As he tried to get up from under all the clutter, the ship was hit again. At that instant he was on all fours, and the steel deck tried hard to break both his wrists and knees. He yelled with the shock of it and flopped over on his side. This time the ship didn't heel over very much. He sensed that there was something significant about that, but his sleep-doped brain was too confused to focus. Then he heard men shouting out in the passageway, followed by a sudden roar of escaping steam coming from somewhere back aft. He thought he could hear the general quarters bugle alarm sounding above that thundering steam leak.

He couldn't use his hands, and both his

kneecaps crackled in pain. He had to pry himself upright with his elbows. He grabbed for his kapok life jacket and battle helmet and dropped both of them when his hands turned to hot rubber. He felt the forward eight-inchers let go up above, their familiar rippling thumps almost drowned out by the steam eruption amidships. More men were yelling out in the main passageway, and he had to hang on to an overturned chair just to stand up. He felt a wave of bowel-liquefying fear sweep through him as he realized *Winston* wasn't coming back upright. Instead she seemed to be slowing in the seaway and listing ominously to port, her main hull girders groaning and grinding beneath him.

Marsh's general quarters station was Sky One, which was a forward five-inch gun director located high up on the superstructure above the bridge. Still hanging on with one elbow, he struggled into his life jacket and tied off the straps, using his better hand and his teeth. His battle helmet had disappeared, so he gave up on that and pushed back through the curtain into the passageway, only to be bowled over by a crowd of damage control repair-party men hustling aft, already masked up and unrolling fire hose in sodden canvas loops. He realized he was still in his socks and ducked back into the stateroom to stuff his feet into his sea boots. He thought he could hear the crack and banging of the five-inch secondary battery guns between salvos of the eight-inchers. Goddamned Japs must be pretty close, he thought. He knew he had to get topside on the double, but getting to his GQ station would require climbing some exterior ladders. There was no way in hell he'd be able to do that: His hands didn't work, and his kneecaps were grinding as he tried to walk across the slanting deck.

He followed the repair-party crowd back toward the main watertight hatch leading topside, realizing as he went that he seemed to be climbing. Then he was shocked to find that they were all sloshing through seawater. That meant she was settling by the bow as well as listing over to port. He actually didn't believe it until he saw a loose battle lantern lying on the deck, its light shimmering through the water.

Great God, he thought: If the second deck is flooding, she's done for.

"Now all hands, abandon ship, abandon ship," came over the ship's announcing system. The words were barely audible above the roar of escaping steam and the rising pandemonium around the forward hatch. The repair-party men dropped all their firefighting gear and began to bunch up at the top of the ladder, where only one man at a time could pass through the round scuttle. Marsh felt the water tugging at his shins and filling his sea boots. He had to jam a forearm into another cableway to keep from falling over.

20

Everyone froze for an instant when the sound of incoming shells screamed through the air topside, followed by the crash of several hits on the armor belt and one huge explosion that rattled the big ladder in front of them on its latch pins. Then everybody was heaving and pushing to get to the scuttle, and there were even more men clawing their way back from the bow to get to that hatch.

"Undog the goddamned hatch," Marsh heard himself shout. "Next guy through, undog the hatch!"

The man at the top of the ladder turned to stare at him for an instant, then nodded and lifted himself through. Another brace of explosions rocked the ship, and they could hear the sound of steel shards whining through the compartments above them, starting a horrible chorus of screams topside. All the red passageway lights blinked out, leaving only two battle lanterns switched on near the ladder. Two more men made it through the scuttle. Marsh decided to just stand aside and let the panicking sailors fight their way up the ladder, everyone yelling at the man ahead of him to move it, move it. His hands were going numb, and it took everything he could do just to stand upright. Then the hatch lifted, and suddenly the men could go up two and three abreast. The water was thigh deep now on the second deck, and the ship was over at least ten degrees to port. He wondered if she would capsize before he got his turn on the ladder. There was light now that the big hatch was open, but it was the searing orange light of a gasoline fire, not battle lanterns.

He finally joined the diminishing stream of men clawing their way up the canting ladder, letting them push him along rather than trying to climb it. The moment he stumbled out into the main passageway from the hatch alcove, he was knocked flat on his stomach by a huge sailor who was running for his life with his eyes squeezed shut. An instant later, a half-dozen more incoming shells hit the superstructure, which was starting to hang over the water like the Leaning Tower of Pisa. One shell went off in the ship's post office, thirty feet forward of where Marsh lay on the deck. Shrapnel flailed the passageway in both directions, cutting men down everywhere, followed by a noxious cloud of smoke and burning paper. He tried to get up but was flattened again by another sailor who landed on top of him, screaming in his ear and bleeding all over him. Without the use of his hands and forearms, Marsh couldn't move. Another salvo of incoming shells hit along the port side, and he was suddenly grateful for the human cover when once again a hail of steel shards ricocheted all along the main passageway. He actually felt the man on top of him get hit and go limp.

Can't stay here, he thought. Have to get outside.

He humped his back to dislodge the wounded

man on top of him. Then he started crawling on his belly over the bodies, now all piled up on the port side of the passageway as the ship leaned into her death roll. He was clambering as much on the bulkhead as the deck because of her list, and his teeth were chattering in fear. He could feel his hands splashing through a stream of blood and worse things as he slithered like a snake toward the nearest main deck hatch. Another barrage of howling shells slammed into the ship. He could hear the thunder of shell-splash water landing on the deck outside the hatch from the near misses. Each hit felt like a punch into his own guts, and he almost vomited in sheer terror.

A dead man was draped across the hatch operating handle, and the hatch itself was perforated with dozens of holes, through which bright white light now blazed into the smoke-shrouded passageway. Marsh nudged the corpse aside and lifted the handle with his shoulder. The hatch swung out by gravity, and, because of the extreme list, he fell through it and slid across the teak deck into the lower part of the lifelines.

He was blinded as the blue-white light from the sixty-inch carbon-arc searchlight of a Jap cruiser lit them up like some kind of baleful ogre eye. The steam escaping from ruptured lines in the engineering spaces drowned out every other sound, including the screams of the wounded littering the deck, their faces contorted in that harsh white light. There was a big gasoline fire amidships where the scout planes were stored, and another one forward, probably from the avgas storage tanks. The water was enveloping the bow by now, and the fire was turning into a cloud of orange-tinged steam. A wave came out of nowhere and buried him, which was when he realized that the portside main deck edge was fully awash. She'll roll at any second now, he thought. Go. Go now.

He took a deep breath, pushed his head and life jacket through the lifelines, and slipped gratefully into the sea. He sensed that there were others doing the same thing. Then he saw one man helping a wounded shipmate through the lifelines. A part of his brain scolded him: As an officer, he should have been doing that, but he was just too damned scared. When his head popped up above the water, he felt the full weight of *Winston*'s gutted forward superstructure hanging over him. There was an avalanche of things falling into the sea from where the bridge had been: signal books, battle lanterns, coffee mugs, binoculars, bodies and body parts, all accompanied by a small blizzard of paper. The roar of steam from amidships suddenly cut off, just as a severed head popped to the surface right in front of him, revealing Jack's chalky face. Marsh cried out in horror, inhaling a mouthful of oily seawater in the process.

The Jap cruiser closed in abeam. They'd turned the targeting searchlight off, and now she looked like a long black dragon, so close that her bridge windows reflected the orange glow from *Winston*'s fires. Marsh could see their topside antiaircraft gun crews staring over at the wreck of the *Winston*. Her towering pagoda masts were clearly illuminated as her gun turrets flashed red and yellow again, fore and aft, followed by the thumping pressure of her muzzle blasts. This time all of the rounds went shrieking over their heads and into the darkness beyond as the bulk of *Winston*'s hull settled out of reach of any more hits. The Jap cruiser steered away and left the scene in search of more prey. She was close enough that he could hear her forced-draft blowers whining across the water as she accelerated into the night. Moments later her wake rebuked the *Winston*'s swimming survivors as they struggled to get away from what was coming next.

Marsh pushed through the warm water, fighting his life jacket as he tried to make progress away from the sinking ship. He remembered practicing the same thing in the natatorium at the academy during seamanship training. He couldn't kick properly because his knees had stiffened into acute angles. He did a crude dog paddle with his equally useless wrists, determined to get away from the ship before she rolled all the way over and took him with her. Still, after a few minutes of painful effort, he couldn't help but turn around to watch. One of the ship's scout planes was fully engulfed in fire to his right, the flames boiling off in bright orange balls as the avgas tanks spilled liquid fire onto the waiting sea. A huge cloud of steam and smoke was rising just aft of amidships, where the tangled steel wreckage of the after superstructure and the stack glowed red and orange. In a few minutes, he thought, he would just about be able to see down her stacks when she settled onto her beam ends. *Winston* hung there, filling with water, as he caught his breath. He could hear the sounds of collapsing bulkheads deep inside the ship banging into the night air. By this time he had drifted forward and was abeam of the bow, which was just about submerged. With the steam leak quelled, the night filled with other terrible sounds: men screaming and shouting, the crackle of fires fore and aft, and, beneath the water, a gathering rumble as *Winston* prepared to die.

Above all the noise, he suddenly heard rapid-fire hammering, steel on steel. A wave slopped over his face, and he had to wipe the stinging saltwater from his eyes. He listened again.

Banging. Someone was pounding on steel back on board. Pounding desperately.

He was maybe fifty feet away, up alongside the bow, but the sound was clear as a bell. *Winston*'s

26

main deck was now hanging over at a forty-degree if not steeper angle. Every piece of loose gear topside was rattling down into the sea. One of the forward eight-inch turrets swung lazily on its roller path with a great squealing noise to point all three barrels directly into the air.

There it was again. Bang, bang, bang. It was coming from the main forecastle hatch. The portside aviation fuel tank that had been burning was now underwater, but he could see that hatch from the light of the scout-plane fire farther aft.

Banging on a hatch. There were men trapped in there.

He swallowed hard. His mouth was dry as a bone despite the constant dunkings.

You're an officer. You know what you have to do.

He did know, but he couldn't make himself do it. As he scanned the expanse of the forecastle deck, which seemed to be getting closer, his limbs felt paralyzed. To his right the remains of the superstructure leaned out over the water, and a small gun director tore loose in a screech of steel. He knew she was moments from capsizing, and that he was much too close.

You know what you have to do.

The hell with that.

You *know* what you have to do.

The port anchor chain rattled as the stoppers let go and the anchor, already submerged, took off for the bottom, three thousand feet below. The sudden noise shook Marsh out of his stupor. He took a deep breath, then began paddling back toward the ship, dimly aware that there were dozens of men behind him, thrashing hard in the opposite direction. Some of them looked at him as if he were nuts.

Bang. Bang. Bang. Clear as a damn bell, the closer he got.

The bullnose was level with the sea by the time he got alongside. The banging continued as he heaved himself over the lifelines up onto the tilted deck, his wrists alight with pain. He had to use his elbows and feet to scrabble like an injured crab across the two-thirds of the deck remaining above water until he reached that hatch. He coiled one leg around the base of a ventilator cowling to keep from sliding back across the slick teak decking.

The hatch was dogged down and dogged hard. The dogging wrench was jammed down into its bracket, its keeper wire intact, but his hands still wouldn't work. He could feel a thrumming through the deck as more shell-holed bulkheads down below gave way, relinquishing more interior compartments to the hungry sea. He tried not to think about what would happen if she rolled now.

He turned on his side, extracted the wrench and set it as best his rubber hands would allow, then straightened out his free leg and kicked at it until the nut loosened and the hinged dogging bolt fell away. He thought he felt his kneecap come off with that first kick. The pain took his breath away. Then on to the next one, and the one after that. He had to hang on to a davit socket with one elbow to get enough leverage, even as the deck slanted over at an ever steeper angle.

Any moment now, he thought, perspiring in the wet air. She's gonna roll.

He went after each dog until, finally, *finally,* the eighth one fell away. The hatch popped up with the force of ten men pushing on it. They erupted out of that hatch like the proverbial bats out of hell, pursued by a whoosh of hot, oily air that was being pressurized by the rising water below decks. More than a dozen white-faced men scrambled out, maintaining discipline, albeit just barely. Marsh lay there, exhausted, as he watched those guys escaping the glowing hell below and roll into the sea like lemmings. Finally, his elbow gave out and he slid feetfirst back across the now near-vertical deck, snagging in the submerged lifelines for a moment but then dropping back into the sea, where he joined the rush to get away. He paddled hard, doing a broken-handed breaststroke, kicking for his life despite the damage in his knees. Just in time, he thought, as he heard an enormous rumbling sound behind him.

No more than a minute later, she went all the way over with a ship-sized exhalation of escaping air, capsizing to port as a few desperate men aft scrambled like log-rollers up the now vertical surfaces of the main deck and then pitched backward, one by one, into the sea, where the ship came all the way over to smother every one of them in an eight-thousand-ton blanket of steel and crashing debris. For one horrifying instant, a hot white cone of steam blowing out of number two stack was pointed right at him, billowing across the orange-tipped waves. He imagined that he could feel its heat even though he was at least a hundred yards away by now. The remains of the gasoline fires aft briefly illuminated *Winston*'s bronze propellers, which were, amazingly, still rotating slowly as she turned turtle and went completely upside down. The red-leaded hull rolled briefly back and forth, probably as the eight-inch gun turrets fell off, and then the bulk of her sagged backward into the waiting sea. Her bow came up for an instant as she twisted, her starboard anchor hanging incongruously up against the lifelines.

Then, accompanied by another howl of compressed air and sheets of water-spray framed by a tumult of shiny black fuel oil, she was gone.

The sudden silence was just as frightening as the sinking. Marsh knew there were other men close by, but he was still somewhat night-blind from those searchlights. Then he smelled the bright stink of advancing fuel oil and began to do an awkward sidestroke to get away from it. There was still some gasoline burning in great flat lakes of fire. He felt an enormous thump from deep beneath him, followed by another and another. There go the boilers, he thought; she's well and truly gone. He wondered if she'd land upright or upside down when she hit the bottom.

The sulfurous smell of bunker fuel oil grew stronger. Then he realized that the gasoline fires had ignited some of the fuel that was still streaming up from the wreck. There were men screaming in the distance as two racing flame fronts caught up with them, and Marsh pushed even harder to get away from the growing conflagration.

He yelped when the black thing erupted out of the sea twenty feet away. Then he recognized what it was: one of the ship's many wood-and-canvas life rafts had torn away from the sinking hulk and popped back up to the surface.

Pushing his body through the light swells, awkwardly because of the bulky drag of the kapok life jacket, he caught up to the raft, quickly pushing one useless hand through one of the rope handholds. With the last of his strength, he hauled himself up partway into the raft. Almost immediately, the low-hanging smoke from nearby burning oil enveloped him, and he had to put his head down flat against the bottom of the raft to get some air. He felt one of the paddles that was still stowed against the bottom and pushed it out of its straps with his right foot. Taking one last deep breath of clean air, he sat back up to start rowing the raft away from the fire, only to feel a searing blast of heat against his face. The raft had drifted *into* the lake of burning fuel oil and was itself now on fire. He yelled with the pain of it and went back over the side, desperately trying to get away from the flames.

Basic training kicked in. Go deep, come back up slowly, open your eyes; if you see fire, push the water away from your face as you surface; grab a breath of air, go back down. It worked, sort of, except there wasn't much air because the fire was consuming most of the oxygen and his damned hands just sort of flopped around. Down again, even as the life jacket perversely tugged him back up to the fire, repeating the maneuver until he could no longer see flickering light above. He surfaced and lay back in the life jacket, truly exhausted. The raft was still visible in the distance, but it was ablaze from end to end.

So much for that, he thought. For the first time he wondered if he was going to survive all this.

Almost unconsciously he kept paddling backward, keeping a wary eye on where the flames were headed, aware now that his life jacket was getting heavier as it inevitably began to soak up water. They said that a kapok life jacket was good for twenty-four hours max before it became totally waterlogged. The fire on the water suddenly blew sideways as a breeze came up, and the air became breathable again.

Where was everybody? There had to be more survivors—he had seen dozens of men abandoning the ship just before she rolled over. He tried a shout but produced a barely audible croak. The right side of his face felt like it had been badly sunburned. He tried again, and this time he heard another voice yelling, "Over here." He turned around in the water and saw another, larger raft about fifty feet away, low in the water from the weight of a couple of dozen men hanging on to its sides. He struck out for the raft with renewed energy and was soon able to stick his forearm through one of the free ropes.

Every other handhold was taken, and there were a dozen men actually in the raft itself, most of them badly injured. He heard someone identify him by name—"It's Mister Vincent"—but everyone else was strangely silent. They were probably as exhausted as he was and were literally saving their breath. The back of his head stung, and he touched it to see if he was bleeding. He felt a flap of skin come off in his fingers. One of the men in the raft suddenly sat up, swore, and pointed. He turned to look, just in time to see a black shape looming out of the darkness, casting a bright white bow wave as she came on.

"She's gonna hit us!" one of the men croaked.

No, she's not, Marsh thought, but it's going to be close—and she's not one of ours.

"Japs!" cried another man. "It's the fuckin' Japs!"

The black cruiser loomed over them in the darkness, close enough to create a powerful pulse of underwater pressure as her thirteen-thousand-ton hull pushed by at twenty-plus knots. Marsh braced for the bow wave he knew was coming and was surprised how good the warm water felt as the wave foamed over the raft. Then a searchlight switched on, followed by a second one. These weren't their big targeting searchlights but close-in devices, signal lamps, throwing off a yellowish glow as they swept the surface before settling on the raft. Instinctively, Marsh knew what would happen next. He yelled for the men to bail out, took a deep breath, let go of the handhold, and pushed himself underwater as deep as he could get with his kapok on. He could feel the twenty-five-millimeter shells tearing into the life raft and hear the rounds buzzing by his ears as they spent themselves in the sea.

He kept windmilling his arms backward underwater until the lights went out and the shooting stopped. By the time he popped back out of the water, lungs close to bursting, the Jap ship had disappeared into the darkness. So had the raft, torn to pieces by one of the AA crews on the cruiser's main deck. There were a few heads in the water, but they were all facedown, bobbing lifelessly in the remains of the cruiser's wake. Another man popped up a few feet away, hacking and coughing as he gulped air. He thrashed around for a minute before taking in the scene in front of them.

"God damn them all to hell," he said, spitting seawater. "Sonsabitches ain't human."

"Just finishing the job," Marsh said. "Allowing us the privilege of a quick death in battle."

The man looked over at him with raccoonlike eyes. His face was covered in a sheen of oil with only the whites of his eyes visible. "You gotta be an officer," he said. Marsh noticed he didn't have a life jacket.

"Lieutenant Vincent, assistant gun boss."

"Monkey-mate Second Marty Gorman," he said. "Wish we had some of them guns of yours."

"Gone to Davy Jones," Marsh said. "You need a kapok."

"They all burned up in two-engine," Gorman said, wiping some oil off his forehead. "Believe it or not, I went out through the torpedo hole. Big as a damn house, it was. I think everybody else was already killed. I'd been down behind the main reduction gear, taking a lube oil sample. I guess that's why it didn't get me, too. Goddamn miracle."

A piece of the raft floated by, and Marsh grabbed it. Gorman swam over and latched on. He was pretty old for being a second-class petty officer, which told Marsh he'd probably been to captain's mast a few times in his career.

"So," Gorman said, "you bein' a lieutenant and all, I guess you're in charge. What do we do now, Cap'n?"

"You can start by getting me a cup of that good engine room coffee," Marsh said, trying for a little levity after the horror of the life raft.

Gorman grinned in the darkness, his big teeth white against the black oil. "Aye, aye, Cap'n," he said. "Right away. One lump or two?"

Marsh managed a grim laugh. "Let's see if we can find some more pieces of this raft. And pray for no more Jap cruisers."

"Fuck them," Gorman said. "What we're prayin' for is no goddamn sharks."

Marsh looked out at the faceless heads bobbing nearby in their life jackets, undoubtedly leaking blood into the sea. "We better get away from all this bait, then," he said.

Gorman relieved a dead man of his kapok, and then they pushed off into the darkness, their arms hooked onto the raft fragment, kicking together like a paddle wheeler, searching for more bits of the raft. It occurred to Marsh that he finally had achieved command at sea: one piece of a bullet-riddled life raft with a crew of one feisty Irishman. Good going, Beauty, he thought. It was going to be a long night.

Dawn brought a wonderful sight: a pair of American destroyers, combing the morning twilight for survivors. By then Gorman had lashed together three pieces of life raft. The two of them were sitting, semisubmerged, on the remains of the float when one of the tin cans came alongside and backed down, her prop wash almost pushing them away from her sides. Marsh saw literally hundreds of men on deck and experienced a pulse of joy: A lot of the crew must have made it off. Then he realized that there were very few faces he recognized. Great God, he thought—what else had happened last night?

Gorman grabbed the cargo net strung out over the side, pulled their makeshift raft up against the steel, and clambered up in his bare feet. Marsh tried to do the same, but his hands simply didn't work. A bosun's mate topside saw that he couldn't climb and tossed him a bowline, which he cinched under his arms so that they could hoist him aboard. He banged his head on the steel plates as they dragged him backward up the side, but at that point, he didn't mind a bit. American steel felt pretty good right about then. They seemed to be in a hurry, probably because they were afraid of Jap subs that might have been left behind to pick off any rescue ships. There were dozens of waterlogged and bloodstained kapoks trailing in the destroyer's wake, already being pursued by shark fins or disappearing in a bump and boil of pink water and slashing teeth. The destroyer was not retrieving any bodies.

Once on deck, Marsh flopped down like a netted fish. He felt the ship push ahead handsomely. An ensign in rumpled khakis appeared, stooped down, and asked for his name and ship.

"There's more than one?" he asked. Marsh's lips were caked with salt and oil, and it was hard to get his words out.

The young officer's face was drawn, and there were dark shadows under his eyes. "*Quincy, Vincennes, Astoria, Winston,*" he recited, probably not for the first time.

"Jesus H. Christ," Marsh murmured. "All gone?"

"All gone," he said, flipping to a clean page on his little green wheel book. "Now—name, please?"

"Lieutenant Marshall Vincent, assistant gun boss in *Winston,*" he told him. "*All* of them?"

"Goddamned massacre," the ensign said, straightening up. "We've been picking up survivors all night. Can you walk?"

"Not really," Marsh said. "I can crawl, I guess."

A deckhand helped him back to the fantail, where there was a line of waiting survivors. He

38

could stand as long as the seaman supported him. Two other seamen were going along the line of survivors, wiping oil off faces and offering a dipper of water to the most recently rescued. The ship's doctor and his two pharmacist's mates were doing triage. There were over twenty blanket-covered forms laid out back by the depth charge racks. Every available square foot of topside space was occupied. Marsh thought the ship's inherent stability was probably being compromised by all this topside weight. He hadn't realized how thirsty he was. The water was wonderful.

He could tell the destroyer's ship's company from the survivors—their guys were all wearing dry uniforms. The rest of them were in various states of soggy disrepair and injury. Marsh apparently had two sprained, possibly broken wrists, second-degree burns to his scalp and neck, and a four-inch-long gash on the back of his head, which he hadn't felt until now. Both his kneecaps were probably cracked, a diagnosis the doc made by flexing his legs and listening to the bones grind with his stethoscope while Marsh tried not to scream. The pharmacist's mate splinted his wrists, gave him a handful of APCs for the pain and another glass of water, and then told the seaman to take him to a spot topside to sit down and rest.

By the lights of what had happened last night, his injuries were trivial. Four heavy cruisers had been destroyed, a thousand if not more men killed in the battle, one-sided as it had been. Another couple of thousand casualties were still being fished out of the sea. The sun hadn't even risen yet, and he wondered if those Jap cruisers were still out there, maybe lurking just over the horizon, waiting to come in and finish the job. He felt suddenly sick again with fear, and he struggled to catch his breath. The man sitting next to him, a chief petty officer with both his legs braced in splints and wire netting, nudged his left elbow.

"Easy there, Lieutenant," he said. Marsh turned to stare at him, only now aware that he had begun to hyperventilate. "You made it. You're gonna be okay."

His hands were bandaged, and both of his legs were splinted in clumsy wraps stiffened with copper tubing. The chief noticed Marsh's splinted wrists.

"Them Jap torpedoes pack a wallop, don't they," he said. "One minute, I'm standing on the deckplates in main control, havin' a ciggy-butt and some java, the next, damn ship's in two pieces and I'm tryin' to swim with two busted wheels. One fish, broke us in half like a damn twig."

"Which ship?"

"The Skinny Vinny," he said. "Gone in ten minutes."

The *Vincennes*, Marsh thought, recognizing her fleet nickname. He lay back against the bulkhead and closed his eyes. "I was in *Winston*," he said. "Two torpedoes, I think. We got some rounds off, but she went dead in the water pretty quick. Then they came in close, punched holes in us with their eight-inch. One came back after the ship sank, shot up the life rafts. Bastards."

"I just transferred off a tin can," he said. "Japs been usin' their destroyers to tow barges fulla army guys into Guadalcanal. We'd find 'em, sink the destroyer, and then shoot up the barges until they was all chum. I guess we can't bitch about them shootin' up a life raft."

"The hell we can't," Marsh said.

He laughed. "Halsey's got it right: Kill Japs, kill Japs, kill more Japs. They started this shit."

Two sailors came by holding a soup kettle between them and asking if anybody wanted chow. Marsh wasn't hungry; neither was the chief, but he asked if they had a smoke. They set the kettle down and fished out cigarettes. Marsh wasn't a smoker, but when they offered him one, he took it. That first drag did more to calm him down than being rescued. He looked down the line of bedraggled men lining the decks and catwalks. Almost everyone, including some of the guys lying in stretchers, had a cigarette going. The smell of good old American tobacco was a pleasant change from the stink of fuel oil, burned

41

flesh, and bloodied uniforms, if only for a minute or so.

The ship was slowing down again. Another raft had been spotted. After a long night, it was going to be a very long day. His third drag on the cigarette reminded him of why he didn't smoke, so he flicked it over the side, laid his aching head back on a soggy kapok, thought about asking for some soup after all, and then fell asleep.

TWO

Midway, June 1942

Lieutenant Mick McCarty looked down at the Japanese Air Fleet with unalloyed joy. Talk about the world's supply of fat targets. They'd flown out almost two hundred miles from the *Yorktown* and found absolutely nothing. One of the other air groups had already turned around, defeated. Their skipper, however, followed offensive doctrine: Start an expanding square search. That had led them to a lone Japanese destroyer, fifteen thousand feet below, who was etching a sharp white wake in the blue Pacific that pointed like an arrow back to the Jap carrier task force she was rejoining. They followed that unwitting Judas and found the carriers with about ten minutes of fuel to spare.

Two ugly gray flattops below were already

executing their own doctrine: When Jap capital ships came under air attack, they put the rudder over and made a continuous wide turn that made it next to impossible for torpedo bombers to line up for an attack. It was also harder for dive bombers to settle into a stable powered descent—but not impossible, Mick thought, and the Dauntless dive bomber was nothing if not a stable diver.

The skipper divided the formation, one for each visible carrier. He went first, rolling onto his back and then pulling through to the vertical, flaps split. Mick was second man in the V and rolled in right after him. He still remembered asking his instructor at flight school why in the hell they had to go upside down to make a dive-bombing attack. Why not just push the nose over? The instructor had said okay, let's try that. The engine quit thirty seconds later. Nose over, you pull negative g's, which causes the fuel flow from a gravity-feed system to stop, along with the engine. Got it? Got it.

It was a beautiful sight, he thought as his excitement rose and the slipstream began its rising wail. The skipper was just a dot below him that became a Dauntless silhouette as he pulled his SBD out of its dive and shot across the ship's stubby, three-tiered bow. A moment later a huge whitewater column rose right alongside the squirming carrier.

A miss, Mick thought, but probably good for some hull damage and some badly frightened engineers down in their boiler rooms.

Mick steadied his bomb-heavy SBD, gripping the stick harder than he needed to, judging the strain on the airframe by the pitch of the airstream. Lead him, lead him, he thought, aiming his bombsight at the point of the arrow-shaped white lines on the carrier's flight deck, bending the Dauntless ever so slightly to match the carrier's turning circle.

Watch your altimeter. He flicked his eyes down to the instrument panel. The altimeter was unwinding so fast he could only see the hour hand. Twelve thousand.

Lead her.

Ten thousand.

More lead.

Eight thousand. Six thousand. Steady. Keep bending into her turn.

Four.

Three. Details of the planes on the target's deck were much clearer now, with little dots scattering all over like ants as the American dive bombers dropped down on them and the deck crews ran for cover.

No cover today, sunshine, he thought. Now.

The Dauntless bucked in satisfaction as the one-thousand-pound bomb left its hooks. He pulled back hard on the stick, having only about twenty-five hundred feet of altitude left in which to get flat. Altitude, as the instructors used to say, is your ultimate friend.

Got that right, he thought, as his eyeballs began to sag with the g's.

He was dimly aware of flak thudding around him, but he had no time to do anything but *will* his barge to get flat and away from all this noise. He felt his chin strap bite into his chest as the g's mounted and his head gained weight. Even his earphones were drooping off his ears.

"Go, Beast!" someone called over the radio. "You nailed his ass. Lookit it burn. Whooo-wee!"

"Cut the chatter," came the skipper's ragged voice. "Work him over. Maintain your interval. *Kill* him, don't just hurt him."

Through increasingly bloodshot eyes Mick finally saw the lighter blue of the sky instead of the deadly dark blue of the ocean lowering into his view and eased off a tiny bit on the stick. As the g-forces relented he was able to turn his head and look back at his carrier.

His carrier.

A fiery bolus of burning gasoline obscured the middle of the carrier where his bomb had hit. As he was looking, there was another big explosion, deep in her guts, sending more incandescent clouds of fire belching out her sides from down on the hangar deck. The carrier's escorts were going every which way, trying to get away from the dive bombers, unaware that not one of the diving planes was interested in anything except that mortally wounded flattop.

We caught them pants-down, Mick thought, probably right in the middle of a launch cycle. Live bombs on the flight deck, avgas hoses everywhere, planes parked all over the flight deck, and all of it just dying to burn.

He leveled off, unconsciously lifting his toes as he realized he was only about twenty feet above the sea. He turned upward to regain some altitude and find the rendezvous point. He'd only carried the one bomb, so now the mission was to get his crate home in one piece without attracting any itinerant Zeros in the process. He turned back east, looking for his mates.

His backseat gunner came up on intercom and congratulated Mick for the direct hit. He looked back and saw that the carrier, *his* carrier, was now aflame from one end to the other and no longer making much way through the water. In the distance another huge column of black smoke was unfolding into the towering white cumulonimbus clouds, which hopefully meant that the other squadron had taken out the second flattop.

He punched the instrument panel in pure glee. I got a *carrier!* Hell's bells, he thought, this was better than the winning TD at his senior year Army–Navy game. Word at the morning briefing was that these were the flattops that had come to

Pearl Harbor. Revenge was sweet, super sweet. It was the best day of his life, and supposedly there were more carriers out there. With any luck, they could get back to the *Yorktown*, rearm, and come back to do it all again before the other two American carriers, *Enterprise* and *Hornet*, even got into the game.

There was lots of excited chatter on the radio, and then he recognized some call signs from the *Enterprise* squadrons. Apparently they'd found a third carrier about twenty miles away and reduced her to a floating volcano. The excitement really wore off when the skipper began calling for fuel-state reports from his various bombers. Mick glanced down at his own fuel gauges, blinked, and looked again. He reached out with a gloved finger and tapped both gauges, hoping at least one of them would move, if only just a little. He called the skipper and reported he was below bingo fuel. That got the tactical net quiet, because it meant Mick could not make it back to the carrier. He was going to have to ditch.

The skipper told him to climb gently to eighteen thousand feet and then go to max conserve. Mick felt a little better when seven other planes were given similar instructions. Assuming they got back to the fleet they'd theoretically have enough altitude to glide, if they had to, to get within range of the carrier's escort destroyers. After that, all they had to do was survive the ditching. He briefed his gunner that they might be going to a swim call.

Damn, he thought. This'll take all the fun right out of it.

With the help of an unexpected tail wind, the gaggle of seven gaspers made it back to their carriers. Mick shifted to the land-launch frequency in time to hear the air boss polling each of the starving seven as to their fuel state. The first two pilots reported that it was no-go for an approach. They were directed to find a tin can and ditch alongside. Number three thought he had enough to make a straight-in approach, but when questioned, he said he wasn't sure. He, too, was told to pick out a destroyer and ditch.

Mick knew that the air boss, a tough, forty-five-year-old commander named Hugo Oxerhaus, wanted no part of a fatal stall right over the round-down followed by a fiery crash on deck. On the other hand, none of the carriers could afford to lose aircraft, especially with the Jap carrier fleet, or what was left of it, only a couple of hundred miles to the west. Besides, he could not abide the thought of ending such a day with a deliberate crash into the sea.

He studied his gauges as he began to let down, then set up switches to transfer everything still left in the wing tanks to the center tank. Might as well have one tank I can count on, he reasoned; the fuel tank gauges became unreliable below 5 percent. He heard his own call sign on the radio and rogered up.

"Request state," the PriFly talker asked.

"Between five and ten percent," Mick lied. He *really* did not want to ditch.

"Confirm you can *complete* an approach." That was Boss Oxerhaus himself talking.

"Get me straight in," Mick said. "If they wave me, I'll have to ditch it."

"You are cleared to the pattern for one approach," the air boss said. "You bolter, no going around, got it?"

"Roger, out."

Mick began his descent. He heard the fuel transfer pump whine angrily as it lost suction and shut it down. The center tank read 5 percent, barely, which meant that he really had no idea how much fuel he had left.

He waited until the last minute to configure the SBD for landing, then executed the Holy Trinity: Hook down. Flaps down. Wheels down.

The broad white wake of the carrier began to narrow as he made his approach. He could see the landing signal officer on his platform, arms out, green paddles fluttering in the stiff wind. The engine sounded fine as he set her up in the groove. The winds were perfect as he came over the round-down. He cut the power when Paddles gave him the chop signal. He held his breath as he felt the hook screeching down the deck, and then came the welcome, neck-wrenching yank of an arresting wire. He heard the gunner whoop with joy. He automatically advanced the throttle to full power in case the hook skipped all the wires or disengaged the one he'd caught and he had to bolter, or fly back off the bird farm.

The engine died in his hand.

The plane shuddered to a stop, its propeller windmilling even as the deck crew was signaling him to taxi clear of the landing zone.

He couldn't do it. The hydraulics died with the engine. He couldn't even raise the tail hook.

There was frantic shouting over the topside speakers, and then a crowd of flight deck crewmen swarmed the plane, manually disengaged the tail hook, and physically pushed the SBD over to one side of the centerline. Fifteen seconds later, another fuel-starved SBD swooped aboard.

Mick took off his flight helmet, wiped his sweat-soaked face, and released the canopy. He looked up. The first face in view was one of the landing signal officers, his paddles stuck under his armpit. He did not look pleased.

"Boss wants to see you in PriFly, Lieutenant," he announced. "Now would be nice."

Ten minutes later Mick was standing tall in the primary flight control tower, which was a glassed-in box on the island, overhanging the flight deck. His squadron commander, Lieutenant Commander

"Dagger" Watson, was with him. They were both still in their flight suits from the carrier raids, their faces red with sweat and their hair matted down like wet moss by their leather helmets. Watson had told Mick to keep his mouth shut and let him do all the talking, assuming they got a chance to say anything.

Commander Oxerhaus was sitting in his thronelike chair, from which he could oversee the entire flight deck. He launched immediately into one of his by now familiar tirades, getting louder and redder in the face each moment: Lieutenant McCarty, known to the entire world as the dumbest aviator and biggest asshole who ever existed, had put the whole air group at risk with a reckless dead-stick landing on the flight deck in the middle of a desperately difficult recovery situation, with fuel-starved aircraft still behind him. He had disobeyed standing orders, obviously lied about his fuel state, and all because he was a little girl who didn't want to muss her hairdo by ditching on a perfectly calm sea within sight of a rescue destroyer, and on and on. When he finally paused for breath, Mick's CO got in a word.

"For what it's worth, Boss," he said, "Mick here planted a thousand-pounder right in a Jap fleet carrier's forward elevator today. That should count for something, I think."

"That's just great," Commander Oxerhaus snarled. "As I understand it, that's his fucking *job*.

It's good to hear that once in his short naval career he managed to do his fucking job. Truth is, I don't care what happens to a Jap carrier. I care about *my* flight deck, *my* flight deck crews, and maintaining some semblance of military discipline in the deck operations of *this* carrier. I'm taking this up with the skipper as soon as this cycle completes, and I'll be demanding this *ass*hole's wings, got it? Now get out of here before I lose my temper."

Watson nudged Mick, and they left the control tower. They went down several ladders until they reached the flight deck, where Watson stopped in the hatchway leading to the deck, took off his leather helmet, and scratched his itchy, wet scalp as the warm Pacific air mixed with engine exhaust streamed past them into the bowels of the ship.

"Sorry, Skipper," Mick said. "I guess."

"You *guess?*"

"Well, the way I see it, I brought my barge home. Last I heard, we needed every plane we can keep these days. I did at least help to destroy a Jap bird farm. Out of thirty-eight guys, only three managed to hit that bastard. Way I see it, no harm, no foul."

"Mick, what if you *had* crashed on deck? Oxerhaus is right: Everybody behind you would be in the drink, which means we'd have lost four planes instead of just one. You took a really big chance. Okay, it worked out, this time, but the potential consequences just don't balance out."

Mick shook his head. "Skipper! We got three Jap carriers today. The barge drivers. The SBD squadrons. Three fucking carriers. C'mon!"

"We had help, Mick."

"Who, the torpedo guys? I never saw any torpedo guys."

"That's because they'd all been shot down by the time we got there. Because they arrived first, all the Zeros were down on the deck, shooting fish in a barrel. The torpeckers gave us a free shot. Get the picture?"

Mick hadn't heard that. "*All* of 'em?"

"All of them. They died so we could get a free ride. So don't think you single-handedly did anything today, except that landing."

"Well, shit, Skipper, I did hit the bastard. And from what I saw, I killed him."

"The word 'we' even in your lexicon, Mick? I was there, too, remember?"

"Yes, sir, of course you were. But I'm sorry. This is bullshit. The plane's back, I'm back, three Jap fleet carriers are toast, and everybody's mad at *me?*"

The skipper studied his flight boots for a moment. "This isn't the first crazy shit you've done, Mick. Some of these senior guys, they keep score, you know?"

Mick had no answer for that. The truth was hard to rebut.

"I hafta say, Skipper," he said finally, "this is

gonna be a day to remember. It's wartime. Everybody takes chances when the chips are down. Hell, guys crack it up on deck on a good day for no obvious reason. I got us a carrier, for Chrissakes!"

"That's not necessarily how the bosses will see it, Mick."

"That's because the bosses're all too damned old, and got where they are after thirty years of peacetime."

"We didn't start this one, Mick, remember? The bosses are the best we have on deck. Admiral Spruance? He's not even an aviator, but he got three Jap carriers today."

"*He* didn't get any carriers," Mick said. "Guys like you and me, *we* got three carriers."

"Like the air boss said, Mick—that's your job. Spruance put you out there, and you did good."

Mick gave up. "Screw it. I need a toddy."

"Go easy on that stuff, Mick," Watson said. "This isn't over. You'll have to see the captain sometime later today."

"Aye, aye, Skipper," Mick said, throwing up his hands in frustration. He headed for the ready room. When he got there, the rest of the bombing squadron pilots were whooping it up after the big strikes. Hands were waving, the tally of Jap planes shot down was growing by the minute, and the lies were expanding to fit their enthusiasm. Someone saw Mick come in, and they all started

54

razzing him for the dead-stick landing, but he knew they were doing it with unfettered admiration. One of his squadron-mates jumped up on the briefing table, stood on one leg like a crane, and hopped across the table with his arms spread out, weaving from side to side, coughing like a sputtering engine and then squatting down on the table and letting out one truly noisy fart.

Everyone roared. Mick grinned, but he still wanted that toddy.

Drinking officially was not permitted on Navy ships, but an unofficial exception had long been in place for carrier pilots, as long as they kept it discreet. Mick retrieved his coffee mug from the board, unearthed the stash, and poured himself a round shot. The rest of the guys were picking on someone else by now, led by the squadron XO. Skipper Watson hadn't come down from topside yet, so Mick decided he should do a team sneak-away before the skipper got back.

The bourbon washed his tailbone in its familiar warmth. He wanted another but thought better of it. Save it for after the carrier's captain chewed his ass for the landing. The *Yorktown*'s skipper was a known war-fighter, though, and Mick figured he would humor the choleric Oxerhaus and then send Mick below with a stern warning and a wink. They needed pilots far too badly to take anyone's wings, especially when the pilot involved in this little stunt had managed to pull it off *and* hit a carrier. He rinsed out the mug and put it back on the board, trying not to notice the mugs that were hanging upside down, denoting the guys who hadn't made it back yet.

As he walked back to his stateroom forward of the ready room, he felt the carrier lean into a wide turn. There was the usual clanging and banging going on topside as the flight deck crews respotted the air group, elevatored any bent birds down to the hangar deck, and got ready to launch the CAP—the combat air patrol. As best he knew, no one had yet located the fourth Jap carrier, which could mean trouble later.

His flight suit stank of sweat, ozone, and hydraulic oil in equal proportions. He really wanted a shower but chose instead to switch to red light in the stateroom and just flop into his rack. His roommate hadn't come back yet, but he was listed as ditched and recovered on the status board. They'd get him back aboard as soon as the rescuing destroyer could get alongside *Yorktown* for a highline transfer.

As he lay back he could hear the first of the CAP fighters taking off, its engine howling at full military power as it roared down the wooden deck. Then another. Go get 'em, tigers. Then he fell asleep.

The general alarm woke him a minute later, or at least it seemed like just a minute. He looked at his watch and saw that he'd been down for almost an hour. He could hear boots running outside in the passageway as the ship's company ran for their GQ stations, urged on by the bong-bong-bong of the GQ alarm. He lay back in his rack. Pilots were supercargo when the ship went to GQ; they either mustered in their squadron ready room or stayed in their own rooms, preferably out of the way, while the fighter-biters launched to engage incoming bandits and the ship's gun crews fought off any bogeys that got through the CAP screen. Then the captain came on the 1MC, the ship's announcing system.

"All hands, this is the captain. Condition Red. Radar has many bogeys inbound. Our CAP is up and will engage, but stay alert. Air department strike down all topside planes and ordnance, and purge all avgas fuel lines. Engineering, double-check condition Zebra; *Enterprise* CAP reports torpedo planes in this strike. That is all."

Torpedo planes, Mick thought. That's *all?* That's enough. He'd seen what Jap torpedoes could do to battleships in Pearl Harbor. He felt *Yorktown* begin to tremble as they brought the speed up to flank and began a sinuous weave. A weave won't do it, guys, he thought. The Japs had it right: Start a circle and stay in it; a bomber might get through, but torpedo planes had a hell of a time with those circles.

The ventilation went off, and immediately the tiny stateroom began to heat up. Mick's room was on the starboard side. Two of the ship's five-inch antiaircraft mounts were about a hundred feet from his room. He considered going to the ready room, which was air-conditioned, but remembered the rule: Once GQ sounds, stay put. Plus, if some pilots stayed in their rooms, they wouldn't lose an entire squadron if the ready room took a direct hit.

The sound-powered admin phone squeaked.

"Lieutenant McCarty," he said. "Solo."

"Okay," said the squadron admin officer. "Stay put."

There's an echo in here, he thought. "Roger dodger."

He lay back on his rack and waited. It wasn't long before he heard the familiar double thump of the escorting destroyers' guns going off, joined a minute later by the louder booms of the light cruisers. When the bogeys penetrated the combat air patrol, the carrier's screening ships closed in a circle around the bird farm to make the Japs work for it. Now that the escorts were lighting up the sky, Mick knew that some of the enemy planes must have made it through. At a certain point, pursuing fighters had to break off any pursuits to avoid flying into the curtain of ack-ack coming up from the screening ships.

He sighed, got up out of his rack, and strapped on his breathing apparatus, steel helmet, and life jacket. The sweat began to pour out of him with all that gear on. He opened the door and looked out into the passageway, which was empty. There were no watertight doors in either direction: If you saw water in this passageway, the carrier had already sunk. He stepped back into his room, latching the door open to get some more air.

Then *Yorktown*'s own five-inchers joined the shooting, rattling the furniture and light fixtures all around him each time they went off. The noise from the guns topside got louder as the massed batteries of forty-millimeter guns joined in. He thought he heard the whine of an aircraft engine coming in and then over the flight deck above, but there was no bomb. Then he heard another one, same deal, lots of close-in gunfire from the antiaircraft guns massed along the starboard catwalks, and that rising-pitch scream of an engine overspeeding, followed by a thumping boom somewhere back aft that shook the whole ship.

Bastard got us, he thought, but *Yorktown* seemed to shake it off, and the guns kept firing. The concussions were shaking the overhead light fixtures, and there was a fine mist of dust raining down from the cable bundles running through the stateroom's overhead. He heard a siren down in the hangar deck but didn't know what that meant. He realized he didn't know much about the carrier herself, other than how to get a plane on and off the flight deck. He sat back down on his rack, still sweating profusely and now unable to lie down with all his survival gear on. It felt weird to be sitting in his stateroom while an intensifying air-defense battle raged one deck above him.

He suddenly found himself upside down on the deck, his ears ringing from a really big explosion. When he cleared his head, he sensed the room filling with smoke. He couldn't see, then realized his helmet had slipped down over his face. He struggled to get up, but there was something wrong with the deck—it was curved up like the hump in a rug, and the aft bulkhead of the stateroom was flattened down over his shoulder. He tried to think, but his brain was still fuzzy from the shock. All he could do was lie there, trying to gather his wits.

"Trapped," he said out loud, and between the rising heat and the smoke, he knew he was going to cook in there unless he did something productive soon.

He tried to move, but the bulky life jacket was caught on something. Then he heard a roar of steam out in the passageway.

That's not right, he thought. The boilers are a couple hundred feet away. The temperature in the room began to soar. What air there was, was beginning to suffocate him.

Gotta move, gotta move.

First, gotta breathe.

He slipped the breathing apparatus face mask up

over his face and pulled the lanyard. There was a brief puff of odorless smoke, and then clear oxygen streamed into the mask.

Okay, he thought. Get out of this kapok, and then get the hell out of this area.

Squirming like an insect shedding its cocoon, he pulled himself forward toward the door, untying the strings on his life jacket. The door itself was now out in the passageway somewhere, and the door frame was a crazy trapezoid of deformed metal. Deafened by the roar of a steam leak back down the passageway, he felt another bomb hit, starboard side and deep. These must be Vals, he thought. That's armor-piercing stuff.

He finally got himself free of the life jacket and made it out the doorway. The passageway was getting dark, with only a few battle lanterns throwing yellowish light here and there. He looked up. There was smoke boiling along the overhead like a giant snake seeking a bolt-hole. The roar of escaping steam was louder out in the passageway, but now it sounded like it was coming from way back aft, behind the island. The smoke was filling the passageway in earnest, expanding down from the overhead toward the asphalt-tile deck, and the heat was getting worse, much worse. The battle lanterns looked like evil yellow eyes, opening and closing as the heavy black smoke searched for a way out.

Right or left? That was the question.

There was hell to pay back aft, steam, smoke, probably a big fire and structural damage. Forward? There was one hatch leading topside at the forward end of this passageway, but there seemed to be an awful lot of stuff heaped between him and it.

Another booming blast sounded off back aft, and this time a bolus of fire came whipping up the passageway. He got as flat as he could and covered his head and face mask with his arms as the flame front shot over him, singeing the hair off the back of his arms and head. Then it was gone. He looked over his shoulder. The smoke back aft had a deadly red glow to it.

Forward it is, he decided.

It was hard. He couldn't stand up because of that maelstrom of hot smoke, coiling and writhing only inches above his head. Each time he got to a knee-knocker he literally had to throw himself over the frame, because by now there was only about twelve inches of air left down low. Just like football practice, he thought, as he wormed his way forward on his elbows and knees.

He finally reached the ladder vestibule leading up to the flight deck. Where the hell was everybody? he wondered. Were the rest of the guys trapped in the ready rooms back aft?

He reached up through the murk for the hatch handle, half expecting it to be jammed, but it wasn't. He rolled over on his back to give himself some leverage and pushed up on the handle, then got to his knees to push it all the way open.

Big mistake.

The moment the hatch cracked off its coaming, the overpressure in the passageway slammed it back against the bulkhead, taking Mick with it before he could let go of the operating handle. His battle helmet came off, and his right arm jammed in the treads of the ladder leading topside. The smoke came at the new airway like an express train, bringing with it enough heat to scorch his flight suit and deform the face mask.

He heard a whumping at the top of the ladder and looked up through his rapidly fogging mask. The hot smoke column, filled with particles of unburned fuel, had found fresh air. Now it had ignited, creating a Roman candle up at the top of the ladder. Mick cringed at the bottom of the ladder, suddenly aware that it was getting progressively harder to get a breath of oxygen from his canister. How much time did he have left? He'd forgotten to set the timer.

Can't go up the ladder, not into that.

Can't go back to my stateroom.

Can't get my arm out of this ladder.

"Oh, shit," he mumbled.

He felt his mind wandering. He realized he'd stopped perspiring, and that wasn't good, not in all this heat. His breathing apparatus made him feel like he was sucking on a bent straw. He began yanking on his arm to free himself from the ladder.

Hot. So goddamned hot.

Then he was free. So free that he was floating in midair and then crashing down again onto the steel deck of the vestibule. The ladder's pins held, but it had come loose anyway because the pin brackets themselves had been broken by an enormous explosion deep down below.

Torpedo.

This time the big ship lurched sideways, and then a second torpedo delivered a punishing belt of energy to the hull that Mick felt in his own guts and knees.

Then he was underwater as the explosion plume from the first torpedo collapsed over the flight deck, dumping thousands of gallons of water down the hatch, washing him clean out of the vestibule and swirling like a drunken spider along the passageway until a knee-knocker stopped him short with an ugly sucker punch to the gut.

He tried to catch his breath, but almost nothing was coming from the canister. He looked up: The Roman candle was out. He realized he only had a minute. He scrambled like a crab along the deck, sloshing through warm saltwater, then scrambled up the ladder and finally into the vestibule, where he spilled out onto the flight deck like a sack of potatoes. An instant later, the Roman candle lit back off, belching a plume of fire thirty feet into the air from the hatch. He found himself rolling because the flight deck was no longer level—the big ship was developing a distinct port list. He rolled into the tie-down chains of a parked aircraft, ten feet from the portside catwalks.

He wiped the mask off his face and breathed in honest seagoing air, even though it was laced with gun smoke from the nearby catwalk AA batteries, which were still blasting away. He wiped his stinging eyes and looked out to sea. Here came yet another torpedo bomber. With his left leg still entangled in the tie-down, he could only watch in fascination as the gunners' tracers converged on the black plane a few thousand feet off the port side, then cheered when it exploded in a white-hot fireball as the twenty-millimeters found the torpedo warhead slung under its belly. The only surviving fragment of the airplane, the radial engine with its spinning propeller still attached, came directly down at the ship and then clattered onto the flight deck like a saw blade fifteen feet from where he lay. The spinning prop dug big chunks of wood out of the deck, one of which whacked him in the arm before the engine cartwheeled its way right over the far side.

Mick lay back, laughing hysterically, and that's how one of the flight deck fire parties found him, knees-up under a badly riddled fighter, lying in a soaked, scorched ball, still laughing about that lone propeller's last fling.

"Crazy fucking aviator," one of the damage control team guys muttered as they scooped him into a Stokes litter. The masts of a cruiser became visible above the canting flight deck as she came alongside to begin taking off the wounded.

THREE

Pearl, September 1942

Two and a half weeks after the debacle at Savo Island, *Winston*'s survivors finally made it back to Pearl. All of the survivors from the four lost cruisers had been taken to Espiritu Santo, a primitive logistics base on an island near Guadalcanal. From there they put them on one of the converted ocean liners serving as troop transports that had brought out reinforcements for Guadalcanal. Sixty-seven more men died of their injuries on the trip back and were buried at sea. In the time it took them to get back to Pearl, there were burial-at-sea ceremonies every third day. It felt to Marsh as if they were leaving a trail of bloodstained mattress covers, weighted down with firebricks from the ship's boiler rooms, all the way back across the South Pacific.

Of the nearly twelve hundred crew in *Winston*, they had lost almost four hundred known dead or missing and presumed dead. The other ships had suffered similar losses. Because the transport carried the survivors from four ships, it took several days to get an organized count. The senior officer to make it off *Winston* was the executive officer, Commander Jerry Wilson. Captain McClain had been torn to pieces by a shell hit directly on the bridge. The XO organized *Winston*'s survivors into three groups: able-bodied officers, chiefs, and enlisted men; the injured but ambulatory; and the grievously injured. Marsh fell into group two, in that he could hobble around even though his hands weren't much use. He was the senior surviving officer in the gunnery department, which was a sobering thought, especially when he found out that of nearly three hundred in the department, only a hundred and fifty were left. The rest were littering the bottom off Savo Island or entombed in the wreck of their ship. That's what happens when you lose a sea-fight, the exec said: unlike in the Army, there's no retreat and regroup option.

Doctors from the naval hospital came aboard to do triage when the transport docked at the shipyard's ten-ten dock just after sunset. The naval authorities in Pearl planned to put the ambulatory survivors in barracks over in the Hickam Field housing area, within walking distance of Hospital Point. Marsh was tasked by the exec to be one of the escorts for the most seriously wounded, who would be going to the hospital itself. The ship's doctors had put plaster casts on his wrists, but there wasn't much they could do for his knees other than Ace bandages. Once he got to the hospital, he could see that there was barely room for all the new casualties. There hadn't been enough ambulances available, so they'd ended up taking some of the badly wounded over to the hospital on the back of Army stakebed trucks.

Marsh could actually smell the hospital as they pulled into the parking lot. The usual Hawaiian ambience of blooming flowers, swaying palm trees, and gentle sea air was overwhelmed by the stench of disinfectant, vomit, and burned human flesh coming from the building, overlaid with the reek of fuel oil that still covered much of the surface of Pearl Harbor itself. It had been almost eight months since the attack, but there was still plenty of evidence lying out in the harbor, crowned by the blackened remains of the battleship *Arizona*'s superstructure over near Ford Island.

The medical staff met them at the door, looking like shell-shock casualties themselves. Doctors, nurses, and pharmacist's mates, gray-faced and pouch-eyed, stared at the incoming trucks with exhausted expressions as the stretchers were unloaded. The men were trying hard not to hurt or jostle anyone. Inside the smells were even worse. The hospital staff had commandeered tables from the officers' club because they had run out of gurneys, so most of the new casualties were laid out right there in the main hallway. With his forearms out of action, Marsh could only stand around and "supervise." All the windows had blackout curtains rigged, which didn't help with the ghastly smell. There was plywood boarding up the windows all along the harbor-side walls, where the office and admin spaces had been shattered by machine-gun bullets.

"Leave it to the Japs to machine-gun the hospital," Marsh remarked to one orderly.

"They were fresh out of bombs," the man responded bitterly. "Welcome to Pearl."

Two weeks later Marsh was summoned to appear before the Court of Inquiry being held at the naval base headquarters. His wrists were healing, but his knees made walking a true misery. They worked fairly well during the day, but at night they seized up like rusty hinges, making mornings really tough. Serious painkillers were reserved for badly wounded men in the hospital. All they could give him was APC pills. The *C* in an APC was for caffeine, so at night his choices were staying awake for hours or trying to sleep with two campfires in his knees. When he did sleep, he had nightmares, which inevitably ended with the blackened superstructure of *Winston* rolling over on him. He was physically and mentally exhausted by the time the call came to testify.

Marsh thought they'd been sent back to Pearl to

recuperate and heal. For the enlisted that was mostly true. The surviving officers, however, were busy night and day dealing with the aftereffects of losing a heavy cruiser. Of the seventy-two officers assigned, forty-one were left, and twelve of those were in the hospital. The rest of them were swamped with re-creating operational reports, making inventories of accountable equipment, writing condolence letters, and checking on their hospitalized shipmates to make sure they were not getting lost in the organized chaos that was the naval hospital. Individually, they all had to recover their own personal situations. Being a bachelor, Marsh had essentially lived aboard ship. It was a great way to save money, but it meant that he'd lost everything when *Winston* went down. He now had to acquire new uniforms, underwear, shoes, insignia, an ID card, and a ration book and then draw up an inventory of personal possessions lost with the ship. He also had to regenerate his service and medical records from memory. After two weeks of picking up the pieces, he was almost ready to return to the relatively simpler port and starboard watches off Savo Island.

Almost, but not really.

He wasn't very proud of his performance at Savo. They'd all talked about what might happen when untested *Winston* finally ran up against the battle-hardened Jap fleet. The enemy had a big base up at Rabaul, at the top of the Solomon Islands chain, which gave them what tacticians called interior lines of defense. The night after the main landings, four cruisers and a couple of destroyers found out what that meant. Now it was September, and the American Navy was still operating out in the Solomons at the end of a long, long logistical tether. So far in this war, Marsh knew that the Americans had had their asses handed to them twice, once at Pearl and again off Savo. The ships out there now were experiencing almost daily air attacks, submarine alarms, real and imagined, and running gun battles with Jap shore artillery. Enemy heavy cruisers were coming down the Slot regularly in search of another night-fight, which meant that every ship out there spent the night at GQ, tightening everyone's emotional and physical bands.

The Marines ashore on Guadalcanal, of course, had it worse: The Navy ships would withdraw out of the amphibious support area when they learned of an impending nighttime visit from Rabaul. All the Marines could do was dig ever deeper into the muddy bowels of Guadalcanal when the offshore shelling began, hunkering down while their planes and equipment roasted in gasoline fires topside. People who'd been out there were telling stories of Marines who looked like walking zombies crawling out of bunkers in the morning to find that Henderson Field, scraped literally out of the jungle by the Japanese, was a collection of swimming-pool-sized craters and burning airplane parts. So, no, he decided, he was not really ready to get back out there, even though he knew that return was inevitable.

He discovered that sitting at that long green table in front of a Court of Inquiry was not pleasant. It really was green: They had draped a green felt tablecloth over a wardroom table. The members sat on one side and the lone witness on the other. The court's stated purpose was to "inquire" into the circumstances surrounding the loss of *Winston* and the other cruisers, with "loss" being the operative word. Marsh had thought that the word referred to the fact that the ship had been lost at sea in combat, but the attitude of those grim-faced captains on the court was more like: You're one of the officers who lost the *Winston*. Lost, as in transitive verb. We want to know why you did that.

A rear admiral from the Pacific Fleet headquarters staff was the president of the court, but he rarely spoke. The other members were four-stripers, and they did most of the questioning. As only a senior lieutenant, Marsh was just outside the main beam of the court's attention, but he still had to answer a lot of questions about the particulars of the gunfight, damage control, what he knew about enemy dispositions the night before, the state of

Winston's equipment—in his case, the ship's secondary battery of five-inch guns—and the overall state of readiness in the ship. Was the crew exhausted? Did the watch arrangements contribute to that? Had they trained in night surface engagements, and, if so, when and how often? Was the damage control effort well organized and effective, or did the crew simply fall apart and scramble over the side?

Marsh answered their questions as best he could, subconsciously defending his ship and her fleet reputation. Of course there had been problems. Every ship had problems—machinery breakdowns, incomplete training, not enough repair parts, the lack of fresh food, the physical exhaustion from eight months of all-out war—but he put the best face on it that he could. He could tell from the court members' expressions that other *Winston* officers testifying before him had taken the same tack, but that didn't seem to bother them. He guessed that what they were really looking for was a sense of the ship's morale and fighting spirit. As four-stripers who'd all had command, they would have expected the same defense of their ship from their own officers and crew.

After three hours, the captain who had been questioning him asked if he had anything to add to what he'd already told them.

His knees had seized up again. Anxious to get

out of there, Marsh said no, sir. Then they surprised him.

"Lieutenant Vincent, I have a question," the president said. He looked positively ancient to Marsh, but there was nothing dull about those bright blue eyes that locked onto his like one of those Jap searchlights.

"Yes, sir?"

"Have you left anything out regarding what you did when you abandoned ship?"

Marsh tried to think, wondering if this was some kind of legal trap. He still wasn't very proud of the way he'd joined that terrified mob of sailors in running for the lifelines, especially when the court had been asking about what role the ship's officers played in executing an orderly abandon-ship.

"I don't believe so, Admiral," he said.

The president leaned back in his chair. "The court has been told," he said, "that you went back aboard *Winston* just before she capsized. Is that true?"

"Uh, well, yes, sir."

"Tell us about that, please."

Marsh told them he'd heard men banging on a hatch and had gone back to open it, and that then they all got the hell away from the ship before she took them with her.

"How did you manage that with two broken wrists and knees?"

"My kneecaps were only cracked, sir," Marsh said. "I kind of used my elbows to get aboard and climb up the deck, and then I used my feet to kick the dogs off the hatch. Some of them were already blown off, so it wasn't as hard as it sounds."

"Why didn't you simply open the scuttle?"

"Oh, well, I'd have had to use my hands, sir. Besides, the operating wheel wasn't round anymore. The deck up there on the foc's'le was humped up and deformed. Otherwise, I think they could probably have gotten themselves out."

"Indeed," the admiral said. "But they didn't. *You* got them out. You went back aboard and got them out. Right?"

Marsh thought about it for a moment, seeing where the admiral was going with this. "Sir," he said, "when I first got topside, I was scared to death. The ship was obviously finished, and we were walking on bulkheads instead of decks. The Japs had one of those big searchlights right on us. I felt like it was centered on me personally, and then they fired a full main battery salvo and I about crapped my trou. I'd seen some guys helping their buddies over the lines, but me? I didn't think. I didn't wait. I didn't help a single soul. I just slid through the lifelines like a rat as those eight-inch shells came in."

"What's your point, Lieutenant?"

"Well, the way I see it, Admiral, the fact that I went back aboard mostly just makes up for the fact that as an officer, the only leadership I displayed was getting into the water."

Marsh couldn't really look at their faces, but somehow it felt good to get that off his chest. He was still ashamed of how he'd cut and run.

"Mister Vincent," the admiral said quietly, "you had every right to be terrified under those circumstances. That doesn't make you a coward. Courage comes in many forms; what you did was not just courageous, it was valorous. Do you know the distinction?"

Marsh shook his head.

"Courage is when you function under fire. *Valor* is when you're scared to death and your brain is screaming at you to run, and yet you still turn around and go back, in your case, to get some people out of a really bad bind. In other words, Mister Vincent, you did all right out there."

Well, Marsh thought, that sounded good—but he still wondered if a couple more guys might have survived if he'd stayed on board to help them off. "Thank you, sir."

"Very well, Mister Vincent. If the members have no further questions, that will be all, sir."

"Thank you, sir."

"You can go now, Lieutenant," one of the captains said when Marsh just sat there.

"Yes, sir," Marsh said. "As soon as I can get my knees unlocked."

The captain got up, came around the table, and

helped Marsh to get up and then to stay up. A second captain took hold of his other arm, and together they got him walking. Marsh felt like a child. He was embarrassed and mostly wanted to disappear.

That afternoon after lunch he met with Commander Wilson, *Winston*'s exec, who had survived the sinking relatively unscathed, at least physically. Being a full commander, he rated his own room in the BOQ. When Marsh knocked on the door and went in, he found him sitting at his desk, which was piled high with paperwork. He was staring at a Naval Academy ring lying on his desk blotter. One side of the ring was the usual burnished gold; the other was encrusted with something black. He looked up at Marsh.

"I've got to clean this up some way," he said, pointing to the ring with his chin. "Haven't the foggiest notion how."

Marsh saw that he was wearing his own ring, just as Marsh was wearing his. "Whose is it?" he asked.

"The captain's," Wilson said. "I took it off his finger when we abandoned. I'm going to send it back to Helen, his wife. The black stuff there is all that's left of him."

"Um," Marsh said. "Are you sure it's his?"

"I wasn't when I retrieved it," Commander Wilson said, "but I found the hand on the remains

77

of the captain's chair. Once I got time to examine it, I could read his name engraved inside."

The hand. Marsh swallowed. "Can't you just wash it off?"

"I suppose," Wilson said.

Marsh suddenly realized that Commander Wilson wasn't all there just then. He had dark pouches under his eyes, a nervous involuntary tic in the side of his face, and what Marsh was beginning to recognize as that thousand-yard stare the war correspondents talked about. "I guess my real problem is what to say in the letter."

Marsh had been using the Navy's standard formula in all of his condolence letters, adding a personal note if he knew the man well enough to get it right. There'd been over three hundred men in the gunnery department, and he certainly did not know every one of them. He could see where the Navy's formulaic language probably wouldn't be sufficient for a letter to the captain's wife, especially with that ring. Realizing that the exec was emotionally exhausted, Marsh made a quick decision.

"Why don't you let me clean that up, Commander," he said.

Wilson handed him the ring without looking at him, his expression revealing that he was back on board *Winston* that terrible night. Marsh took it down to the communal bathroom and held it under hot water to rinse the dried blood off. Then he went to his room, found an old toothbrush, and went back to scrub it some more. The features of the academy and class crests were well worn, almost indistinguishable. The stone was a piece of dull jade that had a crack running across the face. By some quirk of the ring's fit, the captain's full name, engraved in spidery script, was perfectly legible inside the band.

Marsh tried to imagine the captain's wife's reaction when this memento arrived in the mail. Or maybe it wouldn't—maybe the exec would send it to one of the captain's classmates in San Diego, who would then personally bear it to the widow. And what did this say about the exec? He'd probably climbed up to the wreckage of the bridge to see if anyone had survived that final salvo. Surrounded by horrors, he'd still had the compassion and presence of mind to remember the captain's widow.

Big man.

When Marsh returned the ring, the exec asked him how he was doing.

"Hobbling as before, sir," Marsh said, "but better than a lot of us."

"Yes, indeed," Wilson said. "Listen, one of the court's members called, told me about your going back on board to get those guys out. How come I never heard about that?"

"Just like I never heard about you going back up to the bridge, Commander," Marsh said.

The XO blinked and then smiled. "Funny what we do when those dire straits show up, isn't it. Anyway, you'll be getting a medal recommendation."

It was Marsh's turn to smile. "Just what you need, XO," he said. "More paperwork."

"That kind of paperwork I don't mind doing, Marsh," he said. He held up the ring. "This, though . . ."

Marsh went from the base to the hospital by way of the officers' club for supper. Somehow the O-club manager had managed to keep a supply of fresh fruits and vegetables coming in from the island farms, and Marsh tried to eat there at least once a day. He wasn't the only officer there who was hobbling around. They kept a supply of canes at the front door so that the crips wouldn't go lurching into tables. Marsh actually needed two. He asked the manager if he could "borrow" a couple of canes. The manager said he couldn't let him do that, looked around, and then told him to bring them back before he sailed again.

The club was crowded as usual, with seemingly as many men at the bar as in the dining rooms. Marsh had never had much capacity for booze, so he joined some of the other *Winston* officers at a corner table in the dining room, where they traded stories about the court. Then he noticed that the hubbub of conversation out in the dining room behind him had subsided, as if maybe Nimitz himself had come into the dining room.

"For the luvva Mike," Billy Renton, one of the engineering officers, said. "Would you get a look at her!"

Marsh turned in his chair and almost fell out of it. Crossing the dining room toward the buffet was a small group of Navy nurses and doctors. In the center of the group was Glory Hawthorne, dressed in the uniform of a Navy nurse and still the most beautiful woman in the whole world. Marsh was staring, as was every man in the dining room, for the few seconds that it took for them to cross to the lanai and the buffet tables. Then they passed out of sight, even as his memories came flooding back.

Glory Hawthorne.

His roommates at the academy had been William "Tommy" Lewis and Mick "Beast" McCarty. The three of them had been pretty close after plebe year, to the point that, when they did date, or drag, as it was called, they sortied out into Annapolis in a group. None of them had had any money to speak of, so group operations made a lot of sense. Tommy had produced Glory Hawthorne as his date one weekend, and for the next two and a half years Beauty and the Beast had done their level best to snake her away from Tommy. She'd been a stunner even then, in her early twenties and a nursing student at Penn, and she played all three

81

of them like the goggling male fish they were. She was two years older than Tommy, as tall as he was, with shining black hair, a face that belonged in Hollywood, and a body that belonged in bed.

Tommy was the Steady Eddy of their little band and as handsome as Marsh was homely. Beast, the star athlete, naturally made several runs but inevitably bounced off Glory's cool and elegant reserve. Marsh mostly sat on the sidelines and stared longingly at her. Tommy eventually won the match and Glory's heart. They were married right after graduation, in July of 1932. That had been nearly ten years ago, and Marsh hadn't seen either of them since they were married.

On December 7 of the previous year, however, Marsh had found out that Tommy had been the main propulsion assistant in USS *Arizona*. Now he was one of the 1,177 casualties entombed in her wreckage. Marsh remembered seeing his name on the casualty lists and wondering if he and Glory were still married. It had never occurred to him that she might be out here in the war zone. He considered going over to their table out on the lanai to say hello but then decided not to. She probably wouldn't have recognized him in his current hobbling state, and that would have been really embarrassing. He would have looked like any other awkward bore trying to meet the beautiful lady. Maybe, he thought, he'd see her again on one of his hospital visits.

$\bullet \quad \bullet \quad \bullet$

A month later Marsh was surprised by two events: a promotion to lieutenant commander and a Silver Star medal, along with a Purple Heart. The promotion was early by prewar, Depression-era standards, but not these days. He knew that it was more a reflection of American losses in the Solomons and elsewhere than anything special about his own career to date.

The Pacific Fleet commander had decided to break up some of the crews of the cruisers lost at Savo. Normally, if the bulk of a crew could be taken off a sinking ship, they'd be sent elsewhere to new construction as an already cohesive unit. That simply was not possible after the grievous losses at Savo, so along with his promotion came orders to assume duties as the executive officer in a brand-new destroyer, the USS *Evans*, then fitting out at the Boston naval shipyard. By then he was more than ready to get away from Pearl. He never did run into Glory Lewis.

FOUR

"Okay, guys, there it is. Henderson International. I'm seein' no smoke, no big fires, no Zeros, so stand by to break."

Mick clicked his radio mike twice in sequence with the other five planes in the mixed section.

There it was indeed, Henderson Field, on the godforsaken island of Guadalcanal. They were flying southeast down the coast about to break into the pattern for a right-hand approach. To the west was a high hill of jungle-covered rock called Mount Austen, and beyond that was the Kavo Range. The field itself looked like a dark red scar framed by light green jungle. A second scar was emerging out of the tropical bush parallel to the first.

"Where's the Pagoda?" someone asked.

"They took it down," the section leader responded. "Japs were using it as an aim point on the field. They got artillery last night, and they're sayin' hang left of centerline when you go in."

That much was obvious, Mick thought. He could see the black craters all over the field, some of which had already filled with silver saucers of water. There were Seabees bulldozers out on the main runway, pushing red dirt into the holes.

"They gonna clear those dozers?" someone else in the flight asked.

"Negative," the section leader said laconically. "Steer around 'em, best you can. Try not to ground-loop; it tears up the runway and irritates the Seabees."

Steer around the bulldozers, Mick thought. Wahoo. That ought to be interesting in the middle of a rollout, especially with four five-hundred-pounders strapped to his wings. He was the only

Navy pilot in the gaggle. Everyone else was a Marine. They probably thought this would be fun. He got his flaps and gear down and waited to follow the flight leader into the break. He was flying an unmarked Dauntless Avenger, minus the machine gunner in the back. They'd come off the *Hornet* two hours ago, flying in as replacements for the aircraft destroyed by last night's shore bombardment, courtesy of what the Marines were calling the Tokyo Express coming down the Slot from Rabaul.

Mick was now officially an orphan. When the *Yorktown* went down at Midway, her embarked squadrons were either assigned to other carriers or, in some cases, having lost too many planes, broken up. Mick had been tagged, probably at Oxerhaus's instigation, to go into the aviation motor pool, as the orphans called it, at the Kaneohe Marine Corps Air Station on Oahu. The orphans were aviators whose planes had gone down with their carrier, or whose squadrons were now unemployed until new fleet decks came out from the west coast. Mick's injuries had given him a bit of a break at Pearl, but not for long. The extended slugfest on Guadalcanal was nearing its climax, and they needed planes and pilots out there. Any unclaimed orphan who could drive a bomber or a fighter would do, and so when two Marine Corps colonels had come down from Makalapa like a press gang to the naval base,

Mick had raised a bandaged arm and said he was a Dauntless pilot and he was bored.

"Got just the thing for that," one of the colonels called out. "When can you suit up?"

"Mark break," the flight leader called and banked his plane hard right to begin his final approach to the northwest. Mick waited his turn and then joined the spiraling column of planes swooping down onto the Marsden-matting runway. The only thing really dangerous about this landing, not counting craters and itinerant bulldozers, was the fact that he was sporting those five-hundred-pound armor-piercing bombs. If he'd been coming back aboard a carrier, he would have jettisoned any remaining bombs before committing to his final approach, but the air boss on *Hornet* had been adamant: For some unknown reason someone desperately wanted some AP ordnance at Guadalcanal. Mick had been instructed to land with the bombs on board and intact. He wasn't entirely sure what the Marines wanted with AP bombs; they'd be wasted in the jungle mud of the islands, but, as ordered, here he was.

His windshield filled with the sight of a huge black thundercloud that was obliterating the afternoon sun out over what the ship-drivers were calling Iron Bottom Sound to the northwest. He steadied out on final, belatedly ran through the landing checklist in his head, and then put the thing down on the steel runway, watching for errant bulldozers through all the dust from the plane ahead. He tried to forget about the bombs. They weren't armed, he kept telling himself. Their safe and arming plugs were stowed in the backseat. If a bomb came off it would mostly just scare the shit out of the dozer crews.

He rolled out and then taxied behind a pockmarked follow-me jeep to a hardstand, where he shut the barge down. A flight crew swarmed over the plane as he climbed down, asking about any mechanical gripes and whether or not the fifties were armed. A small truck came out to take down the four heavy bombs. He handed over the S&A plugs and then walked across the parking ramp to a large tent marked OPERATIONS. There was a big generator roaring away by the side of the tent. Inside, a bunch of Marines were sitting at tables made from bamboo poles and the tops of ammunition crates. Some were obviously radio operators, others were pounding typewriters, and another half dozen were yelling into hand-cranked field telephones. At the very back of the tent stood a tall, lanky officer wearing a cowboy hat and the gold oak leaves of a Marine Corps major.

"You the Navy guy?" he called out.

"Yes, sir," Mick said, walking back to shake hands. "Mick McCarty, barge driver first class, reporting for duty."

"Aw-*right*," the major said. "Bring us some puncher bombs?"

"I did."

"Good man," the major said. He was sporting a broad Texas accent, and his sidearm was a large, ivory-handled six-gun. "You were at Midway?"

"I was," Mick said.

"Do any good work for Jesus there?"

"Got a thousand-pounder down the forward elevator of a Jap fleet carrier," Mick said.

"You'll do to ride," the major said. "First things first—lemme show you where the club is."

They walked out of the Ops tent across a moonscape of craters, red dirt, oil-soaked sand, blasted trees, and piles of materiel covered in tattered canvas tarps. The major walked with an odd gait, almost as if some crucial part of his brain had lost comms with his legs. He led Mick to another tent, this one with a small sign out front saying O-CLUB. The sign had two bullet holes in it. There was a large crater, easily twenty feet across, right in front of the tent, filled with water. Once inside, Mick found himself in the frontline Marine Corps version of a bar. The chairs were all mortar ammo crates, some of them still containing shells. The tables were empty cable reels. The bar was the wing of a destroyed aircraft, burned at one end and exhibiting several shrapnel holes, supported by two fifty-five-gallon aviation gasoline drums. Mick hoped they were empty. Behind the wing, the booze was stored in steel chests.

"What's your pleasure, suh?" the major asked.

"Whiskey," Mick said. Leave it to the Jarboons, he thought. Set up a perimeter, post sentries and scouts, kill all the nearby Japs, and then get an O-club organized. The Navy would still have been writing the op order.

The major produced a bottle of sour mash and two canteen cups. They sat down at one of the mortar crate tables, and the major poured out.

"Your good health, Lieutenant," he intoned. "Now tell me: What the hell you doing here?"

Mick tipped his cup in a salud and got himself some hair of the dog. He heard a train of dozers go by outside, clattering like tanks. In the distance it sounded like some artillery pieces were going to work at the end of the airfield.

"I'm a carrier dive bomber," he said. "Reasonably good at my trade. I'm also a regular Navy lieutenant. Not so good in that department."

The major poured some more whiskey. "Whose dick you waltz on?" he asked.

"Air boss on the *Yorktown*, to name one," Mick said, "but that was before she got sunk. Don't know if he made it off, but if he did, he'll still be pissed."

The major nodded. "And before that?"

"Well, sir," Mick said, "who can remember all that shit."

The major chuckled. "How'd you get sent out here?"

"Volunteered."

"Oh, my," the major said. "We don't indulge in that vice around here."

"I suspect that my options were limited," Mick said. "That Marine colonel from CincPacFleet said it would be an adventure. He didn't lie, did he?"

The major grinned at him. "No, suh, he did not. Most definitely, he did not lie. This place is every bit the adventure of a lifetime, especially when the Japs come around offshore at night with their big naval guns. It's all the adventure a man could want, even for two lifetimes."

"Are you a pilot, Major?" Mick asked.

"Oh, yes, I am," the major said. "I'm the executive officer of what we call the combined air forces here on our little piece of paradise, otherwise known as the Cactus Air Force. The CO went med-down with malaria, so I'm also acting CO. Now ask me how I got here."

"You're a Marine major," Mick said. "You volunteered, of course."

"Hah," the major said. "You got me. Now ask me why."

"Why?"

"I have a brain tumor, that's why. I have a cancer, or at least all those Navy docs think so. They said there was nothing they could do for me in the way of guttin' and cuttin'. Furthermore, I am certainly going to die."

"Does it hurt?" Mick asked.

The major stared at him for a moment. "You know," he said, "that's the first intelligent question anyone's ever asked about my condition. The answer is no, it doesn't hurt. But I thank you for askin'."

"So you figure, if you're gonna die, why not do it for glory and apple pie? Instead of lying in some hospital, shitting your sheets."

"Pre-cisely, Lieutenant. For glory and apple pie. And for the chance to kill as many of these Jap sonsabitches as humanly possible, seein' as they killed my younger brother at Kaneohe on Mr. Roosevelt's day of infamy. And you know what? Killing Japs on this island is pleasant work. When they come, they come in hordes—and they die in hordes. Actually, though, that's not why *you're* here."

"But I *like* to kill Japs."

"Don't we all, suh, don't we all. But: We need a guy like you to help us kill *ships,* not a buncha yella-bellied, buck-toothed, rice-crappin' squirm-worms out there in the high weeds. I'm talkin' *big* ships. Heavy cruisers. Battleships, sometimes. We need someone knows how to plant him a big AP bomb right where it hurts on a big ship."

"I can help you, there, Major."

"Day or night?"

Mick finished his whiskey and put the tin cup down. "Day, no problem. Night? Never tried that."

"Night's when they come, though," the major said. "Night's when they come, and that's when the glorious Yew-nited States Navy seems to be either going elsewhere or adding to the litter in Iron Bottom Sound out there. All our fine carriers and such move their precious asses out of harm's way when them Dalai Nipponese come down the Slot, hissin' and spittin'. That leaves us helpless jungle bunnies sitting here while those big bastards cruise offshore and shoot the place all to hell. It's bodaciously noisy, too. Man cain't hardly sleep."

"And you want to go up at night? Do some dive-bombing, what, in the moonlight? With no visible horizon?"

"Exactomundo, pardner," the major said. "As you will find out, it beats the hell out of being down in the bunker, wondering if the next round's gonna come through all those grass-reinforced balsa-wood logs."

"Oka-a-y," Mick said. "I can see getting off the deck. I can see maybe getting set up on a cruiser or even a battlewagon, if there's enough moon, or star shells, maybe. But here's the problem: You gotta know when to drop and, more importantly, when to pull out."

"Ain't no problem, there, Lieutenant. You drop

when the little bastards look up, squint real hard, see you comin', and start to say oh-shit in Japanese."

"Actually, Major, you drop when there's enough altitude left to pull up and get away, and that depends on being able to see the horizon. That's real hard to do in the dark."

"Did I say it would be dark? It won't be dark. There's always plenty of light around here when them big ships come. Burning tents, oil drums, airplanes, ammo dumps, even the jungle burns sometimes. Lots of damn light."

Mick shook his head and grinned. The major finished his whiskey. "The real problem," he said, "is the strip, and that's because it's usually full of big-ass holes."

"So where do we land?"

"I propose to land on the beach, Lieutenant," the major said. "Them bastards never shore-bomb the beach."

Mick just stared at him. He'd seen the beach when they'd landed this afternoon. It was maybe forty feet wide, steeply slanted, with palm trees right alongside. "Any more of that whiskey in there, Major?"

"You bet," the major said with a grin. There was some noise outside, and then the rest of the flight came pushing through the tent's flaps. "And did I say welcome to Cactus?"

Outside the big black cloud arrived, releasing a

torrential rainstorm that momentarily drowned out any further conversation.

Land a Dauntless on the beach in the dark, Mick thought. These guys had been out in the jungle far too long. On the other hand, the bombing mission sounded interesting. The Japs would never expect dive bombers coming off Guadalcanal at night. For a damned good reason, he had to admit.

The next morning Mick joined the rest of the hung-over pilots in the Ops tent at daybreak. He'd been assigned to a single tent out along the runway, halfway between the duty strip and some crude hardstands back in the woods. The Marines had learned from bitter experience not to keep aircraft anywhere near the airstrip at night. The Jap cruisers had started using special fragmentation warheads on their shore-bombardment shells, which reduced unprotected parked planes to metal shreds. The major, not noticeably any worse for wear except for a slight tremor in his hands, gave the brief.

"Morning, Breakfast Clubbers," he said, pulling down a well-oiled plastic map of the island. "Welcome to yet another fine Navy day on Guadal-fucking-canal. Here's today's deal."

He told them that a two-regiment push had begun that morning north of the Matanikau River and that they would be providing air support for the grunts.

"For our lone carrier new guy, the bombs are small, two-hundred-fifty-pounders, but the advantage is you can carry four under each wing, and a two-fifty will tear *up* some Jap ass when they're in one of their holes."

Mick raised his hand. "Who controls the strike?" he asked.

The major smiled. "It ain't a strike, Lieutenant. It's escort duty. We fly in two-plane sections. Each section works for a forward air controller, what we call a FAC. A FAC is a second lieutenant with a radio, a view of the forward areas, and a death wish. Your section comes up on the FAC's freq and you get a target. One guy rolls in on the target, the other guy flies cover in case the Nips have an AA gun nearby the target. You drop, you climb out, you wait for the next call. Once you're out of bombs, you become the wingman, your buddy becomes the bomber. When you're both dry, you RTB, rearm, refuel, go do it again until sundown. The FACs have a mortarman with 'em so they can use willy-peter smoke rounds to mark the targets. Friendly front lines will be given in local landmarks, such as a buncha Marines waving at you and pointing at the bad guys. It's easy, actually."

"Bandits?" someone asked.

"We get Jap bombers from time to time, sometimes twice a day if the weather's good. We keep fighters up on CAP stations. The funny thing is, the Nips don't seem to coordinate their fighters with their bombers, so y'all should not see any Zeros."

"If we do?"

"Pickle your baby bombs and go get 'em, Lieutenant. That's why God put those fifties in your wings."

"Are there gunners for our SBDs?" another pilot asked.

"Negative," the major said. "It saves weight for more bunker bombs."

There were no further questions.

"That's it, then, boys and girls," the major said. "Breakfast on the flight line. And remember, out here we never come back with live ordnance. Find something suspicious beyond friendly front lines and crap on it if you're out of called targets. Okay? Let's roll."

Breakfast consisted of a cigarette, a canteen cup of serious coffee, and a warm mystery-meat sandwich, slathered in ketchup, mustard, and hot sauce to hide the mold. Then they launched. Mick figured that if he ran out of fuel, he could burp in the general direction of the engine and it would keep right on going.

FIVE

By early November, Mick had settled into the Cactus Air Force. They bombed, strafed, dodged friendly artillery shells whizzing through their assigned airspace, missed things and hit things. It was obvious from the radio that the ground troops were very happy that they were there. It was, Mick discovered, more fun than fleet work, and when they finally quit at sundown, he always felt like he'd done some good work for Jesus, as the major irreverently put it.

As his section came in for a landing one evening, later than usual, he noticed a couple of Seabee dozers working out on the narrow beach. One was dragging its blade backward, smoothing down the sand its treads were packing. The other was pushing over palm trees, dropping them onto the sand strip. When they all rendezvoused in the O-club tent, Mick asked the major about the dozers.

"As you saw, there ain't really a beach here," he said. "Not like back in the World, anyway. So they'll tear up a fifty-foot-wide strip of palm trees parallel to the water, level it, smooth it all out, and then lay the dead trees back out on the sand. That way, when Washing Machine Charlie comes for his nightly look-see, he don't see a landing strip.

He sees a buncha dead trees. But if he could look closer, he'd see that each tree has a wire attached to it. One dozer can run the beach after dark and pull every one of those things out the way. Tomorrow evening, see me after chow, and we'll go take a pasear down there."

Oh-oh, Mick thought. He'd been hoping the major had forgotten about his crackpot idea of going up at night. He'd done night hops at P-cola during training; they all did, but it was tacitly acknowledged that only specially trained pilots would do night ops, and they would be fighters, not bombers. Dive bombers over water were strictly visual weapons. Bombers over water at night had no visual reference to tell them when to pull out of a dive, and all that light the major had joked about would be at the airfield and not out in the sound.

Supper was a metal tray of Spam chili served over a glop of sticky rice, captured from the Japs when the Marines' own food supplies had run out. When Mick started to weep and wheeze from the chili heat, the O-club mess sergeant brought him some thick slices of bread and a quart of beer.

"Eat it all, boys and girls," the sergeant said. "This is the last meat night unless we get us a transport sometime soon."

Mick left the O-club tent an hour later, still trying to find his voice over the lingering fire of the chili. Thinking of Spam as meat required a certain suspension of disbelief, but it had actually tasted pretty good as soon as the fire overwhelmed his taste buds. The S-2—the intelligence officer— had provided the pilots with some special Spam cans to drop over the jungle. Spam on each end and a grenade with the pin pulled stuffed in the middle. The word was out that the Japs were starving, and the Marines thought it only fair to share.

Some of the guys had stayed to drink, but Mick was tired and didn't want another hangover. Because of the late hour, there were, of course, no lights along the airfield or anywhere else within the American perimeter. He knew roughly where his tent was back in the margins of the airfield, but he'd never tried it on such a dark night. He fished out his red-lens flashlight to find his way to his hardstand tent. A figure with a rifle appeared out of the dark.

"Whoa, there, Nelly," the Marine said softly. "Douse that fuckin' light."

Mick stopped and turned off the flashlight. "How do I find my way back to my tent, then?" he asked.

"You get one of us to take you, Lieutenant," the man said, shining his own red flashlight on Mick's flight suit for just an instant before switching it off. "Otherwise, a sniper will put one through your head."

"They that close?"

"Oh, yeah. They send out onesies and twosies after dark, put 'em in trees out there in the jungle with a seven-seven. You show a light, you'll git you a toe tag. Follow me, sir."

Mick obeyed the unknown Marine, grateful for the help. It fascinated him how loosey-goosey things were here at Henderson Field as compared to the carrier Navy, and yet how well the Marines had wired their hard-won base to take care of important business.

The sentry left him at his tent, reminding him to show no lights and to make sure he knew the way to his bunker. Mick knew where the bunker was in relation to his tent, but he'd never actually gone down into it. By then he could see reasonably well using the meager ambient starlight, so he walked the thirty yards from the tent cluster to the bunker, which was basically a dozer-scrape in the ground protected by palm-tree logs and sandbags. He groped his way down the crude steps, turned right and then left through the direct-fire baffle, and turned on his flashlight. The bunker was twenty feet long, twelve wide, and some ten feet below the surface. There were three benches made of planks and ammo boxes shaped in a U around the sides of the bunker. The overhead, which was made of steel shipping pallets, was supported by palm-tree trunks spaced every three feet across the wet dirt floor. The air was even hotter and more oppressive than topside and smelled faintly of eau de latrine. There was an inch of muddy water on the floor, and a rodent of some kind scuttled away when he turned on his flashlight.

He backed up the sandbag steps and went to his tent, where he checked his cot for insects and snakes with the dim red light, arranged the mosquito netting, and dropped onto the cot with an audible sigh. He knew the Marines out in the bush had no such luxuries as a net and a cot, and he wondered how they stood the constant insect assault. He left both tent flaps open to get some air, although it didn't seem to make much difference. He felt for the M-1 carbine under his cot and lifted it to lie next to him. He remembered the Marine gunnery sergeant during plebe summer indoctrination grasping a rifle in one hand and his crotch in the other while reciting: *This is my rifle, this is my gun. One is for killing, the other's for fun.* He made sure it was chambered and then set the safety.

He exhaled forcefully, sending forth a cloud of garlic and hot sauce. He thought he could hear small insects falling to the ground outside the net. *Damned* good chili, even though he thought he could feel the Spam moving around a little. Spam did that.

The next day passed pretty much like every other day at Cactus. Evening meal had been so-called hand-grenade stew on more Jap rice. It was made by taking all the different kinds of canned C-rations, blending them together, and pronouncing it stew. The troops had even more interesting names for it, and the hot sauce was in great demand. Afterward, Mick started back to his tent but then remembered that the major wanted to see him. He went to the Ops tent to find him. The major was studying a sheaf of radio messages at the back of the tent. When he spied Mick, he waved him back.

"Coast watchers on Choiseul reportin' three Jap heavy cruisers and some tin cans headed our way. They should arrive sometime between zero two and zero three hundred hours. I propose to go hunting, and I need me a wingman."

"How much moon we got?"

"Little over three-quarter, twenty-three hundred moonrise, with clear air. I've got the dozers pulling palms right now. Let's go take us a little walk."

They went down a long path to the beach area, where one dozer was hauling palm trees off the flattened sand while two more waited at the far end of their makeshift runway. The major said the strip was a little over two thousand feet long.

"This won't support an SBD," Mick said, feeling the packed sand with his flight boots.

"I was able to 'borrow' some of the repair rolls of Marsden matting for this little deal. They gonna lay down one section of metal, wide enough for us to launch side by side, for one thousand feet of takeoff roll."

"I understand that the main runway might not be there when we come back," Marsh said, "but why can't we take off on the main?"

"Because we won't know the sneaky bastards are here until shells start landing. We'll only get one shot at this, so we can't launch early and take a chance that they show up late with us outta fuel. We have to wait for the shooting to start. *Then* we launch."

Mick kicked the sand once again. "I can see us getting off here, but coming back?"

"They're gonna leave this metal here once we launch. If they need it over on the main, they'll roll it up, and then we'll do it the hard way."

"Automatic ground-loop," Mick said.

"Nah," the major said. "We'll be at least a thousand pounds lighter when we come back. You feather the prop, keep her real flat, slightly nose up, and come in gear-up. Drag your hook like you was tryin' to get a carrier wire, then ease her down into the sand. Piece'a cake."

Mick looked at the major in the darkness. He was grinning like a Cheshire cat. Mick realized he was looking at a madman.

"Think of it this way, Lieutenant," the major said. "This'll surprise the hell out of them Japs. They'll go back tonight, report goddamn night dive bombers operating over the 'Canal? Spook 'em good. We can only do it once, but they won't know that."

We'll only do it once because we're both going to be dead, Mick thought. "You do understand that the opportunities for vertigo here are just about unlimited."

"What the hell, Lieutenant, *you* know how to do this. I'm a fighter guy, but I'll just do what you do. C'mon, whaddaya say?"

The man is NAFOD, Mick thought. No Apparent Fear of Death, as they called it back at Pensacola. He had terminal cancer of some kind and didn't care if he flew himself and his tumor into the sea.

Mick did care. On the other hand, the major had a point: The Japs would in fact be stunned. Right now they owned the night. American dive bombers working at night would really upset their planning. Even better, they'd have to assume there was an American carrier in the area that they hadn't known about.

"Okay," Mick said. "Just once, though."

"That's all the planes we have," the major said helpfully. "Brief at twenty-three hunnert, strip-alert launch, probably go up around zero deuce thirty."

The fun actually didn't begin until 0240. Mick and the major had been sleeping in their respective cockpits at the northwest end of the ribbon of Marsden matting since 0030. Each of them had two of Mick's five-hundred-pounders strapped under his wings and a full load of fifty-cal. The starting crews had draped mosquito nets off the wings and slept on the hard-packed sand underneath the planes.

At 0240 what looked like heat lightning appeared behind them out over the sound, followed by the rolling thunder of heavy guns. A minute or so later there were corresponding explosions inland, to their right, as the incoming began landing on and around Henderson Field. The crews scrambled out from under the planes to start their engines. Once they were ready, Mick saluted the major and began his roll. The major waited until Mick's plane was ten lengths ahead of him and followed suit, not wanting his engine to ingest too much sand.

Between the moonlight and his fully night-adapted vision, Mick could see pretty well. He lifted off while still rolling on metal, cleaned up, flattened out to gain airspeed, and then began his climb. He didn't look back—it was the major's job to fly form on him. They went southeast, keeping low, and then curved back around to head way out over the sound to avoid flying through the arc of the shells being lobbed into Henderson Field by the Japanese ships. Mick couldn't see the ships yet, but he could see their muzzle flashes.

"Arming now," he called to the major. "Taking angels eight."

"Roger eight." The major sounded cool, calm, and collected. Mick did not feel any of those things. Takeoff had been the easy part.

At eight thousand feet they got a good view of what was going on at the airfield. There were some fires burning where the runway should have been. Closely grouped explosions showed where the cruisers' salvos were landing.

We should have brought flares, Mick thought. He could see the guns flashing and the shells landing but still could not make out the actual ships.

"Can't see 'em," he reported.

"Me, neither," the major said. "They gotta be creepin' down there somewhere."

"Let's go down-moon," Mick said, hoping for a silhouette. There was no point in making a dive into the gloom below if he couldn't see the target. He put his barge into a gentle turn toward the azimuth of the moon and then continued around 180 degrees to fly away from the darkened ships below. After a few minutes, he told the major he was going to drop down to angels three and fly back up-moon. The major rogered and followed him down.

From three thousand feet he was able to see the flashes of all three ships firing and establish a rough lineup on their formation. He still couldn't see the ships themselves, but maybe if they flew right by them, then went right and executed a two-seventy, they might get a silhouette. The problem with that was that they'd be bombing at right angles to the ships' movement, whereas doctrine called for dropping along the ships' line of advance to maximize the target footprint.

He told the major what he wanted to do. The major had a better idea.

"Let's go down to five hundred feet and strafe 'em soon as we see 'em. If we can start a fire, even a small one, then we can bomb the little fucks according to Hoyle."

"Sounds good to me," Mick said. They were passing over the gun flashes, which now were much brighter than they had been. "Descending for a two-seventy."

Once again the major followed him down, and as soon as they had the gun flashes ahead, he pulled abeam of Mick's plane so they could both shoot at the same time. Mick was hoping that the sound of the Japs' big guns had drowned out the roar of their own engines as he stared down into the darkness just below the flaring blasts of the cruiser's outbound salvos.

There. Shapes.

"Tally," he called.

"Roger tally. Light 'em up."

They were maybe two thousand yards away when they started firing. Mick descended some more, carefully watching his altimeter to level off at three hundred feet. The major matched him perfectly. The ships' masts were known to stick up as high as a hundred and fifty feet. At half a mile the ships were finally visible in the moonlight, and Mick concentrated on the middle of the three with both guns, laying down long bursts and seeing the tracers curving down into that dark mass of steel. They'll know we're here now, he thought.

"Break right, *now*," he called as they flew over the ships. "Angels three."

He knew they had to turn away from the trajectory of those big eight-inch guns or risk being shot down, if not by the main battery guns then by the mass of twenty-five-millimeter AA guns arrayed along each side of the cruisers. As they climbed out to three thousand feet behind the ship column, Mick looked back and saw a few lines of tracer trying to follow them out. He also saw a small red and yellow fire down there on the water.

"Angels seven," he called.

"Roger seven. Bombs this time?"

"Roger bombs," Mick said. "Pickle one bomb at tail-end Charlie like we briefed, then bank right, climb out, and do it again."

"Copy."

They maneuvered back astern of the ships, which were no longer visible in the gloom. The major was behind him, keeping close enough to see him but far enough back to give Mick time to dive, release, and escape. Once they gained altitude, the small fire became visible again. Mick lined up on that from seven thousand feet, waited until they were much closer, and then rolled into his attack dive.

This was the dangerous part. He had only a few seconds to line up on that tiny spot of fire, establish a lead, drop, and then make a climbing turn back to altitude. With no visible horizon reference, this was no time for target fixation, and he hoped the major understood that. He set out his dive brakes to give him time to line up and still keep an eye on his altimeter. As his altimeter passed through thirty-five hundred feet he released the first bomb.

"Bomb away and I'm coming right," he called, cleaning the brakes up. "Taking angels seven."

"Roger right to seven."

There was a large flash of light from down below, followed by a second, dimmer one a few seconds later. As they climbed back up to seven thousand feet, Mick could see a much larger fire down below them. Even better, by the light of that fire they could now see two wakes. The Japs had finally figured out they were under air attack, and were executing air-defense doctrine: Speed up, start a circle.

"I see two wakes," the major called.

"Roger two wakes and one fire."

"Let's take the easy way out," the major said.

"Go hit that bastard again. Those other pogues are gonna be too stirred up."

"Roger," Mick said.

"Dropping back," the major said.

They rolled in again on the one ship that was most visible, with a large fire in her center. More importantly, she wasn't turning. The other two had stopped firing on Henderson Field and were evading out to sea, away from Guadalcanal. They were firing wildly into the darkness, which made them more visible than before, but not like the one they'd hit.

"Rolling in," Mick called. "Same deal as last time."

"Roger deal."

This time Mick aimed well ahead of the fire, then realized that its intensity had just eliminated his night vision. He had no choice: To aim, he had to look at the fire. He flicked his eyes at the altimeter but could no longer read it. He suddenly had no idea of where he was in the attack profile. In a moment of panic, he pickled the bomb and turned out.

"Bomb away," he called. "Outbound for angels ten."

The major didn't reply, and Mick turned to look as he climbed out. He saw a large white shape rise up in front of the fire down below. "Missed it," he muttered, not realizing his mike was hot. Then his night vision disappeared entirely when a very large explosion blossomed below them, a fireball that started out bright yellow and then turned to red.

"I didn't," the major said. "Nailed that bastard."

Had to be a magazine, Mick thought. Not big enough for a main, but maybe one of the AA magazines. "I believe you did, sir," he said. "Now for the hard part."

"Na-a-h," the major called. "Now you join on me."

"My night vision is fucked."

"I'll turn my lights on," the major said. "Piece'a cake."

The big red fireball had gone out down below as they cleared the area. They couldn't see what they'd achieved, but they didn't see any more salvos headed onto the island, either. The major checked in with Base Ops as they made their first sweep over Henderson Field. It became obvious that the runway was out of action. There were several fires burning along the strip, although Mick couldn't make out exactly what was burning. They went into a wide orbit overhead while the major coordinated the beach landing with Ops on a different frequency. He wondered if that cruiser had gone down or was now limping back to Rabaul. We'll need to check that out in daylight, he reminded himself. A cripple in daylight offered a tempting target. Then the major came back up.

"Runway's clobbered. They gonna run some vee-hicles down to the beach strip, put some headlights on the sand."

"Hope those Japs have gone home," Mick said. "Nothing like giving them an aim point."

"Well, hell, if they start up again, we'll have even more light on the beach, right? B'sides, they cain't hurt sand."

Mick grinned in the darkness of his cockpit. One crazy bastard over there. "The metal still there?"

"That's affirma-hotchee, big guy," the major said, "but they have to get it back over to the field. Some bigwig inbound from Pearl at first light, so let's hustle-bustle."

The major took the lead, flying a downwind leg at about five hundred feet along the beach. They could see four jeeps' worth of headlights pointing out to sea on low beam. As they went downwind, Mick could see the lights but not the sand. Oh, well, he thought. When the major crashes and burns, *then* I'll be able to see the sand.

He slowed his barge to minimum speed, deployed flaps but not wheels, and followed the major around. Hook down, flaps down, stand by to feather the mill and then polish this trusty bastard's belly.

No, wait: The metal strip was still there! Wheels down, hook back up.

He felt a cold sweat on his back as he realized

his near-fatal error. He swallowed hard. This was going a long way past crazy shit.

He scanned the dark ocean off to his left as he descended, half expecting a blizzard of eight-inch shells to appear among the jeeps parked below. Then he saw the major's landing lights flare up as he crossed the imaginary threshold and landed in a swirl of blowing sand, rolling out the full one thousand feet of matting before coming to a stop.

My turn, Mick thought. He lined up on what he hoped was the centerline of the metal strip and set up his controls for a slow, nose-high, full-power approach onto a field he couldn't see—and then he could: The troops down below had positioned over a hundred flashlights in the holes of the Marsden matting, all pointing back and up toward the approaching planes, establishing a centerline of tiny white dots.

Piece'a cake, he thought and put her down, carrier style, right at the leading edge of the metal. It was a noisy landing, with lots of bumps, but he was able to taxi back up the hard-packed sand and shut it down right behind the major's plane. That's when he realized how hard he'd been gripping the controls. The canopy came back and there was the major, standing among a small crowd of grunts who were all clapping and cheering. Apparently the word was already out on the main field: The two nutcases had driven the Japs away. As Mick climbed out he could see a clutch of dozers rumbling down the beach, rolling up the metal strip, while another one was already pulling palm trees back onto the beach.

Back at the main field the repair effort was in full swing, with more dozers pushing dirt and sand into craters while infantrymen fought some oil fires in the nearby jungles and the offline dozer drivers, blades in the air as shields, shot snipers out of the trees. The jeep took them to Operations, where they received another enthusiastic reception. Mick let the major tell the story, with much gesturing and a full measure of expanding aviation bullshit, two cruisers absolutely sunk with direct hits, the rest of them, at least five, hightailing it out of there in a big panic, all trailing smoke and fire. Mick perched on an ammo crate, sipping some coffee that one of the sergeants had thoughtfully laced with whiskey, while the major provided the night's entertainment.

"Who're the bigwigs coming in at sunrise?" he asked the sergeant, who was watching the show with a big grin.

"New skipper's arriving," the sergeant said. "Cactus Air Force is going uptown."

Mick asked him what that meant.

"New skipper's a brigadier general," the sergeant said, rolling his eyes.

"That gonna take all the fun out of it?"

"Generals often do, Lieutenant," the sergeant

said. He looked at his watch. "You better get you some shut-eye. You're launching again at zero seven hundred."

The morning brief came and went, and they lifted off to go work the weeds. At three that afternoon, Operations called a stand-down for all hands so the new skipper could address the squadron pilots. Mick was surprised to see that the major wasn't present for the evolution. Then he learned via the sergeants' grapevine that the new general had grounded the major after learning about the night dive-bombing caper the night before. There went all the fun, Mick thought, just like the Top said.

The brigadier gave them the usual team effort, highest professional standards, the whole world is watching what we do here, it's going to be a long haul, but victory will be ours speech. Then he said there'd be a beer muster in the O-club tent in thirty minutes. Dis-missed. They all stood at attention in the sweltering heat as the general walked off with his aide and the nervous-looking operations officer. By this time, Mick was the only Navy pilot attached to the Cactus Air Force, so he decided to let the Marines do their buzz-cut bonding all by themselves. He went to find the major.

The major, it turned out, was holed up in the sergeants' version of a Navy Acey-Deucy club, which was a kluge of three CONEX boxes welded together behind high sand berms down near the beach. A lone generator struggled with wet air to provide power for two fans and one freezer. The freezer held the beer and was thus in the most secure part of the club. The major was visibly drunk but greeted Mick like a long-lost brother. A sergeant with one leg brought Mick a frozen beer and then left the two of them to talk.

"Why ain't you at the big damn deal?" the major asked.

"Couldn't find my XO, is why," Mick said.

"Not XO anymore," the major said. "They got a full bull in there now. I'm getting sent back to San Diego."

"Aw, please, don't throw me in *that* briar patch, B'rer Fox," Mick protested.

"Ain't like you think," the major said, "but never you mind. You need to get up there, git you some face time."

"Fuckit," Mick said. "Face time is usually how I get in trouble. This beer ever gonna thaw?"

"Gimme that," the major said. He pulled out a knife and cut away the top of the beer can, then passed it back to Mick. "Cactus snow cone."

Mick chewed on his beery slush. "All it needs is a Spam sandwich to make it four-star," he said.

A very young-looking second lieutenant showed up in the opening to the CONEX box. "Excuse me, sir," he said to Mick. "Are you Captain, I mean, Lieutenant McCarty, sir?"

116

"Who the hell wants to know?" the major asked, suddenly looking like he might want to fight.

"Uh, excuse me, sir, Major, but the general wanted to know where the Navy, uh, lieutenant was, sir. On account of he was missing beer muster. Sir."

The major gave Mick a sympathetic look. "Generals," he said. "They keep score, don't they. Better getcher ass up there, Lieutenant. Sir."

Mick thanked the shavetail and told him he'd be right along.

"Major," he said. "It's been a professional privilege to be on your wing and to have you on mine. Thanks for last night."

"Like I promised when we met," the major said, "we had us an adventure, didn't we. You'll do to ride, old son. Now you better get a move on before I get drunk and embarrass the sergeants' mess here."

They shook hands, eye to eye, and then Mick left to go up the beach and past the pile of neatly arranged dead palms. By the time he got to the beer muster, the general had already left on an inspection tour of the airfield's defenses, leaving the pilots to do what they did best. Mick joined right in. Sometime after dark, he staggered into his tent, his head already hurting from the formaldehyde preservatives in the beer, and dropped onto his cot. The last thing he remembered to do was to make sure his carbine, loaded and chambered, was safe like a steel baby in his arms.

In his dreams, a siren was wailing to the accompaniment of several police whistles. The sound of a giant buzz saw rose up and then drowned out all the lesser noises as he climbed toward consciousness. Then he was levitating, pressed up against the canvas fabric of his tent while his eardrums flattened inward and all the breath was squeezed out of his lungs by the explosion of a pair of fourteen-inch shells outside.

He fell back onto the dirt floor where his cot had been, stunned and spitting sand out of his mouth. A wad of rank canvas tent fabric and the mosquito net dropped down on top of him like a shroud, followed by the tops of several palm trees and then a rain of dirt and sand that seemed to go on for goddamn ever. The inside of his ears felt wet, and all he could hear now was a loud hum. Then he felt two more shells land, not so close this time but still near enough to press even more debris onto him with the double shock wave. He tried to draw a breath but got a mouthful of netting instead.

Bunker, he thought, twisting to get on his side. Gotta get to the bunker. He felt rather than heard more shells landing, some close, most distant, great big shells that hammered the ground with jaw-rattling power.

He tried to move sideways but couldn't. It felt like there was at least one tree trunk pressing down directly on the tent, along with several hundred pounds of dirt, palm fronds, and other things. More shells were landing, but these were trending farther away, in the direction of the landing strip. They were also different. They weren't pounding the ground but seemed to be going off in the air, followed an instant later by a hail of steel fragments shredding the palm groves and anything else that had the misfortune to be vertical out there.

He decided to relax, wait for help. As long as he stayed on his side he could draw a breath, and the mound of debris above him was probably protecting him from the shrapnel that was decapitating whole trees and reducing any unprotected airplanes to aluminum confetti. The shelling seemed to go on forever. He wondered if the major had gotten off on one of his night bombing sorties. Then suddenly it ended, abruptly as it had begun.

His head hurt, and he was thirsty. The air in his tomb seemed hotter than before, if that was possible. He wondered just how much shit was piled on the remains of his tent. Would they find him? Was there anyone left alive out there to even look? The general had told the pilots about the possibility of Jap battleships coming down from Rabaul to work over the airfield, especially after last night's dive-bombing attack. Most of the guys had thought he'd been exaggerating, adding a little drama to his own arrival on the island and throwing some shit at the major. Mick had missed the speech, fortunately, because he would have asked the general if the battleships would still come now that there were night dive bombers on the island. He'd experienced some eight-inch howitzer fire during advanced flight training down in Texas, but these shells had been bigger. Much bigger. Maybe the general had been right. Mick hated that thought.

Breathing was getting harder. His lungs worked, but there simply wasn't much breathable air.

Great, he thought. I'm gonna suffocate down here under all this debris. Okay, hotshot, he told himself; can't just lie here anymore. Nobody's coming to rescue your worthless ass. This is like the *Yorktown*: time to *do* something.

He wiggled around under all the debris to see what would move and what wouldn't. He was able to reach the survival knife sheathed on his right lower leg and pull it straight up to his waist, but he couldn't turn his hand to apply the big knife to the canvas. He squirmed some more, but his movements shifted something on top of him, and now his legs became immobilized as a load of sand slid down to bury them under serious weight. He was afraid to cut through the canvas only to admit a ton of sand right in his face. He felt the cold steel of the carbine barrel against his right cheek, but the rifle wasn't going to get him out of here.

Buried alive, he thought, and then banished the thought. He felt something wet on his cheek. He hadn't felt the sting of a cut, but it was definitely wet. He was able to get to the tiny flashlight on his flight suit with three fingers and turn it on. In the red glow of the light he could see a black stain on the canvas, a stain that was slowly growing.

Oh, Jesus, he thought. I'm in a crater, and the groundwater is filling it up. Just like all the craters he'd seen when he landed that first day.

He felt a drop hit his cheek, and then another.

Wait a minute, he thought. Groundwater would be coming *up,* not down. He flicked his tongue out to the side of his mouth.

Salty.

Not water.

Blood.

It was blood, and it wasn't his. Not good.

He closed his mind against the ghastly images that were rising in his imagination. He'd made the mistake of looking down into the flight deck catwalks of the *Yorktown* as they were taking him over the side to that cruiser. The flight deck crews had used fire hoses to sweep body parts off the deck into the catwalks. As the wounded carrier listed farther and farther to port, the catwalks had become a scene right out of *The Jungle.*

He closed his eyes and tried to slow his breathing. He knew that when the air ran out he'd start breathing his own CO_2, and that would put him to sleep. His ears were still humming like a big generator, so he wasn't sure he'd even hear rescuers outside calling to see if anyone was under all the debris. The drip on his cheek continued. He closed his eyes and tried to think of a way out.

A while later, something hit his arm. He looked sideways in the dwindling light of the flashlight. It was a piece of rebar. It withdrew as quickly as he identified it. Then it came again, this time hitting his chest. He yelled.

Silence. He strained to hear something over the humming in his ears. Then he thought he heard voices. Angry voices. Disgusted voices.

The probe came again, this time barely visible, on his left side.

He understood. There must be a body on top of him. The probe had come up bloody, and the rescuers were moving on.

He yelled again, but it was really hard to get enough air. Even to him, his yell sounded more like a squeak. Then he remembered the carbine.

Was its barrel full of dirt? Would the damned thing explode if he fired it? So what? he thought.

He twisted his wrist, reached into the trigger guard, and pulled the trigger.

Nothing happened.

The safety was on. He tried to move the tab, but his fingers couldn't get enough leverage.

With a desperate push, he got the safety off, put his finger back into the trigger guard, and pulled the trigger. The carbine bucked backward, slamming his right hand against the sand. It felt like it was broken.

The noise was overwhelming in his tightly packed dirt grave. Gun smoke filled the air pocket. His whole hand stung, and his fingers seemed suddenly full of pins and needles. He pulled the trigger again, not with a squeeze of his finger but more of a spasm. The second blast really hurt his bleeding eardrums, but he was determined. If I'm gonna die, I'm gonna die trying, he thought, ears or no ears.

Moments later, hands were scrabbling through the dirt, and he got his first breath of clean air, and then another. It took them five minutes to dig him out. A face kept telling him he was going to be okay and not to fire the carbine anymore, okay, Lieutenant? The face looked to be fifteen, tops. Very young, and very scared. "Me, too, pal," he mumbled, spitting out some more sand.

Once they hauled him out, they put him on a litter. He protested that he could walk, but the Navy pharmacist's mate ignored him. "It's okay,

Lieutenant," one of the kids said. "You're gonna be fine, but let's try the jeep just for grins, okay?" As they drove him out of the camp area, he saw in the headlights that the bunker, or the crater where the bunker had been, was already filling with groundwater. There were bloody *things* floating in that water. He repressed a wave of nausea as he realized that everyone who had sought shelter in the bunker was now hamburger.

Several oil fires up and down the taxiways and the hardstands illuminated the field. Mick couldn't see what was burning, but the runway was really torn up and there were pieces of airplanes everywhere, even in trees. Amazingly, the Seabee dozers were already out, their diesel engines roaring at full power, some pushing loads of sand and jungle dirt into the huge craters while others jammed the wreckage of the planes into the jungle or laid their buckets down on fires to smother them. The occasional tracer round spat out from the edge of the field as perimeter defense troops dealt with snipers out in the near jungle.

The pharmacist's mate had the jeep in first gear, which was painfully noisy to Mick's bludgeoned ears. Mick asked him what had happened.

"Jap battlewagons," the young petty officer said. "Fucked everything up. You could see 'em, offshore, big-ass clouds of fire, and then those shells comin' in, wa-wa-wa, *boom!*"

"You were *watching?*"

"Yes, sir," the kid said proudly. "I was sleepin' in one of the meat wagons? Wasn't nowheres else to go, so I opened the back doors and watched."

"You didn't run for your bunker?"

"Us medics don't have no bunkers, Lieutenant. If we're in a bunker, we can't see where we're needed, right?"

"Right," Mick said, lying back at last. Medics, he thought. Someone back at pharmacist's mate school had told them that they were invincible, God bless 'em.

A chief pharmacist's mate was doing triage at the field hospital, which was a long tent surrounded by litters spread all over the ground. Mick said he wasn't really hurt. "Other than this," he said, holding up his right hand. "This doesn't work so well right now."

"No need to shout, Lieutenant," the chief said, examining the hand. "I'm right here."

Mick stared at the man. "I was buried alive, Doc," he blurted out, surprising himself when he said it.

"Scary, was it?" the chief asked, making notes on his triage pad.

"Are you shitting me?"

"Not a pound, Lieutenant. Me? I'd'a drowned in my own piss. Listen, you want a Section Eight, I can start the paper."

"Hell, no," Mick said. "I want to go get that

battleship. Tell the major I'm ready to beach-party with him again."

The chief frowned. "Um," he said. Mick had to bend forward to hear him over the bloody hum in his ears.

"What?"

"The major tried to take off when all this shit started. Hit a crater, ground-looped, burned."

"Fuck!"

"Yeah," the chief said.

"Shit," Mick said. "Shit. Shit. Shit."

"That's what everybody's saying."

"He told me he had a brain tumor," Mick said. "That since he was gonna die anyway, he might as well take some Japs with him."

The chief medic smiled. "Brain tumor, hunh? Not exactly."

"I wondered."

"Yeah, well, what the major had was a drinking problem. A flight surgeon had to clear him each morning before the brief. Thing was, I think that ol' boy could fly better hammered than most of the boot pilots flying stone cold sober. So, yeah, they let him go kill Japs. You know he was an ace?"

"I believe it. He was a leader, is what he was."

"That's gospel, Lieutenant," the doc said, rubbing weary eyes. "So, you ready to launch and go find some Japs?"

"I need some coffee," Mick said, "and maybe

one small taste of bourbon whiskey. But then? Hell, yes."

"Bourbon whiskey," the doc said, patting him on the shoulder. "That sounds familiar."

His shoulder hurt when the doc patted him. Hell, everything hurt. Except his rapidly enlarging right hand, and that worried him.

He got his shot of medicinal whiskey, which was horrible, and then made his way to the Operations tent, which somehow had survived the bombardment. There was a new enormous crater in front of the tent, over which a plank bridge had already been built. The generator had been disabled by the blast, so the men inside were operating with flashlights. The big problem was that there weren't any planes left. The Japanese battlewagons had blown Henderson Field into a mud-mire, and most of its aircraft were in charred pieces out among the few palm trees still standing.

"No planes at all?" Mick asked.

A Marine warrant officer looked up at him with bleary eyes, a cigarette going in each hand. "Yes, sir, there's four. But there's no gas."

"If I can scrounge up some gas, can I get one of the four?"

"Could you sign for it with that hand, Lieutenant?"

Mick looked down at his right hand, which was now almost twice its original size. He tried to make a fist, but nothing happened. It still didn't hurt.

"Well, fuck me," he muttered. "Lookit that piece of meat."

"Keep you and it out of that field hospital," the warrant advised. "They got a new surgeon over there, came in with the general. Likes to cut shit off."

"Might as well," Mick said. "I can't feel the damned thing."

He went back over to the triage tent and told the chief pharmacist's mate he couldn't feel his hand anymore.

"You will," the chief said. He reached into his pocket and pulled out a small pill bottle. He gave Mick two pills. "When it starts to hurt, take 'em both, and be sitting down when you do. Preferably somewhere safe. That right there is seriously strong stuff."

Mick went out the back entrance and walked down what was left of the open-air flight line. When he came to the regular field hospital tents, he saw that many of the forms in their shabby litters had their faces covered in bloody blankets. There were only a few fires still going now out along the runway, and what sounded like a brisk small-arms firefight had erupted at the other end of the runway. He realized he could hear again. He rubbed the dried blood off his neck and crackled his eardrums a couple of times.

His right hand now felt like a lead boxing glove. The carbine must have broken it when he'd fired it underground, he thought. Otherwise he felt relatively okay. A little shaky-Jake, maybe, and his flight suit smelled like a latrine, but he was alive, unlike these poor bastards. He stepped into the hospital tent and asked a blood-spattered pharmacist's mate for a sling. He rigged the sling, cadged a tin cup of coffee, and went back outside, where he sat down on a stump.

He felt like he should be writing a letter home to tell someone he was still alive. The only problem with that was that he had no one left at home to write to. His father had been the vice president of his hometown bank when the crash came. He'd committed suicide when the bank failed in 1929 and revealed some damning irregularities. His mother had withdrawn into mute madness a year later, and Mick, their only child, had thrown himself into his varsity football career at the Naval Academy. His mother was now in a state home for the insane. He wrote her letters from time to time, but the last time he'd gone back to see her, she might as well have been on Mars.

He surveyed the devastation around the field and decided to stay right where he was. It was like being back on a carrier after an attack. If an aviator couldn't fly, he was expected to stay the hell out of everyone else's way. For the next hour he watched more jeeps come grinding in to the field hospital, litters sticking out of their backseats, with far too many of them carrying people to the parking lot morgue. He slipped off the stump, leaned back against it, and went to sleep.

At sunrise, two R4Ds touched down on the freshly repaired main strip. They taxied up to the field hospital and shut down in a cloud of blue exhaust smoke. Mick recognized them as the military version of the redoubtable Douglas DC-3, rigged out as aeromedical transports. The field hospital people came out and began loading the most seriously wounded into the waiting transports. A Marine first lieutenant came over from the Ops tent, spoke to one of the pharmacist's mates, and then headed for Mick. He was extremely thin from malaria and was walking with a cane. Mick figured he must have weighed a good ninety pounds.

"You Lieutenant McCarty?" he asked.

"Yup."

"You're supposed to ride the medical flight to Santo."

"What for?"

"That," the man said, pointing at Mick's hand. "You can't fly with that, so they want you there for treatment. There's a real hospital there."

"I can fly with the other hand, you know."

"Hey, Lieutenant, I'm just the messenger boy,

okay? That's the word from the CO. If you can fly, you stay. If you can't, you go get fixed."

"What'd you do in real life?" Mick asked.

The guy grinned. "FAC," he said. "Sniper shot my knee off. Now I run errands here at Ops. Good deal, hunh?"

Mick shook his head, got up stiffly, and walked over to the nearest transport. He was immediately conscripted to help load the wounded. When they saw he couldn't use his right hand, they stationed him on the appropriate side of each litter so that he could carry with his left hand. Fair enough, he thought. My legs still work.

When they were ready to go, he told the loadmaster that he was supposed to go to Santo. The Army Air Corps sergeant looked at him blankly for a moment. "Ain't no seats in there, Captain," he said.

"It's Lieutenant," Mick said. "Naval air. I guess I can stand up."

"It's two hours, Lieutenant," the sergeant said.

"The general said I have to go to Santo," Mick replied.

"On you go," the sergeant said. "Hustle up, though. They're sayin' there's an air raid inbound from Rabaul."

They launched five minutes later, bumping and banging over the rough repairs on the runway. Several of the wounded cried out in pain as the heavily loaded transport gunned it down the strip, its engines shooting flames out the exhaust pipes, and lifted reluctantly at the very end of the matting. Mick found himself a cubicle at the back of the plane in the life jacket locker. He put on a kapok so that it would support his head, sat down among the stash of life jackets, and leaned back on the remains of the Ops generator that was being sent on to Nouméa for repairs. Forward of him were racks and racks of litters hung on the sides of the transport, four high. He could see pharmacist's mates and a couple of Navy nurses tending to the wounded, hanging bottles, wiping brows, handing out pills and sympathy. The pilots let some exterior air in as they climbed through five thousand feet, and for the first time since he'd been on the island, Mick experienced air-conditioning.

His right hand was beginning to throb, though. He pulled out the two pills. Take 'em both, the medic had said—but if something happens, I don't want to be zombied up here, Mick thought. He decided to take one, keep one. In fifteen minutes he was sound asleep.

Seemingly seconds later he was yanked awake by the sound of twenty-millimeter cannon shells blasting through the back of the aircraft, and then pinned to the left side of the fuselage as the pilots tried to jink away from what had to be a Jap fighter behind them. Mick tried to gather his wits, but his brain was numbed by the pill. He felt the heavy shells whacking the generator at his back while others slashed by his head and down the full length of the transport. He heard screams as some of them hit wounded men, and then the Douglas went way over in a left bank, pulling g's that forced Mick hard against the floor. The interior of the cabin was filling with smoke, and one engine absolutely didn't sound right.

There was another hail of gunfire from behind the aircraft, and both engines quit in a gasp of oil and shattered pistons. The only noise now was that ominous airstream howl of an aircraft fully out of control, going down in a wide left spiral.

Well, fuck me, Mick thought. I've tangled with Zeros before, but now I'm gonna buy the farm as a *passenger?*

The smoke in the cabin grew thicker, and Mick instinctively turned his face into the stack of life jackets as the plane's dive steepened, the sound of the slipstream outside rising to a crescendo. At least there were no more rounds slamming into the transport's innards, but that fact hardly made a difference.

Going down, Mick thought. Gonna hit that concrete surface of the ocean at three hundred knots, and then we'll find out if all the preachers were right or wrong.

Strangely he was not afraid. He'd been in combat, he'd had some near misses, and half the guys he'd been flying with were already dead. It was as if this were simply a natural outcome. He remembered the unofficial slogan of some of the *Yorktown* pilots: *Fly Navy. Die Navy.*

That refrain sounded a bit off to his drugged brain, but there was nothing he really could do about it, was there, he thought. He wondered if the pilots up front were already dead, but then the transport banked sluggishly back to the horizontal. He began to lean the other way, toward the aisle. The g-forces grew in his belly as the plane pulled up, leveling for a ditch in the Pacific.

No, no, no, Mick thought. Too fast, much too fast: You can't ditch at this speed. You fly flat, pull up the nose, stall the bastard ten feet over the water, keeping her wings level, and close your eyes. Assuming you still had engine power. From the sounds of it, though, these guys were trying to fly that proverbial rock the instructors were always talking about.

The light coming through the portholes changed from white to blue, and he felt the nose come up and hold. He braced himself into the pile of life jackets and waited. The big generator behind him had probably saved him from the storm of bullets from that Jap fighter. Now he prayed that the thing was firmly lashed down or it was going to crush him when they hit.

He felt the tail keel pounding waves, and then the plane slammed into the water with a vicious crash. The chorus of screams from the wounded was overwhelmed by the roar of water along the plane's sides. Then it was suddenly silent, but only for a moment. The groans and moans of the wounded men strapped to the hull of the transport were terrible to hear. The aircraft remained relatively level, but Mick already felt water rising around his ankles. He checked his own extremities, disentangled himself from his nest of life jackets, and looked forward along the aisle.

The interior was filled with dust. The patients were still all strapped in lengthwise in their tiers of litters on either side of the aisle. Then he saw the sheen of seawater on the floor. The light coming through the portside portholes was white at the top but going green at the bottom.

Get out, get out, *get out!* a soundless voice was screaming in his ear.

He climbed over a pile of equipment boxes and headed forward through the center aisle, trying not to look at the wounded men, their bandages all red with new bleeding, some moaning, some crying, bandaged hands reaching for him as he went forward.

There were three bloodied nurses piled up in front of the cockpit door, which itself was riddled with bullet holes. Two of the nurses were either unconscious or dead, but one was trying to extricate herself. He reached her and pulled her to her feet, very much aware that the water here reached his knees. The main hatch was on the left side, back by where he had been sitting. He started pulling her toward the back of the aircraft, but she resisted.

"The wounded," she mumbled. "We have to get them out."

He looked down at her. Brunette. Plain, round face; terrified brown eyes. Bloody uniform, hands, and wrists.

"How?" he asked. "They can't swim, they can't even float."

"You've got a life jacket—where are the rest of the life jackets?" she said. "I'll start unstrapping."

"We have to open the hatch before the plane sinks any deeper," he said. "Otherwise the water pressure will seal it."

"You open that hatch, we'll flood," she said, and then she realized that it was hopeless. She was looking past him, back into the cabin, at the tiers of litters, stacked like the remains in a catacomb. The lowest tier was already awash. They were the most seriously wounded, and many were already unconscious. Mercifully, Mick thought.

He could see that she understood. Moving the wounded was impossible. Open the hatch, the plane would flood and sink rapidly. Leave it closed and they'd go down with it. At the rate the water was already coming in, there was absolutely nothing that could be done for the wounded. They were aboard the plane because they were so badly hurt they couldn't even move. Now they were all going to die.

"Are they alive?" he asked her, pointing at the two inert nurses.

"I don't think so," she said in a small voice, her fingers brushing all the holes in the cockpit door. "There were so many bullets."

Behind them there was a crash and a yell of pain as one of the Marines, who had managed to unstrap himself and his litter, fell to the floor, where he floundered faceup in foot-deep water. Other wounded men were shouting now to let them out, while still others, the ones who knew what was going to happen, just sobbed or cried for their mothers. The air was getting unbreathable as the plane settled into the sea, its heavy engines beginning to drag the nose down.

Mick sighed and took her by the arm, and together they sloshed back along the aisle, stepping over the man on the floor, who was now quiet, no longer struggling, his wide-eyed face already under half a foot of water. When they got to the hatch, Mick pulled the operating handle to the open position. It didn't move. He grabbed a stanchion on either side of the hatch, swung both legs up against it, and pushed hard. His swollen right hand came back to life with a lance of pain that nearly made him faint, but the hatch handle moved a few degrees, and then a few more. A small wall of seawater flooded in, and as it did, the angle of the floor deepened toward the nose. He shoved the hatch up.

"Get out, now!" he shouted at the nurse, who seemed unable to function. She was still looking back at all the wounded strapped to what was going to become their coffin, her hands at her mouth, her eyes filling with tears. He would have pushed her into the gap at the bottom of the hatch, but it was taking everything he had just to keep that gap open. The structure of the plane gave off a low groan as the fuselage was subjected to reverse stresses, and then the plane began an ominous roll to the right. Even so, the water was streaming in now, much of it flowing aft from the cockpit door. A porthole on the right side burst, and the plane began to really fill. The roll to the right exposed the bottom of the hatch for a moment, and Mick, who'd been pushing on it to hold it open, felt himself falling into the opening as the hatch popped up. The river of water coming in threatened to sweep him back into the cabin, so he let go, grabbing the nurse by one ankle and pulling her out of the airplane as they went into the sea.

When they surfaced, the left wing was rising into the air above them, its engine spewing steam and oil beneath the badly bent propeller blades. The nurse was floundering right in front of him and crying hysterically. He grabbed the front of her shirt with his good left hand and started a half-ass backstroke to get away from the plane and the growing slick of high-octane aviation gasoline on the water. For some reason they were drifting forward along the hull of the transport. Mick felt something, a rumble of some sort, and looked up. The left wing was dropping back into the sea. He kicked hard, still dragging her with him, as the huge sheet of aluminum slapped the sea ten feet away, stinging his eyes with a flat, hard sheet of spray.

Right wing broke off, he thought. Momentarily exhausted, he stopped swimming and took stock of his passenger. She had fainted and was now a dead weight on him and the sole kapok. He treaded water for a few minutes and looked around. The blue Pacific stretched to the horizon in every direction. He thought he could see the tops of the Kavo Range back to the northeast, but he couldn't be sure. Had the pilots managed to get out a Mayday?

He focused back on the plane, which appeared to have reached some state of equilibrium in the sea, albeit with just the very top-line of the fuselage and the tail fin showing. The only sounds came from the portside engine, which was making clicking sounds as it cooled in the ocean. The top of the main hatch was barely visible. There was no more screaming inside the cabin.

We need a raft, he thought. He'd seen what looked like inflatables lashed to the bulkhead right by the main hatch. Would the damned thing float long enough for him to get back inside and snatch a raft?

He shook the nurse, then yelled at her. Her eyes fluttered open and then widened in shock. "Wha-a-a . . . ?" she exclaimed.

"Tread water," he ordered, letting go of her as he began to untie his kapok. She went under immediately but then popped back up, spluttering.

"Take this jacket," he said. "I'm going back inside, see if I can get a raft."

She just stared at him blankly until he got the last string off and then dropped the already sodden life jacket into her arms. She failed to grab it, and a small wave began to take it away. He swore, retrieved the kapok, spun her around in the water, and manhandled her arms through the holes. He tied a single chest string and then let her float. She was sobbing again, her small fists pressing against her eyes.

The plane was now more than fifty feet away, barely visible except for the vertical stabilizer. He wondered why it didn't sink but prayed for another five minutes as he set out for that hatch.

By the time he got alongside, the top of the hatch was underwater and the top-line radio aerial was level with his face. He saw a large wrinkle developing in the skin just above the hatch as the left wing flexed in the underlying swells. He took one deep breath and then went under the partially opened hatch and into the cabin. There was some ambient light, but not much. Everything was illuminated in seawater green. There were hundreds of white shapes suspended in the interior, which he realized were probably bandages. Hanging onto the hatch coaming with his left hand, he grasped around in the darkness where he thought he'd seen the rubber bundles. He made sure not to look forward into the main cabin. He couldn't find the rafts, and now he needed air.

If she's floating, he thought, there has to be an air pocket. He took a big chance and went all the way into the cabin and let himself float up to the ceiling, where there was indeed an air pocket. It was foul and extremely wet air, but it beat breathing water. He took a couple of breaths and went back down into the murk around the open hatch, which was now just a greenish square of light against the gathering darkness. This time he found one of the rafts. He tugged on it, but it was lashed down and he couldn't find the release snaps. He was again running out of air. He began to panic as he heard structural breakup noises crackling in the water around him. He went up, got more air, and went back down twice more but could not find a way to release one of the rafts from the bulkhead.

On the third try his left hand found a D-ring. From his training days at Pensacola, he knew that D-rings were actuators.

Screw it, he thought and pulled hard. The raft began inflating in a noisy rumble of CO_2. He grabbed one end of the raft, now beginning to bulge like a loaf of rubber bread, and pulled himself over to the hatch coaming. If this works, the pressure of inflation ought to break the straps, he thought. If it takes too long, the raft will inflate and be stuck inside the plane.

He pulled some more, trying to position the writhing bundle of rubber in the hatchway, but then he was out of air. He let go, went out the hatch, and lifted to the surface, accompanied a moment later by two loud bangs and then the entire fifteen-man life raft. By the time he got himself alongside the raft and his left arm through one of the straps, the plane's tail had disappeared. There was no dramatic underwater convulsion. One moment she was there, the next she was gone, gliding like a razor blade into the depths with her cargo of the very unlucky.

He hung alongside the raft for a few minutes, getting his breath, and then rolled over the side into the raft. Then he sat up and looked around for the nurse.

He couldn't find her.

He got up on his knees, trying to get his sight line a little higher, and yelled out over the empty waves. Even if she'd passed out again she'd be floating, he thought. I know I got that one strap tied on her. He stretched to see better and kept shouting. He tried to stand up, but the raft was too unstable. After ten minutes, he quit. She was simply gone. The seas were maybe one to two feet, but he could see at least a few hundred yards in every direction.

Nothing.

He sat back down on the rubber bottom of the boat and examined his throbbing right hand. It was no bigger, but it looked darker, as if there were blood pooling under the skin. He heard something in the water and looked up. A large dark gray fin was cutting through the water nearby. He remembered her bleeding hands. That might explain where she went, he thought, suddenly very glad for the raft.

The seas remained relatively calm, and the morning was not yet half over. Take the rest of the day off, Lieutenant Jonah, he told himself. He tried not to think of all those wounded guys, strapped down tight in their litters as the plane filled with water. He felt really bad about not having saved any of them, but on the other hand, what could he have done? Pushed their broken and bleeding bodies into the water so they could drown sooner?

Still.

He heard what sounded like an airplane engine and rolled over. He scanned the bright sky but couldn't find it.

Japs? Coming back to machine-gun survivors? He'd heard all the stories.

The sky appeared to be clear, but then he saw there was a light haze at about five thousand feet. The plane seemed to be executing a square search, but there was no point in waving or doing anything else. If he couldn't see them, they couldn't see him, either. After a few minutes the plane droned off to the northwest, back toward Guadalcanal.

Mick got back up on his knees and took another look around for the missing nurse but still saw nothing except a few more shark fins in the distance. He rousted out the raft's supplies bag, in which he found C-rations, water, and cigarettes. He drank one can of water but, after the horrifying scene inside the plane left the food alone. He ignored the two short-handled paddles strapped into the gunwales; he was too tired to start paddling. First he'd see which way the raft seemed to be drifting. There were some inflatable life jackets in another bag. He put one on but left it deflated. The jacket had a battery-operated light, which might come in handy if they came out later in PT boats or perhaps even sent a destroyer. He knew that rescuers would be out if, and only if, the pilots had had time to get a Mayday out when the Zeros jumped them. If not, nothing would happen until the aeromedical flight failed to arrive in Espiritu Santo. By then he would have done some serious drifting. He set up one of the sun flaps, lay down against the rubbery side of the raft, and dozed.

He awoke at sunset. The evening sky was red and orange, with enormous cumulonimbus towers building across the western skies. He scanned the horizon to see if he could make out any aspects of land but now saw nothing, not even the high ridges on Guadalcanal. The seas were still pretty calm. His face felt sunburned from the reflected light, but otherwise, with the exception of his throbbing right hand, he was none the worse for wear. The raft was equipped to sustain fifteen survivors for a week, so as long it stayed afloat and he stayed in it, *and* no Jap planes saw him, he would probably survive. He found one of the keeper lanyards, snapped it to his life vest, and then restowed the supplies pouch. He also found the flare gun and six rounds of flare projectiles. He made sure he knew where the bailing bucket was. If the weather on Guadalcanal had been any example, sea conditions could change rapidly out here. He still wasn't hungry but forced himself to eat part of a C-ration and drink one more can of water. He remembered he still had one more pill. He fished around in his trouser pockets and produced one badly crumbled tablet. He took it anyway and went back to dozing.

He was awakened by a rainsquall around midnight. There was no thunder and lightning, just a sudden cold downpour that seemed to flatten the seas. He lay back, opened his mouth, and used the rain to rinse away the taste of the pill. With his head flat on the rubber bottom of the boat, he thought he heard, or more likely felt, a deep vibration in the water.

He sat back up. It was a starless night with the tail end of that rainsquall drifting overhead, but now he could definitely hear the rumble of one or more big diesels. PT boats? The engines sounded too big for that. A Jap destroyer? He shivered in the dark at the thought. He couldn't remember if destroyers were diesel or steam, but he thought they ran on steam turbines. He cupped an ear and then turned in the raft to locate the sound, but it seemed to surround him. Whatever it was, it was coming nearer by the minute. Finally he thought he could pinpoint the direction. He wasn't too worried about a collision—the rubber raft would bounce off the hull of a ship unless it was a direct, cut-it-in-half hit.

Should I signal? That was the question. What if it's a Jap? He was pretty sure that he was roughly south and east of Guadalcanal. The Japs were based north of the island, so there was no reason for one of their warships to be this far south. That's what the guys at Pearl Harbor had thought, too, he remembered.

The rumble grew louder, but he still couldn't see anything in the rain-washed darkness. Then he could. A black bow emerged out of the darkness, low down on the water, pushing a gray-white bow wave ahead of it. He could see a line of holes along the near side and then what looked like a deck gun topside.

A submarine, running dark on the surface—but whose? He had only seconds to decide.

He reached down to his life vest and switched on the one-battery white light. It almost blinded him in the darkness, so he felt rather than saw the bulk of the sub slide by. Just for the hell of it, he yelled out, "Hey, rube!"

A moment later the raft wobbled in the water as the sub's wake pushed it away. He felt the spray from the engine exhausts blowing in his face and smelled diesel oil. Then the engines slowed down. Had they heard him?

He broke out a paddle and used it to turn the raft so that he faced the direction of the engine noise. The sub was running totally dark, so he could only listen, but he kept the light on. It had a single battery that wouldn't last long, but in the almost absolute darkness it shone like a lighthouse.

The engine noises seemed to die away in the distance. He quit paddling and sat back on his haunches, not knowing what if anything would happen next. He thought about turning off the light to save the battery, but if they did turn around, that would be the only way they'd find him. Maybe he should fire a flare.

Ten minutes later he was startled when something big nudged the raft sideways from behind him, and when he looked up, there was the submarine's bow, right overhead. There were figures out on deck, shining red flashlights down on him.

"Douse that white light," someone called. Mick switched it off.

A rope ladder came whistling out of the dark and thumped into the life raft. Mick didn't hesitate. He pulled the ladder taut and scrambled up the slippery wet rungs until two strong hands pulled him on deck.

"Who are you?" a voice asked.

Mick identified himself.

"Pilot?"

"Yeah, Navy, but I was a passenger this time." He told them what had happened. He heard a ripping noise alongside, and then the rope ladder was being pulled back aboard. He heard air escaping from the raft as it began to sink, and then arms were leading him to a hatch in the foredeck. He climbed one-handed down a really steep ladder, with one sailor below and another above. The hatchway and the entire interior of the submarine were also red-lighted. His ears popped when they shut the big round hatch at the top of the ladder.

An hour later he was sitting in the tiny wardroom with the executive officer. The submarine had submerged; the captain was concerned that another ship or sub might have seen Mick's white light. Mick's wet flight suit had been exchanged for someone's spare khakis, and he was busy giving a debrief about his last twenty-four hours. The exec, a weary-looking lieutenant commander, just shook his head when he heard about the wounded on the evacuation flight. He looked at Mick's guilty expression.

"You were not responsible for that," he said. "Goddamned Japs did that. The plane was marked, right? Red crosses?"

"I think so," Mick said. "It was still pretty dark when we took off. I never looked."

"Bastards worship death," the exec said. "We pulled a survivor out of the water, after we sank one of their tin cans? He was unconscious, bobbing around in a life jacket. When he came to, on deck? Found our doc working on him? He bit the doc's hand and then rolled right back over the side. Now we don't bother."

"The Marines sure as hell don't bother," Mick said. "So where will you take me? Back to the 'Canal?"

"I guess we can," the exec said. "Or you can come with us to Darwin."

Mick grinned. "Gosh, XO, I'd have to think about that. Darwin, Australia, or Guadalcanal. That's a real tough one."

"Right," the XO said. "Let's find you a rack."

SIX

USS *Evans* was one of the new Fletcher-class destroyers, twenty-two hundred tons full load, sixty thousand steam turbine horsepower turning twin screws, five single five-inch gun mounts, and two quintuple torpedo tube mounts. The ship's complement was about three hundred twenty souls. Marsh was executive officer and therefore second in command, otherwise known, and universally addressed, as XO. After commissioning, shakedown, and some three months of accelerated tactical training at Guantánamo, *Evans* slipped through the Panama Canal and transited to Pearl Harbor in the late summer of 1943 as one of twelve escorting destroyers for an aircraft carrier, the new USS *Lexington.*

Before leaving Pearl, Marsh had gone around to the barracks and looked up a few of the enlisted petty officers who'd made it off *Winston.* Commander Wilson had suggested he do that when he gave him his new orders. Find some *Winston* guys to take with you to your new ship, he told Marsh. They'll be a big help in a precommissioning crew. Marsh had talked to Machinist Mate Marty Gorman, five petty officers from the gunnery department, and Lieutenant

(Junior Grade) John Hennessy, who'd been in the navigation department. They were all as eager to get out of Pearl as he was, so Commander Wilson made the arrangements.

The word in the Pacific Fleet was that Guadalcanal had been pretty much secured and that there were operations being planned to move American forces up the Central Pacific island chains, starting with the northern Solomons. That said, nobody at the deckplate level felt the war was even close to going decisively America's way, especially when *Evans* crawled through the minefields outside the channel, entered Pearl Harbor, and steamed by the melancholy wrecks of the battleships *Arizona*, *Oklahoma*, and, behind Ford Island, *Utah*.

"Damn, XO, what is that smell?" one of the ensigns asked.

"It's exactly what you think it is, Mister Cauley," Marsh said.

They were standing out on the port bridge wing, and the smell in question was a combination of bunker oil, bottom mud, and burned electrical insulation, overlaid with a sickening thread of decaying human flesh. *Arizona* was right where she'd died that awful morning, her head bowed down and every visible inch of steel still above water burned black and even white in some spots. *Oklahoma*, which had turned turtle after being torpedoed at her moorings, had been righted and pushed up against the shore at Ford Island and was now streaming harbor water from her many cofferdams as pumps down below labored day and night to get her truly afloat.

"I thought," Ensign Cauley said, "I mean, didn't they get, uh, the bodies out? After it was all over?"

Marsh thought Ensign Cauley was amazingly innocent, even for an ensign, USNR, with ninety days of Officer Candidate School and a whole six months of naval service under his belt. The captain glanced over at Marsh from his bridge chair and rolled his eyes.

"There's reportedly over a thousand men still inside *Arizona*," Marsh told him, "and they're never coming out. They just got *Oklahoma* right side up a few months ago. Some of the human remains coming off *Oklahoma* are coming through those pumps, okay?"

Cauley swallowed at that lovely image and went back to rubbernecking as they closed in on the destroyer piers. It had been a year and a half since the attack, but there were still signs aplenty of the devastation. Some of the other stricken battleships had already been refloated. Repaired well enough to go back to the mainland, they were in navy yards on the West Coast being refurbished for further service. Looking at *Oklahoma*, though, Marsh found it hard to believe that any of those battered leviathans would ever raise steam again.

They'd heard the Navy was going to leave *Arizona* and *Utah* where they lay.

The carrier had gone into the shipyard piers to have aircraft hoisted aboard. Her escort destroyers had been ordered to tie up at the destroyer piers complex in the East Loch. Ensign Lee, the assistant gunnery officer, had the conn, and the navigation officer, Lieutenant Hennessy, had the deck. The captain was watching intently, ready to take control of the landing in case the junior officer did something remarkably dumb. As everyone knew, ensigns did that often. The rest of the crew manned their special sea and anchor detail stations for entering port, with first and second divisions topside fore and aft, ready to handle mooring lines, and Fox division waiting amidships to run out fenders. The engineers, universally called snipes, were on station down below in the firerooms and engine rooms. The navigation department was manning up the pilothouse, the Combat Information Center, and the signal bridge.

Marsh's job, as the executive officer, was to make sure that everyone was on station and ready to do whatever needed doing to bring the ship alongside another destroyer already moored at the piers without breaking anything. He normally stayed up around the bridge area while the captain and whichever junior officers had the deck and the conn actually maneuvered the ship into the designated berth. Once the ship was pointed fair at the berth, there was nothing more for him to do. He would spend the next few hours ensuring that fuel, provisions, mail, cargo, repair parts, new personnel, ammunition, and visiting staff officers all got aboard in good order.

Marsh's day finally slowed down to a gentle chaotic rumble at around five, so he and the captain headed for the officers' club. Everyone except the duty section personnel went ashore for some much-needed liberty time. Captain Warren was a three-striper, or full commander. He'd been chief engineer on an antiaircraft light cruiser, and command of *Evans* was his reward for keeping that ship afloat after one of the many savage naval gunfights in the Solomon Islands campaign. He and Marsh had some dreadful experiences in common, so as CO/XO partnerships went, theirs was pretty good. Marsh was young to be an XO, and the captain already had taught him much.

The destroyer squadron commander, a youngish-looking four-striper, was holding court at the main bar with his skippers. The captain dutifully joined the commodore, while Marsh joined up with a bar stool and a much-needed Scotch. The first one was perfect; the second even better. A man wearing slacks and one of those riotous Hawaiian shirts sat down next to him. He introduced himself as Dr. Ernie King and then ordered bourbon.

"What ship?" he asked. Apparently it was obvious that Marsh was a fleet officer. He told him he was XO in *Evans*.

"That's a tin can?"

"Right. We're in the *Lexington* task group."

"Yeah, I saw her pull in today. She's bigger than the last *Lexington*. You guys do the exciting stuff."

Still mindful of the *Winston*'s sinking, Marsh told him that exciting was overrated. King laughed.

Marsh asked if King was attached to the naval hospital. He was. He inquired if he knew of a nurse named Glory Lewis, or possibly Hawthorne. King looked at Marsh with sudden interest.

"Lady Everest? Hell, yes, I know her. I'm a surgeon, and she's one of the team leaders in our ORs."

"Lady Everest?"

"Can't be climbed," he said with a comic, leering grin, "but, boy, we all wish differently. You actually know her?"

Marsh gave him a very brief history of his acquaintance with Glory. King nodded somberly when Marsh mentioned her connection to the *Arizona*.

"You know," he said, "I think that's what makes her so desirable, besides the obvious female attributes, I mean. She's almost ethereal. Withdrawn, quiet, a little bit sad. All you want to do is hold her."

"All?"

He grinned again, as if some kind of machismo demanded it, but then his expression changed.

"Truth is," he said, "there are lots of pretty nurses, but Glory Lewis is in a class by herself. She's so goddamned beautiful, and yet she's not in the least 'available.' I saw her at the base chapel last Sunday. Dressed in these somber clothes she wears when not in her hospital gear. Her face framed in this gauzy black go-to-Mass veil. Heart-stopping; that's the only term I can come up with. Goya would have been dying to paint her. She's as distant as the morning star. Every man in the chapel was looking at her, and she was completely oblivious."

"Her husband was my roommate at Annapolis," Marsh told him. "He was quite a guy."

"Had to have been," he said, lifting a finger to order another bourbon. "She's the best OR supe we have over there, too. All business, all the time. No joking around, no bullshit, no mistakes. But even when she's covered up in a full mask, all the cutters have to be careful not to look at her. She's that distracting."

"Well I remember," Marsh said.

"You're in port—why don't you call her? Go see her."

Marsh told him he wouldn't know how. He didn't want to point out that on the scale of handsome he still rated a distinctly negative number. Just like in the courage department, he reminded himself.

"Oh, hell, that's no problem. Call the hospital. Ask for the staff duty officer. Tell her you're trying to contact Ensign Lewis. They'll get ahold of her for you."

"She's an ensign?"

"They're all ensigns, except for one old bat who's in charge of all the Navy nurses. She's a jay-gee. I'm a commander. Whoopee. The rank means nothing—it's just a way to keep the girls in officers' country, if you know what I mean."

"What's that number?" Marsh asked.

An hour later he was walking down the palm-lined street on Hospital Point where all the nurses' quarters were. The buildings were old verandah-style, two-story houses that had been converted to dormitory residences for the medical staff. The staff duty officer had taken his message, called back a few minutes later, and told him that Ensign Lewis was in surgery but would be able to meet him at 1800. As he drew near the quarters he saw a large hole in the street. He immediately assumed it was a bomb crater but then realized it was simply evidence of the eternal battle between the diggers and the fillers at the Naval Base Public Works Department. Some things never changed.

As he came up the walk to the house, a pretty,

sweet-faced young woman smiled at him from one of the deck chairs. She was wearing what he later learned was called a muumuu, a full-length, flowing, flower-printed and tentlike garment.

"Hi, there," she said. "Who are you?"

Marsh told her his name and said he was there to see Ensign Lewis. Since he was in khakis, he didn't have to tell her his rank. She introduced herself as Sally Adkins and said she'd go get Glory. She was back in a minute and said that Glory would be right along.

"Where you from?" she asked. "And are you a commander or something?"

Marsh sat down next to her in a wicker chair. "I'm a fresh-caught *lieutenant* commander," he told her. "I'm the exec in a destroyer with the *Lexington* group. She's called the *Evans*."

"Wow," she said, and he was surprised to see that she was truly impressed. Up close she appeared to be in her late twenties, with gorgeous blue eyes. "What's 'fresh-caught' mean?"

"Recently promoted," he said. "I'm originally from San Diego, California. How about you?"

"I'm from St. Louis, but I've been to San Diego. I did my Navy nurse training there."

"These days, if you're in the Navy, you've been to San Diego."

"You're wearing one of those big rings—did you go to Annapolis, too?"

"I did, but it seems a very long time ago."

"Gosh," she said. "We don't see many Annapolis men, at least not upright and walking around, I mean. Let's see, if you went to Annapolis, you must have had one of those funny nicknames they give each other—what was yours?"

"Beauty," said a hauntingly familiar voice behind him. "Hello, Marsh."

He turned around, stood up, and forced himself to speak. "Glory," he said. "I'm so very sorry about Tommy."

It wasn't the way he'd planned to start the conversation, but the sadness framing her face positively demanded it.

"Thank you, Marsh," she said, glancing reflexively across the nearby harbor at that blackened pile of steel jutting out of the water next to Ford Island. "It was a terrible waste. Let's go for a walk. I've been inhaling disinfectant all day. I desperately need some fresh air."

"Nice to meet you, Commander," Sally called as they started down the front steps. "Come see us again."

Marsh said he would, and then they went down the stairs.

"Sally's such a dear," Glory said. "The men love it when she comes on the ward, and she's been especially nice to me. We actually share a room here in the nurses' quarters."

"I'd lost track of you and Tommy after the

159

academy," he said. Many if not most wives and families had remained stateside when the Pacific battle fleet moved to the advance base in the Hawaiian territories. "How long had you been in Pearl?"

"Since the fleet came out from California," she said. "There was a naval hospital right here, so I decided to come along. What with the war in Europe going so badly, we'd talked about my going back stateside, but . . . we just put it off."

"Family?" he asked. "Kids?"

"No," she said with a wan smile. "Tommy'd been considering going engineering duty officer. He said he wanted to wait until then, when he'd be working in a shipyard and be home every night. But, again, with all the war talk . . ."

Marsh nodded. Another of his classmates had become tired of eternal sea duty and made the transfer from the line to EDO, as it was called. Now that the country was at war, he was stuck in a naval shipyard, while his line-officer classmates were getting promoted and going to interesting and exciting places. Like Savo, for instance.

"And you, Marsh? Married yet? Family?"

"Me? Married?"

"Well, yes—why not?"

"Look at me, Glory—I haven't improved much in the looks department since the boat school. Most guys aren't even willing to introduce me to their sisters, even the homely, one-legged ones."

She laughed, although he suspected she might have been just going through the motions when she'd asked the question.

"We had Amish nearby when I was growing up," she said. "They admired plain people."

"Plain? Listen, kids still ask me if I live under a bridge with the rest of the trolls. That's when they've run out of rocks."

"Do our classmates still call you Beauty?"

"When I see one," he said. "Right now my name seems to be XO."

"XO," she said. "That's pretty good, Marsh, at just eleven years. As a battleship man, Tommy told me that it'd be fifteen years at least to exec, and twenty or more to command."

"That's all changing pretty fast," he said, as they reached the tip of Hospital Point. The buoys out in the entrance channel were flashing on low power, with their seaward-facing lenses reduced to small vertical slits. He told her about his experiences in *Winston* and that he'd actually been at the hospital last August. She chided him for not calling her, but he reminded her that he hadn't known she was in Pearl. That wasn't quite true, of course, not after seeing her at the O-club, but the truth was he'd been reluctant to renew their acquaintance so soon after Tommy's death.

"Were you admitted?"

"No, I wasn't that badly hurt. If you could maintain vertical, they wouldn't let you in."

"August 1942," she said. "Savo. I remember that. The burns cases were the worst. We lost most of them, I'm afraid. Although I might be wrong—by then my days had become such a blur."

"I can't imagine."

"Yes, you can," she said. "Especially if you were in *Winston*. All those poor cruiser men were in a state of ambulatory shock. Talking, walking, but not looking at you. Still out there, on the sea, or in it, I guess."

"Yes, indeed," he said, remembering all too well. Jack's eyeless head popping up in the sea beside him. He banished the image. "You have no—"

"Don't I?" she said softly.

He had to think about that for a moment. "If you don't mind my asking, Glory," he said, "where were you? On that day?"

"Right where we're standing, Marsh."

Dolt, he thought. "You watched? You saw?"

"Oh, God, yes. The Jap planes came right overhead, on the way out of Pearl. Some of them shot up the hospital, just for fun, I guess. And of course I knew where the *Arizona* was berthed. I'd been out aboard the Friday before, for dinner in the wardroom. I saw her go, Marsh. I saw that blast of fire and smoke come straight up the stack."

"Good Lord," Marsh whispered.

"I *knew*, Marsh. Jesus Christ, I *knew!*"

She swayed for a moment, and he held her shoulders then while she wept silently. She kept murmuring it: I knew, I knew, I knew.

"It's passing strange," he said, the scent of her hair in his face. How many times had he dreamed of holding Glory Hawthorne, but not in these sad circumstances. "When the second torpedo hit *Winston*, I *knew* we were done. She trembled after the first hit, kind of like an overstressed guitar string. But after the second hit? She turned sodden, like a bag of wet laundry, as if she didn't care anymore. Her plates groaned, and then they started breaking, big hull sections snapping like glass, rivets pinging in the dark down below. She made this terrible groaning sound as she gave in to the sea. Like you, I *knew*."

She composed herself and pulled away, but not too far. "I feel so, what's the word?"

"Guilty?"

She looked at him with those shining eyes. "Yes! Guilty. There I was, standing on the seawall, and there went Tommy with the rest of the engineering department, up the stack of the *Arizona*, just little specks of carbon in a boiling black and red cloud. On a Sunday! God *damn* them, Marsh. God *damn* them!"

"We're working on that, Glory," Marsh said. "Believe me, before this is all over, Japan will burn in hell. I promise."

She heaved a great sigh and turned away from

him, staring once again out across the darkened harbor. He reluctantly let his arms drop. The only bright lights over there now were the temporary spotlight stands over on Ford Island, where humming strands of cable were straining to hold the battleship *Oklahoma* upright while they pumped her out. He remembered what he'd told Ensign Cauley.

"Glory," he said, "we're in for just a couple days. How about dinner somewhere?"

She turned to look at him. "Oh, I don't know, Marsh. That would be too much like Annapolis. The four of us, scouting Crabtown for the cheap eats? Fish and chips at the Greek place? Home brew served in a Coke glass?"

"That's the past, Glory."

She sighed. "I'm not sure I could stand it, Marsh. No Beast, no Tommy, can't you see?"

"*I* could stand it, Glory," he said, surprising himself.

She blinked in surprise. "Ah," she said.

"I mean, look, forget it. I understand—"

"Oh, Marsh. I'm so sorry. I've grown so accustomed to thinking only about myself, haven't I. Of course, let's go somewhere."

"Um."

She smiled, and the night briefly glowed. "I have the day off tomorrow, most of which I'll spend sleeping in. So: tomorrow night, around six. Come in a taxi. I know a little place in Aiea."

164

· · ·

Glory Hawthorne Lewis lay in the bathtub, watching her toes and fingertips wrinkle in the cooling water. She was dreamily thinking back to those happy weekends down at the Naval Academy, where she was inevitably the star attraction of their usual foursome. Tommy Lewis, Beauty Vincent, Beast McCarty, and, of course, herself. Beast, the star athlete, big and bold, with those challenging eyes and roaming hands, flaunting his aggressive maleness with every pose. Tommy the brain, a slash, as the midshipmen called the really smart ones, and the only one in the group who could make her belly tingle with just one gentle touch. And Beauty, poor Beauty, with a face only a caricaturist could love, intensely shy because of his looks but with an almost tangible longing for her in his face whenever he thought she wasn't looking. She was secretly glad it was Marsh Vincent who'd reappeared in her life and not Mick McCarty.

Their dinner together had been a quiet affair, with lots of reminiscing about Annapolis while they both gamely danced around the unseen presence of Tommy's ghost hovering out there on the verandah. She called him Marsh, not Beauty anymore, as if to emphasize the point that they were both different people now. Glory, the widow, whose daily fare was to wade through the bloody tapestry of an OR; Marsh, the executive officer,

165

on his way west to grapple with the horrors of war at sea and generate more business for the hospital.

It had been almost two years since the attack on Pearl Harbor, and the restaurant had been crowded with noisy white faces as the ever-growing staffs up on Makalapa Crater became increasingly confident that they were going to win this thing and punish the treacherous bastards for what they had done. She'd asked Marsh if that same sentiment prevailed in the fleet, but he'd kept his own counsel, saying only that they took it one watch at a time. She'd idly asked if he had anyone back in the States who might be a marriage prospect. His answer had stunned her.

"I'd like to marry *you*," he'd said.

Her face flushed again as she recalled that moment. She'd thought she had the evening under control.

"I've been in love with you since Crabtown," he'd said. "I've just never had the courage to say that to you until now."

"Marsh," she'd said, struggling with her own emotions, "I don't know what to say."

"You could say yes," he'd replied with a lopsided grin.

Then he'd reached across the table and taken her left hand, where she still wore her Naval Academy miniature and her wedding ring. His hand had been warm, but to her, those two lumps of gold felt conspicuous.

"Look, Glory, I know that was presumptuous. I guess war encourages direct speech. Time seems more valuable now."

"Does this have to do with love or something else, Marsh?" she'd finally asked.

"What something else?"

"Desire, Marsh. Desire. Do you really know me, or are you in love with the pretty girl you used to hang out with back at Annapolis?"

"Pretty doesn't do you justice, Glory," he'd said.

"I suppose so, Marsh. That's also why I know all about desire. Men see me, they desire me. That's been true ever since I was sixteen. Now that I'm thirty-three, my looks color every interaction I have with a man. Doctors, orderlies, patients, strangers in the O-club, even passing sailors on the base."

"So you wish, what—that, just once, men would appreciate you for the woman you are?" he'd asked with a straight face.

She'd laughed out loud at that hackneyed line, and he'd grinned back at her.

"I know, I know," she'd said. "The lady doth protest too much. Look, I loved our time together back at Annapolis. I was the center of the universe every time I went down there for a weekend, and what woman doesn't like that? I fell in love with Tommy because, well, because I did. But I also loved my good times with Beauty and the Beast."

"You're telling me my image of you now is simply something I've created in my own mind?"

"Of course you have, Marsh. It's what people do. All of us. You were the shy one. You were a man who'd never muster the courage to say what you just said. And me? I was a giddy prom queen with an admiring court of three dashing midshipmen. Now you're the second in command of a destroyer, and I'm a war widow. Neither one of us is the same person."

"Okay," he'd said. "I'll grant you all that. So let's start over. My name's Marsh Vincent. I went to the Naval Academy. I've heard you did, too, in a manner of speaking."

She'd looked at him and sighed. "Aren't you forgetting someone?"

"Tommy?"

"Yes, Marsh. Tommy. The man I married."

He'd let go of her hand and looked away for a moment, then picked up his drink before speaking.

"Glory, that's not Tommy down there in the *Arizona*. Tommy's gone to wherever the good ones go after they die. You and I are still present for duty, at least for now."

"My head knows that, Marsh. My heart's not so sure. Next you're going to tell me that I have to get on with my life, that I can't linger in widow's weeds forever."

"Something like that, Glory. It's not like you can go join Tommy."

"Would if I could, Marsh."

He'd smiled at that and decided to fold his tents. "Me, too," he'd said. "I really admired Tommy. Mr. Straight Arrow. Literally born to succeed, and he had the good grace to always be surprised when he did."

She remembered that he'd said that without the slightest hint of sarcasm. Apparently she wasn't the only one who missed Tommy Lewis. Beast had once described Tommy as a prince. When she asked what that meant, Beast had explained that some men were just more valuable than others. Tommy, who'd sailed through the academics, was the first to help his struggling classmates get ready for their exams, and he could do it without ever making another midshipman feel beholden to him. Smart, good-looking, genuinely friendly and kind. Even back then, everyone knew that Tommy was special.

"Goddamned war," Marsh had said. "When this is over, I'm finished with the Navy, assuming I make it through."

"What else would you do?"

"I have no idea," he'd said. "Law maybe, like my dad. But certainly no more of this. I've come to dread being on the sea."

"You'll probably feel differently once you get your own command. That can't be too far away."

He'd laughed. "The closer I get, the more scary command looks," he'd said. "You have all those lives right in your hands. I don't think I'm strong enough. I know I'm not experienced enough."

She'd made the obligatory protestations, and then they'd gone on to talk about naval careers, other people they knew. She remembered feeling relief that the matter of his proposal had been put back in its box. They'd both been pretending: she that she hadn't flatly said no, and he that he had even asked the question.

She pulled the plug with her toes and got out to dry off. She held Marsh in great affection, but he would never stir the spark in her that Tommy had. She had agreed to write him, mostly because he so badly needed someone to talk to. He *thought* he was in love with her, but she knew better, even if he didn't.

The bathroom door opened, and Sally came in, wrapped in a towel.

"Save me some hot water?" she asked brightly. "So how was your big dinner date with that commander? He's cute."

"Hardly a date, Sal," Glory said. "Just old friends. And he's a lieutenant commander."

"Hah," Sally replied, sitting on the edge of the tub to start the water. "I saw the way that poor guy looked at you, and you haven't had dinner out with anyone since I've known you."

That was true, Glory thought, but she didn't want to pursue this line of conversation. Sally draped her towel over the rack and stepped into the oversized ceramic tub. Glory did a quick appraisal. Not bad, she thought. Maybe a little too full in the hips, but she was such a sweetheart, lively, a ready smile, those startling baby blues, and a pretty face. She'd make some lucky guy a great catch.

Like Marsh, perhaps?

"Hey, Sal?" she said. "I need a favor."

Sally Adkins wrote her first letter that very night to the nice commander with the improbable farm-boy face, excuse me, *lieutenant* commander, she thought, giggling. She wondered if he'd be disappointed, hearing from her and not from her gorgeous roommate. Sally was used to writing letters. The senior nurse at the hospital, Lieutenant McHale, had quietly suggested to all the nurses that they adopt some of their patients as pen pals, especially the ones headed back to war. Mail is what they live for out there, she'd told them. They had to use that crinkly white airmail paper and envelopes, and every letter supposedly had to be cleared by the hospital censor, a rule honored more in the breach than in fact. Sally had five pen pals, all Marines, and she had become highly proficient in dashing off a one- or two-page letter filled with trivial news from the home front.

She did realize that she'd been more than a little smitten by Lieutenant Commander Vincent. He was a senior officer, and yet he'd been polite, kind, and easy to talk to, at least until Glory Lewis had appeared. Then she might as well have vanished from her chair. She chided herself for the petulant thought. Every woman might as well vanish once Glory came into a room, because men could simply not take their eyes off her. The fact that she was not in the least bit approachable in the romantic sense seemed only to double her allure. No wonder Mr. Vincent, who'd apparently known her for years, was still carrying that torch. There'd be no way Sally could compete with Glory Lewis for any man's attention.

Unless.

She thought about it, and the idea took her breath away.

Suppose she did write Mr. Vincent but signed the letters as Glory Lewis? Or maybe just G. L.?

He would be ecstatic, of course, and she? She could indulge her imagination in ways not possible with the ordinary pen pal letters. It might lead to real love letters. She'd always wanted to receive love letters, and to respond in kind. What harm could it do, at least for a while?

Wait: Suppose he came back to Pearl—ships often did. He would then approach Glory thinking she loved him as much as he loved her, and Glory would be caught flat-footed. She'd find out what Sally had been doing, and then there would be hell to pay. And Mr. Vincent? He'd be crushed when he found it had all been a deception.

She shook her head. No. That would be mean.

Well, what if she wrote him letters and didn't sign them at all? Or perhaps signed them as "secret admirer"? They weren't supposed to put their full names on the envelopes anyway, just initials and their room numbers at the nurses' quarters. The mail clerk came through the building once a day, dropping letters on one of the bunks in the individual rooms. If she did that, the return address would be S. A, Room 232, Nurses' Quarters, c/o Fleet Post Office, Pearl Harbor, Hawaii. Glory wouldn't open a letter addressed like that—she'd assume it was for Sally.

Would he figure it out? Would he even remember her? Signing her real name might inspire a "ho-hum, that's nice" reaction, but a secret admirer? That would make it more interesting, and maybe, just maybe, she could get him to look at her instead of pining away for the unattainable Lady Everest.

Why not?

Dear Mr. Vincent, she began.

SEVEN

The *Evans* left Pearl a day earlier than scheduled. That kind of surprise creates a painfully hectic day for the XO as he tries to compress all the things that were going to be finished up into one day instead of two. The first four destroyers cleared the minefields set up around the entrance to Pearl Harbor and assumed their screening stations. They were followed by the carrier and the rest of the screening ships. *Evans* came out tail-end Charlie and had to bend on some knots to catch up with the formation. Once the carriers got out of port, they tended to run fast, as that was one of the better ways to frustrate lurking submarines. *Evans* strained into her assigned station two hours later and was then able to slow down to a brisk twenty knots. As usual, Marsh had no idea where the formation was headed, other than west, always west. What they were going to do when they got there was still a secret; the top brass did not share grand strategy with lowly destroyers.

Evans's tactical world centered on protecting the aircraft carrier from air and sub attack while the carrier flung out planes who did their work miles away, hundreds of miles away sometimes. Periodically the captain would get a special message laying out the objective for upcoming air strikes, and he would share these with the officers. Otherwise, though, the rest of the crew were operationally in the dark when it came to the big picture. Marsh didn't mind: The secrecy reduced his worry horizon to the actual horizon; there were usually problems enough in that confined space to occupy his entire day.

The ship secured from special sea detail and set

the regular underway three-section watch, which meant that the deck watch officers would stand bridge watches of four hours on, eight off for as long as *Evans* was motoring from point A to B. Once in the objective combat zone, they would tighten that up to port and starboard watches, six on, six off, which gave the ship half the crew on station throughout the ship, on the bridge, in engineering, and all the gun stations, ready to fight. The downside was that people were usually exhausted after a few weeks of port and starboard, as Marsh well remembered from his *Winston* days.

The ship had been in its screening station for an hour when the sonar control room called up to the bridge to report a sonar contact. Marsh was going through some admin messages with the captain on the bridge when the report came up over the captain's intercom, affectionately known as the bitch-box. The captain looked at Marsh, sighed, and shook his head. Apparently every time a formation came out of Pearl, one of the screening destroyers inevitably got a sonar contact. It almost always turned out to be a false contact, but the entire destroyer screen had to react anyway when the ship in contact sent out the initial report. All destroyers had to set general quarters for the hour or so it took to decide that the contact was a whale or other marine life. It was especially annoying when the ship reporting the contact happened to be a "new guy" to the Pacific Fleet, as the *Evans* was, fresh off the East Coast and new construction to boot.

"We're going to get razzed about this," the captain said, as he reached for the talk-between-ships radio handset and nodded to the officer of the deck to sound general quarters.

"Probably," Marsh said, "but we have to go take a look."

Evans left her assigned station and turned toward the bearing of the sonar contact, which was north of the formation track. The carrier, hearing *Evans*'s report, automatically increased speed to thirty knots and got the hell out of the area, beginning a broad zigzag pattern to foil any long-range torpedo shots. The destroyer squadron commodore, well aware of the false-contact reputation of the waters around Pearl, detached one other ship, USS *Hodson*, from the screen while the rest of the formation went galloping over the horizon with the bird farm. Marsh went down to the Combat Information Center—the CIC, known as Combat on the intercom circuits. One of the first things he had to do was to ensure that there were no American submarine submerged transit lanes nearby. He checked the chart and found that there were none.

"All stations reporting manned and ready for GQ," the OOD reported. "Material condition Zebra is set throughout the ship."

"Very well," the captain said. "Arm the depth charges for one hundred fifty feet."

In the CIC, two officers began the tedious process of establishing the plotted track of the contact. Any contact was presumed to be a Japanese submarine until it was proved otherwise. Sound-powered phone talkers connected to the sonar control room muttered constantly to the plotters as the operators down below fed bearing and range data to Combat. Back on the fantail, the depth charge gunners were taking the safety locks off the five-hundred-pound depth charges. The five-inch gun crews were ramming shells into the breeches of the gun mounts. Anyone topside with binoculars was looking for signs of a periscope.

The captain, who was senior to the skipper of the *Hodson*, assumed local tactical command and put the other ship on the fence, as it was called. This meant that she steamed in a big circle around the ship in contact. The tactic called for the ship in contact to cue the ship on the fence with ranges and bearings until that ship, too, established sonar contact. Once both ships held contact, one would drive down the bearing and right over the top of the sonar contact, releasing her depth charges. The ship dropping the charges would, of course, go "deaf" as soon as she passed overhead, because the sonar could not hear anything through the ship's own propellers. The attacking ship would then go out onto the fence and reestablish contact, after which the second ship would then drive in and make an attack. The maneuver would be repeated until something happened.

First, however, there was one last thing to do: Uncle Joe. These were the code words, transmitted over the underwater telephone, which were meant to give an American submarine one last chance to identify herself as an American by surfacing immediately. The sonar operators would transmit the words "Uncle Joe" repeatedly into the water, using the underwater telephone. If they received a reply, or an American sub popped up between the ships, they all went on about their business. If nothing happened, the presumption was made that the contact was a bad guy. The destroyers were then free to make an attack, which would begin at once.

The captain called sonar control, located down on the third deck. "Sonar, conn, what's the quality of your contact?"

"Medium definition, steady return, echoes clear and metallic. He's running just in and out of the layer, estimate two hundred feet."

"Pretty sure it's not marine life?"

The leading sonarman, Chief Ripley, replied. "Yes, sir, it looks pretty good. I know there ain't supposed to be any Japs this close to Pearl, but . . ."

"Never mind that, Chief. They weren't supposed to be around here back on seven

178

December, either. If the contact goes mushy, let me know."

"Aye, Cap'n," Ripley said. He'd been assigned to *Evans* from the antisubmarine warfare school in Key West and was a sonar expert. If Ripley thought it was real, there was a chance it was. The captain ordered the fantail crew to reset the exploder depth on the charges to two hundred feet.

The *Hodson* now reported that they, too, had intermittent contact, and the plots on the two ships were generally in agreement. Their evaluation of the contact, however, was possible large marine life. As in, let's play with it but not waste too many ashcans, okay? We know you guys are new to this game.

The captain surprised Marsh by ordering *Hodson* to make the first attack while *Evans* maintained the fence. They rogered for that order and bore in at eighteen knots to run over the top while *Evans* steered out to maintain a good sonar contact on what was coming. Moments later the sea erupted into six huge waterspouts as *Hodson*'s charges went off at two hundred feet. *Hodson* put her rudder over and turned out to join *Evans* on the fence, reporting, as expected, that they had lost contact.

"Still got him, XO?" the captain called in.

"Affirmative, ready to go in."

"Cue the *Hodson* back onto the contact. Then commence our attack."

It took the Combat team five minutes to steer *Hodson*'s sonar team via radio back into contact. Then control of the ship was passed into CIC, where Marsh ordered the OOD out on the bridge to turn the ship onto an intercept course with the contact and increase speed to eighteen knots. The release of the depth charges was controlled from CIC because they were the only ones who could see the whole tactical picture. The idea was to give the order far enough in advance that the men actually rolling the charges did it right in front of the contact as the ship passed overhead.

"Roll one," Marsh ordered. "Roll two." A brief pause. "Mark center."

The K-guns thumped charges out to the port and starboard sides while the rest of the depth bombs rolled silently off steel tracks mounted over the stern. Moments later they felt the undersea hammerblows start up.

"Sonar has lost contact."

The *Evans* made a wide turn away from the detonating charges and back out to the fence. *Hodson* had maintained contact and was cueing *Evans* to get back on target, but they were now reporting a truly mushy contact. Marsh knew that this was typical following the explosion of depth charges that deep. The turmoil in the water could persist for over an hour, making good contact very difficult. *Hodson* still thought *Evans* was dealing with marine biologics. Their radio operator sounded bored.

The *Evans* sonar team got back on the contact a minute later and reported the same evaluation: The contact was losing definition, the course track was becoming random, and the depth estimates were all over the place. Okay, Marsh thought, we've done our duty and probably killed yet another innocent whale. Time to call it off.

Then they heard a thundering boom from outside, and a moment later everyone felt an underwater shock wave envelop the hull.

Evans heeled sharply to port and increased speed. The bitch-box lit up. "All stations, this is the captain. *Hodson*'s been torpedoed. Blew her bow right off. We've got a live one. Bridge has control."

"Combat, aye," Marsh replied. "I'll get out on the HF and notify the commodore."

While Marsh made his report on the long-range radio net, the ship began turning again, and now there was a high sense of urgency among the Combat team plotters and phone talkers. All the routine had gone right out of the situation, especially when the next report came over the bitch-box.

"All stations, sonar! Torpedo noise spoke, multiple fish, bearing three three zero!" The sonar operator's voice was high-pitched.

Marsh froze for a moment as his guts coiled in a cold wave. Then he looked up at the course indicator, which showed which way the ship was headed at that instant: 320.

Marsh didn't have to say anything. The captain himself would have the conn now, and he would try to comb the tracks of the oncoming torpedoes. After *Winston*, Marsh knew all about Japanese torpedoes. He was suddenly very afraid but knew he couldn't show it. If *Evans*, no, if the captain did this just right, the torpedoes would come screaming past her on either side at nearly fifty miles an hour.

He felt helpless. The plotting crew was standing around the plotting table like statues, transfixed as he was by the stream of reports coming in from sonar: strong up-Doppler on the noise spokes, two, possibly three torpedoes, range now under one thousand yards, coming right for *Evans* as the ship heeled slightly in another tight turn. Then Marsh got hold of himself.

"Hey!" he yelled. "Reciprocal of the bearing! We've got a pigboat to kill. Get that track going again."

They all bent back down to the plot. By now the bridge team should have been able to see the approaching wakes, although Jap torpedoes sometimes left no wake at all. Marsh called for a visual bearing, but, understandably, no one on the bridge was answering. Then he could hear the shouts of the signalmen topside as they spotted the incoming wakes.

Marsh told the CIC gang to brace for impact and lifted his own body up on his toes, mindful of what had happened to his knees aboard *Winston*.

A very long minute passed. None of the men dared to look at one another.

"Noise spokes in the baffles!" called sonar. There was an audible group exhalation in CIC. The fish had passed down either side and were now acoustically invisible in the turbulence of *Evans*'s own wake. They would howl out behind the ship until their fuel ran out and they plunged to the bottom. The plotting team got back to the business at hand.

Marsh sent out the best estimate of the submarine's range and bearing to the bridge while sonar tried to refine the target through the residual wakes of the torpedoes. Finally, with the captain running down the bearing from which the fish had come and Combat calculating the best dead reckoning position for the sub, they let fly with everything. The sea around *Evans* erupted in thunder, and sonar once again went deaf as the ship maneuvered back out to the fence to regain contact.

"No echoes," sonar control reported.

With their plotting team blind, Marsh went up through the charthouse passageway and out to the bridge. Everyone out there looked pretty shaken.

About three miles distant, *Hodson* was smoking heavily forward and already down by the head. Everything forward of her forward gun mount was gone. More ominously, there was an enormous column of dense black smoke coming straight up from her number one stack, which meant they probably had a big oil fire in the forward fireroom, probably caused by the torpedo hit rupturing a fuel line on a boiler front. Marsh could see men in life jackets and helmets swarming topside, humping fire hoses in both directions. He went back down to Combat in time to hear that sonar still had no echoes.

Marsh stared and stared. Torpedoes, his nemesis. The bright morning sun became those battle searchlights, and he heard the screams of the men in *Winston*'s passageway as the eight-inch shells punched through and cut everyone to pieces. He felt *Winston*'s blackened bridge leaning over his head and heard the bodies hitting the water from four decks up.

"XO!" the captain said. "Snap out of it!"

Marsh hadn't realized how long he had been standing there, but the captain had. "Yessir," he said automatically, then went back inside.

With her bow gone, *Hodson* was no longer in the sonar game. Marsh conferred with the plotting team, and then they passed a search sector to the sonar team. "Search sector is two four zero to one six zero true, range twenty-five hundred yards."

The only sounds now were the reports coming over the bitch-box from sonar and the coaching orders from the CIC plotting team. The captain had kept the conn and was maneuvering the ship in a broad weave to foil another torpedo attack while keeping the bow, and thus the sonar, pointed at the best estimated position of the sub. His voice was calm and precise, and Marsh, feeling anything but, tried to emulate that.

"Conn, signal bridge. Big-eyes has oil and stuff coming up."

"Conn, aye," the captain said. "Bearing?"

The signalmen came back with a relative bearing. Marsh looked over at the gyro compass repeater, converted it to true, and gave the bearing to the plotting crew, who would add the sighting to the plot and try to figure out which way the sub was headed. They had to assume that the oil and debris slick was a decoy, released by the sub to make them think they'd got him.

"What do you think, XO?" the captain called in.

"We fired on a dead-reckoning estimate," Marsh said. "Blind luck if we got him."

"Yeah, that's what I think. Let's let him know that. Right standard rudder!"

The captain asked for an attack bearing. Marsh had to tell him that the plot was still cold.

"Your best guess, then, dammit," he snapped.

Marsh gave him their best guess, and then he went back up to the bridge. He took another look at *Hodson*. The black smoke column hadn't diminished one bit, which meant they had a serious engineering space fire going. Up forward there were no flames, but the pall of grayish smoke seemed to be increasing, boiling out of ruptured hatches on the peeled-back forecastle, or what was left of it. She had settled farther by the bow, which meant that they'd probably flooded the forward magazines. Otherwise, she looked reasonably stable. If the sub shot at her again, though, she was dead meat.

Evans drove in at twenty knots and laid down another pattern, set this time for two hundred fifty feet. They were assuming that the sub had gone deep to get beneath an oceanic acoustic layer. The sonar still had no echoes. Radio reported that they'd sent out the incident report to the carrier group. Because they were using high-frequency radio, they'd first had to encrypt the message; HF radio signals at sea could be heard in Japan, even all the way from the Hawaiian Islands. Marsh picked up his binoculars and did a sweep of the near horizon.

He listened as the captain talked to the skipper of the *Hodson* and asked him if they could handle their damage while *Evans* continued the hunt. The reply was brief: Affirmative, we're handling it, go get the bastard. As the captain hung up the radio handset, *Hodson* blew up in a shattering explosion. Either the fires had reached a magazine, or the sub had finished her off. One second she was there, the next there was only a towering cloud of smoke and a half-mile-wide circle of splashes as bits of the ship and her crew of three hundred fell back into the sea. Marsh, aghast, clamped down on his fear and hustled back down to Combat.

If it had been the sub, there was no way to tell from which direction the torpedoes had come. Their plot showed where the *Hodson* had been, their own position, and their best guess as to where the sub was. Marsh stabbed a pencil down onto the plot and had the talker tell conn to head zero eight zero, which would take them past the spot where *Hodson* had blown up. He gave sonar another calculated search sector, but they reported that the explosion had made the sonar useless until *Evans* got past the smoking boil in the water that had been a twenty-two-hundred-ton destroyer a minute ago.

Minutes passed. Marsh, dry-mouthed as the rest of them, listened as the captain and the signal bridge appraised the scene, still weaving every thirty seconds to throw off the sub's attack solution. He went back up onto the bridge, where he could see men in the water as *Evans* drove toward the still-turbulent oil slick. He then hurried back to the boat deck to supervise as the captain slowed the ship for just a minute so that the bosun's mates could throw some life rafts over the side to the survivors. The very few survivors. Then *Evans* sped up again and began an expanding-square sonar search. An experienced sub skipper would have taken the opportunity of the *Hodson*'s sinking to go deep and slink away, satisfied with one kill. The captain handed the conn back to the officer of the deck with instructions to execute a broad weave on top of the expanding square.

"He was gutsy enough to take on two destroyers," the captain said. "I think he'll stick around. He missed a shot at the carrier group, but he also knows the main body's gone over the horizon. It's one on one now, and he's already put one of us down."

That was not a comforting thought, but Marsh realized the captain was probably right. For a moment he wondered they should maybe take the hint and take *themselves* over the horizon at high speed. There were men in the water back there, though, and killing, or at least holding down, a Jap sub lurking off Pearl was nothing if not one of *Evans*'s primary duties as a destroyer. What they really needed was another three or four tin cans to even things up. The problem was that their encrypted contact report might take hours to get through the communications station ashore, and by then the carrier group could be two hundred miles distant. Then one of the lookouts sounded off.

"Aircraft, two, bearing zero eight zero relative, elevation angle thirty, inbound!"

Everyone on the bridge with binoculars swung around to the starboard side to search the skies. Two aircraft out here had to be American, Marsh thought, unless of course the Japs had snuck a carrier back to the Hawaiian Islands, a feat not unheard of.

"SBDs," the captain said. "Admiral must have got curious as to what two of his tin cans were still doing back here."

The planes came overhead, waggled their wings, and then circled *Evans*. They were flying clean, except for belly tanks for extended range. Combat established comms with the flight leader and told him what was going on. The pilot rogered for the report, flew over the sparsely populated life rafts behind *Evans*, and then departed to the west, climbing for altitude so that their VHF radios would have a longer reach. Then the flight leader came back up, reporting a thin oil slick visible on the surface, four miles away to the west, and running an east-west axis.

"Hot damn!" the captain said. He swung around in his chair. "Captain still has the conn," he announced. "Right standard rudder, come to two seven zero. All ahead full, turns for twenty-two knots." Then to Marsh, "XO, go back inside, talk to the airedales, give them an estimated position. Let's see if we can get this bastard."

Marsh went back to the flight leader and asked if one of them could remain on station and give them an overhead view. The leader detached his wingman to stay with *Evans* and then positioned himself high over the moving oil trail. The ship drove west toward the new estimated position, very much aware that the sub would hear them coming before they got contact on him. The captain approached the EP at twenty-two knots while executing a random zigzag so as not to make it too easy for the sub skipper to take another shot. He told Marsh that this was no time for buck fever.

The captain then got on the ship's announcing system and briefed the crew as to what was going on. He told everyone topside to keep a sharp eye peeled for a periscope. The sea was a little choppy but not too rough. If the Jap stuck his scope up high enough, the *Evans* or her airborne helper-bee might get lucky.

At twenty-two knots, it was about twelve straight-line minutes to the EP, but with the zigzag it was going to be more like twenty. *Evans* could go faster, but above twenty-two knots, her own hull noise drowned out the precious echoes coming back from the sonar ping. Marsh didn't want to think about what was going through the *Hodson*'s survivors' minds as they watched *Evans* head for the horizon. The bald fact was that they had provided rafts for far more men than were in the water. Must have been a magazine hit, he thought. She'd gone in an instant. They waited nervously, praying for no more torpedo noise spokes.

"Sonar contact, two niner zero, range fifteen hundred yards."

"Combat, conn, conduct urgent attack—straight in now, XO."

That's what they did. The captain slowed slightly to give the sonar a better listen, stopped the zigzag, and bore right at the contact, depth charges primed in a depth ladder ranging from one hundred fifty to two hundred fifty feet exploding depth. Then the pilot of their one-plane air force came up on the radio shouting something about a torpedo, followed immediately by an excited call from sonar control.

"Conn, sonar, torpedo noise spoke, on the bow, high up-Doppler!"

The Jap skipper must have understood the significance of their stopping the zigzag. He'd fired one down the throat and was probably going deep again. The Doppler confirmed that it was coming straight at *Evans*.

"All stations, conn, torpedo wake in sight—it's going to pass down the port side. Combat, have all the depth charges reset for two hundred fifty feet and stand by to fire."

"Combat, aye," Marsh answered, as one of the phone talkers passed the word back to the fantail.

191

Now the question was: Would the sub turn as he tried to evade deep? And if he did, which way? Their one-plane air force made the call for them. The slick was beginning to drift right. Marsh checked the true wind. It was coming from the other direction. Right drift meant the sub was turning right.

"Conn, Combat, range to contact is five hundred yards. Come right in a slow five-degree rudder turn, now."

"Conn, aye, coming right."

"Roll one!"

Evans laid down a standard pattern and then made a sharp evasive turn. Marsh marked the plot where they made that turn because their rudders would create what was called a knuckle, a tight whirlpool in the water that the sonar could see and confuse with a real contact. The charges started going off, deep and satisfying. It felt good to be doing something about *Hodson*, even if they didn't get him on this pass.

The ship swung around in a big circle and slowed to fifteen knots, trying to get back in contact. The plane still circled above them at a few thousand feet. If anything came up from the sub, he'd be the first to see it. Then they waited, constantly changing course to defeat another torpedo attack. The plotters fed constant estimated range and bearing data to the sonar operators down below, trying to focus their search, but the cluster of depth charges had so badly disturbed the water that all the sonar could see was a cloud of turbulence.

They waited some more, weaving this way and that just like the aviators did. Fly straight and level in a dogfight, someone will kill you. Marsh decided once more to go back up onto the bridge.

Everyone who had binoculars was looking hard for any signs of debris or other indications they'd hit him. The sea was picking up out here, and the relative wind blew a gust of stack gas back onto the bridge wing.

Suddenly the signal bridge called down, "Our plane's diving astern of us, one seven zero relative!"

They looked aft from the port bridge wing in time to see the SBD strafing something back in their wake, and then the sub broached right into a hail of gunfire. Without being told, the after five-inch guns began to fire as the plane cleared out, shooting over at first and then punching five-inch shells into the black mass of the sub as she wallowed in their wake about a half mile behind them, her front half sticking out of the water as if she were stuck in ice. The captain turned the ship to open an arc of fire for the forward guns, and then all five got into it, along with one of the after forty-millimeter mounts. The noise was terrific, but no one was complaining. A cloud of gun smoke blew back over the bridge wing, filled with sulphurous confetti from the powder-can wads.

The sub's bow began rising straight up into the air, and then she hung there. Marsh couldn't tell if it was an I-boat, but he did see at least three direct hits from their main battery on that black, now almost perpendicular shape. Then she began to slide backward, spewing air and sheets of shiny diesel oil into the sea. The SBD kept well clear now to avoid getting shot down by the hail of gunfire that was still exploding all around where the sub was collapsing back into the sea. Marsh ran back down to CIC, knowing what they had to do next. The captain was ahead of him on the intercom.

"All stations, cease firing, cease firing. Combat, conduct an urgent attack on the sink point, bearing zero eight five, range six hundred yards."

The captain drove them over the point where the sub had sunk, and they rolled a short pattern, again set deep. Then they drove away from that point, slowed down, and waited while the sonar went into the passive mode and listened. They had a speaker in Combat that allowed them to hear the actual sounds of the sonar and any returning echoes. Their depth charge attack had created a long acoustic waterfall of white noise, but then came the sound they'd been waiting for, a sound they'd only heard before on training tapes: the rumble and crump of a hull collapse as the sub sank below its crush depth on its way to the bottom, some twelve thousand feet down.

Marsh called the plane and asked him to verify a large oil slick and debris field that should be coming up shortly. The SBD was already skimming the scene at about two hundred feet. He reported that he could already see it and that there appeared to be bodies in the slick. That was as good a confirmation as they'd ever get. Subs sometimes released oil and trash to make pursuing destroyers think it was all over, but not crewmen.

"Combat, conn, secure from GQ. I believe we got ourselves a kill there."

"Combat, aye, plotting a course back to the EP of *Hodson*'s people in the water."

Marsh sent the plane home, telling him they'd take the survivors of *Hodson* back to Pearl and then, unless otherwise directed, rejoin the task force. The pilot said he'd relay the message and report that they'd sunk the sub. Marsh thanked him for equalizing the odds.

It would take the ship about a half hour to get back to the estimated position of *Hodson*'s survivors. Marsh went below to the officers' head, where his bowels testified explosively to his compelling fear. Then he went to his cabin, shut the door, and lay down on his bed. He pulled a pillow over his face and began taking deep, difficult breaths, forcing himself to blank out the horrific images of the morning. *Hodson* without her bow. Then that fiery pall on the water, surrounded by fragments of the ship and her crew. The raucous scream of the Jap torpedoes clearly audible over the sonar speakers. The boil of bodies and oil coming up from the depths as the submarine imploded in the absolute blackness of the deep.

There was a quick knock on the door, and then the captain was standing next to his rack. He was still in full battle dress, and he had a white china mug in his hand, which he handed to Marsh. The mug contained an inch of bourbon whiskey.

Marsh, hugely embarrassed, tried to scramble out of his rack, but the captain put a firm hand on his shoulder and forced him to take the mug.

"If it's any comfort," the captain said, "I've already had one. Knock it down, XO, and then get yourself back on the line. This happens to all of us."

Then he was gone, ducking through the door but still banging his helmet on the frame. Marsh gulped the whiskey down and promptly choked on it.

This happens to all of us.

All right, then.

He took some more deep breaths, washed his mouth out so that he didn't smell of booze, and went back topside to take charge of picking up the survivors.

It took them an hour to round up the life rafts. When they arrived, there were only about three dozen or so men visible in the water, and some of them were not moving. That was a sobering head count. *Hodson* had had a crew of at least three hundred. The Jap torpedo, sub- or ship-launched, was still one of the most potent weapons in the war. *Evans* put down her motor whaleboat to corral the life rafts so as to minimize the time the ship spent stopped in the water. There was always the chance that the sub had had a partner on this bold mission, and everyone topside could hear the sonar going out at full power, searching all around them. Once they recovered the rafts and what was left of *Hodson*'s crew, they set course back to Pearl. It seemed to Marsh that the only way he got into Pearl Harbor was on a mission to get people to the naval hospital.

The entire evolution in port took six hours, and then they were steaming back out of Pearl and headed west to find the carrier group, which by now was more than three hundred miles west and opening. There'd been a line of ambulances waiting on the pier to shuttle the wounded over to Hospital Point. *Evans* had recovered thirty-seven alive and twelve dead. They'd hoped for more, but a magazine explosion takes the whole ship at once, as anyone who'd seen the *Arizona* knew firsthand.

Marsh watched the unloading of the survivors from the starboard bridge wing. The train of ambulances headed off to the hospital. For a moment he fantasized about going with them, just to see Glory. Then reality intruded. The chief engineer asked if he could take an hour to on-load some fuel oil before they left. Marsh told him to set it up and then forgot about seeing Glory. He sent for the gunnery officer to see if he could rustle up some more depth charges, too. Fuel they could get from the carrier; depth charges had to come by Higgins boat from the depot.

Just before sailing, a truck arrived and unloaded six aviators who needed a ride out to the *Lexington*, along with several bags of mail. Killing a Jap sub had been satisfying; getting mail was truly important. Marsh was busy filling out the after-action incident report on *Hodson*'s sinking and their successful fight with the Jap sub, so he didn't get to meet the flyboys until the ship was clear of the minefields and on her way west again. One of them was none other than his academy roommate Mick McCarty, known back then as Beast.

Mick still looked like the dashing football star he'd been at Annapolis, tall, handsome, extremely fit, and full to the brim with Irish charm and bullshit. It was a little bit awkward when Marsh saw that he was still wearing lieutenant's railroad tracks while Marsh, his classmate, was already a lieutenant commander. He shook hands with the other flyers, had an ensign show them where they'd be bunking, and then sat down in the wardroom with Mick. That's when Marsh noticed Mick's right hand was encased in a leather glove.

"Damn, Beauty," Mick said. "I thought you'd be better-looking by now, but you're uglier than ever. Congrats on those oak leaves, by the way."

"Thanks, Beast," Marsh said. "What's that British Army toast? 'Here's to a long and bloody war'? How long you been in Pearl?"

"Two days, two nights, long enough to get a hangover and to see Glory Lewis. Did you know she's in Pearl?"

Marsh told him about meeting her and having dinner one night. He observed that she hadn't recovered very well from Tommy's death in *Arizona*.

"Man, that was obvious," Mick said. "I had some high hopes that I might comfort the grieving widow, but she made it pretty damn clear that wasn't on the table. What a waste of a beautiful woman."

Mick had been an enthusiastic and apparently successful skirt-chaser the whole time Marsh had known him. Single, engaged, married, widowed, blind, crippled, or crazy, they were all fair game for Mick. Back at the academy, he was forever bragging about his conquests. He had a theory: It took five rejections to get one yes, so all you had to do was talk to six women and you were guaranteed to get some. All except Glory Hawthorne, who'd had a lot of fun teasing Mick to distraction.

"So what are you flying these days?"

"SBD-5s," Mick said. "Tried for fighters, didn't have the grades at flight school. But Midway was fun."

"You were at Midway?"

"I helped get the *Kaga*," Mick said. "Best moment of my life. Better than beating Army. Put a thousand-pounder through her flight deck and watched her burn all the way back to *Yorktown*."

"Now that's something to talk about," Marsh said. "I had to go swimming when *Winston* went down, although we made up for it a little bit today when we got a Jap sub."

"There you go," he said. "Like Halsey says, kill Japs, kill Japs, kill more Japs."

"We're headed to join up with his Big Blue Fleet," Marsh said. "The scuttlebutt around Pearl is that we're starting to win this thing."

"Lemme tell you something, sport," Mick said, frowning. "The Japs aren't done by a crock of crocks. Last time I came back to the bird farm my plane was so full of holes that they pushed it over the side once I crawled out. They are the fightingest bastards I've ever seen. This is definitely gonna take a while."

"I suppose you're right," Marsh said. "Midway

must have been a real kick in the buck teeth, though."

"Don't get me wrong," Mick said. "We're gonna win this war. We're gonna push and push, and then we'll drive 'em all the way back to the emperor's bathroom, and then we'll blast the little bastards into submission—but it won't be any cakewalk."

"We found that out today," Marsh said. "We had that sub dead to rights, and yet he still managed to plant one in *Hodson*'s magazines. We brought in just over ten percent of the crew, and some of them aren't going to make it."

"I was still onboard *Yorktown* when the *Hamman* got hit," Mick said. "She was right alongside, helping *Yorktown*'s ship's company fight the fires. One minute she was there, the next she was gone and *Yorktown* was abandoning ship."

"Jap torpedoes. We were lucky today."

"What was it Napoleon said? If I have to choose between a smart general and a lucky one, I'll take lucky every time?"

For some reason, that made Marsh shiver. He was still seeing those Jap searchlights every time he closed his eyes and thought about *Winston*. Mick saw his reaction.

"Oh, hell, Beauty," he said. "Look at it like an aviator: If it's your time, it's your time. In the meantime, always empty your guns and don't worry about shit you can't change. Bull Halsey is headed for a horseback ride in downtown Tokyo, and *all* us snuffies're gonna ride the whirlwind. Me? I'm looking forward to it, long as I can stay out of any more trouble."

"Yeah," Marsh said. "I suppose you're right. So where've you been since *Yorktown*?"

"Would you believe Guadalcanal, and then Darwin?"

"Darwin? What the hell were you doing there?"

"Flying with the Aussies and Dugout Doug MacArthur's Air Force. That's what happens when you become an orphan."

"I don't understand 'orphan'—you mean after *Yorktown* you—"

"Got fired from a big-deck squadron and became a soldier of fortune, so to speak. It's a long story."

"I've got to get topside," Marsh told him, "but later—I want to hear it all. You need our doc to take a look at that claw there?"

Mick raised his gloved right hand and looked at it as if for the first time. "This hand?" he said. "Nope. As long as no one officially knows about it, I can keep flying."

EIGHT

After a bath, Glory slipped into a muumuu and went out to the verandah of the nurses' quarters. It was just after midnight, and she had brought down one lone cigarette. Everyone she knew at the hospital smoked, but she consumed precisely two a day: one with her first morning coffee, and another before going to bed at night. She smoked in private because her mother had drilled it into her that ladies did not smoke in public. In these days of global war, Glory knew those rules of female propriety were hopelessly old-fashioned, and yet she still abided by them whenever she could.

The moon was somewhere behind the building, but the night was clear with just a hint of a tropic breeze coming in from Diamond Head. The bougainvillea was in bloom, along with a few stray orchids. It was almost too beautiful, she thought. Sally had said she'd be delighted to write to Glory's "handsome" lieutenant commander, as long as Glory did, too. Glory had promised to write and then realized she didn't have his address. She'd have to check with the Fleet Post Office to find out how to send mail to the USS *Evans*. Or perhaps not, she mused. If Sally struck up a warm correspondence, then she wouldn't have to.

She heard voices coming from the darkness of the street. The Pearl Harbor blackout was still being observed, so there were no streetlights. Finally she saw shapes moving up the sidewalk toward the nurses' quarters. Four nurses in uniform were accompanied by a tall, dark-haired man wearing khakis. The girls were giggling like teenagers surrounding a movie star, and Glory guessed this must be the new surgeon everyone in the nurses' lounge had been talking about. What was he doing here?

She rubbed out the cigarette on the rocker of the chair and bent forward to get up and go inside. Then she realized she was naked under the flimsy muumuu, a fact that would be obvious to anyone who saw her in the doorway. She sat back down and adjusted the fabric so that it draped less revealingly.

The nurses came up the walkway, saw Glory, and happily introduced her to Dr. Stembridge. He was indeed tall, dark, and very handsome, and his voice was soft and refined, with a hint of New York City.

"Nurse Lewis," he said, taking her hand and squeezing it gently. He had to bow slightly because Glory had remained seated, and it seemed a movement to which he was accustomed. His hand was soft and rock-hard at the same time, a surgeon's hand.

"Doctor," she replied. "Welcome to Pearl."

"Oh, c'mon, Glory," one of the girls said. "Say aloha—we're in Hawaii!"

"I don't speak Hawaiian," Glory said. "I think it sounds silly when Americans use their words."

There was much rolling of eyes and then several giggling good-nights and thanks-for-walking-us-backs. The verandah emptied out quickly, but Stembridge hesitated. He appeared to be sniffing the air.

"Is that bougainvillea?" he asked rhetorically. He went to the side of the verandah. "I haven't smelled that since a trip to the Botanical Gardens. And those look like orchids."

"Yes, all of that grows almost wild here," she said from her rocking chair. "If you like flowers, you'll love Hawaii."

He came back and sat down sideways on the top step. "You're an OR supervisor, correct?" he asked.

"Yes, I am. OR Two."

"Super," he said. "I look forward to working with you. Where did you train, if I may ask?"

"Penn," she said.

"Very good," he said. "That's a first-rate school. Have you been working since you graduated?"

"We got married at the Naval Academy after Tommy's graduation," she explained, "but then he went to sea right away, and so I went to work. There were a few years where I didn't work, but mostly I stayed with it. It paid better than the Navy."

"Most anything does," he said with a wry smile. "Is your husband in the Pacific Fleet?"

"For all eternity," she said. "He was MPA— assistant engineer—in *Arizona*."

He inhaled and then blew out a long breath before replying. "Wow," he said. "I'm surprised you haven't left Hawaii."

"They needed me, especially right after the attack. They offered me a commission immediately, and I took it and moved on base. Our apartment downtown got requisitioned, so, if nothing else, I needed a home, I guess."

"Makes perfect sense."

"Then 1942 wasn't such a great year, either. So here I still am."

"Inertia has its way, doesn't it," he said. "I know how that works. I lost my wife and two children early last year. A truck hit them head-on. The Merritt Parkway, of all places. Not supposed to be trucks on that road. Turned out the driver was drunk."

It was her turn to say wow.

"I was working in New York City at the time. I took a month off, found myself going crazy, so I went back to the grind. It just seemed like the thing to do."

"Yes, exactly," she said. A breeze came up and stirred the fabric of her muumuu, pressing it against her breasts. She sensed that he was looking.

"Now I smell lilacs," he said. "Let me guess: This is the end of a long day, you've just had a bath, and then put on some lilac water."

She felt her cheeks redden. That was precisely what she had done. Her rearrangement of the fabric hadn't worked at all. She suddenly felt exposed.

"Sorry," he said, putting up a hand. "My wife used to do that, too. In fact, the lilac water was our secret signal."

"Secret signal?"

"You know. You were married. I'd be working late, reviewing records in my study, and she'd show up wearing not much at all. I'd smell the lilacs and then she'd be right there." He laughed softly. "As in, time for bed, and now would be nice."

She felt her breath catch. She and Tommy had done something very similar. She looked straight ahead, really feeling the red in her cheeks.

"I'm sorry," he said. "I've embarrassed you again, haven't I. I'll go now. It's been a pleasure to meet you and talk a little. Tomorrow it will be much more formal, I assure you."

"Good night, Doctor," she managed.

He nodded, doing that formal little bow in the process of starting down the steps.

"You didn't embarrass me, by the way," she called after him. "You just caught me unawares."

He turned around. "That happens to me all the

time," he said. "I keep telling myself I'll get used to it, but then I wonder. Good night."

The next time Glory saw Surgeon Stembridge was in OR Two. The patient was a Marine with a through-and-through gunshot wound to the chest. One lung had been partially compromised, and a rib had been shattered near the exit wound. The patient had been prepped and anesthetized by the time Stembridge entered the OR from the scrub room. He came to the side of the operating table and introduced himself to the nurses.

"Good morning, ladies," he said. "I'm Dr. Allan Forrest Stembridge, thoracic surgeon. Please tell me your names, and a little bit about your training."

Glory, being the senior nurse, went first, describing her nurse's training and her work experience. She was followed by the other four nurses. Ordinarily there would have been another surgeon present, but the naval hospital was running five operating rooms, and with a heavy flow of casualties coming in from the climax of the Solomons campaign, there were no spare surgeons. Stembridge took it all on board, listening carefully and with such fierce eye-to-eye concentration that a few of the nurses stumbled with their résumés.

"Thank you," he said. "My turn. I'm forty-six, graduated from Brown and then Harvard Medical College. I've been doing thoracic surgery for fourteen years, lately specializing in traumatic injury. This will be our first operation together. I will debrief Nurse Lewis when we're finished, and she will in turn debrief you."

He then asked the anesthesiologist if the patient was stable and ready for surgery. The doctor tending the mask said that the patient was stable but somewhat precarious, having only one functioning lung. Stembridge glanced up at the X-rays hanging from light boxes above the table.

"Super," he said. "Then we'll need to go fast. Ladies, step up, please."

Ninety minutes later he was done, and Glory was exhausted. Stembridge had become like some kind of a machine, cutting swiftly and seemingly without a pause to see what he'd done or where he was going. Neither of those things appeared to have been in question, ever. The quiet scramble to keep up with him had had some of the younger nurses tripping over each other to get instruments into those ever-demanding hands. Prior to closing he had announced the sponge count, in and out. Glory, as supervisor, always kept a running count, and he was right on. Usually the surgeons roughly kept track but really depended on one of the nurses to make damned sure.

When they were finished, Stembridge left the table to go sit down in a far corner of the OR for a few minutes before the next surgery began. The anesthesiologist, an older doctor, nearing sixty, gave out a low whistle as they began their preps to remove the Marine to recovery.

"Superman," he murmured. "He's here."

Glory took off her mask, hairnet, and gloves. "That was pretty amazing," she whispered.

"Let's see how he does after six of 'em," the gas-passer said.

"That kid going to live?" Glory asked.

"Maybe," the doctor said, "but probably not. Long time getting here. You know—operation was successful, comma . . ."

By the end of the day, which came at around seven in the evening, Glory was ready to concede Stembridge the title of Superman. Each operation had been like the first, with the same fiery concentration, a sense that time was being altered when he was working, the frantic silence as hands came from everywhere across the table to hand him the next instrument, preferably before he called for it. When their last patient had been rolled into recovery, the OR crew was ready to drop. Stembridge reappeared in the doorway and called for Glory to meet him in the hospital cafeteria in fifteen minutes.

Her feet hurt, and her brain was awhirl. She'd never seen anything like this guy, and only then realized that she already was dreading the post-op conference.

"Glad it's you and not me, honey," one of the girls said. "That guy's not real."

"Scrub it good, Doris," Glory said. "He'll be back tomorrow morning, and so will we."

Glory went to the nurses' locker room and changed out of her scrubs and back into her day uniform. Then she went to the cafeteria to find Superman. He was already there, having a coffee and a cigarette. He waved when he saw her come into the room and stubbed out his cigarette when she sat down.

"Don't do that on my account," she said. "I have two a day, but the rest of the time I feed my cravings from other people's cigarettes."

He smiled, and when she saw the lines in his face, she realized that perhaps even Superman was tired.

"It went well today," he said. "We need to work on your people's anticipatory readiness."

Glory raised her eyebrows.

"By that I mean they're slowing me down somewhat. If a bleeder pops, I expect suction and then clamps. I shouldn't have to ask for either one."

She nodded. "I recommend you ask anyway," she said. "Normally you'd have an assistant surgeon in there. The girls have to get used to you. Some surgeons get angry if the nurses presume to anticipate them."

"That will soon not be a problem," he said.

"Really," she said. She knew two surgeons who

could be real jerks about that, and they were both older than this guy.

"I guess I should tell you," he said. "I've been brought in here as *chief* of surgery."

She blinked. She'd thought he was just another surgeon, drafted or cajoled out of civilian life to aid in the monumental task of salvaging the thousands of young men being harvested by this war. Then she saw the silver oak leaves insignia on his shirt collars. He was a *commander?*

"That's right. I chose OR Two as my theater because the hospital CO said you were the best OR supervisor we had."

"That's an exaggeration," she said. "I've had more experience in more hospitals, but there are plenty—"

He waved his hand to shut her off. "Me, too," he said. "So here's what I'm going to want from you. I watched you today. You didn't know it because you were watching everyone else like a hawk. When one of your girls was about to screw up, you intervened, quietly, inconspicuously, before she gave me reason to squawk."

She shrugged. "That's just my job," she said.

"I'm going to float through all the ORs. It'll be at random. Once I have a complete picture, I'll corral the surgeons and get them calibrated to my standards. I want you to rotate with me, and then I want you to calibrate the OR teams to *your* standards."

"That's going to hurt some feelings," she said. "Besides, I think some of the other OR supes are as good as I am, if not better."

"We'll see," he said. "If that's really the case, we'll move on to the next one. Five ORs in one facility is a pretty big surgical suite, especially for a small hospital like this. Can you imagine twenty?"

"Good God, no," she said.

"Well, start thinking about it," he said. "We're beginning, just beginning, to advance on Japan. They've demonstrated that surrender is not an option. When we have to invade the Home Islands, the casualties are going to be in the hundreds of thousands. Before that happens, the teams here are going to be staged forward as seed corn for over a dozen forward-based hospitals. My job is to ensure they're ready for that."

"And why me, again?"

"I move fast, Nurse Lewis. You saw that today. I make a judgment, and I act on it. Doesn't always pan out, but usually it does. I need someone closer to my own age to be my assistant, and the fact that we've both been through a similar personal loss, well, that actually makes things easier."

"What?" she asked, surprised that he had interjected a personal note.

"I assume you're still not over the loss of your husband, certainly not with that wreck still sitting out there in the harbor. And I miss my wife terribly. You and I are going to work closely. I'm saying that I want our relationship to be strictly professional."

Glory was taken aback by that. "What other kind of relationship would we have, Doctor?"

"Don't get mad," he said. "Young nurses are impressionable. They tend to fixate on older doctors. You've seen that."

"And us old battleaxes don't fall for that?"

He grinned at her. "Correct," he said.

"Even when the doctors are tall, dark, and handsome?"

"Even if the nurses are stunners in their own right," he said. "C'mon, Glory, don't be a pill. You know I'm right."

"Oh, it's Glory now?"

"Right. And please—feel free to call me Doctor." She tried to maintain her expression of indignation, but the twinkle in his eye was unmistakable. He was most definitely having her on. Finally she smiled. "Very well," she said. "This should be interesting."

"Then you'll do it?

"There's a war on, Doctor. I'll do whatever I can to help."

He leaned back in his chair and beamed at her. "Super," he said.

Glory met with the other four OR nurse supervisors in the nurses' lounge. The operating rooms were all shut down for sanitizing. The first one finished was then designated as a ready room in case a plane came in overnight from the western Pacific with urgent surgical patients. Three of the four nurses had been here since December 7. The fourth was brand-new.

"Okay, ladies, you're wondering why I asked everyone to come down for a meeting," she said.

"This has got to have something to do with that new surgeon," Etta Mae Beveridge said. She was the closest in age to Glory, and they were friends.

"Is it true he's a full commander?" Janet Wright asked.

"Yes, he is, and that's kind of why we're meeting," Glory said. "He's not just another surgeon. Apparently he's been sent here as the chief of surgery, and to get us all ready for a big expansion."

"Here?" asked Etta Mae. "There's hardly room for what we're doing right now."

"Not here," Glory said. "Somewhere out west. He didn't exactly say where, or even when, but this has something to do with when we invade Japan."

There was an immediate outburst of excited gabbling at this news, but Glory quickly brought them back to the business at hand. She told them what Stembridge wanted and then waited for their reactions. She didn't expect what happened next.

Etta Mae started giggling, and the other nurses soon joined in.

"What?" she asked.

"Oh, honey, you're such a peach. You think he chose you to be his assistant because you're the oldest?"

"Well, I am the oldest, and I've been a surgical nurse longer than anyone else here," Glory said. "I feel like I ought to apologize in advance to the rest of you, though."

"Glory," Etta Mae said, "a man who looks like that did *not* pick you out because you're the *oldest* woman in this motley crew."

Glory felt herself reddening. "There was absolutely nothing—"

"Oh, we know, we know—and you don't have to apologize. We'll help out any way we can. Just watch yourself, dear heart. He will be looking for a *close* working relationship, unless I miss my guess."

"Hell, I'm ready for a close relationship with him," said Janet. This provoked more hoots of laughter, and Glory realized that her first official meeting as Stembridge's new assistant was totally out of control, even if they were entirely wrong about him. And her.

The next evening, Glory was sitting out behind the nurses' quarters with the rest of the girls, nursing a beer and cooling her weary feet in the long green grass of Hospital Point. The ever-present tropical breeze was blowing through the palms and riffling the water in the harbor entrance channel, which was only a few hundred feet away. The sun had set, but there was still a beautiful tropical afterglow.

"Oh, look," one of the nurses said. "That's an aircraft carrier, right?"

Glory shaded her face to look into the sunset. Sure enough, the bulky silhouette of an Essex-class carrier was pointing into Pearl, followed by a long line of smaller ships.

"I think it's *Lexington*," another nurse said. "Scuttlebutt in the cafeteria was that she's coming in for a week."

Glory was always surprised at the speed of ships coming through the narrow reef channel. Tommy had told her that there were strong currents off the outside reef and that ships had to scoot in order to maintain good steering control. The carrier came abeam of Hospital Point and passed the nurses in their lawn chairs at a distance of only a few hundred yards. Many of the crew were topside on the flight deck, and sailors were waving at the nurses, who were waving back. They could hear the sound of the big ventilation fans under the flight deck overhang. An announcement being made down on the hangar deck echoed across the water as the ship's wake broke over the coral flats between the channel edge and the shore. Glory sneezed when a strong whiff of sulfurous smoke from the carrier's single massive stack wafted over the lawn.

Lexington, she thought. That will mean Beast, and possibly Beauty, if his ship was still assigned to the *Lexington* group. She knew they'd both be calling, probably as early as this evening. She made up her mind to put them off, and then to make sure that if she did see them, it would be with both of them together. She was pretty sure that Marsh would be satisfied with that arrangement, and Beast? He would simply have to cope. The last thing she needed was an evening spent trying to keep Beast's big hands off various parts of her anatomy, especially once he got some booze in him.

"I'm going to turn in," she announced. "My feet are killing me."

"Sure you don't want to come with us to the O-club?" one of the nurses asked. "With a carrier in, it'll be jumping tonight."

"Jumping is precisely what I don't need right now," Glory replied. "Anyone calls, somebody please just take a message."

It almost worked. At eleven, one of the girls, Betty Billings, knocked quietly on Glory's door. Glory, who'd been just about to turn off the light, put down her copy of *Time*. "What now?" she asked.

"There's this really big guy down on the lanai?"

218

the girl said. "He's got two mai tais, and he said if you didn't come down and have a drink with him, he's coming up."

"He damned well better not," Glory said, reflexively pulling up her sheet.

"Glory—he's *huge*. I think he's a pilot. I can't stop him if he really wants to come in. Please?"

"Betty, just tell him to go away, and if he doesn't, call the base shore patrol. They know what to do with drunks."

"He's not drunk, I swear. Well, not very. He's kinda cute, too. He says he knows you're here because he checked with the hospital."

"Glo-reeee!" a voice called from the downstairs hallway.

"Oh, for God's sake," Glory said.

"Glo-reeee!"

"All right," she said. "Go down there and tell him to shut up and I'll come down."

Ten minutes later she pushed open the front door of the quarters and looked around. Beast was sitting in one of the rattan armchairs at the far end of the front porch, balancing a large, fruity-looking drink in each hand. Glory had put on cotton pajamas and a long bathrobe. She went over to where he was sitting and pulled up a chair. She'd put a few curlers in her hair just to make herself frumpier.

"Beast, for cryin' out loud—what are you doing here?"

"I'm in love. I'm also in lust. And just a bit drunkit."

"No kidding."

"Yeah, well, what can I say. You're the best-looking thing west of San Diego, and I just had to see you. Like my jeep?"

"*Your* jeep?"

"Yeah, my jeep," he said, draining half of one of the mai tais. "Over there. The one with the spiffy aerials."

"And you acquired the jeep how, exactly?"

"Army pukes. They think they own the place. Leave the keys in their jeeps when they go to our O-club. Who the hell would steal a jeep, right? Couldn't walk so well, so I drove. Here, this one's for you. Didn't spill a drop, even if I did drive on the grass a coupla times."

"Mick," she began.

"Beast," he said. "Hate Mick. My CO calls me Mick. I'm gonna get fired, I think. Again. Not a team player, is what they've been saying. Even though I'm an ace. Twice over, in fact. Twelve Nips, gone to Jesus. Or Buddha, maybe. Yeah, Buddha. He's the one likes Japs. Take your mai tai, for Chrissakes, my arm's getting tired."

She took the fragrant drink and set it down on the arm of her chair.

"An ace means you've shot down five enemy planes, yes? I seriously doubt they'd fire a pilot who'd managed that."

"Twice," he said, followed by a burp. "Damned rum. I can feel the hangover coming."

"So maybe stop?"

He looked at what was left of his drink. "Stop? I never stop. Never. Isn't a woman in the world who's ever told me stop, stop." He leered at her. "Not you either, Miss Glory of the heavenly breasts, legs—"

"Stop," she said. "There—now it's happened. Look at me."

"All I want to do," he mumbled. "Look at you."

She thrust her left hand into his face. "See this ring?"

"Oh, God," he said. "That's your miniature?"

"Yes, it is, Mick. Still there, too. So you can quit with the masher routine. Why are you going to get fired?"

He finished his mai tai and threw the glass over his shoulder into the shrubbery.

"I lost two wingmen. Skipper says it's my fault. Says I'm a glory hound." He looked over at her for a moment and tried to leer. "He has no idea, actually," he said.

"How do you 'lose' a wingman?"

"Wing*men,*" he said. "Two of 'em. It's all the rage these days. No more solo fighting. You go up in pairs. One guy's the shooter, the other guy's the wingman. Shooter's job is to kill the Jap. Wingman's job is to protect the shooter from all the Jap's buddies. Statistics. Now it's all about statistics."

221

"I thought you were a bomber pilot?"

"I used to was," he said. "Not much to bomb these days, so I transitioned to fighters. Big mistake. These people take everything seriously."

"I take it you were always the shooter?"

"Oh, hell yes," he said. "You gonna drink that?"

"No, I'm not, and neither are you." She poured the drink into the bushes.

"Hey," he said. "I paid good money for that hooch."

"Too bad," she said. "You've had quite enough."

He leaned back in his chair and let out a long sigh. He was enormous, she thought. She wondered how he fit into a cockpit.

"You're supposed to talk, see?" he said. "You're supposed to be a team. You always let your wingman know what you're gonna do, so he can cover you."

He took in a long breath and let it out. The scent of rum filled the air. "But that's not me, okay? I'm a lone wolf. I do crazy shit in the air. Japs, they go by their rules, just like all our fighter jocks these days. Execute the approved doctrine. I show up, start my crazy-Beast shit, poor rigid bastards can't figure out what's happening, and then I smoke 'em."

"How did this do in your wingman?"

"Wing*men*," he said again. "Two of 'em. Rookies, that's how they start, flying wing on the more experienced guys. Show 'em how it's done, okay?"

She nodded.

"Like I said, I do crazy shit. Drop my gear in the middle of a dogfight. Turn upside down. Go head-to-head. Nips can't believe what they're seeing. Then I start shooting. Hell, it's not hard. Word is, they lost most of their best carrier guys at Midway. These land-based Japs are mostly all nuggets now. But it takes all *my* concentration. Can't be worrying about a goddamned wingman."

"So, what—they get left behind in the middle of one of your stunts? And then the Japs gang up on the rookie?"

He gave her a surprised look. "Yeah, babycakes, that's exactly what happened. Twice, for my sins. Jesus, you're too beautiful for words."

"Mick," she said, "your Irish is showing. This is the rum talking."

"No, it isn't," he said. "I've carried the torch for you since boat school, ever since, well, you know. Ever since Tommy, too." He put up a hand. "I'm sorry. I shouldn't have said that. Tommy was the best. Best man, got the best girl. Okay. But that doesn't mean a man can't dream."

"You're out of bounds here, Mick. You need to get back to the ship, sleep it off. We'll blame it all on the booze. Then we'll forget about it."

He seemed to relax into the chair, his huge frame going soft, his knees spread wide, and his hands hanging down. She was surprised to see a defeated expression creep over his face.

"I'm a case, Glory," he said quietly. "I think I hit my peak at the Army–Navy game, first-class year. After that, I've been a professional fuckup. If the war hadn't come along they'd have boarded my ass out a long time ago. Midway was my best day as a pilot. Now they want to send me to the amphibs. Backwater Navy. No more fleet carrier ops. All these big-deck skippers are on the make, heavy duty. No place, no time for a killer-diller like me, ace or no ace."

"We all do our part, Mick," she said gently. "You guys out there in WestPac, pushing the Japs back. Back here we do twelve on, twelve off, day in, day out, on this phony paradise island, putting the pieces back together. One day, we're going to win, and then what?"

"Fucked if I know," he said, "but I actually dread the thought of that. Peacetime? Guy like me? I'll be lost. No, I'm gonna go out in a blaze of—hah—Glory!"

She smiled at him then, and he grinned back, removing the past decade from his face. She suddenly realized that that was what he'd come for.

"Marry me," he said.

"What for?" she asked.

"Because I lo-o-o-o-ve you," he cooed.

"Sure you do."

"I do, I really do."

"You want to marry me?"

"Yep."

"Then give up booze, stay away from O-clubs, hew to the straight and narrow path of righteousness, and become a model naval officer."

"Jee-sus, Glory," he complained. "You sound like my wife already!"

They both laughed, and suddenly it was okay between them.

"You know who really does want to marry you, don't you?" he asked.

"He drive a destroyer?"

"He does indeed. And he would give up the booze, hew to whatever the hell that was, and do anything else you asked. Brother Marshall's been in love with you from the very beginning."

"I know," she said.

"But."

"Yeah, but," she said, wishing just now that she hadn't thrown the mai tai into the bushes. "Let me try to put it all into words."

"I'm all ears," he said. "No, I guess that's Beauty's line."

"You approach women like a caveman. Me hero, you wo-man. On your back, wo-man. Beauty? He stands off in the corner, the perfect gentleman, his heart on his sleeve, waiting for a woman to recognize that golden heart, right over there."

"And Tommy?"

"Bastard."

"He won the day, Glory. Only fair."

"Tommy was the smart one. He never did make advances. He never put his arm around my shoulder and his hand on my backside. He just took my hand one day and said, 'Come with me.'"

"Don't say backside," he said. "Say derriere. God, I love that word. The French know a thing or two."

"I was talking about your hand, Beast."

"That one doesn't work so good anymore," he said, holding up the black-gloved right hand. "This one, however . . ."

"Mick," she said.

"Glory Hawthorne," he said.

"Glory Hawthorne *Lewis*," she said.

"Not anymore."

"Forever, Mick. Forever."

He stared at her, and she saw a longing, a desperate longing. She would never have expected that, not from him. It startled her, and then aroused her, for the first time since that terrible day. She clamped down on that feeling, immediately.

"I have surgery at seven," she said. "Time for you to go home."

"Home."

"Let me call you a taxi. Leave the stolen jeep.

The shore patrol is probably already looking for it."

"Glory, Glory, Glory. It must be hard being you."

"Hard?"

"All these men, pressing in. Desiring you, lusting after you, loving you, approaching you, and lingering when nothing happens."

"It happened once, Beast," she said. "That was enough."

"Never."

"Always."

He puffed out a breath. He nodded. "Okay," he said. "I tried."

"Yes, you did."

"I'm going to die out there, you know that?"

"I hope not."

"One way or another, I will. When I get into that airplane, strap in, taxi up to the midships hold line, and then give it full military power, release the brakes, gun that bastard down the centerline and right off the bow, dip down a little, scare the bridge while I kiss those green waves with the landing gear, that's when I'm *alive,* Glory. Really alive."

"I can't imagine."

"You let me love you," he said. "You'll get the picture soon enough."

There was no answering that, she thought.

"Okay," he said, after a moment. "I guess I'm officially a pumpkin."

"Good night, Beastie McCarty. Fly low and fast, now."

"Keep me in mind, beautiful lady. And remember, one Roman candle trumps a hundred sparklers."

Beast walked away from the nurses' quarters on unsteady legs, which he immediately attributed to having been at sea for a long time. Couldn't be the booze, because he still needed another drink. When he got to the bar at the O-club, he found the staff putting chairs up on the tables. He sat down at the bar and ordered another mai tai.

"Sorry, boss," the bartender said. "We closing up now."

"You can make one more," Mick said. "I know you've got them all premixed. Just add the rum, and I'll be quiet."

The bartender was a large Samoan, with a placid and friendly face. "No can do, boss," he said. "I've closed out for the night. You've had plenty. Lemme call you a taxi."

"I don't want a fucking taxi," Mick snarled. "I need another drink."

The bartender just shook his head and moved away. The guys stacking chairs out on the floor were watching but not alarmed. They'd seen this a hundred times before. Tonight, though, when the bartender turned around, he found Mick behind the bar, rooting around for the mai tai mix.

"Hey!" the bartender shouted when Mick, who couldn't find what he was looking for, began sweeping bottles onto the floor with a loud crash. The cleaning crew stopped working. There was entertainment.

"Stay out of my way," Mick said. "You won't make me a drink, I'll do it myself."

The bartender, who was as wide as Mick was tall, sized him up for a minute, then shrugged. "Hey, Benny," he called across the room. "Call the HASP."

Mick ignored him, poured a large amount of rum into a glass, added some mix, and then walked over to a table in the corner and sat down. Five minutes later, the Hawaiian Armed Services Police arrived in two of their distinctive jeeps. Four of them came into the bar area. One was an Army officer, the other three Navy enlisted. The officer was a diminutive, bespectacled first lieutenant who came up to Mick's shoulders; he was wearing Army khakis and highly polished boots and sported a Colt .45 on a pristine white holster belt. The three sailors were all large, strong men. They wore plastic helmets and pressed dungarees with white leggings and carried batons in their gloved hands.

The officer approached Mick at his corner table. "Let's see some ID, Lieutenant," he said.

"Up yours, Army," Mick said. "My uniform's my ID, and I'm not bothering anybody."

"ID, please," the officer said again while his three military policemen spread out behind him.

Mick ignored the officer and examined the three big HASP policemen. "You guys want some action?" he asked, finishing his drink and gathering himself to get up.

"Love some," said the largest of the three. "Or you can come with us, peaceable like. We'll all go downtown, see the nice man at the Navy desk, do some paperwork, and then you can sleep it off in one of our officer rooms."

"I'm not going anywhere," Mick said. "With you or anyone else. So why don't you pussies just beat it."

The officer looked over his shoulder at the big man, who nodded and then slapped his baton against his thigh. The officer stepped aside as they moved in. Mick got up and started forward, fists ready, only to trip over the officer's extended foot and fall flat on the floor. When he tried to get up, the HASP went to work on him with their batons, whaling on his upper arms, thighs, elbows, shins, and knees. When Mick stopped resisting, the big guy stepped in and tapped him once expertly behind the right ear, and Mick was out for the count.

The next morning, Mick found himself in the officer wing of the drunk tank at HASP headquarters in downtown Honolulu. He felt nauseous and badly hung over. His head throbbed with a vicious headache, and every one of his major muscles hurt from the baton workover. There was a large knot behind his right ear, and every time he tried to stand up he got dizzy. He finally stopped trying.

The steel door clanked open, and a HASP cop handed him a mug of black coffee. "Head's down the passageway to the right. If you gotta puke, do it down there. You puke here, you clean it up. Use the head, then come back here and wait. Sir."

Two throbbing hours later Mick was taken out front to the booking desk, where they gave him back his wallet, watch, and academy ring. Two more HASP cops were waiting. The desk sergeant told him he was going to take a ride back to Pearl, where somebody wanted to see him.

"I'll just bet," Mick said.

"Easy way or hard way, Lieutenant?" the sergeant, a middle-aged Marine, asked. The HASP cops, ever optimistic, had their hands on their batons.

Mick waved a hand. "I'm all done," he said.

"Smart move," the sergeant said. "Go with them, please."

The two cops put him in the right front seat of a HASP jeep, with one of them driving and the other sitting right behind Mick. The fresh air felt good, but when they arrived at their destination, Mick groaned. They'd taken him to the naval base headquarters building. There were senior officers in there, and the last thing Mick wanted to see right now was a senior officer. His uniform was wrinkled and stank of booze. He had not shaved, and his head felt like a fermenting pumpkin. He figured he was probably black and blue all over, but the HASP guys knew where to hit a fella so that his uniform would cover the bruises.

The cops parked the jeep and escorted Mick into the building, where they took him to an office and told him to take a seat. The label on the office's outer door read NAVAL BASE ADMINISTRATION. They then stood at a casual parade rest behind him until a yeoman came through from the inner office and said the commander would see him now.

Mick got up and followed the yeoman through some batwing doors into the inner office. There he confronted none other than Commander Hugo Oxerhaus, sitting in a wheelchair.

"Who says there's no God," Oxerhaus said, rubbing his hands together.

Mick spent the next three weeks temporarily assigned to the naval base headquarters as Commander Oxerhaus's brand-new personal assistant. He spent his nights in hack at the BOQ and took his meals in the naval station's enlisted mess hall. He was forbidden to consume alcoholic beverages or to enter any of the island's military officers' clubs. Because of the HASP incident, Mick's squadron had issued temporary administrative duty orders leaving him behind when the carrier sailed.

His days consisted of manning a desk in Oxerhaus's outer office while dealing with an unending stream of personnel issues and the attendant mountains of paperwork. Once an hour Oxerhaus would yell for him to "get in here" and then chew him out for one administrative infraction or another. Oxerhaus was confined to a wheelchair after breaking his back on a ladder trying to escape the sinking *Yorktown*. He made Mick wheel him to the head when necessary and then stand outside until he was ready to be wheeled back to his office.

The other officers working at headquarters left Mick alone, being very much aware of Oxerhaus's special ability to humiliate an individual all by himself. It took the full three weeks for Mick's body to heal from the HASP beating, during which he learned that such beatings were standard operating procedure for the HASP when dealing with troublemakers. When he complained about it, the other people looked at him as if he were nuts: Everyone on the island, including civilians, knew not to mess around with the HASP, ever.

He also found out that being denied alcohol was its own special form of hell. For the first three nights of his confinement he was able to talk some transient aviators into bringing beer back from the club, but then Oxerhaus made him swear on his personal honor that he would not drink while in hack. Mick kept his word, but the transition from drinking man to abstinence made his nights worse than his days.

His right hand, which had been healing at a glacial pace since the incident on Guadalcanal, was now turning colors again, courtesy of a HASP baton. He worked to keep it out of sight as best he could, because he was sure that if Oxerhaus ever focused on it, he'd use it as a way to board him out of naval aviation. Mick did not want to spend the rest of the war at this naval station backwater. In his third week of BOQ restriction, however, Oxerhaus did notice the hand. He surprised Mick by sending him to see the senior flight surgeon over at Kaneohe Air Station. The doctor gave him a general physical exam and then sat down with him to talk about his hand. Mick explained how it had been injured and then reinjured.

"That HASP love tap didn't help things," the doctor said. "If you were looking for a way out of naval aviation, this could certainly be your ticket. But that's not what you want, is it?"

"Absolutely not," Mick replied. "All I can do is fly and kill Japs, and that's all I want to do. But lately I'm getting the impression that the fleet carrier Navy is equating spit-and-polish procedures with Japs in the water. I admit to being a little rough around the edges, but I'm starting to wonder if the Navy really needs people like me anymore."

The doctor, a fifty-year-old commander in the Medical Service Corps, got up and shut the door to his office. Then he produced a pack of Camels, offered one to Mick, and lit one for himself. Mick had been an indifferent smoker until he'd quit the booze, but now he was well and truly hooked.

"Naval aviation *is* changing, Lieutenant," the doctor said. "I'm seeing it every day. Back in early 'forty-two, it was all about survival. Extended peacetime, the Depression, the pay cuts, all that turned a Navy career into a longevity game where people kept their jobs by keeping their heads down. Someone had to die or retire for someone else to get promoted. The Japs helped thin out the upper ranks here in Pearl, but now the smoothies are getting into it. Careers are being advanced, reputations polished. I'm seeing senior aviators more afraid of screwing up than they are of Jap fighter pilots. You academy?"

Mick nodded.

"From the size of you, I'll bet you played ball and you were good at it."

"They seemed to like me back then," Mick said. "Called me Beast. They even had a special cheer whenever I lined up."

"Yeah, I went to an Army–Navy game once in Philly. Great stuff. And you've seen some good action?"

"I got a carrier at Midway, if that counts."

The doctor nodded. "That where you ran into Oxerhaus? On the *Yorktown*?"

Mick was surprised. "You know him?"

The doctor took a deep drag on his cigarette and then ground it out in his ashtray. "Yeah, I know him. Had to deal with him back in Pensacola, before he became air boss on the *Yorktown*. Guy's a prick, always has been. Did you know his wife left him for another brownshoe?"

"What flavor brownshoe?"

"Three guesses, Lieutenant, and the first two don't count."

"An SBD guy?"

The doctor nodded. Mick just shook his head.

"So the first thing we have to do is get you out of Oxerhaus's clutches, or he'll bury you there at that naval station. The way we do that is to send you back stateside for treatment. Special surgery, maybe, then some rehab. I'm thinking the training command, back at Pensacola."

"Will surgery fix this?" Mick asked, holding up his battered hand.

"Probably not," the doctor admitted. "Eventually, the circulation in that hand is gonna shut down, and then you may lose it. But I've got the authority to order you back stateside, and that will get your ass out of that paperwork cage."

"When could I go?"

"I'll write the orders today, and I'll write the medical report in such a way that the docs back there will get the bigger picture. After that, it'll be up to you to figure out how to get back to a big-deck and killing Nips. Deal?"

Mick finished his cigarette. "Best offer I've had all year," he said. "Deal."

Marsh was surprised to see a letter on his bed when he got back to the cabin. It was one of those tiny airmail envelopes, smelling faintly of a woman's perfume. It had been mailed three weeks ago, according to the frank from the Fleet Post Office in Pearl.

Glory?

The return address only had initials, but there it was: the nurses' quarters at Pearl.

Glory had written him. He felt his heart leap.

He opened the letter, trying not to tear the flimsy paper. His hands were wet from the rain, and he immediately smeared the ink on the top of the almost transparent paper.

Dear Mr. Vincent,
I hope you are well and keeping safe, or as safe as you can be out there. I so much enjoyed seeing you the last time you were

here. The days seem to fly by, as they probably do for you, too. We're all working as hard as ever, and I'm sure you know why better than we do. There are more people coming on staff every day, it seems, and new medicines and techniques as well. Our mutual friend has been reassigned to work with a senior surgeon in preparation for an even bigger upgrade to the facilities.

I hope you have time to write back. I'd love to get to know you better. Until then, keep safe.

A secret admirer

Marsh re-read the letter and then smiled. This had to be that young nurse he'd met on the front porch of the nurses' quarters when he'd gone to see Glory. He was a little disappointed that it wasn't Glory herself writing him, but he could understand that, too.

Glory was never very far from his thoughts, when he had time to think, which wasn't that often. The ship had been going full bore since leaving Pearl as the Big Blue Fleet waged a war of attrition on various Jap bases in the Solomons and farther north. In a way, though, he knew she was moving away from him. Truth be told, he had to admit, it was only in his imagination that she'd ever been moving *toward* him. He had hoped that with Tommy gone he might have a chance to resume at least his long-distance love affair. After the Pearl visit, even he could see that she was still very much in love with her departed husband, and that no man was going to invade that longing anytime soon. Nevertheless, he'd jumped at the chance to start a correspondence with her as a way of maintaining contact. There was always the chance that she'd finally grow tired of mourning Tommy, and if that happened, he wanted to be right there, if only on paper.

A secret admirer. He smiled again. Sally, that was her name. Sally something, beginning with an *A*. Well, he'd certainly write back—it was nice getting mail from someone, and she had mentioned "our mutual friend." Perhaps by writing Sally he might keep in touch with Glory. They were roommates in the quarters, and sometimes they probably talked about people they knew. Or wrote to.

There was a knock on the door. The bridge messenger said the captain wanted to see him on the bridge.

"Be right up," Marsh said, folding the letter and putting it in his to-do basket.

NINE

Pearl, October 1943

Glory was proud that she had not become seasick, although the flat, calm waters off Honolulu may have contributed to her achievement. She and fifty other medical staff from the hospital were on board the Navy's newest hospital ship. Superman had set up an orientation tour so that people from whom the advance base invasion augmentation teams would be formed would at least know what a hospital ship looked like.

This one looked a lot like an ocean liner, which she had been just seven months ago when they painted her white, then put a green stripe around her sides and enormous red crosses on her stacks, sides, and top decks. The main dining room and ballroom had been converted to operating theaters, and the forward and after holds to medical supply storage compartments. The six hundred individual staterooms could hold up to four patients each. The ship's crew was made up of all merchantmen, not Navy, and, of course, there was no armament onboard whatsoever. Everyone knew there were no guarantees that the Japs would respect all those red crosses, especially after they'd sunk the Australian hospital ship *Aurora* in 1942. This one, called the

Salvation, was almost thirty thousand tons, much bigger than *Aurora*, and she'd just finished a three-week fitting-out period in the naval shipyard at Pearl.

Today's sea trial, as Stembridge called it, was mostly for the benefit of the shipyard engineers, who ran ship's systems tests while the medical people checked out the operating rooms and all their equipment. They'd come out of Pearl early that morning and had circumnavigated the island of Oahu for the entire day. Glory was truly tired after a day of going up and down companion-ways, into the main holds, and through all of the sickbed staterooms with Stembridge as he conducted a whirlwind inspection, he with a flashlight and she with a large notebook, writing down what seemed like a few thousand discrepancies. They'd then done a mock operation in one of the four ORs, where they quickly discovered that the anesthesiology systems had everything but a way to pipe the various gases to the table, among other things.

It was now an hour before sundown. Glory stood with Stembridge up on the starboard side of the navigation bridge, right behind the ship's expansive pilothouse. Stembridge was comparing notes with the ship's superintendent from the shipyard. Glory had stepped out of her uniform shoes and was enjoying the feel of cold steel against her aching white-stockinged feet. The island of Oahu lay to starboard at about twelve miles, pale green in the yellowing light of late afternoon. The city of Honolulu was in view as they sailed past Diamond Head. Farther to the west she could see the masts of warships in the Pearl lagoon, interspersed with yard cranes at the shipyard.

The master of the ship, a ruddy, round little man with the face of a leprechaun, stepped out onto the bridge wing to have a cigarette and a mug of coffee before entering port. He was a merchant officer from the Moore-McCormack Lines, from whom the ship had been requisitioned. His uniform was a navy blue jacket with four stripes, white trousers, and an open-collar white shirt. With that face, Glory thought, the four stripes looked incongruous, but based on how the crew treated him, he was fully in command.

Up above, on the signal deck, two Navy signalmen were shooting the breeze with the ship's civilian signalman. One of the Navy guys pointed toward Pearl and said, "Hey, we're getting a light." The other Navy man turned around, squinted over at Pearl, and then asked the merchant sailor, a fifty-year-old with a large gray beard, to uncover the ship's signal light. Glory stared across the water in the direction of the naval base and finally saw a lone, yellow light winking at them urgently from among the forest of masts and stacks. The older Navy signalman told the other one that he would read while the other wrote down the message. The merchantman with the beard seemed content to let the Navy guys do their stuff, exchanging a wink with the master one level below, the old hand letting the eager beavers play Navy.

"Probably a challenge," Stembridge said at her elbow.

"What's a challenge?"

"A code, either a number or a word, that changes every day. Any ship approaching Pearl gets challenged. If she doesn't come up with the right code word in reply, they tell the Army at Fort DeRussy over there to open up with their sixteen-inch coastal guns."

She gave him an arch look. "Of course they do," she said, believing not a word of it.

"Baker Tare, stand by to write," called out the reader. He was looking through a pair of binoculars clipped to the top of the lamp while holding down the light's signaling arm to give the signal lamp at the base a target. The other man began filling out the message blank, which he held on a clipboard.

"Easy, Mike, Easy, Roger, Golf, Easy—emergency."

The master, overhearing that, frowned, took his cigarette out of his mouth, and flipped it over the side. Then he listened to the reader calling out the rest of the message.

"Yoke, Oboe, Uncle, break it—You."

"Able, Roger, Easy, break it—are."

"Sugar, Tare, Able, Nan, Dog, Item, Nan, Golf—break it—standing."

"Item, Nan, Tare, Oboe—break—into."

"Mike, Item, Nan, Easy, Fox, Item—oh *shit!–minefield!*"

Glory heard the master's china mug shatter on the deck. She had just turned to see where he'd gone when suddenly a mountainous thump hit the ship and lifted the bow twenty feet into the air, followed by an enormous explosion of dirty, smoke-filled water that rose a hundred feet and then fell back onto the forecastle like a tidal wave. The ship shuddered along her full length and then began to slow, her bow dipping down into the sea before coming back up again.

Glory found herself sprawled on the deck, along with Stembridge and the ship's superintendent. All three of them had turned to the ornate wooden railing to begin pulling themselves upright when the ship hit a second mine, again at the bow. This one produced a smaller water column but seemed to punch the ship much harder. A third mine went off in a sympathetic detonation off the starboard side, but far enough away that they saw it rather than felt it. The ship, which had only been making ten knots, slowed to a stop, and this time the bow was not coming back up. As Glory watched in horror, the forward-most sixty feet of forecastle deck folded down right in front of the H-shaped kingpost and collapsed into the sea. The kingpost followed it in a rattling crash of dismounted winches and thrashing wire cables.

The master, white-faced, stepped out onto the bridge wing and told the signalmen to send out an SOS to the naval station. Glory could hear other voices shouting inside the pilothouse. The master ran back in, shouting orders of his own. The ship's superintendent followed him into the pilothouse, yelling something about organizing a shoring party. Above them, the Navy signalman began to work the signal light's metal arm so fast Glory could hardly see his hand. The merchant-man with the beard was nowhere to be seen.

"Let's get below," Stembridge said, grabbing her arm. "Get all the troops in one place. This damn thing might sink on us."

As if he'd been overheard, the ship's announcing system crackled to life on the topside speakers all along the upper decks.

"This is the captain. We've hit a mine. Two mines. Engineering department damage control team muster at the number three hatch with shoring gear. All medical passengers assemble on the port side, that's the seaward side, boat deck, with your life jackets. Lifeboat captains lower away the portside lifeboats to the rail and stand by."

As they hurried across the catwalk behind the

pilothouse to get to the port side, Glory felt the deck beginning to tilt. She realized they were going slightly downhill. They stopped to let some crewmen, already in their life jackets and steel helmets, come racing up the portside stairway ladder. The looks on their faces said it all.

"Where's your life jacket?" Stembridge asked.

"I have no idea," she said, feeling suddenly like an idiot.

They rushed down the first ladder, and then Stembridge saw a life jacket locker mounted to the inboard bulkhead. He opened it, gave one to her, and then began strapping one on himself.

Glory just looked at it. It was blue-gray in color, soft and spongy, with a confusing array of white strings hanging down like the tentacles on a jellyfish. It had a tarlike smell. She might technically be a naval officer, but she had no idea what to do with this thing.

"Turn around and hold out your arms," Stembridge ordered. He pulled the jacket first over one arm and then the other, whirled her around to face him, and began tying strings. "I think we can get all of our people into two boats. I'll deal with the boat captains; you corral everyone and get a muster. Make sure no one's still belowdecks. Got it?"

She nodded, which was difficult because he had knotted the neck string right up under her chin. He was looking down into her eyes.

"Scared?"

The downward tilt on the ship was increasing. "Yes."

"Good. Focus. Everyone else will be scared, too, so they'll do whatever someone in authority tells them to. Give orders, not suggestions. Tell everyone to muster together, near one or two boats. Then get a head count."

They felt the engine trembling, followed by a whipsawing motion through the ship's structure that rattled the outside fittings. The engine shut back down. Stembridge appeared to be listening.

"Propeller shaft's probably broken," he said.

"Is that bad?"

"Means we can't back out of the minefield," he said. "Hope Pearl's sending tugs. Right. Let's go."

The portside boat deck was already crowded with the people from the naval hospital, all struggling with the unfamiliar life jackets. A half-dozen ship's crewmen, also in life jackets, were busy lowering the six portside lifeboats to the railing level. The ship was heavily down by the bow now and continuing to list to port. As Glory arrived, she heard the crewmen directing some of her people to grab boat ropes so that the boats didn't swing out too far from the railing. There were gates in the railing, all of which were now open. She saw Sally Adkins, called her over, and then told her to help take a muster of the medical people. Sally promptly told the nearest people to

247

fall into ranks. Most of them just looked at her.

"Just like OCS, goddammit," she yelled. "Now fall *in*."

Glory saw one of the merchant seamen nodding approvingly as the pretty, blue-eyed blonde took charge. She looked for Stembridge but couldn't find him in all the commotion. The noise on the boat deck subsided as doctors, nurses, orderlies, and med techs fell into ranks, looking like rows of blue-gray pumpkins in their bulky kapoks. Glory heard a whoosh, followed by a second one, as the bridge personnel fired red distress rockets into the evening air. Then Stembridge appeared.

"Do we have everybody?"

"Sally's taking a muster," she said. "When do we get into the boats?"

"The captain thinks they can contain the flooding to the forward holds, but they can't use the engines. The problem is we're adrift on the edge of a minefield."

"How in the hell—"

"Navigation error. They turned toward Pearl too soon. There's a destroyer coming out, and she's bringing tugs. The captain recommends we stay aboard for now." He surveyed the uneven ranks of medical people, the front row holding on to the life rails to keep upright. "Let me talk to everybody. You take one of the docs and do a quick tour of the OR spaces. Make sure no one is down there."

All the lights were still on inside the ship, but it was deathly quiet as they went down two decks to what had been the dining and ballroom area. *Salvation* was not a steamship. She had a diesel-electric power plant, where a set of large marine diesels drove generators, which in turn drove a single electric motor coupled to the propeller shaft. They could hear the diesels idling a few decks below, and, except for the unusual slant of the deck and some dangling light fixtures and overturned furniture, they would never have known the ship had hit not one but two sea mines. Ordinarily there would have been up to twelve hundred passengers and crew on board, but now there was only the basic crew, the shipyard engineers, and the medical team.

As they walked quickly through all the medical spaces, Glory sensed that the doctor was in a hurry. She asked him why.

"If we hit another goddamned mine, we don't want to be down here, do we."

She hadn't thought of that, and stepped up the pace. She'd been dealing with patients who'd survived sinking ships for two years. It had never occurred to her that she might become one herself. After checking the four operating rooms, they went forward to make sure the recovery wards were empty, and promptly got lost. Glory felt a surge of fear when she realized that neither one of them knew exactly how to get back topside, and the fact that they were both holding on to the passageway bulkheads to stay upright wasn't helping.

Then they heard a noise that sounded like an injured animal. It was coming from beyond the large steel door ahead of them, on which the words MAIN GALLEY were printed. She realized that the door was really a watertight hatch. The doctor went ahead and grasped the operating handle.

"Wait!" Glory called from behind him. He turned to look at her. She pointed toward the bottom of the door, which was dripping beads of water from the bottom up to about a foot above the hatch coaming.

"Oh, hell," he said. "It's flooding. We can't open this door."

At the sound of his voice, the whimpering noises from the other side grew louder. "I think we have to," she said. "There's someone in trouble on the other side."

"We do, and if that's the ocean, we'll never get it closed. That could sink the ship."

They stared at each other, intensely aware that they were probably right at or even below the waterline, especially with the ship down by the head. Then the sound became a man's voice, but it was masked by a burbling noise, as if he were trying to shout through water.

"We can't just leave him," Glory said.

"Okay," the doctor said. "Damned thing's probably going to sink anyway. Stand back."

He lifted the handle but forgot to step out of the way. The water pressure on the other side immediately punched the door open and pinned him between the bulkhead and the hatch. A wall of greenish water two feet high swept past them into the OR passageway, nearly knocking Glory off her feet. Beyond the hatch they saw a tangle of piping that had come down from the overhead. One of the pipes was pumping water into the galley passageway, and beneath the mess they could see the figure of a man on his back trapped by all the debris. They plunged into the pile of metal, heaving and twisting as best they could until the doctor grabbed her arm and pointed. They could see the man's Oriental face, which was now under perhaps six inches of water. His eyes and mouth were wide open.

The doctor swore. It was too late. They climbed back over the pile of piping and tried to close the hatch. They had to wait another minute for the water level to equalize between the two spaces, but then they were able to get it closed and dogged back down. Their khaki trousers and shoes were soaked. Glory felt exposed with the wet fabric clinging to her lower body, but the young doctor was more interested in all that water.

"That whole compartment is going to fill up eventually," the doctor said. "We'll have to tell somebody about that. Maybe the engineers can get that water pipe shut off."

"Fine," she said, "but first, how do *we* get out of here?"

"Let's try going back the way we came," he said, and together they went squelching back up the slippery inclined tiles toward the operating rooms.

It took them ten minutes to find their way back out of the medical complex and up to the boat decks. The sun had set, and now most of the light came from the ship's own gallery lights. They reported to Stembridge, who went up the ladders to the bridge to tell the captain what they'd found below. Glory went to find Sally.

"Everybody's here," Sally said. "There's a destroyer right out there, but I think it's stopped."

"I would, too," Glory said.

Sally eyed Glory's wet trousers. "What happened to you down there?"

Glory explained, and Sally shivered at the thought of the man drowning under all that wreckage with help so close.

They could see the shape of the destroyer and its running lights. Behind it in the distance were four smaller shapes, each with a white bow wave visible in the twilight. The hospital ship's bow-down attitude seemed to have stabilized, as had the port list. Glory stared out at the twinkling reflections of the ship's lights on the flat seas. She wondered how close they were to any more mines. The fact that the destroyer wasn't approaching worried her, and it was clear that the quiet crowd on the boat decks fully understood why the rescue ship hadn't closed in. The topside speakers came on.

"Deck department lay down to the fantail to receive tug and hawser."

They watched as a six-man crew went aft along the main deck to take a hawser from one of the tugs. A grim-faced captain came down from the bridge to reassure the medical people. He told them that the two mines had essentially blasted the same part of the ship, but at least she was no longer flooding.

"That tin can out there is providing navigation positioning for the tugs. They've turned on the navigation aids ashore so we can get a three-point fix in reference to the minefield. We're in it, but just barely. The tug will hand up that towing hawser and pull us in the direction of safety. Then they plan to put the rest of the tugs alongside and take us into the shallows near Pearl."

"Why not into the harbor?" Stembridge asked.

"We're too far down by the head," the captain said. "They'll send out some caisson floats, get the bow up, then we can get over the reef. That's going to take all night, folks, so if you want, go inside to the lounge nearest the boat decks and have a seat. But keep your jackets handy."

"How did this happen?" one of the doctors asked.

"The navigator made a serious mistake, that's how. Anyway, this will be your last night on board. Mine, too, probably."

It did take all night, and Glory found herself making a bed out of a sofa in the lounge, using another life jacket as a pillow. The ship's main galley had been fully flooded by the broken water line, but the captain's galley managed a soup-and-sandwich meal at about eight that evening. By the next morning, the ship was being held just off the entrance channel while partially flooded caissons were cabled onto the remains of the bow. While this work was going on, the medical staff was removed by personnel boats from the naval station and returned to the landing at Hospital Point. It was only later in the day that she learned that the destroyer had been USS *Evans*, where Marsh Vincent was the XO.

Marsh wrapped up his day at 1800 and went to the O-club for dinner. Then he walked over to the nurses' quarters. The carrier group was going to sail in the morning. He wanted to see Glory if that was possible, but when he got there Sally met him out on the front verandah.

"Glory's exhausted," she said. "She's asleep. But you can visit me if you'd like."

"My secret admirer," Marsh said with a warm smile. "You bet."

Sally brought out two beers from the nurses' secret hoard, and they sat out in the shadows of the verandah. Marsh had not known that Glory or the other medical people had been on board the *Salvation.*

"You had a close call," he said. "One more mine, or if either one had hit her on the side, she'd have gone down like a ton of bricks. As it was, they barely got the caissons out there in time."

"I guess sometimes ignorance *is* bliss," she said. "They didn't tell us much, just to muster up on the boat deck and stay near the lifeboats."

"*You* were there, too?"

"I was the musterer-in-chief on the boat decks," she said proudly. "I even gave an order, and everyone obeyed."

He gave her a mock salute. "Well done there, Chief Sally. If you weren't so pretty I'd shanghai you for the trip west right this minute."

Her eyes sparkled. "Then we wouldn't have to write, would we," she said.

"Those letters have been wonderful," he said. "I didn't realize how much I missed getting mail until you started writing. I got one from Glory, but then I guess she got busy."

Some of the sparkle went out of her eyes, and Marsh realized he'd just made an error, mentioning Glory.

"She's more than busy these days," Sally said.

"Superman has practically made her into his chief of staff for the expansion project, and she still has OR duties."

"Superman?"

"Oh, that's just what everybody calls him. Dr. Stembridge, chief of surgery. Tall, dark, handsome, very fast in the OR, knows everything, sees everything, jumps buildings with a single bound . . . *and* he keeps Glory flying along behind him every minute."

"Got it," Marsh said. He wondered if their association extended beyond the hospital and then realized he had no right to ask that question. "Will any of the staff here come west with the new hospital ships?"

"Not if they keep running into minefields," Sally said, "but yes, that's part of the expansion project. Superman is running training classes on mass casualties, triage, and what he calls two-stage surgeries. That's where they do a minimal, stabilizing repair, move on to the next patient, and then come back later and do it right."

"This sounds like invasion planning to me," he said.

"You'd know more about that than we would."

"Not necessarily. We know the carrier's flight schedule each day, and when they expect air attacks. Beyond that, the tin cans are mostly in the dark. Our world stops at the visible horizon. Has Beast been by?"

She made a face and looked down at her shoes for a moment.

"Okay, what happened?"

She told him about Mick's late-night visitation. Marsh just shook his head. "Did he get into trouble for all that?"

"No one knows. The whole quarters got to listen to him until Glory sent him packing. After that, we haven't heard."

"I was going to try to see him on this visit, maybe run into him at the club." He looked at his watch. "I've got to get back. We're sailing in the morning. That's a secret, by the way."

"Sure it is," she said. "Only the whole base knows."

He laughed. "A lot different from December 1941, isn't it."

"Except in our business," she said. "If anything, we're seeing more casualties than in 'forty-two."

"This war's getting bigger and bigger," he said. "After Midway I think we were down to two aircraft carriers in the whole fleet. Now the new *Lex* is one of six carriers, and that's just in our task group."

"The Japanese must know how this is going to end," she said.

"They worship death," he said. "An 'honorable' death in battle is the highest achievement they can attain in their lives. I believe we're going to have to kill every stinking one of them before this is over."

"On that lovely note, Commander," she said.

"Sorry," he said. He covered her hand with his. "You will keep writing, won't you? I live for your letters."

"Of course I will. I'll even try to get Glory to write at least once."

He looked her in the eye. "Forget Glory," he said.

"Can *you* forget Glory?" she asked.

"I'm trying," he said. "I'm learning that everything I ever thought about her existed mostly in my own pointy little head. So now I'm trying to grow up."

She squeezed his hand. "Don't be too hard on yourself, Commander Marsh. Glory Lewis breaks hearts just by walking by. She puts the rest of us way back into the shadows."

"Not that far back, secret admirer." He leaned forward and gave her a brief kiss on the cheek. "Stay out of minefields, okay?"

She reached up, put both arms around him, and gave him a lingering kiss on the lips. "Hurry back, Commander Marsh," she whispered. "Life is short."

Marsh flagged down a base taxi that was headed back to the destroyer piers. There were two other lieutenant commanders in the cab. One was a submariner and the other a destroyerman. Based on the fumes, they'd had a great evening. The destroyerman asked Marsh what ship he was on. Marsh told him he was XO in *Evans*.

"XO," the submariner said. "Pretty damned young to be an XO, aren't you?"

Marsh shrugged. "I don't feel that young anymore," he said.

The other two laughed at that. It turned out that the submariner was the exec on a fleet boat, and the other officer the exec on his destroyer. The submariner leaned forward from the backseat. "Care for a little advice there, XO?" he asked.

"Absolutely."

"Find a handkerchief, get that lipstick off your face. Otherwise someone on the mess decks with a grudge might write your wife."

"Not a problem," Marsh said. "Don't have a wife."

"Well, in that case, leave it right there. The crew'll love ya."

He nudged the other officer, and they both laughed hysterically, as only drunks can. Marsh smiled, but for entirely different reasons.

Glory didn't know who had come up with the idea for a hospital staff beach party on Waikiki, but it hadn't taken too long to organize. Everyone was ready for a break, and the hospital's commanding officer had managed to tap into some money from something called the welfare and recreation fund at the base. The party was held on a Sunday afternoon behind the Royal Hawaiian Hotel, and only the duty section personnel remained in the hospital. Everyone else had shown up at the beach via the Navy shuttle bus system that ran from Pearl to downtown Honolulu once an hour. There was beer and soft drinks stuffed into ice-filled GI cans, along with a hard-liquor tiki bar back up the beach.

Glory had come with a group of nurses, including Sally and three of the other OR supervisors. They'd all changed in the outdoor ladies' bathhouse and then joined the crowd of doctors, nurses, admin people, orderlies, and some staff officers from Admiral Nimitz's Pacific Fleet headquarters up on the hill at Makalapa. The ratio of men to women was about six to one, which suited most of the ladies just fine. Glory, like many of the other women present, did not know how to swim, so she confined her water activities to wading in the shallows, while other more adventuresome people swam out to the protective reef and tried their hand at surfing. She was also being careful not to get her new one-piece bathing suit wet, as she was afraid that it might become much too revealing. She'd bought the suit downtown on impulse almost six months ago, and this was the first time she'd actually worn it out in public.

Sally, her adventuresome roommate, had talked her into it.

Late in the afternoon a crew from the hotel came down and fired up a pit-style barbecue. Glory had to move her beach blanket once the smoke started up. As she was doing so, she saw Stembridge waving her over to his little group under a clump of palm trees. She recognized two of the women there but none of the men. Stembridge introduced her as Glory Lewis, surgical coordinator at the hospital. The men were all staff officers from the Pacific Fleet headquarters. She listened absently to all the names and then joined the group on a large beach blanket, sitting next to a Captain Somebody, who was wearing a Hawaiian shirt over his khaki swim trunks.

Behind the group was a small beach hut, containing a narrow bar and a lone bartender who was presiding over an oversized Waring blender. Stembridge signaled that they needed another round. A moment later the barman brought frozen concoctions of some kind to the group, and she took one. She sniffed the glass. It smelled of crushed pineapple and various tropical fruits. Thank God, she thought, it's not one of those head-breaking mai tais. In fact, she didn't smell any liquor at all. She took a sip. It was delicious.

"Like it?" the captain asked. He was in his

fifties, gray-haired, and discreetly giving her bottom the once-over whenever he thought she wasn't looking.

"Yes," she said. "It's nice. What's it called?"

"Missionary's Downfall," he said with a grin. "They take a ripe pineapple, slice the top off, extract the core, then make vertical cuts in the fruit from the inside. Then they fill it with Five Islands gin and put the top back on. Set it outside in the sun for a few days so the pineapple begins to ferment, then chill the whole thing. Usually they bring it out with a straw, but tonight they scooped out the good stuff and blended it with ice. One's lovely. Two, and you'll be the star of the evening."

She smiled. "Thanks for the warning. I'm not much one for stardom."

"You ought to be in the movies," he said, letting his leg drift over to hers. "You're certainly beautiful enough."

"Thank you, kind sir," she said demurely, knowing where this was going. She looked over at Stembridge and flashed a silent "help" look at him. He said something to the cute young nurse at his side, got up, and came over to where Glory was sitting.

"Like that stuff?" he asked.

"In a careful sort of way," she said. "The captain here was explaining how it's made."

"That's a state secret, Captain," Stembridge

said. "Takes all the fun out of it. Glory, come meet the fleet surgeon."

He offered his hand and pulled her to her feet. She smiled at the crestfallen captain and walked across to meet yet another doctor, tugging her rubbery swimsuit down in the back. She noticed that Stembridge didn't let go of her hand as he introduced her to the senior doctor in the Pacific Fleet. She quietly disengaged and then shook hands with the elderly captain, who was visibly on his second or perhaps even third Downfall. He was so drunk, in fact, that all he could do was nod and smile, nod and smile. She looked at Stembridge.

"*You* sent the signal," he said. "Consider yourself rescued. Hey—the music's on. Let's dance."

The hotel had piped music from one of the bands inside to the tree-mounted speakers on the lanai dance floor, which was basically a low wooden platform on the sand in the middle of a small grove of palms. Lawn torches scented with citronella gave off a yellowish light.

She felt unusually self-aware, dancing bare-legged with this handsome man wearing nothing but his swim trunks. Some of the other women had wrapped colorful beach skirts around their waists, and Glory wished she'd done the same. It was doubly awkward because they'd taken their drinks with them onto the floor. Her swimsuit fit like a second skin, and its bullet-bra top made her breasts stick out like impudent dunce caps. The bottom of the suit barely covered the tops of her thighs. She saw Sally dancing with one of the officers from the fleet headquarters. Sally was wearing a suit similar to Glory's, except hers appeared to be made out of even thinner material. The poor man with her was having a tough time concentrating on not stepping on her feet or his own arousal. Sally winked at her over the man's shoulder.

Stembridge seemed to be making sure he didn't bump into her body, and she was being just as careful not to make physical contact. There was no avoiding his intensely masculine presence, though a mixed aura of perspiration, suntan lotion, and a hint of something far more elemental. He was a well-made man with no body fat, long, strong arms, and hands hardened by years of surgery. She sipped her drink, still pretty sure that there wasn't much booze in it, couldn't be, not with all that ice and fruit juice.

Another couple bumped into them from behind her, and she felt the unmistakable brush of exploring fingers across her bottom. She flinched away and right into a full-length contact with Stembridge. For just an instant, she stopped moving and so did he. They were touching from top to bottom, and she felt a sudden flash of desire that she hadn't experienced literally for years as his hard body made firm contact with the front of her swimsuit.

Then the music stopped, and they hastily broke apart. Stembridge, pretending that nothing had happened, was looking over her shoulder and heartily greeting someone new and then introducing Glory, who was still trying to recover her voice and her composure. They joined the line that was forming for the barbecue, everyone talking, no one listening. By this time, Stembridge was behind her in line, and she was once again intensely aware of him, as if their bodies had unfinished business to conduct. She downed the rest of her drink in one long gulp and put the wide-mouthed glass down on a table near the barbecue. She was glad that it was getting dark, because she was sure there was a red flush rising on her neck. Or maybe it was just the Downfall. Now that she'd finished it, she realized that, yes, there had been a wee bit of alcohol in that thing. She wasn't drunk, but she'd never been a serious drinker, and it didn't take too much to make her head spin.

"Let's sit over there," Stembridge said when they had their plates. He was pointing to a tiny table just off the dance floor. Once they were seated he asked if she needed another drink. She'd wobbled just a bit sitting down.

"One of those was quite enough," she said, "but please don't hold back on my account."

"Me?" he said. "I don't drink. This is just ice and pineapple juice, so I don't have to listen to 'real men' razzing me for being a teetotaler."

"That makes you something of a rare bird in the Navy," she said.

"Got to like the booze much too much, early on," he said. "Quit while I still could. Self-control is important to me."

"I usually need a drink at the end of the day," she said. "One cocktail, one cigarette. My two vices."

"Only two?" he said with an easy smile. "Sounds like a dull life."

"Mmmm" was all she said, looking past him at the afterglow of the sunset over Diamond Head.

Back at the nurses' quarters, Glory went straight to the bathroom, still wearing her suit. She'd seen two of the other nurses taking their leave of the party right after dinner and had joined them on the empty bus. Stembridge had been gracious about her leaving early, saying he'd be on the next bus back himself. They had an official pass to be out after curfew, but they were still restricted to the military bus system.

She stepped into the communal bathroom and turned on the lights. There was no trace of her flushed skin from earlier, although her eyes were a bit bloodshot from a combination of the sun and that sneaky drink. Her hair had that lank, lifeless look that came from too much salt air. Just for the hell of it, she turned on the shower and stepped in, still wearing her suit. She rinsed her hair and then got back out to examine herself in the mirror. She'd been right about the bathing suit: Soaking wet, it had become just barely transparent, displaying some rather private areas of contrasting color. She'd have to remember that, the next time she went beaching.

Once in bed, she let her mind wander back to that moment on the dance floor. It was one thing to be conscious of a man's desire from a safe distance. It was quite another to feel it so directly. She'd been startled by the strength of her own response. Had she been hiding herself under false pretenses these past two years since Tommy had died? At least Stembridge had had the good grace not to tell her, as every other man eventually told her, that she had to rejoin the human race, start living again, et cetera. In fact, he'd never put a foot wrong in that department, and yet what she'd felt on the dance floor had been unmistakable. Did that mean simply that he was a normal, healthy male of the species, or was something more subtle going on between them? Was it possible he was working some kind of reverse psychology on her? Pretending he didn't desire her to the point where she'd notice, and then maybe go on the sexual offensive herself?

Listen to me, she thought. Being Lady Everest for the past two years had simplified her life immensely. Why change now?

Still.

TEN

Pearl, December 1943

On Christmas Day, the captain, two engineers from the shipyard, and Marsh stood on top of the starboard engine reduction gear casing while the chief engineer unlocked the access plates. The *Evans* had been sent back from the Tarawa operation after a loud, rattling noise in the starboard engine forced an emergency shutdown. The reduction gears, weighing several tons, translated the 24,000 RPM of the steam turbines to the low-hundreds RPM of the ship's propellers. Reduction gear repairs required the services of a shipyard, so once again *Evans* was back in Pearl.

The crew, of course, was heartbroken to be in Hawaii for the holidays instead of out on the gun line, to the point where the captain had wondered out loud to Marsh if whatever was loose in the reduction gearing was indeed an accident. He'd checked with Chief Gorman to see if there was anything to that, and the chief had laughed it off. Marsh tended to agree with him—their guys were a pretty gung-ho bunch when it came to shooting things up. While no one was going to pass up two weeks' worth of liberty down on Hotel Street, Marsh thought that the notion of self-inflicted sabotage was pretty far-fetched.

Since they were going to be in the yards for two weeks, it was decided that *Evans* would be regunned, having put the allotted number of rounds through her five-inchers during all the shore-bombardment operations. This involved taking off the five gun barrels and replacing them with new ones, followed by a tedious process called a battery alignment. That project, plus the inevitable laundry list of broken pumps, valve repairs, hull preservation, and the accumulated mountain of low-priority paperwork, meant full workdays for the entire two-week stay.

The good news, of course, was that, as XO, Marsh could take every night off, and that meant he was going to see a lot of Sally. Their letters throughout the grind of 1943 had drawn them much closer, and he was really looking forward to being with her. They'd only been gone since early October, but it had seemed longer. Marsh knew that there was one personal minefield he had to avoid: Glory. He could still remember the subtle change in Sally's expression when he'd mentioned Glory's name after the incident with the hospital ship. He'd told her then to forget Glory, and had promised himself that he would park all his adolescent pipe dreams in the memory locker for good. As he stood watching the engineers dive into the inner workings of all that oily bronzed gearing, though, he had to wonder: Forget Glory? Now that he was here in Pearl, that would be a lot easier said than done, until he remembered that Sally would probably have a role to play in that little project.

"What are you smiling about, XO?" the captain asked.

Marsh just shook his head and said, "Nothing, Captain."

The captain looked at him and then shook *his* head. "It's that nurse, isn't it," he said. "God help us. I do believe my XO's in love."

Sally came back into the room from the bathroom with her makeup kit, took one look at Glory, and said, "That's not fair."

Glory smiled, kissed a tissue, and examined the lipstick mark. She'd taken some time with the war paint tonight. She normally used very little makeup. It was expensive, and hard to get, and not a little unfair to parade down a ward of badly injured men tarted up like a chorus-line girl. Tonight, though, she had gone all out, with a dark blue, low-cut ball gown, heels, and her hair done up by a downtown hairdresser. She was wearing

270

her one good pair of nylons and three strategically placed dabs of Lanvin's Arpège.

"Okay," Sally said. "Who's the intended victim?"

"Superman," Glory said. "I think he's been playing a game with me."

"Everyone else thinks you're an item," Sally said. "Not true?"

"Not even close," Glory said.

"But you're always together. Surgery, meetings, all those committees."

Glory turned to look at Sally. "We're getting ready to commission twenty-two field hospitals," she said. "Even I don't know where they're going, but we're looking at three thousand medical personnel. That's business, Sally. War business. You ever find me *not* here at night?"

"Well, no," Sally said, "but you know how the girls gossip."

"Don't be one of them."

"Okay, okay. Sorry. So what's the game?"

"Ah, well, that's the point. Superman has never put a foot or a hand wrong. Never made a pass. Never copped a feel. Holds my hand on the dance floor while talking over my shoulder to someone else."

"I get it," Sally said. "Deliberately ignoring the best-looking woman in the hospital. Finally got you wondering—lost my touch?"

Glory smiled again. "Possibly. So, tonight? I'm

going to make an entrance. I'm going to walk right by him, flash him the fifty-thousand-watt smile, and then I'm going to ask the first officer I meet if he'd like to dance. Then the next one after that. Make a little stir. My contribution to their New Year's celebration. Flirt shamelessly with everyone. Except Superman."

Sally raised her eyebrows. "And what happens when one of your unsuspecting victims gets the wrong idea? Lady Everest is finally thawing out? How do you turn off that fire once you start it?"

"Easy," Glory said. "Marsh Vincent will be there tonight. He called earlier, did I tell you? If I have to, I'll run to him for safety."

"Commander Vincent isn't exactly indifferent to you, Glory. You run to him, looking like that, you may get a surprise."

"Then maybe Superman will come to the rescue. We'll find out how dedicated he is to his little game."

Sally frowned. "Glory—this isn't you."

Glory slipped into her gloves. "It is now," she said. "Besides, Sally, what do you know of me, really?"

"I know I've lived in your shadow for almost two years. You've been devoted to the memory of your husband. You've put up with an army of horny guys who want to take your pants off, and you've done it with dignity. Suddenly you're going to play party vamp?"

Glory felt her face getting red. She thought of a hundred slashing comments she could make. Instead, she simply turned back to the mirror. "See you at the party, Sal," she said.

When she turned back around, Sally had gone.

"Dammit," she muttered as she got her purse.

Sally was right, of course, and Glory could not explain exactly what was going on, other than as a culmination of things: Stembridge's long campaign of physical proximity coupled with studied indifference, the waves of wanting coming from every other healthy male she encountered in a world where the men outnumbered the women twenty to one, the abnormal juxtaposition of being beautiful while pretending to remain aloof from the earthy tensions of human desire. Superman had let his own guard slip for just that delectable second on the beach, as had she. There was no denying that sudden flash of desire, even if he had covered it up immediately with his usual false bonhomie.

She appraised herself in the mirror one last time. There was color in her face, and her lips were almost too red. The snug-fitting gown, the gloves, the heels, the sheen of wartime stockings, the whole package fairly shouted, *Look at me.* Tommy wouldn't have let her out of the house looking like this. He'd have undone everything and hustled her off to bed.

She smiled at that memory, but then the smile

faded, much as Tommy was fading from her life. War, she thought—the original no-one's-to-blame divorce machine. She'd done nothing wrong, he'd done nothing wrong, and then this goddamned war had split them apart like a meat cleaver, and with the same stunning finality.

Face it, babe, she thought. Beast was right. Tommy is gone forever.

But I'm not. I'm still here.

Maybe it was time to live again, assuming she still remembered how.

She sat down by the upstairs window and watched as the nurses walked over to the officers' club in a large group, most of them wobbling uncomfortably in heels they hadn't had on in weeks. She waited until the main group just about reached the club and then went downstairs to the front verandah and sat down again. She could see the entrance to the club from the porch. She watched the stream of white dress uniforms going through the big glass doors. The New Year's Eve party had started officially a half hour ago, but she wanted to wait for a quorum of potential victims before she made her entrance.

Marsh *had* called a few days earlier, but what she hadn't told Sally was that he'd been calling for Sally, not her. She was glad for that, especially if it meant he'd gotten over his infatuation with her. He was such a nice guy. His homeliness was actually endearing. The two of them were perfect for each other, and they'd be even happier when Marsh finally realized that. Men were so damned slow sometimes. She'd been surprised to find out *Evans* was back in Pearl so soon after their last visit, but Sally had been positively beaming lately. She felt a stab of resentment: The war had snuffed out her marriage while bringing those two together.

Then she remembered that Mick McCarty would probably be in the club tonight. She wondered what he'd do when he saw her in her man-killer regalia. He'll laugh out loud, that's what he'll do, she thought. Give it to Mick: He had a very low threshold for BS. The only problem would come if he was really drunk. She could always turn to the nearest group of officers, and they'd hustle him away from her so fast his head would spin.

And Stembridge? Really, what would he do? At every Navy social occasion they'd attended, he'd always broken off from whatever group he was with to greet her with a warm familiarity, a familiarity he'd never actually earned. Of course people thought they were an item. The fact that she'd been pretending for months she wasn't the least bit available and he'd been pretending he wasn't interested probably looked like some kind of mutual campaign to fool everyone else.

He was interested, though. She *knew* he was. All she had to do was stand just a tad too close to hear his voice change. That was one of his problems—he never stopped talking, lecturing, instructing, informing, arguing. On the other hand, he was indeed Superman in the OR. His eyes would light up over that mask as he peered down at the latest challenge, followed by the usual scramble to keep him supplied with instruments. Sometimes he'd leave the OR between surgeries, and she occasionally wondered if he was getting a hit of pure oxygen or perhaps something a little more chemical. She knew that wasn't likely; the docs who were dependent on some kind of pills usually became more and more so, to the point where they just crashed and burned. Stembridge was just Stembridge—all energy, intelligence, polite impatience, and absolutely maddening reserve when it came to reacting to the guarded wiles of Glory Lewis. She checked the flow of traffic at the club, saw that it was diminishing, and decided it was time to go break some hearts, and one in particular, unless he really surprised her.

Marsh spotted Sally as soon as she came through the doors with the herd of nurses. He was one of at least a dozen officers to roll in on the group like a bunch of fighter planes, peeling away from the bar in an echelon formation of flushed faces and choker white uniforms. Ordinarily he'd have been late, but the skipper knew about Sally and had ordered him to cut loose on time and hand over the day's remaining crises to the ship's duty officer. He'd also gotten them rooms at the BOQ, using his clout as a commanding officer, so that neither of them had to stagger back to the ship in the wee hours in front of the crew.

Sally gave Marsh a big hug, much to the disappointment of two other guys who'd had her targeted.

"Buy me a drink, sailor?" she said softly.

"You betchum, Red Ryder," Marsh said and whisked her away from the swarm.

They snared a table for two against the wall and just looked at each other. No matter what she says, Marsh reminded himself, we do not mention or even think about mentioning GL. Gazing into those blue eyes, he found that determination getting easier by the moment.

"I never expected you guys to be back so soon," she said.

"What'd you tell the boyfriend, then?" Marsh asked.

"Which one, smarty? There's at least, oh, I don't know, four, five?"

She was wearing a shiny green longish dress, tight on top, with layers of interesting lace and nylon underneath. The outfit accentuated her lush body. Marsh always considered himself a leg man, but that tight top was hard to ignore.

"Eyes in the boat there, sailor," she said with an arch smile.

"You wore that here," he said. "I'm supposed to pretend you're one of the boys?"

She took a deep breath, which did amazing things to the dress and all the lacy bits underneath. Definitely not a boy. Before he could gather his wits, the band started playing and she wanted to dance. Me, too, he thought. Slow and close, if possible.

They'd drifted dreamily through two numbers and were headed back to their table when Glory made her entrance. Even the guys in the band noticed, Marsh thought, because their timing went off the tracks for a second or two. The bustling crowd of officers at the bar turned like a drill team to stare before the bolder ones began to make their way through the dancers. Then Marsh noticed a table of older officers across the room, whose shoulder-board insignia indicated they were all Medical Corps. One guy in particular stood up when Glory arrived, a tall, dark-haired, and very handsome full commander.

"What are you looking at?" Sally said from below his right shoulder.

"Trouble, I do believe," he said.

She turned to look and then whistled softly. "See the tall guy? The commander? Watch what happens."

They sat down and watched as Glory made her way like the Queen of Sheba across the floor, slowly peeling her gloves off, one at a time. The commander got about five feet away and started to put out his hand. Glory turned one of her tungsten smiles on the poor guy, wiggled the fingers of her right hand in his direction, and then walked past him and straight into the nearest group of panting lieutenant commanders. The group closed around her like a mass of white chain mail and swept her back to the bar. Glory was talking to them as if she'd known them all for years. The tall commander stood there for a second, looking like a stunned bird.

"That was planned?" Marsh asked.

"Oh, yes," she said. "That's Dr. Stembridge. Her boss, actually. They call him Superman at the hospital, because he's always saying 'Super!' And also because he's an incredible surgeon."

"Not so super just now," Marsh said. "I think I want to hear this."

She drew apart from him and gave him a look.

"I'm all grown up now," he said, "but there has to be more to this story. I wonder if she knows Beast is here."

Sally looked alarmed. "*Is* he? Oh, my. This might get really interesting. You'll have to ply me with lots more liquor, though."

"Champagne do it?" Marsh asked.

"Every time," she giggled. Her shining blue eyes banished all thoughts of Glory, who remained invisible behind her screen of white uniforms. Marsh decided to try some boldness of his own.

"Did I tell you I have a BOQ room tonight?" he said.

"Did I hear you mention champagne?" she replied, studiously ignoring any mention of a room.

"Ah, yes, you did," he said. He signaled a passing cocktail waitress that he needed something. Once she'd taken his order he caught Sally trying to suppress a grin.

"What's funny?" he asked. He almost had to shout over all the noise in the dining room.

"How long did it take you to get up the nerve to tell me that?"

"About five seconds," he said.

"I'm impressed," she said. She leaned back in her chair, smoothed her hands through her hair, and ran a stockinged foot up the inside of his right leg under the table.

"Why don't we open that champagne somewhere else, then?" she asked.

Marsh tried to say okay without whimpering too much, his interest in the back story of Superman and Glory long forgotten.

Glory found herself in possession of at least five cocktails and an equal number of anxiously attentive young men. It felt wonderful, even though she knew that at some point she'd have to do some maneuvering. It was almost like being back at Annapolis, with a crowd of Navy men pressing in on her, all with high hopes and all with no chance whatsoever. She saw some of the other nurses surreptitiously watching her. She stared back at two of them, who quickly turned away. She avoided looking over at the doctors' table, not wanting to stir up any more unnecessary trouble.

All of them wanted to dance with her, but she said she needed another drink before she was ready for that. The five drinks in front of her became ten, and she dutifully tried them all, albeit in tiny sips. The noise in the club was growing as the band tried to make itself heard above the muted roar of conversation. Two tables of aviators were getting a little rowdy, but they were still in the amusing stage. The sheer number of people was defeating the overhead fans, and she felt herself beginning to perspire underneath all that makeup. She turned around and leaned back against the bar, carelessly thrusting her chest forward and then scanning the room to see what was happening. Unexpectedly, she locked eyes with Mick McCarty.

They stared at each other for a long moment while the buzz of anxious conversation all around her retreated into the background. Then Mick grinned that damned Irish grin of his. She couldn't help it: She smiled right back.

She could almost hear him saying it: I go with

the first girl who smiles. Then he was there, cutting her out of the crowd like a pro, substantially bigger than everyone around her, and then they were together on the dance floor. Mick never could dance, but he could definitely hold a woman and make her not care one whit about his dancing ability. His right hand rested just far enough below her waist to make her aware of it.

"Hey, beautiful," he said, imitating one of the downtown bar girls. "I love you so fucking much."

She giggled. "I heard a story about you, that you were in hack," she said to his shoulder.

"In hack, in trouble, in pain, in the drunk tank, in Pensacola, in a rehab clinic, and now back out here in pineapple paradise. Tomorrow or in a day or so, back to sea, this time in the Big E."

"They're taking you back?"

"Not willingly," he said, "but believe it or not, we've got more carriers than aviators just now, so they kinda had to."

She squeezed his left hand. "Why are you still wearing your gloves?" she asked.

"My right paw doesn't look so good right now," he said. "That was the rehab mission. It works, but it looks like Frankenstein made it."

"I'd forgotten," she said, as the band wound down one dance number and then shifted into the next one.

Just then Stembridge appeared. "May I have the honor, Lieutenant?" he asked, tapping Mick on the shoulder.

"You want to dance with me?" Mick asked innocently.

"Not my type," Stembridge said, "but she is."

Mick looked at Glory, who nodded almost imperceptibly. "Don't go far," she whispered.

Mick gave Stembridge a quick mock bow and went back to the bar. Glory offered her hand, and Stembridge stepped in. They began to dance as the crowd closed in. Glory waited for him to say something, but he didn't. Okay, she thought. I can play this game. Just for the hell of it, though, she moved into him, pressing one thigh and then the other where it might do the most good.

"I do believe I'm being disciplined," he said finally.

"Whatever are you talking about?" she asked and bumped him again.

"Oh, hell," he said. "I don't know. You and I have been close for months, but not really. I'd love to take you to bed, but every time I even think about making a move, you've . . ."

"I've what?"

He sighed. "You've nothing. I guess I've been too busy being Superman. I'm sorry, Glory. I should have paid more attention."

"Is that what you think I wanted? Attention?"

He moved away from her. "Yes, I do. You may not have known it, but, yes, that's what I think you wanted. Attention. A suitor, even."

She looked away. He'd seen right through her. That's exactly what she'd wanted, and, truth be told, she'd been dishonest about it. To him, to herself.

"It's been two years," she said. "Since that awful day. Perhaps you don't understand."

"Clue me in."

"I've been the object of every man's attention since I turned sixteen. Tommy was—special. He didn't play games. He fell in love with me and I fell in love with him. That was precious. All the rest of it? That was, I think, lust."

"Lust is human," he said. "We poor men are wired for lust. Tarzan see Jane. Tarzan *want* Jane. Jane better lie down, or Tarzan will get out the club."

"How convenient," she said, looking up at him. "Poor me, the big strong man says. I'm permanently disabled by a short-circuit between my brain and my—"

He put a finger on her lips, then pulled it away and examined the lipstick. "Poor me, indeed," he said. Then he smiled, and so did she. "I keep asking myself: Am I in love with Glory Lewis, or is it just desire?"

"Come to an answer yet?"

"I want to know you as a woman. Not as a

medical colleague, not as an OR supe, not as my chief assistant, but as a lovely woman. But I've felt all along that that can't happen until you're ready to *be* a woman again. I felt as if it would be wrong for me to, oh, what's the right word—push?"

Then Mick was back. He tapped Stembridge on the shoulder, perhaps a little harder than necessary. "Commander," he said. "May I have the honor?"

Stembridge stepped back, his gaze locked with Glory's. "I guess I should have, after all," he said. He nodded to Mick. "Lieutenant."

Then he was gone and Mick had her enclosed in those massive arms. She wanted to look back, to say something to Superman, but the moment passed, probably forever. For some strange reason, she felt a small pang of regret. Then she felt Mick.

"Hey, I brought you a drink," he said.

"So you did," she said. "Hopefully there's more where that came from."

"The world's supply," he said.

She drained half of it and then handed the glass back to Mick. Then, looking directly into his eyes, she moved in and pressed her body against his. "Change of plan," she whispered.

"Really," he said, a knowing grin spreading across his face.

"Really," she replied. "I'm going to the ladies'.

You go out front and have a cigarette. Then we'll take a walk or something."

"Something," he said. "Definitely something."

By the time they got back to the nurses' quarters, he was walking close behind her, letting those big hands roam, while she kept her mind blank and let him do it, whatever he wanted, until they fell into her room upstairs and she pushed him down onto her bed. There was no need for any more talk, and she knew it. He started to get back up, but she shook her head and then took her clothes off, slowly at first but then faster as her own need welled up. Mick stripped his clothes off in a flurry of uniform pieces, then lay back on the bed at full staff. Glory stared at him hungrily for a moment, then slid down on top of him, letting her breasts flatten up the length of his thighs as she stretched out and upward on his body.

"Go fast," she murmured.

"I remember," he said and then drove himself deep inside her. She gasped once, convulsing in a shallow release almost before she knew it. Then Mick grasped both her hips and started in, his eyes drinking in that heavenly body and the way her swaying hair obscured her face as she matched him. After a little while she came again, this time with a gut-wrenching force and a cry of deep release. He pulled her to him and kissed her hard on the mouth while he arched his back and went even deeper, never stopping for a moment until she pulled away to catch her breath. In a moment she was prone on the bed and he was taking her from behind, those massive arms locking her into a violent, bruising embrace as he went for his own ride. He was hurting her now and she struggled, but then her body betrayed her and she once again rose to it as a wave of bliss overtook the pain and she felt him empty himself deep inside her.

She collapsed on the sweat-soaked sheet, trying to get her breath. Mick stayed with her, doing an awkward stationary push-up so that she could breathe. She was startled to see that the sheet was smeared with her lipstick and made to wipe it off except that her arms wouldn't work. Her whole body felt like a mass of gelatin, every inch alive and quivering. He lowered himself to the bed alongside her and pulled her into a strong embrace, his breath smelling of Scotch as he buried his face in her damp hair and listened to her pounding heartbeat.

She thought of Tommy then, how he would never have taken her this way. Tommy loved her deeply but had never mustered this depth of sexual need or physical violence. Tommy was the brain. The gentle, loving brain. Mick was the Beast. She waited for a sense of guilt, but nothing like that came. She'd been emotionally dead for the last two years, but not anymore. She thought briefly of Marsh, fondly even. He was with his

Sally, and she was perfect for him. Stronger than he was but a sufficiently wily woman to never let him know that, even as she gathered him in to precisely where he belonged. She felt Mick stir beside her. He began to stroke her bottom.

"Ever hear the story about the sex surveyor?" he asked.

"Nope."

"Sex surveyor turned up on a housewife's front porch, asked if he could ask her his survey questions. Didn't want to come in or anything, just ask his questions. She said sure. So he went through his list, then got to the last one. Which was: Do you smoke after having sex?"

"And?"

"She said, 'You know, I've never looked.'"

She laughed, and then they both looked.

"Not yet," she said.

"Let's work on that," he said.

"First, where's that world's supply?"

Marsh led Sally though the door to his BOQ room and locked it behind them. He was carrying the sweating bottle of champagne and realized there was nowhere to put it. The BOQ rooms were more like cells than hotel rooms: a single metal bed, a metal dresser, a closet, a sink, one chair, and a steel kneehole desk. The communal showers and bathrooms were down the hall. He put the bottle down on the desk, not sure of what to do next. Sally went to the bed and sat down, then indicated he should sit next to her by patting the bed.

"We need some ice," he said. "A bucket or something. And some glasses. I forgot glasses."

"That's the last thing we need," she said, kicking off her shoes. She patted the bed again. He sat down next to her. To his surprise, she bounced back up and then stood in front of him. Then she turned her back.

"Zipper, kind sir," she said. "Please."

"Right," he said. He reached up and undid the little hook at the top of her dress and then lowered the zipper. It went a long way down the soft curves of her back. She reached over her shoulders with both hands, did something, and the dress slid to the floor. She was wearing a full-length slip, under which was a girdle, among other filmy female things.

For a moment he just sat there, his hands on her hips, the white nylon of her slip silky to his hands. Then he leaned his head forward, pressing his forehead into the small of her back, drinking in the scents of her perfume and rising arousal.

She flicked the straps off her shoulders, and the slip slid down her back, bunching at her waist. She said not a word, but he knew what was expected. He gathered the slip and pulled it down over her hips, still pressing his forehead into her back. Then he moved his hands over her waist and hips, as if to smooth the fabric of all the remaining underthings. She leaned back against him as he ran his hands down and then back up her thighs, softly but knowingly, his own excitement building. He stripped away the rest of her underwear until she was naked in front of him. Then she turned around, encircled his head with her hands, and told him to kiss her like he meant it.

An hour later Sally lay with her back to his perspiring chest, her hair in his face and the rest of her melted against him. When he opened his eyes he saw the champagne bottle on the table. It was still sweating, but not as much as he was.

God *damn!* he thought. She must have read his mind, because she squeezed his hand and let out a contented sigh.

"I think we missed New Year's," he said.

"I seem to remember some fireworks," she said. "Does that count?"

Marsh grinned in the darkness. "You bet," he said.

She was quiet for a few minutes. He thought she'd drifted off to sleep, but then she sighed.

"What?" he asked.

"A new year," she said. "I can remember when New Year's was purely fun, with everyone looking forward to what was coming next. Not anymore."

"I suppose anything can happen over the next twelve months," he said. "The bastards may even give up. They have to know by now they can't win this thing. And Roosevelt will never negotiate with them. Not after December seventh."

"You really believe they'll give up?"

"No," he said, after thinking about it. "It's not in their blood, apparently. I heard that we had to kill forty-seven hundred Japs to take Tarawa, and that we lost nearly one thousand of our own guys dead in the process. Another two thousand wounded or missing. There were just seventeen Japs left alive when it was over."

She sighed again. "Then this war will go on forever."

"It won't," he said, "but it's gonna seem like it. Tarawa was tiny—maybe a half mile across at its widest point. Wait until we have to go into the Home Islands."

"Happy, happy New Year," she said.

"It is right now," he said. "Let's see if that champagne is still drinkable."

"Champagne makes me tipsy," she said. "No telling what might happen then."

"One way to find out. Let me up."

"Up?" she asked innocently.

Sometime after midnight, Marsh walked her back across the lawns of Hospital Point to the nurses' quarters. When they arrived at the front steps they were surprised to see a woman sitting in one of the chairs, her face in shadow.

"Glory?" Sally asked as she started up the steps. "Is that you?"

Marsh followed Sally up the steps and then stopped short. Glory wasn't sitting in the chair—she was sprawling. Her expensive hairdo had come apart, and the straps of her evening gown were missing. The fabric across her front was riding dangerously low, and she was barefoot. The glazed expression on her face said she didn't really care what she looked like.

"Glory, honey," Sally said, going down on one knee. "What's wrong? What happened?"

Marsh thought he knew. She had finally succumbed to Mick, and from what he could see, Lady Everest had been well and truly conquered. She saw him looking at her and gave him a lopsided smile.

"Well, Marsh," she said. "What do you think of your dream girl now, hmm?"

Sally shot him a warning glance over her shoulder and then tried to lift the fabric of Glory's gown.

"Oh, hell, Sally, don't bother," Glory sighed. "It's thoroughly used goods just now. Anyone have a cigarette?"

Sally stood back as Marsh stepped forward with his duty pack of Luckies. Glory took one, stuck it in her mouth, and then cupped his hand when he extended his lighter. She might be putting on a brave face, he thought, but he felt her fingers trembling. He wanted to reach out and hold her but knew that was impossible. She took one deep drag, blew it out sideways, looked over at Sally's face, and then gave him another crooked, lipstick-smeared grin.

"I guess I'm not the only sinner on the porch tonight, am I?" she said. Even in the semidarkness, Marsh could see Sally's face go red.

"Ah, well," Glory said. "Happy damn New Year. What better way to usher in yet another year of world war than with a good, wholesome romp in the hay. God knows I needed it." She hiccupped, put a surprised hand to her face, and then did it again. "It got just a little bit drunk out tonight," she said.

"I think it's time we got you upstairs," Sally said.

Glory took a drag on the cigarette and then pitched it into the bushes. "What, am I intruding?" she said. "Three's a crowd?"

"Glory, *please*," Sally said. Marsh started to say something but thought better of it.

"Okay, you two," Glory said and lurched forward out of the chair. Her gown immediately fell down, exposing her white breasts as she stood up. Marsh could not take his eyes away.

"Well, looky here," Glory said, cupping her

breasts with both hands. "Like all this, Marsh? Want to hold them for me? Mick sure did."

"Glory!" Sally cried.

"Oops, I forgot," Glory said, swaying a little. "It's yours he wants, not mine. Right. Fair enough. Fair enough."

She reached down for the bodice of her gown and covered up as best she could while trying to remain upright. Sally took her by the arm, gave him a weary look, and helped a very drunk Glory Lewis into the building.

Marsh sat down in the chair from which Glory had just risen. There was a lingering scent in the chair, a heady blend of perfume, cigarette smoke, booze, and seriously aroused woman.

He tried to keep his brain in neutral, not wanting to dwell on the obvious fact that Glory was finally completely beyond his reach. His feeble efforts not to recall her nakedness weren't working. Then he realized that it wasn't the end of the world after all.

Sally had *not* been drunk when she sat back on that bed. Tipsy, maybe, but the look on her face had been that of a woman with a plan who was not going to be denied. Their lovemaking had been exciting, even the inevitable comic bits as they explored all the various ways they fit together. After that, she'd been all business, radiating an urgent, primal need with nothing romantic about it, at least not until the second time. That had been much slower, gentler, deeper, her kisses lingering as his own emotions welled up after years of a relatively sterile bachelorhood. They were in love, and they'd just confirmed that in the only and best way they could.

And Mick? What had happened here? Glory looked like she had been roughly handled, and that made him wonder. Was all that slutty dialogue just the booze talking or something else, a woman who'd finally realized she needed a man and who'd found just exactly what she was looking for? In all his fantasizing he'd never imagined Glory as a woman with all her clothes off, hands on hips, telling him or some other man: Okay, sport, here it is. Fuck me if you're man enough. She'd been right all along: He'd formed some dreamy, love-soaked image of this woman, without ever considering what it might be like if she ever said yes.

He heard Sally coming back downstairs. He stood up and went to the screen door. She stopped behind it but did not come out.

"So," he said. "Happy New Year again, secret admirer."

She smiled. "I have to get back upstairs. The room's a disaster area. Right now she's decorating the bathroom. She thinks Mick went back to the club."

He glanced at his watch. "Club's closed," he said. "Has she said anything? Was this—"

Sally shook her head. "She says she needs a bath, that she needs to scrub and scrub hard, as she puts it. Poor thing. So many men have lusted after her for so long since Tommy died. And now . . ."

"I was one," Marsh said.

"Well I know," she said through the screen.

"Until you came along," he said.

She smiled again. "Good answer, Commander. Very good answer. Think you can come see me before you guys go back out to sea?"

"If the XO will let me off the ship one more time, I will."

"I thought *you* were the XO."

"Why, yes I am. I guess that's a yes. Night-night, secret admirer."

Marsh walked back across the lawns to the officers' club, which was indeed at darkened-ship. There were a few official cars in the parking lot but not a soul about that he could see. He did hear one, though. Someone was singing in a low voice over near the front door of the club. The beer song. *Twenty-nine bottles of beer on the wall, twenty-nine bottles of beer . . .*

He walked over and found a bleary-eyed Beast, still in his whites, with his tunic unbuttoned and a bottle of beer in his hand. He was sitting on the front steps of the club. For some reason his white shoes were off and sitting next to him. He looked up as Marsh approached, tried to focus, but then gave it up.

"I'll go quietly," he announced. "Don't fuck with the HASP if you know what's good for you."

Marsh sat down on the step above the one Mick was perched on. That put his face level with Mick's.

"It's Beauty," he said quietly. "Not the HASP."

"Beauty Vincent, as I live and breathe," Mick said. "You get to third base with that Sally-Wally tonight? She was positively cookin' with gas, man. Lady with a mission. I thought I saw you guys sneakin' out."

Marsh didn't say anything. Mick took another swig of beer, examined the empty bottle, and then threw it into the bushes, where it clinked against others already expired there. Then he looked sideways at Marsh.

"You've been back to the nurses' quarters, haven't you."

"I took Sally back, yes," he said. "We found Glory out on the front porch."

"Was she now," Mick said and then let go an enormous belch. "Came out to cool off, I imagine."

"Cool off."

"Yeah, classmate, cool off," Mick snarled. "'Cause when I left she was still so hot her lipstick was melting. You don't like hearing that, do you, lover boy?"

"That's between you and her, I guess," Marsh said. "None of my business."

"Bull*shit!*" Mick spat. "You wouldn't have come looking for me if that were true. You think I raped her, don't you?"

Marsh finally looked back at him. "Thought crossed my mind, Mick," he said.

"'Cause it was *me,* right? Mick McCarty, fleet fuckup. Got the girl drunk and then had my evil way with her. Is that it? That what you think?"

"What should I think, Mick?"

"Okay, Mr. Lingering Eye. I'll tell you what to think. That was always the difference between you and me when it came to Glory Hawthorne. You think. I *do.*"

"Lewis," Marsh said.

"What?!"

"Lewis. Her last name is Lewis."

"Not anymore, classmate. Tommy Lewis is toast. Tommy Lewis, old Mr. Three Point Eight, he's just part of that bad smell you get when you walk downwind of Ford Island. No, sir, there was no Lewis tonight. She let me know that in no uncertain terms, too. I don't know what was going on between her and the pretty doctor, but tonight? No more Lady Everest. Out on the dance floor, all the way back to her room, and then when she pushed me down on that bed and looked me in the eye, it was time to get to it in a big, big way. I've

298

got the fingernail grooves in my back to prove it. Wanna see?"

"No. I don't want to see."

"But somehow *I'm* the bad guy here, hunh?"

"I think you took advantage."

"And that pisses *you* off? You who never had the balls to make the first move in your whole life? The guy who liked to watch? I remember you, classmate, when our little gang would go out cruising Crabtown. Mooning from a distance, so desperately in lu-u-u-v, but not man enough to take what was on offer."

"Glory was *never* on offer," Marsh said.

"Little you know, snake," Mick said. "Here's a secret—this wasn't our first time, okay? My only problem was that back then? I wanted her so bad and I fucked her so hard and she climaxed so big, I scared her, and then she ran to Tommy, and Tommy, that old slash, made exactly the right moves and won the girl. Didn't know all that, did you?"

Marsh was stunned. "No, I didn't."

"Listen to you," Mick snorted. " 'No, I didn't.' Because you were too scared. I'll bet you've been scared ever since this war started, haven't you? This is *man's* work, classmate. Warrior's work. You better hope that cute little nurse doesn't find out what you're really made of, because she'll write your fluttery ass off just like Glory did."

"Glory made her choice a long time ago, Mick,

and it wasn't me or you. Nothing to do with being scared."

"Bullshit. You're still scared, aren't you? Scared every day you're out there with the Big Blue Fleet. Been scared since you first went to sea, am I right? And now? Watching you still pining like a damn dog around Glory? Time's gonna come, Vincent. Time's gonna come when you'll get to meet the elephant, as the Civil War boys used to say, and that's when you'll find out what you're made of. Personally, I think you'll fuck it up."

That stung. Marsh told himself it was just the booze talking. He said nothing.

"Oh, get the fuck out of here," Mick said disgustedly. "Right now I'm a sailor on liberty. I just got laid, now I'm gonna get really drunk, then I'm gonna puke. Then I'll go back to the ship with the rest of the liberty party. And tomorrow or the next day we'll go back to sea, find some Japs, and kill 'em all."

"And Glory?"

"What about her?"

"What happens to her?"

"Happens? What the *fuck* are you talking about? Oh, I get it. You're a gentleman and she's a lady. Yeah. Okay: Here's what happens to Glory. She retires to a convent, takes the veil, and gives her life over to Christ to make up for the stain on her sacred honor, caused by a guy most appropriately nicknamed—Beast!"

Marsh got up and started to walk away.

"Eat your heart out, Beu-tee-e-e," Mick yelled after him. "She's a woman, not a saint. They all are. They're *women,* first and last. Everything else, all that love and romance, that's just our imagination. God put 'em all on earth so we could breed 'em, nothing more."

Marsh turned around to stare. Mick suddenly grinned back at him.

"Now that's the look you want, Tiger. That I-want-to-kill-you look. Practice that in front of a mirror. Think of me making Glory yell, if it'll help. Then when the day comes and you're looking Death in the face, lay it on him. Sometimes he blinks. Now get outta here. I gotta piss."

Glory sat on one of the park benches at the very tip of Hospital Point and listened to a bugle playing taps over the outdoor announcing system at Hickam. The night was settling in as the yard tugs huffed back to their piers across the harbor and the steady stream of aircraft going in and out of Hickam began to thin out. She tried to ignore the dark wreck of *Arizona*, visible against the lights on Ford Island as little more than a black lump in the harbor. They'd removed her salvageable guns and the great bulk of her superstructure, so now she looked more like a dead animal than a warship. The removals did not change the fact that *Arizona* was now a tomb. There'd been talk of trying to remove all the bodies, but a diver's report had settled that issue. The damage to her internal structure made work inside much too dangerous.

If she sat on the far right end of the bench, she couldn't see the ship at all. She lit up a second cigarette, telling herself that it was to ward off the seaside mosquitoes, and watched the channel buoys blinking. She concentrated on trying to keep her mind empty when she came out here, and lately the cigarettes seemed to help. The events of New Year's Eve were never too far from her mind, and today's argument with Sally hadn't helped things. It had been trivial, but the tension between them had, if anything, built since that night. She knew it was mostly her fault and that she was going to have to solve it pretty soon or get a new roommate.

She heard someone coming across the grass from the quarters, took one last drag on the cigarette, and pitched it over the seawall.

"Well, speak of the devil," she said when she saw it was Sally.

"Devil is it now?"

"I was just thinking about how to apologize for being such a bitch. It's all my fault, and I am truly sorry. Please forgive my bad behavior."

"That'll do it," Sally said, "and you don't have to throw away your cigarette on my account."

"Old habits," Glory said. "My mother would be appalled to see me smoking in public."

"Mine had a three-pack-a-day habit," Sally said. "It finally killed her, too, back in 'thirty-nine. I even got to watch. How are you doing with Superman these days? I don't see the two of you joined at the hip so much."

Glory laughed quietly. "I think he got the shock of his life at that party."

"Not used to being upstaged, is he."

"I did kind of throw it in his face," Glory said.

"That's what he gets for taking you for granted. Probably did him some good."

"Probably why I'm back to all day in OR Two and not spending my days in perpetual meetings. When I think about it, that's an improvement."

"I have a delicate question to ask," Sally said.

"Let's see if I can guess," Glory said. "Is there any biological reason for me to be throwing up in the bathroom every morning before everyone's up?"

"Um, yes, that's the one."

Glory sighed. "Why not?" she asked the night air. "Why should my life presume to get back to some semblance of normal when the whole world is turned upside down?"

Sally didn't answer that one. They sat there in the dark for a few minutes before Glory continued. "And no, I'm not in search of some back-alley abortionist, if you're curious."

"You'll *have* the baby?"

"Of course I will. The baby didn't do anything wrong. It shouldn't be killed for my indiscretion."

"How will you manage that?" Sally asked. "I mean, once they find out, they'll—"

"They'll what? Banish me to Molokai with the lepers? It's not contagious, the last time I checked. I can work up through the second trimester. After that I'll go on medical leave of some kind. The chaplain says there's a Catholic convent downtown where women in my 'delicate condition'—his actual words, God love him—can go to deliver and then get the baby adopted."

"Wow" was all Sally could manage.

"The hard part will be dealing with everyone in the hospital. Lady Everest finally got hers. Knocked up like any common sailor's girlfriend."

"It'll be a couple months before you show," Sally said. "Maybe even longer."

"Oh, I can't imagine anyone *saying* anything, but they'll think it. Even if they don't think it, I'll believe they're thinking it. I'm just sorry that my first child wasn't Tommy's. We'd talked about it, but he was afraid that, with war coming, something might happen. And, boy, did it ever."

"Who, I mean, do you, um, oh my goodness, I didn't mean—"

Glory smiled. Poor Sally had embarrassed herself. "Do I even know who the father is?"

"No, no, no, I didn't mean anything like that," Sally protested.

"It's okay, Sal, relax. I do know, and no one else needs to know, especially not Marsh Vincent or Mick McCarty. They have enough on their plates right now. This is my problem, and for now, my secret. The rest of the world can either like it or lump it."

ELEVEN

Mick grabbed a second cup of coffee and then dropped into a chair at the back of the ready room as the air intelligence officer got ready to start the brief. The whole squadron was there, and the Big E's air-conditioning was barely keeping up. Topside he could hear cables scraping on the flight deck as the various flight deck crews, called "shirts" for their color-coded jerseys, got the launch ready. He'd been with Bombing Eight for seven months now, ever since his short stint in P-cola. It was going okay, so far. He wasn't going to get promoted anytime soon, but he hadn't managed to piss off anyone of consequence. Yet.

He flexed his hand. For the most part it was doing what *he* wanted, although it still didn't look right. The flight surgeon had kept his word. The doctors back at Pensacola told him pretty much the same thing about his hand, that it was one of those borderline injuries that could be a ticket out of aviation if he was tired of it, or that he could do some surgery and rehab work and get the hand quasi-operational. Mick had opted for the latter, which had turned out to be a lot more painful than the original injury. He'd gone back to drinking, but the daily tempo of flight operations in the training pipeline meant that he had to keep it under control. He'd finally been cleared to go back to war and then caught up with the *Enterprise*, which had been in Pearl for Christmas through New Year's just before the Central Pacific offensive really got under way. He had not exactly been a patient and understanding flight instructor, and the CO of his training squadron was beginning to complain about the number of "downs" Mick was handing out. Mick was failing new guys in their flight syllabuses, and he was beginning to complain about the levels of chickenshit and Mickey Mouse rules in the training command. The transfer orders came just in time.

It had taken him two weeks to catch the hops he needed to get out to Pearl and catch *Enterprise*. As the buzz of conversation in the ready room rose, he reflected on the events of New Year's Eve. Glory had finally rejoined the living, and his groin quivered with the memory of that tumultuous night. He was sorry about his encounter with Beauty Vincent, but Jesus, that poor bastard took everything so seriously. It had been like meeting up with Sir Galahad and trying to explain why he'd spent the entire night with Maid Marian. Or somebody, he thought. Maybe it was Guinevere. Anyway, he hoped that hot little blond nurse had calibrated the poor bastard's pecker once and for all. Marsh was an XO, and there was some hard fighting coming up. The Japs would fight to the last man, and they obviously expected the Americans to do the same thing. Now that the Marines were going into Guam and Saipan, there were rumors that the Jap battle fleet might come out, after having taken a powder through most of 1943.

"Gentlemen," the air intelligence officer began from the podium. The room full of chattering aviators ignored him. The squadron CO, Commander Bill Blake, stood up, put two fingers in his mouth, and whistled. When the room got quiet, he nodded at the intelligence officer.

"Gentlemen," the bookish-looking lieutenant commander began again. "The Japanese carrier fleet is at sea."

There were low cheers around the room.

"As you know, our task force has been fighting off land-based air strikes for the past two days. The brass is calling it shuttle bombing. Carrier air comes at us from way out there, then goes to a nearby island strip, refuels, rearms, and hits us again on their way back to their home carriers."

"There's a cure for that," the skipper said.

"Not until we know where they are, Skipper," the briefer said. "As of this moment, we have not located the enemy carriers."

"But they know where *we* are?" the skipper asked.

"As long as we're tethered to Saipan, apparently they do. We've got picket submarines out looking, three hundred fifty miles or better, so we're expecting a sighting report at any time. Your fighter buddies have been busy, but you guys won't launch until we get a solid posit."

"We know they're coming from the west—why not go out there like they did at Midway and just find the bastards?" Blake asked.

"Because Admiral Spruance remembers what they brought with them at Midway. He doesn't want to get sucked into a battleship-versus-carrier action. His mission, *our* mission, is to protect the landings going on right now at Saipan."

"But, shit, we've got seven big-decks, plus eight light carriers. Surely we could spare a couple to go hunting Jap carriers? We only had three decks all in at Midway."

"Skipper," the intel officer said, "that decision's way beyond my pay grade, okay? For now, let me show you what we *think* they're bringing to the party."

He put up a chart, provoking some low whistles from the front row, where the senior officers in the squadron sat. Mick couldn't see the chart from the back row, but there seemed to be a lot of ships listed.

"Five big-decks, four light carriers, five battlewagons, the usual gaggle of heavy cruisers and tin cans. Pretty much the whole of what they call their Mobile Fleet. Probably six, seven hundred aircraft total, including the stuff they've stashed ashore."

That number produced a moment of silence. The fighter squadrons from the three nearby battle groups had been scrambling all morning against raids from the west and north. So far, only a few Japanese planes had made it through the screen, including one that had almost scored on the Big E.

"As I said before, no bomber raids will go out until we have a much better fix on where their carrier formations are."

"The day's a'wastin'," Commander Blake said. "It's already fifteen hundred. If we have to go a couple hundred miles out and back, you're talking swim call tonight."

"If I may be permitted an educated guess," the intel officer began, but stopped when everyone started laughing. The skipper waved his hand to shut it off.

"You guys are probably not going anywhere today. If it's any comfort, the fighter people are claiming huge Jap losses, and I mean *huge*. Seventy bogeys down here, thirty over there, thirty-seven of forty-two over Guam, counts like that. Even by fighter pilot BS standards, that's significant."

More laughter. The fighter guys were notorious for inflating their scores, which their after-action gun camera films inevitably deflated. Bomber pilots, on the other hand, were always scrupulously honest. Every ship sunk was at least a cruiser, if not a battleship.

"Anyway, if half of what the fighter-biters say is true, when we do find the Mobile Fleet, it ought to not be too bad getting in."

Easy for you to say, Mick thought. The ship's intel officers stood behind them in every way— usually *way* behind them when the shit started. A lot depended on whether or not their own fighters could go with them. If not, even a few hundred Zeros over the Jap carrier formations would be no cakewalk.

The briefer went through weather conditions expected over the Marianas for the next two days and the general plan of movement. He stressed that Admiral Spruance would not leave his Marines uncovered, by which he meant that the American carriers would stay close to the invasion forces. That in turn meant that when they did launch, it could be a long flight, two hundred miles minimum, maybe more. Getting out to the targets would be guaranteed. Getting back aboard safely would not.

When the briefing was finished, the skipper stood up. "Guys, since none of us is really night qualified, it's too late to go carrier hunting today. They can't hide that many carriers for too much longer, and then we're gonna throw the book at them. Hit the sack early, and be ready at first light."

That night in one of the carrier's two wardrooms Mick listened to the fighter pilots whooping it up over the day's action. They were calling it the biggest bag of the war, with literally hundreds of Japanese planes shot down or destroyed on the ground and with relatively few casualties among the American formations. The battle groups were finally headed west to find the Jap carriers, and tomorrow promised to be the dive bombers' day.

The entire squadron was in the ready room by 0700, waiting for the final brief and the order to launch. All available fighters had taken off at dawn, headed out for their combat air patrol stations seventy miles from the Big E. To the pilots of Bombing Eight, however, the day turned into one big washout. The fighters came back and went out again, but with fewer engagements being reported. The intel officer had come into the ready room twice to tell them that they were still waiting for locating data on the Jap carriers. By 1300, Mick had gone back to his stateroom for a nap. At 1430, a call came from the ready room: One of our subs has located the Jap Mobile Fleet with sufficient precision that a strike launch has been slated for 1530. The sub claims one carrier sunk, but lots more out there desperately needing attention.

Mick got up, washed his face, got his gear, and returned to the ready room. The final brief was short and sweet: Fly west by southwest for two hundred eighty miles and blast the Nip bastards. Frequencies and call signs were on their knee pads; the weather should be CAVU in the target area. Every American carrier was going to participate in the strike. Any questions?

There was only one problem that no one wanted to talk about: By the time they got back, it would be almost dark. Mick waited for someone to point out the obvious: A night recovery after an opposed strike and then a long flight back was a prescription for many accidents. Theoretically, all the pilots were night qualified, but in practice, except for some very specialized squadrons, this wasn't true. They'd all done some night approaches on well-lit outlying fields at Pensacola, but, in general, combat operations were a daytime affair for the carrier Navy. One crash on the deck with a gaggle of waiting planes stacked up behind the bird farm, all low on fuel, could spell disaster for the whole air group, as Commander Oxerhaus had pointed out so vividly.

No one said a word. The elephant in the room went unnamed.

"Bomber pilots, man your planes," came over the announcing system.

Skipper Blake stood up. "Okay, guys: Here's your chance to repeat Midway. Let's go get 'em."

As Mick strapped on his parachute and survival vest, one of the squadron's two ensigns, Georgie White, came over to him. He and Mick had become pinochle buddies.

"Mick," he said, "I don't think I can do this."

"The mission, or the getting back aboard part?" Mick asked.

"Night landing," George said. "I can't do that. I *know* I can't do that."

"Say something to the skipper?"

"Yeah," Georgie said.

"What'd he say?"

"That if I downed myself, I'd regret it for the rest of my life."

"That's helpful."

"Well, shit, I know what he's saying. But the rest of my life will end the first time I try a night approach. I barely passed at P-cola, and even my instructor said, if it weren't wartime, he'da given me a down right there and then."

Mick checked his knee pads. "Here's the thing, Georgie: We're sending a couple hundred bombers against the Jap carriers. If the fighter-biters can be believed, which is always a stretch, there won't be much opposition."

"I know, I know."

"But: We're all gonna come back low on fuel and flying in the damn dark. One guy prangs on the round-down, the rest of us are gonna be in the soup."

Georgie nodded.

"So if you really don't think you can do that, don't go. Don't kill yourself and your gunner."

"They'll take my wings, Mick."

"So you go do something else. Or go home. You've done your bit."

"Jesus, man, I don't know what to do."

"Well, my advice? Go see the skipper, tell him you want out, that you don't want to put other guys in the drink because you *know* you can't do night landings. Is that the truth?"

"Yeah, I think it is."

"Well, there you go, Georgie. Nobody can fault you for telling the truth. He can big-deal it all he wants, but really? It's just another strike. I gotta go."

Mick went topside to his plane and was strapped in by his plane captain. The Big E had already turned into the wind, producing a forty-five-knot relative wind across the deck. The shirts were all leaning into it as they directed the various aircraft to unfold their wings, lock them down, and then taxi into the conga line. Signal halyards on the

314

island were standing straight out in the stiff wind, with the Fox flag two-blocked, indicating an imminent launch.

His gunner, Petty Officer Jimmy Sykes, was already in. A single thousand-pound armor-piercing bomb was slung under the fuselage. With that big a bomb, the wings were clean except for two drop tanks. Around him twenty-three dive bombers were already turning up, with some being signaled to the midships line for launch. A bluish cloud of engine smoke was streaming aft from all the waiting bombers. The plane-guard destroyers behind the carrier were shimmering in all the exhaust smoke. Mick looked around for Georgie but didn't see him. Then a shirt was waving at him, and he slid the canopy forward and got ready for takeoff.

An hour and forty minutes later, they saw the first wakes, as the Japanese capital ships began to turn into their defensive circles. From fifteen thousand feet, the ships below were small black dashes on the dark blue sea, their wakes creating bright white lines that pointed right at them. There'd been no fighter opposition. Mick reluctantly concluded that, for once, the fighter guys had been telling the truth. A few flak bursts were popping below them, red winks blooming into dirty black shreds. On signal they dropped their external fuel tanks.

Commander Blake called the bombing order,

told everybody to arm, and led the attack down against the biggest carrier. One after another, the dive bombers rolled onto their backs, pulled in, and started down.

"I've been here before," Mick mumbled to himself.

"Look at all those damn ships!" Gunner Sykes said.

"Hang on, Jimmy," he said. He split his flaps and rolled in.

He was the seventh bomber to roll down into a steep dive on a carrier that was already smoking. He saw enormous columns of water erupting all along the big ship's sides, and the glow of a large fire aft on her flight deck. He felt rather than saw the antiaircraft fire coming from the escorting cruisers and destroyers, but he definitely saw the bomber ahead of him plant one right on the ship's flight deck. There was a puff of dust and debris, and then a world-ending explosion as the ship's entire flight deck mounded up and then collapsed into a ball of orange fire.

Mick pulled out of his dive and turned away. The Dauntless creaked and strained with the weight of that big AP bomb as he pulled left, trying to get flat.

No point in wasting another bomb on that baby, he thought. She was done for. He looked for another target as the skipper came up on the strike circuit and called off the rest of the bomb run, ordering the squadron to head west, looking for another carrier. At that moment, however, Mick saw a battleship pop out from under a cloud. He was lower than he liked to be, just over nine thousand feet, and there were more and more thumps of black flak appearing around him. What caught his attention was the fact that the battlewagon wasn't circling. It was running northwest, as if trying to get away instead of protecting the nearest carrier.

Mick made a snap decision. Instead of following the rest of the squadron, he rolled in on the battlewagon and then went straight down until the big ship, looking more like a heavy cruiser now, began to fill his windscreen. He adjusted the telescopic sight of the Dauntless to point right at the ship's bow and then, at four thousand feet, released the bomb.

Immediately he banked to the right and began to pull back on the stick, aiming to level off at sea level well forward of the target, scramble out of the engagement area, and rejoin the squadron.

"Holy shit!" Sykes exclaimed over the intercom.

"Did I get him?" Mick said, straining to get the words out as the g-forces flattened his face and made his vision go red.

"Oh, God, *yes,*" Sykes said. "Lookit that!"

Mick got the Dauntless level at about two hundred feet over the sea, banked right, and looked back at his cruiser. He saw an enormous column of black smoke, boiling with red and orange fire, rising from where the ship had been.

He pulled right again and flew back toward the evolving catastrophe, dipped the nose, and fired his forward guns. He didn't care about doing any damage. What he wanted was for his gun cameras to record what had happened to the Jap cruiser. They flew through the fuming cloud of smoke and fire, the aircraft bumping and sliding in the hot turbulence. I must have hit a magazine, he thought. The ship had simply disappeared.

He climbed back up to altitude and started looking around. The Jap fleet was dispersing in every direction, with newly arrived formations of American dive bombers falling out of the sky to litter the sea with armor-piercing bombs. There were several stationary columns of black smoke mingling with the puffy white clouds covering the Philippine Sea. He glanced at his fuel gauges and pulled back on the throttle. No bomb, no more work for him to do. Time to loiter, join up with the squadron, and head back to the carrier. As he looked around, he realized that the sun was setting. He focused on the radio, made sure he was on the right freq.

A few minutes later, he heard Commander Blake gathering up his chickens after everyone had expended his useful ordnance. Mick listened for a few minutes, caught sight of some contrails to the north, and headed for the gaggle. He was very grateful for not having sighted a single Zero. Fifteen minutes later he joined up with the rest of Bombing Eight. There were two planes missing. He settled into the echelon formation and checked in with the skipper.

"Where you been, McCarty?" Commander Blake asked.

"Got me a cruiser," Mick said. "I was lined up on that carrier, but she blew up. So I went hunting."

"We did, too, McCarty," Blake said. "We missed you."

Oops, Mick thought. Gonna hear about this later. By rights, he should have followed them after breaking off his bombing run.

The sky to the east was getting darker by the moment.

"Are we in trouble, Lieutenant?" Sykes asked over the intercom. He wore a split headphone, one ear for intercom, the other ear set on the tactical frequency assigned to their squadron.

"Aren't we always, Jimmy?"

There wasn't too much interpilot chatter on the way back to the carrier. The pilots were concentrating on their fuel states and thinking about the landings to come. Mick had Sykes dig out the ditching checklist for their plane, and together they went through it. During the hour or so that it took to get back to the carrier, the skipper drew up a verbal order-of-landing list as a function of who would have the least fuel left when they caught up with the ship. *Enterprise* reported she was heading west to shorten the transit distance, but as everyone knew, that wouldn't solve the darkness problem.

Mick ended up as tail-end Charlie on the list because he had the most fuel remaining, not having been with the rest of the squadron on their pursuit of other carriers. No longer in the heat of the moment, he knew he should have stayed with the squadron. It had just seemed the logical thing to do, he thought. No point in wasting a big bomb on a carrier that was already aflame from one end to the other, and he'd absolutely blasted that other big Jap. He also knew, however, that this wouldn't help his reputation in Bombing Eight. Gunner Sykes had told him that he was already being called the Lone Ranger by some of the squadron pilots. There'd been some guys from his first squadron on the *Yorktown* who were now department heads in this squadron, and his reputation as something of a maverick had preceded him. He was also older than most of the replacement pilots coming to Bombing Eight.

One day he'd heard two ensigns talking about the "curious" fact that the Lone Ranger had been the only survivor from that medical evacuation crash off Guadalcanal. He'd braced them up about that, and they'd immediately retreated into ensign-versus-senior-lieutenant formality. The next day he'd had Sykes paint a white horse on the side of his barge. After that, Mick pulled into his own shell, flying as professionally as he could but keeping himself apart from the camaraderie of the squadron. People left him alone, and that was fine with him. He'd gotten a carrier at Midway and a cruiser today. They could talk behind his back all they wanted, but they couldn't take those achievements away from him, and the gun camera would back him up. Fuck 'em if they couldn't take a joke.

The skipper came up on the radio and declared that they had reached the rendezvous position with the carrier formations. Couldn't tell it by me, Mick thought, looking into the well of darkness that was the sea below.

There was no moon, and a high, thin overcast was blocking most available starlight. Everyone started looking for a home. Any home. The skipper put the ten planes of his squadron into a circular orbit at eight thousand feet and reported in to the *Enterprise*. They could hear other squadrons doing the same thing, and it wasn't long before the first ditching calls began to come out over the Mayday frequency. Then suddenly there was light, everywhere. Each of the big-deck carriers had its red *and* white flight deck lights on, and several battleship targeting searchlights were pointed straight up into the air to act as beacons for the returning planes. It looked like a Hollywood premiere night, and it was a heartwarming sight. Mick wondered what brave soul had made that decision. Probably Admiral Mitscher—Spruance wasn't an aviator. Of course, if there were any Jap subs lurking nearby, the carriers would be meat.

"Bombing Eight, Big Easy, cleared for the break," came the radio call. "Call your states."

Commander Blake came up and read out the landing order by side numbers and then directed the first plane to make his approach. The rest of them were to follow him down to a five-thousand-foot holding pattern above the break circle, which itself was only a thousand feet above the sea surface.

"Which one's ours?" Sykes asked from the gunner's seat.

"Damned if I know," Mick said. "That one, I guess. But if we have to, I'm gonna land on the first carrier that smiles at me."

Sykes just laughed. "Hi-yo, Silver," he said.

The first guy to make an approach was one of the ensigns. Mick watched his wing lights spiral down toward the back end of a carrier, presumably the Big E, line up on the deck, and then fly right over the carrier and back off the front end.

"Bolter, bolter," came the PriFly radio call. "Try it again, two-niner. Next in line, hold in the break."

Two-niner, he thought—that's Georgie. With literally a ringside seat, Mick watched the struggling ensign pull his bomber around in the left-hand pattern, line up again, and this time settle into a pretty good-looking approach, right up to the point where he landed in a brief sheet of fire along the portside catwalks and then went cartwheeling over the side. An escorting destroyer immediately drove into the area of the crash and began lighting up the sea surface with searchlights, but all Mick could see was a cloud of steam and smoke drifting over the water alongside the carrier's wide white wake. Georgie, Georgie, he thought. You should have listened.

"Green deck, green deck, three-one, commence your approach."

Wow, Mick thought. Normally they'd have closed the deck down until they could inspect the arresting gear and clear away any debris. Side number thirty-one must be running on fumes.

He checked his own fuel tanks. After the nearly two-hundred-mile trip back, he was good for another fifteen minutes or so, assuming the gauges were working reliably. He continued circling at low cruise power, watching the other guys in the squadron trying to get aboard.

Three-one made it on the first pass. Three-six boltered twice and then was told to ditch alongside another escorting destroyer, having lost a main mount on his second attempt. The skipper

323

got down on his first try, but the plane after him ran out of fuel during his approach, stalled, and then augured straight into the carrier's wake before he could set up for a ditch.

God damn, Mick thought, this is going to cost us more planes than the Japs did today. Then he was startled by the appearance of a star shell off to the north, and then another and another. As he was figuring out what to make of that, one went off about ten thousand feet over the Big E, lighting up the carrier and the flight deck in its magnesium glare. Someone's really taking chances tonight, Mick thought. As the parachute flare descended through the crowd of waiting planes, a second one went off back up at altitude. It turned the night into day, and the next three planes landed safely on their first pass. Then it was his turn.

"Here we go, Jimmy," he said. "Hang on."

He lined up on the carrier's stern and watched the landing signal officer's illuminated wands as he came onto the glide path. At the last moment, just as the LSO indicated the cut command, the star shell illuminating *Enterprise*'s deck winked out. There should have been another one lighting off above it. Instead, for a critical instant, Mick was totally blind. He got one fleeting image of the after five-inch mounts along the starboard side and then felt a terrific wallop as he landed. He reflexively firewalled the throttle, which was standard procedure in case the hook didn't catch, and the next moment found himself flying off the bow and then settling toward the black ocean in front of him.

Still at full power, he pulled the nose up and braced himself for impact, but the Dauntless struggled back into the air and he was able to lower the nose, gain some airspeed, and exhale.

"Two-seven, state?"

"Two-seven, I've got enough for another pass, maybe two," Mick called.

"Roger, two-seven, and execute your pattern. We have a green deck."

"Two-seven," Mick replied, acknowledging the order to try again. "You okay back there, Jimmy?" he asked his gunner. He thought he smelled engine exhaust.

"Uh, yessir, but we got a problem, I think. The deck's gone, back of my seat. It's breezy back here."

"Two-seven, this is Boss."

"Two-seven?"

"Two-seven, your tail hook has been found on the flight deck. Pick a destroyer, put her down, Lieutenant."

Goddammit, Mick thought. Here I am with all the gas I need and now I have to ditch. Shit!

"Two-seven, wilco," he acknowledged. He banked out of the pattern and went looking for a destroyer, of which there were plenty around the carrier. His night vision wasn't totally back yet, but it was coming. More star shells were popping now above the formation. Where were you when I needed you? he wondered.

"Okay, gunner-man," he said. "Swim call. Check your vest, turn on your light, and push on the back of my seat. Canopy coming back."

Mick turned on his landing lights and flew past a destroyer some three miles off the Big E's port side. He saw men rushing on deck to man their motor whaleboat and others assembling on the forecastle around the rescue swimmer davit.

"If I can do this right, we'll hit flat, and then the nose will pitch straight down. Roll out either side and get away from it. If we go inverted, remember to follow your bubbles, and don't inflate your vest until you're clear of the aircraft. Just like in the Dilbert Dunker, only noisier, okay?"

"Got it, boss. Low and slow, please."

"Low, slow, and flat," Mick said and put down the flaps. He kept the gear up so that they'd be clean at water entry.

He flew past the destroyer, with his landing lights still on so they could follow him in the dark. When the destroyer skipper realized he was going to ditch on their starboard side, he turned on some searchlights pointed down at the water to give Mick a visible surface reference.

Those boys have done this before, Mick thought. He banked left into a one-eighty, leveled out about a half mile behind the tin can, and started slowing. The object of the game was a slightly nose-up flat stall just above the water and right alongside the destroyer. He started into his final turn.

As he came in on the destroyer, he could see he was going too fast, much too fast. If he did stall it, he'd be way out in front, and time was of the essence if they were going to be rescued. He poured on the power and went around. As long as he had gas, he could do that until he got it just right.

The second approach was better. He started the descent much farther back, and this time he felt the big bomber shuddering as it lost most of its lift only a few hundred yards behind the ship. He let her settle until he could no longer see water over the nose and then pulled slowly back on the stick. A moment later she hit with a gut-flattening bang and immediately flipped upside down. A wall of water flooded the open cockpit. Mick waited for the regulation three-count for the initial turbulence to subside, then hit his latches, felt the harness go slack, and kicked down, away from his seat, just as he'd done a dozen times in the Dilbert Dunker training back at flight school. A second later he was bumping his head on the wing, and then he popped up to the surface behind it. He fired his Mae West life vest.

He looked around for Jimmy but couldn't see

him, so he started yelling his name. The plane was going vertical now, submerged to the star emblem on the rear fuselage. Amazingly the landing lights were still on underwater, showing the silhouette of the sinking plane against green water. He thrashed around the tail, shouting for Jimmy, but still couldn't find him. For the briefest instant, he thought he saw Jimmy's waving arm silhouetted against the green glow under the plane. Shit! He was still in his gunner's compartment. As Mick jackknifed to go get him, the landing lights winked out and the plane slid past him into the depths of the Philippine Sea, the portside horizontal stabilizer pushing him roughly out of the way. When he popped back up to the surface, defeated by his inflated Mae West, the ship's boat was alongside and several hands were reaching for him. He forced himself to stop fighting and let them pull him into the bobbing whaleboat.

Damn, he thought. Damn, damn, *damn!*

"What's that, Lieutenant?" a young ensign in a bulky kapok life jacket shouted at him over the noise of the boat's engine. "You okay? You hurt anywhere?"

"Not yet," Mick murmured. "Just my right hand. And my gunner."

He let them position him in the back of the boat. Somebody threw a damp blanket over his shoulders. He wanted to ask them to look around for Jimmy, but he knew that was pointless now.

There were white searchlights everywhere around the scene of the crash, and the gray steel sides of the destroyer were already closer. If Jimmy had been on the surface, they'd have seen him.

Mick closed his eyes against sudden tears. He wasn't the Lone Ranger. He was fucking Jonah himself. Just like on the medevac plane.

One day later Mick sat down with the squadron's informal accident board and debriefed both his part in the strike and the subsequent ditching. The board consisted of three officers, Bombing Eight's XO and two lieutenant commanders from the *Enterprise*'s other bombing squadron. A yeoman sat at one end of the table, taking notes. Commander Blake and the ship's assistant air boss were in the room, but they were there strictly as observers.

When Mick was finished, the board members had some questions about why he had lost control during the final moments of his landing and what, in his opinion, had happened to his gunner. Mick knew that the purpose of the board was to gather the facts while they were still fresh in everyone's mind, not to apportion blame for knocking his tail hook off and losing his gunner in the course of the ditching. He described how the star shell had wiped out his night vision and then disappeared right when he needed it most. Then he recounted the ditching.

"Was Petty Officer Sykes injured during the strike operations?"

"No, sir. We were both fine. We went through the ditching checklist together on the way back. I didn't like the first pass, so I went around to make sure we went in nearer that tin can. He was braced, vest on, and reported ready for impact."

"Any idea what happened?"

"We hit pretty hard, despite my best efforts, *and* the plane flipped. Once the water came in, I lost comms with Sykes. I did what we were trained to do in the Dunker. Once on the surface I swam around the tail looking for him." He hesitated.

"Yes?"

"Well, the landing lights were still on as the plane went down. I think I saw his arm sticking out of the gunner's compartment as the plane sank. I'm not positive. She went down pretty quick, and then the lights went out. I got about a one-second look."

The board members looked at each other, but no one commented.

"I tried to go down and get him, but my own life vest prevented it. Then the rescue boat was there and they were hauling me in."

"So he may have been trapped in the aircraft?"

Mick sighed. "It's possible, sir. Or he may have been unconscious or even dead, and it was *his* vest that was lifting him partway out of the gunner's compartment."

The XO asked him some more questions about his control settings at the time of impact and then asked the other members if they had anything else. Neither of them did. The XO looked up over Mick's shoulder, nodded fractionally, and then had one more item for Mick.

"You broke off during your dive on that carrier. In your after-action report you said you didn't think she was worth another bomb because she was already burning. Then you stated you rolled in on what you described as a heavy cruiser and hit her, causing that ship to explode and disappear. Is that all correct?"

"Yes, sir." Mick's right hand had begun to hurt again. He realized he was clenching his fists at the questions.

"We can't document that, of course, because no one else saw it happen."

"I dove on the explosion plume and fired my forward guns, trying to get it on the gun camera. But of course . . ."

"Yes, that film was lost with the plane. Okay: Why didn't you join up on the rest of the formation when they headed west?"

"I lost track of them in the dive. By the time I pulled up, everyone else was gone. The sky was full of flak bursts, there were ships going everywhere, and it took me some time to avoid flak and get back up to safe altitude because I still had that thousand-pounder hanging."

"Your radio working?"

"Yes, sir, but I was busy. The Japs weren't happy that their carrier was burning."

"And when you got clear?'

"I looked around for another target."

"Did you try to communicate with the skipper while you were looking?"

"Uh, negative, sir. I figured they'd gone after another target and that by the time I rejoined, the action would be over." Even as he said it, Mick knew his excuse sounded pretty lame.

"Oka-a-a-y," the XO said. "And would the fact that you remained behind in the area of the carrier attack account for your having a relatively good fuel reserve when everyone came back?"

Mick flinched. That hurt. "Yes, sir, probably," he admitted finally. "After I dropped my bomb, I went back to altitude and then looked around for a friendly gaggle. But I didn't go anywhere; I just orbited high enough to stay out of the flak."

"And your radio was working, right?"

He keeps saying that, Mick thought. He knew what the XO was implying. "Yes, sir. I could hear the chatter of an attack going on, but since I wasn't there, it didn't seem right for me to break into that looking for a steer."

"So you orbited, and then?"

"Saw eastbound contrails, checked in, and joined up."

"Was the cruiser you hit still burning at that point?"

"She was gone, XO," Mick said. "I believe that bomb got into a magazine. She disappeared in one really big blast, and when the smoke cleared, there wasn't anything down there. Not even any Jap tin cans."

Mick heard a door open and close softly behind him but didn't turn around.

"Well, okay, Mick, thank you. Let me remind you that this is an informal proceeding, not a court-martial or a pretrial hearing or anything like that. We have your written report, plus the report of other pilots, and we've interviewed the PriFly people and the LSOs on what happened out on the flight deck. Assuming you've recovered physically from your ditching, you will resume your normal duties."

"Aye, aye, sir."

"That is all."

When Mick got up to leave, he saw that the skipper was no longer in the room.

A week later Mick received orders to join Composite Squadron Eleven, based on an escort carrier. The squadron exec knocked on his stateroom door and asked if he could have a minute. He told Mick that one of the escort destroyers, the *Evans*, was being detached the next day to join the Seventh Fleet, which was assembling to support MacArthur's invasion of the Philippines. Mick would ride the *Evans* down to the area of Leyte Gulf and there transfer aboard the escort carrier *Madison Bay.*

"I'm being shit-canned, right, XO?" Mick asked, pretty much knowing the answer to his question.

"Um, not exactly," the XO said. "There's been a fleetwide draft for pilots to beef up the light carrier forces. They needed two bomber guys, and we and one other squadron got tagged to give up one each."

"Unh-hunh."

"Let me put it this way, Mick. Ordinarily the skipper would be throwing a temper tantrum in CAG's office for having to cough up an experienced fleet pilot."

"But this time, he just signed off and had another cup of coffee."

"They requested you by name, Mick."

"Sure they did."

"The air boss weighed in, I think."

"Ah. And losing my gunner, that didn't help."

The XO was silent for a moment. "About a quarter of the pilots who ditched that night were not recovered. We all know what happens when you go from a hundred twenty knots to zero in ten feet. If you're not sitting just right, you break your neck. That's most likely what happened to Gunner Sykes. So, no, that wasn't it."

"Too much Lone Ranger, maybe?"

"Maybe. Tell me this: Would *you* want you as your wingman?"

Mick had to think about that one. From a fighting competence point of view, hell, yes—but as a team player? "Wingman is fighter stuff, XO," he said.

The exec just looked at him. Mick sighed and finally nodded.

"Anyway," the XO said, *"Evans* will be alongside to refuel tomorrow morning sometime. You'll highline over then. Ship's bitch will have your paperwork ready by zero eight hundred tomorrow."

Mick nodded. "Thanks for telling me in person, XO. Should I bother with departure calls on the CO and CAG?"

"Do as you please, Mick." He closed the door behind him.

"Don't I always?" Mick said to the closed door. The Carrier Air Group commander doesn't know me, Mick thought. The skipper did, though, so no departure calls definitely meant he was being fired. He couldn't win for losing.

TWELVE

Following their unscheduled holiday break at Pearl, *Evans* spent the next eight months with the Third Fleet as it battered its way up the Central Pacific island chains. As a lowly tin can in the *Enterprise*'s screen, they were not privy to any of the grand strategic plans. Every destroyer's mission remained plain and simple: Protect its carrier, and run errands in the task force formations as assigned—move people, rescue downed aviators, run off snooping aircraft, steam as a plane guard behind the carrier during land-launch operations, refuel from the carrier or an oiler every third day, conduct training exercises and gunnery practice, train up the new guys on board, repair broken machinery, eat, and sleep when they could.

The ship routinely went to GQ just before dawn and again just at sundown. They shot at and hopefully downed any enemy aircraft that evaded the outer ring of combat air patrols thrown up by the carriers all day. Occasionally they were detached to join an amphibious group for inshore naval gunfire support duty, where they fired five-inch into the jungles on both named and unnamed islands. Sometimes the Jap army artillery fired back, but *Evans* seemed to lead a charmed life, never once being hit. Marsh remarked about that once to the captain, who said they were simply overdue. The captain was more afraid of mines than of Jap artillery. By this point in the war, *Evans* didn't fire a gun that wasn't under radar control. The Japanese were still mostly using optical fire control or sighting down the barrel.

By September of 1944, the United States was closing in on the Philippines, MacArthur's holy grail and the scene of an especially painful defeat for America on the Bataan Peninsula. The Pacific had been divided by the high command in Washington into two command areas: General Douglas MacArthur commanded the South West Pacific Area, and Admiral Chester Nimitz the rest of the Pacific Ocean. For the past year, MacArthur's Army and Navy forces had been working their way north from Australia through New Guinea and Borneo, while Nimitz's Navy and Marine Corps forces had been blasting Japs out of the Solomons and then grinding up the Central Pacific to destroy the huge Jap bases at Rabaul and Truk Lagoon before concentrating on the Marianas Islands of Guam, Tinian, and Saipan.

From time to time elements of Halsey's striking fleet were detached to augment MacArthur's Seventh Fleet operations. In early August 1944, the captain had been given a heads-up that *Evans* was going to join the light carrier formations being assembled for the initial invasion of the Philippines. The target was the island of Mindanao, later changed to Leyte, which was south and east of the main island, Luzon. Three weeks before that, however, Marsh got a surprise. The captain called him aside in the wardroom one night after dinner and handed him a message. It contained the promotion list from commander to full captain. *Evans*'s captain was on the list, and he'd received news that he was going to be the commissioning skipper of a new Baltimore-class heavy cruiser.

"This means a change of command, XO," he said. "As if you had nothing else to do."

Marsh congratulated him while stifling a groan. Even out here in the western Pacific war zone, a change of command meant a full week of inspections, reports, audits, briefings, fitness reports, and all the other trappings of handing over absolute command of a warship from one commanding officer to his successor. It would all have to be done on top of the day-to-day operations with the carrier force. Department heads, who were standing six on, six off watches, would have to give up sleep to prepare briefings for the new captain on the material condition of machinery in their departments, an overview of their officers, chief petty officers, and enlisted men, an accounting of all high-value equipment, and then a physical inspection of all their spaces in the ship.

Usually a change of command would be scheduled for a period of time when the ship was going to be back in port, but for the Big Blue Fleet there was little in-port time, especially for the destroyers. The only time offline *Evans* got was a few days at one of the island anchorages, where the crew could go ashore, sit on a beach, and have a few beers and a softball game. If they were really lucky, they might get back to Pearl for Christmas, as they had in December 1943—although the fact that they *had* been pierside in Pearl for the past Christmas would actually work against their chances of getting back anytime soon.

"Just what we need," Marsh said. "Do you know the new CO?"

"I do," the captain said, "and that's one of the things I need to talk to you about. Let's get some coffee and go topside."

They headed up to the bridge. There they went out onto the downwind bridge wing to watch the stars come out. A few miles away the *Enterprise*, showing red and amber flight deck directional lights, was recovering the last of the evening combat air patrols. There'd be no more flight operations until just before dawn, when the entire carrier task group would launch their dawn patrols. It was one of the consequences of Pearl

Harbor that the Navy day now began at dawn. Prior to the sneak attack, a Navy ship company's day in port began in earnest around nine in the morning, pretty much like their civilian brethren.

The port lookout moved into the pilothouse to give them some privacy, but even so, the captain kept his voice down. There were no bigger gossips in the world than sailors.

"The new CO is Commander Bill Hughes," he said. "He's a classmate."

That spoke volumes: The captain was completing his commander-command tour, promoting to four stripes, and on his way to an even bigger ship. His classmate was obviously a little bit behind the career power curve.

"I haven't seen him for several years," he said, "but the nature of your job here as exec is probably going to change, and I think I owe you a heads-up."

"That sounds ominous."

"Well, I had some reservations when you were sent in as XO, mostly because you were so junior. On the other hand, you had recent and downright vivid combat experience, you'd won a Silver Star for bravery, and you were academy. And you've done damn well."

"Thank you, sir."

"I mean it. The crew and the wardroom respect you, and that brings me to what I have to tell you: Bill Hughes is a notorious screamer."

Marsh's heart sank. He'd heard of that type, officers who knew only one method of command: absolute tyranny, accompanied by a perpetually furious personality. They found fault with everything and everybody while demanding the highest standards of professional performance and discipline.

"This is what you need to know," the captain said. "You will have to become the buffer between the CO and the rest of the ship's company. The Lord Protector of your officers and enlisted men. That doesn't mean that you become a disloyal subordinate: The captain is the captain. But when he loses his temper and verbally demolishes a junior officer in front of his subordinates, then you are the one who gets that JO to come around to your stateroom after hours, where you'll explain that whatever he did was not an act of high treason. That the CO just lost his temper, and that he's not going to have him shot on the fantail at dawn. You get the picture?"

"Who will do that for me?" Marsh asked, being only halfway facetious.

The captain grinned in the dark. "That's the hard part, XO. If destroyer command is going to work, the CO and the XO have to merge professionally and, if possible, personally, as I think you and I have managed to do. With Bill Hughes, you are going to be operating in the lightning rod mode."

341

"Sounds great."

"What I mean is this: Try to set it up so that he yells at *you* rather than the troops. You know, chain of command. When he does yell at the troops, do damage control as best you can. Otherwise they will become dispirited. It's bad enough to have Jap planes dropping torpedoes at you, only to then have the skipper scream at you for not shooting the bastard down *before* he dropped his torpedo."

"Tell me this, then: If I'm the guy he spends most of his time screaming at, what chances do I have of getting a decent fitness report?"

"You started out in cruisers, didn't you?" he said.

"Yes, sir. Three in a row."

"The cruiser Navy is a little more formal than we are in the tin can Navy," he said. "We sound the GQ alarm. A cruiser blows a bugle call. We stand watch in our short-sleeve wash khakis; a cruiser bridge requires a long-sleeve shirt and tie. A cruiser skipper occasionally visits the wardroom for dinner. A destroyer skipper eats in the wardroom with the rest of the officers."

"I remember all that," Marsh said.

"Well, the tin can Navy's a much tighter community, especially when it comes to professional reputations. I'm talking about the regular officers now, not all these ninety-day wonders. If the ship does well, accomplishes her missions, and doesn't run aground, then even a lousy fitness report from someone like Bill Hughes would be interpreted as a mark of respect for you. The people who sit on promotion and command screen boards know how this works, and they also know about screamers like Bill Hughes."

"If he has this kind of reputation, why is *he* getting a command?"

"I don't know—some admiral called in a marker somewhere, maybe? There's probably a shortage of qualified skippers. We've lost a lot of middle-grade officers these past two years. Hell, you were at Savo: Three American cruisers had their entire wardrooms decimated. How many prospective XOs and COs did we lose, just in one night?"

Marsh thought back to *Winston* and could remember at least a half-dozen officers who would have gone on to command, except that now they were asleep in the deeps of Ironbottom Sound. The wind blowing through the pilothouse hatch was warm enough, but even so he felt a chill. Silver Star not withstanding, he still felt in his own mind that he had not distinguished himself that night. Beast was probably right, he thought: When the day came to face a real battle, he'd probably clutch up. He was starting to feel that way about the new commanding officer, and he hadn't even met him.

"And here's one last thing," the captain said. "What I've told you tonight? You can't share this openly with the wardroom. All you can do is protect the good guys as best you can. You cannot openly denigrate the captain, or you become part of the problem. No matter how you feel, you must rigidly support the chain of command."

"These guys aren't dumb, Skipper. They'll see right through that."

"Yes, they might, but remember, discipline is the only thing that keeps a ship going, especially in wartime. If a popular and respected XO becomes openly disloyal to the captain, then the crew loses confidence in the captain. Then along comes one of those moments of extreme peril, where he gives an order, the exactly correct order, and someone questions it. Then everybody dies."

"Suppose it's the wrong order, though?"

"That's the deeply embedded hook in the military seniority system, XO. A junior officer can never know whether or not his boss might be privy to information that he, as the junior officer, is not. If you think it's a mistake, you can say that, but once the CO shakes his head and says no, do it, you must comply. Somebody has to be the ultimate authority, and that's the captain. That's why he gets that great big cabin."

That was a joke, of course; the captain's in-port cabin was maybe eight feet wide and twelve long. Marsh knew what he was talking about, though.

"Sometimes I feel that we're all actors," he said. "Pretending that we have the answers to everything."

"A surprising amount of this command business *is* an act. I don't mean play-acting in the Hollywood sense. I mean that when you're the captain, everyone is watching you, every moment. So you have to present a calm, confident, wise, compassionate, patient demeanor, even if personally you are none of those things."

"Yes, sir, I understand that, I think. But what if you're the XO and the captain doesn't live up to those rules?"

"Then you have to fill in for his professional failings while not appearing to. In the end it's not about the XO or the CO—it's all about taking care of the ship and her people. You concentrate on doing that, and your fitness reports will take care of themselves, one way or another. It's actually a beautiful system."

"Did you know all about this when you took command?" Marsh asked.

"Nope," he said with a smile. "The screening boards select officers for command based on their potential to step up and fill the shoes. Sometimes they get it wrong, but for the most part they get it right, as I think you'll find out when your turn comes."

Marsh shook my head. "The closer I get . . ."

The captain chuckled in the darkness. "Yeah, I

know. That's the amazing thing, when you think about it. We regulars are more afraid of screwing up professionally than we are of the Japs and their bombs and torpedoes. I think you'll do just fine when the time comes, and it'll come sooner than you think."

"I just made lieutenant commander," Marsh said. "I'm years away."

"You're probably one year away, XO. If nothing else, Bill Hughes will be superb training for when you get your own ship. On how *not* to act under fire."

"And a free education at that."

The captain laughed quietly. Marsh was going to miss him.

Commander Bill Hughes came aboard a week later, after a long trip from Pearl through a succession of waypoints across the Pacific and finally to the *Enterprise*. The *Evans* came alongside the bird farm one fine morning and Hughes and his seabag were highlined aboard. He was a tall, rangy officer, with a narrow, bony face and pronounced dark circles under his eyes; he was obviously exhausted by the long trip to join *Evans*. The captain gave him his in-port cabin and moved himself to the even tinier sea cabin right behind the bridge. Commander Hughes slept for the first twelve hours of his stay on board. He even slept right through the next morning's dawn gunnery practice, with five-inchers banging away fore and aft.

Commander Hughes was accompanied by a second officer, who was as short and round as Hughes was tall and thin. He was Rabbi Sidney Morgenstern, and he was *Evans*'s brand-new chaplain. Marsh had not known they were getting a chaplain, and his surprise showed when they met on the midships highline platform.

"Welcome aboard, Rabbi," he said after Morgenstern introduced himself. "Are you rotating through the screen ships or are you our new chaplain?"

"I think I'm all yours, XO," he said with a grin. "We had three rabbis on the *Bunker Hill*, and I was voted most likely to become expendable, so they sent me to a tin can."

"Well, let's find you a berth, then," Marsh said. "We have maybe three men aboard who are Jewish, but I assume you can counsel anyone who needs it, right?"

"Absolutely," he said. "That's why I have the Star of David on one collar and the cross on the other. Same God, last time I checked in."

Marsh handed the rabbi over to the supply officer and went to catch up with the new skipper. As the exec, his job was to coordinate the turnover process and the actual change of command ceremony. It all went pretty well over the next week, with only a few custody signature items such as binoculars having to be "surveyed" because no one could find them. After it was all over, and Captain Warren had been highlined off to begin his own long journey back to the States, Commander Hughes called Marsh into his cabin for the customary here's-how-I'm-going-to-run-it conversation. He was not especially friendly, but Marsh sensed that was more his professional demeanor than any antipathy toward him.

"Everybody gets one mulligan," Hughes said. "After that, when someone screws up he's going to hear from me. I will not tolerate incompetence or slack behavior."

Marsh nodded. There really wasn't any response he could make to that, other than perhaps to point out that, in the main, the *Evans* was sailing with a crew made up of last year's high school class and a wardroom of ninety-day-wonder reservists. It wasn't so much that they were incompetent as it was that they were necessarily ignorant of how everything was supposed to work.

"This is a good, solid crew, Captain," Marsh told him. "They're willing, but they're still green. If they screw up, it's usually because they don't know any better."

"Then we need to beef up the training program," Hughes said. "You can't be doing OJT when the Japs come calling."

On-the-job training, however, was precisely

how much of the U.S. Navy had trained during 1942, as Marsh knew firsthand. The heavy casualties in that year and the next reflected that. He'd been sent into an exec's job with absolutely no training, other than having watched his own exec in *Winston*. It also didn't help that there was a great deal of turnover among warship captains. About the time the rest of the ship's company had gotten used to a new skipper, another one seemed to show up to take his place, as there were many commanders eager to get the command-at-sea box checked off.

"Give me your appraisal of the individual officers, please," the captain said. "Start with the department heads."

In *Winston*, there had been a four-striper as captain, a three-striper as exec, and five lieutenant commanders as department heads. Every officer on board except the doctor, the supply officer, and the chaplain had been regular officers and academy graduates. By 1944, things were very different: The skipper and Marsh were academy professionals. Every other officer on board was a reservist, with the *most* experienced department head having not quite three years of sea duty under his belt. The captain nodded when Marsh finished going through the list.

"I'm an impatient man, XO," he said. "I've never learned to coddle people. I tell them what I want and I expect them to deliver, whether it's chasing rust out on deck or keeping a spotless engineering space. If they don't measure up, I tend to yell. Don't take it personally. It's just how I do things. You may find yourself mending fences for me with the wardroom and the crew from time to time."

Marsh almost laughed, given what Captain Warren had told him. At least Hughes was being honest about himself, he thought. A screamer who could admit he's a screamer was better than one who didn't see anything wrong with acting that way.

Marsh hadn't counted, however, on just how explosive his temper was. It happened at the end of one of their refueling evolutions. The ship would come alongside the carrier every third day and receive and hook up span-wires, down which a thick black hose would roll. Once the hose was plugged into an on-deck refueling connection, the carrier would start pumping, and the engineers would open and close valves down below to distribute the fuel oil to the various tanks lining the ship's bottom.

On this particular occasion, the snipes managed to overfill one of the forward fuel tanks. When that happens, the fuel oil comes spurting out of tank vents all along the main deck, covering men, the deck, and the sides in a viscous film of heavy black oil. Since it's the receiving ship's job to tell the providing ship when to stop pumping as her tanks get close to full, there's never a question as to who screwed up. To make matters worse, there's always a gallery of senior officers lining the carrier's island catwalks watching to see how well the tin can is being handled alongside. It was hugely embarrassing for *Evans* to blow black oil all over herself.

Captain Hughes said not a word, but after the *Evans* broke away from the carrier to regain her assigned station in the screen, he summoned the chief engineer, the main propulsion assistant, and the oil king, who was a senior boiler-tender chief petty officer. Then he proceeded to detonate. Marsh stood behind the captain, studying the steel deck beneath his feet, while Hughes went on and on, practically foaming at the mouth. Marsh was pretty sure the rest of the crew could hear it all over the ship; the bridge watch team certainly got an earful. The oil spill had been embarrassing. Marsh thought this temper tantrum was downright humiliating.

Afterward, the captain sat back in his bridge chair and asked him what was on tap for the day. One moment ago he had been almost purple in the face. Now he was calmly asking about the day's schedule of events, as if he had some kind of off-on switch for his temper. After Marsh recited the evolutions planned for the day, the captain instructed him to conduct an informal investigation into how the engineers had managed to foul up the refueling so badly this morning.

"I'm guessing an inexperienced fireman misread a tank sounding," Marsh said. "Or we got a bubble."

"Don't guess, XO. I need to know precisely what happened, and thereby where we need additional training."

Marsh got together with the chief engineer and the main propulsion assistant, Lieutenant JG "Swede" Bolser, after lunch. It was as he had "guessed." During refueling, a fireman apprentice was stationed at every tank's sounding tube on the deck above to periodically measure the level of fuel oil in the tank with a steel tape. A fireman named McWhenny had put the tape in upside down. It was as simple as that.

Marsh told the chief engineer to put something on all the tapes that would make it impossible to put the wrong end in the tube and then to hold a training session for all the junior firemen assigned to sounding duties.

"Is he going to take McWhenny to mast?" Lieutenant "Kit" Carson, the chief engineer, asked.

"I hope not," Marsh said. "The kid made a mistake, that's all."

"Based on the captain's reaction, I thought *we* were going to be taken out to a yardarm somewhere."

"He'll get over it," Marsh said. "It's embarrassing to foul up in front of all those airedales."

"Well, Swede and I are going to be spending a lot of time down in main control this week," he said. "I don't ever want to be screamed at like that again."

"Then don't screw up," Marsh said. "Because that's what he'll do."

"It'll be interesting to see what happens when the Japs come. He starts screaming like that, people are gonna get rattled, and then we'll have a real problem."

Which is exactly what happened two days later after the carriers had made a strike on Guam. The Japs launched a retaliatory raid against the task group, a few dozen Kate bombers accompanied by just enough fighter escorts to keep the carriers' own fighters fully occupied. The Kates went after the three big carriers, but most were driven off or shot down. One, however, came after *Evans*. He'd been hit trying to get at a carrier and was now trailing a lot of smoke. Having overshot his target, he was flying at about one thousand feet but losing altitude. Marsh suspected the pilot knew he was never going to make it back to his base and had decided to take at least a destroyer with him, because he put his damaged plane into a shallow dive and headed right for *Evans*.

The ship was shooting with everything she had—the five-inchers, the forty-millimeters, even the short-range twenty-millimeters. Since he was coming straight in, there wasn't much of a fire-control problem. Marsh saw pieces of the plane come off as shells and bullets whacked into it. His general quarters station for an air raid was back on the secondary conning station, which was behind the after stack. That way, if the ship got hit on the bridge, the second in command would still be alive to take over, but for now Marsh had nothing to do but to watch. The gun noise was incredible, but even with every gun blasting away, he could hear Captain Hughes from a hundred fifty feet away screaming at the weapons officer to get that bastard. Marsh thought the captain should have been conning the ship in evasive maneuvers, but instead the *Evans* was going straight as a die at twenty-seven knots, making it easier for the pilot to set up his aim point. He released three bombs just as one of their five-inchers put one right into his belly tank. The Kate exploded in a ball of burning aviation gasoline, but those three bombs kept right on coming, and Marsh and his two phone talkers instinctively ducked behind a splinter shield.

The first bomb landed in the water about a hundred yards away and went off in a tremendous explosion that Marsh thought must have scared the absolute hell out of the snipes down below. The middle one hit the back of the signal bridge, behind and above the pilothouse, bounced off with a loud clanging noise, and went cartwheeling into the water without going off. The third went over the forward stack and detonated two hundred yards away. Bits of the bomber landed in the water all around the ship, and its tail assembly went skipping across the sea like a flat rock before finally sinking out of sight.

The relief was as dramatic as the sudden pressure drop when all the guns ceased firing. The only sound that Marsh could hear in those few moments of stunned silence was Captain Hughes, still screaming at the weapons officer for having let that Kate get so close. Marsh thought it surreal, and then the normal noises of a destroyer going full bore through a light chop intruded and everybody went back to scanning the skies for more Kates. Five minutes later Marsh was summoned to the bridge, even though they were still at GQ and some of the screening destroyers nearby were blasting away at unseen enemy planes.

The captain was visibly furious. He pointed to the forward five-inch guns with a shaking finger and commenced a tirade about mount fifty-one not even firing on the incoming bomber, while mount fifty-two had put several rounds right into the water. At that moment, mount fifty-one, the forward-most five-incher, let go with one round to starboard, away from the formation. The sudden bang startled everybody, especially the captain, who had his back to the bridge windows. He jumped, and his steel helmet went sideways on his face, making him look ridiculous.

"I'll find out what happened," Marsh said quickly, not wanting him to see any snickering on the faces of the bridge crew. "I'm guessing—"

"I told you," he yelled. "No guessing! Facts. I want to know facts. That bastard almost got us, and two of my five guns weren't even in the goddamned game! Go find out now, right now!"

"Shall we secure from GQ, Captain?" the officer of the deck inquired. "Combat says the raid is over."

"No!" he replied. "Keep everyone on station until I *know* what happened with those two guns."

The gunnery officer, Lieutenant "Killer" Keller, was at his station up on Sky One, the forward and highest gun director on the ship, two levels above the bridge. Once again, Marsh was pretty sure he knew what had happened: Mount fifty-one had had a hang-fire, and fifty-two had probably lost elevation synchronization with gun plot. He climbed the ladders to the director, and Killer confirmed his suspicions.

Mount fifty-one had gotten off thirty rounds before the thirty-first failed to fire. Since it was technically a hot gun, the rule was that they trained the gun at the enemy or in a safe direction and waited ten minutes before dropping the breechblock, extracting the defective shell, and inserting a clearing charge. If a hot gun experienced a hang-fire and the crew opened the breech immediately, the defective powder round could cook off from the heat of the previous thirty rounds and blow the gun mount right off the ship. Hence the prescribed ten-minute wait.

"And fifty-two?"

"They lost electrical power," Killer said. "Went to manual control. New kid on the pointer seat. Forgot to point in all the excitement."

"Wonderful," Marsh said. "The captain is not pleased."

"So we heard," Keller said with a rueful grin. "Japs probably heard it too. But looky here: We got us a souvenir."

One of the signalmen, a third-class petty officer, was holding up the badly bent tail-fin structure from the Jap bomb that had failed to go off when it bounced off the signal bridge. Both of the officers noted the wet stain on the front of the signalman's dungarees.

"Give you a little skeer there, sigs?" Keller called down over the wind.

The kid grinned back at him. "You should see what Pettybone did," he called back. "Had to throw *his* dungaree trou over the side."

This was more like it, Marsh thought. Guy pissing his pants and then laughing about it. I'd have probably pissed mine, too, he thought, but this was the way it was supposed to be in the tin can Navy—up close and personal. What had happened was hardly unusual: Lots of things went off the tracks, especially on a relatively new ship. The power loss to mount fifty-two was probably caused by the vibration of all the guns firing at once tripping a breaker somewhere. The new kid getting the naval version of buck fever as he watched his first real live Jap bomber come at him was by no means without precedent. Somehow, Marsh thought, he had to find a way to make the captain understand these facts of life and relax a little bit. He'd come from a staff assignment, where perfection was achieved on a typewriter. He was in the real, frontline, down and dirty Navy now, and he had to realize that perfection out here did not exist.

That's not how it went. The captain wanted the new gunner's mate moved to a different GQ station. He wanted the chief engineer to personally check every circuit breaker in the gunnery electrical system to verify operability. He kept the entire ship at GQ while these orders were carried out, even as Combat sent out recommendations to steer *Evans* back into her assigned antisubmarine station out behind the carrier. As for the hang-fire, the captain declared that those were peacetime rules, and in the heat of battle they were to clear a hang-fire immediately and get that gun back on the line.

Marsh dutifully carried out his orders, although

later that evening he brought the captain the operating procedures manual from the Bureau of Ordnance for the 5"/38 naval gun, which specifically stated that hang-fire rules were to be followed regardless of the operational situation, since a cook-off with the breech open could lead to a magazine explosion and the loss of the ship. The captain read it, closed the book, and gave Marsh a sour look.

"It's my ship, goddammit, and *I* will make the decision on what to do with a hang-fire. Assuming, of course, that I know about it. Tell me this: Why didn't they report that they had a hang-fire?"

He had Marsh with that question. Marsh had assumed they had made a report. "I'll have to find that out," he said. "That's standard procedure, too."

"XO, let me tell you something. To use your favorite expression, I'm guessing you *assumed* they had. You *guessed* they'd lost power or had this problem or that problem. You have to stop that. Assuming and guessing is unprofessional: You have to *know*. You *have* to know. *I* have to know."

"Yes, sir. I'll work on that."

"What's the chain of communications from the gun mount to me on the bridge?"

Marsh described the sound-powered communications links for control of the gun systems.

"So if they have a hang-fire, the gun reports to main battery plot, plot reports to Sky One, who reports to Combat, who reports to me on the bridge?"

"Yes, sir."

"And you are not in that loop?"

"I have a barrel switch back at my secondary conn station, so I can listen to any sound-powered phone circuit I want to. My phone talker is tied to the command circuit, the 1JV, so that I can take over if something happens to the bridge."

"Like a bomb hitting the signal bridge because two of our guns didn't work."

"Yes, sir, just like that." Marsh hadn't mentioned the "souvenir." Somehow it didn't seem like the best moment.

"You know, that's pretty cumbersome. I think that the best place for the XO would be in Combat, where he would have the tactical picture right in front of him, instead of being back behind number two stack with his shirtsleeves in the breeze."

His voice was calm now, and he was thinking aloud. Marsh suddenly realized there was a big brain in there, and maybe all the shouting had to do with frustration rather than anger.

"But if we take a hit up there, say right between Combat and the bridge, the two most senior officers in the ship could be lost at the same time."

"You're in there for an antisubmarine action."

"A torpedo isn't going to hit the bridge," Marsh pointed out. "Remember the *San Francisco*, off Guadalcanal? They took a hit on the bridge that killed the admiral, the captain of the ship, the admiral's staff, and all the ship's bridge officers except one. The communications officer ended up taking over not only the ship but effectively the whole task group until the shooting stopped."

"I know," he said. "Let's do this: I want to have a meeting in the wardroom tomorrow with the gun boss and the chief snipe, assuming we're not dealing with Jap bombers again. I want to sort out our internal communications so that something like a hang-fire doesn't have to go through four separate phone talkers before I know about it."

"Aye, aye, sir," Marsh said.

And so it went from that day forward. Anytime something went wrong, Captain Hughes would scream and yell, embarrassing himself as much as the officers he was mad at. This would be followed by an uncomfortable discussion between Marsh and the captain, where he would be as calm and in control then as he had been out of control earlier. In each case Marsh learned something valuable, he realized, while striving to protect the department heads and even the junior officers from the captain's wrath.

The ship's company, interestingly, did not hate the man as Marsh half expected them to. After a

361

while, they came to expect and endure the temper tantrums, because he would inevitably explain why he got so mad, what had to be fixed, and why it was important in the context of a warship in the battle zone. There was little arguing with his rationale. Marsh just wished he wouldn't make it so unpleasant, but that was his nature, and he was, after all was said and done, the captain. Chief Marty Gorman, promoted twice now since *Winston*, offered Marsh the lower-decks view: Captains are issued from above just like spare parts for the engine rooms. Some are noisier than others, but they all serve a purpose.

Sometimes Captain Hughes would personally take a hand to show everyone how something was supposed to be done. On one occasion, *Evans* had had to shut down one of her four boilers for maintenance, and, upon relighting it, the snipes managed to lay down a cloud of black smoke that was very visible within the carrier formation. It got so bad the flag officer over on the carrier sent *Evans* a flashing-light message telling them to knock it off. The captain treated the engineers to his usual verbal fireworks and then went below to the forward fireroom and personally lit off the boiler, while making all the boiler-tenders watch him go through the procedure. Marsh had to admit: There was very little black smoke when he did it, and he also demonstrated to the snipes that he knew how to line up the fuel pumps, the blowers, and the burners to get a proper light-off with no smoke.

One of the five-inch gun mount crews managed to break a powder case in the process of loading a round during gunnery practice, spilling macaroni-sized powder grains all over the hot amplidyne motors and the interior of the gun mount. Once again, there was lots of noise on the bridge, followed by a visit from the CO to the offending mount, where he personally ran them through their paces on how to properly load, ram, and close the breech. He actually operated the loading control panel, demonstrating that he knew both how and when to cycle the appropriate machinery and that, if *he* knew how to do it, then by God they ought to know how to do it without risking a flash explosion in the mount. It took them two hours to clean up all the spilled powder, during which he kept the entire ship closed up at general quarters. Marsh thought he was punishing the crew for the mistakes of just one battle station and finally said so. The captain reminded him that a mount explosion was still possible until all the powder had been cleaned up and said that was why he kept the ship at GQ, not to punish anyone but in order to be ready to deal with such an event.

Marsh realized then that Captain Hughes was thinking differently than he was. The captain was always mindful of the bigger picture, even while diving in and getting his hands dirty in a fireroom or a gun mount to make his point. He had seven years seniority on Marsh, and it seemed to him that those seven years made Hughes a hell of a lot more qualified to be the CO than Marsh would ever be. Except that three weeks later Marsh became the captain when Captain Hughes killed himself.

It was another one of those situations where a small group of sailors managed to screw up what should have been a simple evolution. One of the lifeboat davits had turned up a cracked davit arm. The shipfitters went out to weld it back together, but first all the metal had to be cleaned. Once they got the davit arm cleaned up and ready for a weld, they discovered that three of the four bolts holding the frame of the arm to the main deck were broken. They sent a fireman apprentice to go get a power drill, and then one of them proceeded to punch several holes in the frame trying to drill out the broken bolts. A chief came by, saw the mess in progress, and, unfortunately, imitating his captain, started yelling at them.

The captain, who happened to be one deck above, looked over to see what the fuss was about. He then came down to the davits, saw the hash the fireman had made out of what should have been a simple job, and grabbed the big drill to show him how to attack a recalcitrant bolt. He then proceeded to drill perfectly through the bolt head, through the shaft, and then right into a 440 volt cable running underneath the davit arm base. There was a sickening humming noise, a purple-white flash that seemed to envelop the captain, and then a sudden stink of cooked meat. A breaker popped in main control, and a moment later the sound-powered phone in Marsh's cabin squealed at him in a manner that told him it was serious.

By the time he got to the main deck, horrified sailors had managed to get the captain unstuck from the steel of the main deck, but it was obvious that there was nothing that could be done for him. His mouth was open and contorted in a snarl worthy of a feral animal, and the whites of his glaring eyes were literally cooked. Two of the younger sailors were feeding the fishes over the side, and Marsh, too, felt a moment of extreme nausea when he looked at the scorched body. The ship's pharmacist's mate came running with his black bag, took one look, and shook his head. He didn't have to say anything. He sent two men to sick bay to bring up a body bag.

Rabbi Morgenstern showed up right after he heard the pharmacist's mate called away to the port boat davits. He knelt down next to Commander Hughes's rigid body and tried unsuccessfully to close his eyelids. Then he put on a narrow shawl and began to recite the Twenty-third Psalm. The sailors standing around took off their hats, as did Marsh. The rabbi got up from the deck and told Marsh he'd make the arrangements for a burial at sea. "That's usually my job," Marsh told him.

"Not anymore," the rabbi said. "You're the captain now, right?"

Marsh was taken aback. The rabbi, of course, was correct. Marsh went up to the bridge and called for a signalman to bring down a message blank. The ship was within visual range of the carrier, and Marsh didn't think that this news was appropriate for the TBS voice radio circuit, to which all ships in the group listened. Lieutenant John Hennessy, the navigation department head, looked over his shoulder as Marsh wrote up a terse report. When he was finished, Hennessy told Marsh that he'd forgotten something.

"What?"

"Sir, you have to say that *you've* assumed command."

"They'll know that, for Chrissakes."

"No, sir, that's not what I mean," Hennessy said. "You have to make a log entry, and then you have to inform the task group commander who, by name, rank, and serial number, is now in command."

"Oh," Marsh said. "You're right."

For Marsh it was a more than interesting moment. Before this awful day, he had been the de facto leader of the wardroom, with the subtext being that he was one of them against, or at least afraid of, the captain and his rages. Following the advice of Captain Warren, Marsh had been shepherding the wardroom, while being very careful not to say or do anything that they could interpret as insubordination. Now that he was the captain, if only in an "acting" capacity, John Hennessy was going to be the acting executive officer. The change in Hennessy's tone and body language, and the "sir" when he spoke to Marsh, were tacit recognition that everything had changed.

"All right," Marsh said. "You're the next senior in line. That makes you acting XO, so *you* write the message and make sure it has all the right stuff in it, okay?"

"Aye, aye, sir," John said. Before this moment, he would have said, "Got it, XO." That invisible but tangible gulf between the ship's company and the captain was already opening, and it made Marsh more than a little uneasy.

They jointly made the requisite log entry, and Marsh formally assumed temporary command of USS *Evans*. A flashing-light signal went out to the *Evans*'s squadron commodore, embarked on one of the other destroyers, five minutes later. The commodore came right back with instructions to initiate a JAG-manual investigation into the circumstances and saying that Marsh's temporary assumption of command had been duly noted. An hour later the Japs sent a large raid of land-based bombers against the task group, and *Evans* went back to the work at hand, blasting away at the big black planes whenever they came in range. This time all the guns worked just fine, almost as if to give Captain Hughes a proper send-off. After securing from general quarters, *Evans* went alongside another destroyer and transferred their doctor over so he could conduct a postmortem exam. That evening, the ship's company, led by the rabbi, conducted a formal burial at sea, after which Marsh took a mug of coffee up to the bridge and sat in the captain's chair for the very first time in his life. It hadn't seemed appropriate until they'd committed Captain Hughes to the deep. It still didn't, and he wondered if he was doing the right thing.

Remembering what Commander Wilson, *Winston*'s XO, had done, Marsh had removed Commander Hughes's academy ring before the burial and put it in his safe. He wasn't sure at that juncture who was supposed to write the condolence letter, himself or the commodore, so that night he crafted a letter to the captain's widow expressing his profound sympathy for the loss of Commander Hughes in an operational accident at sea. He enclosed Hughes's academy ring, bundled the package into an official Navy correspondence pouch, and addressed it to Hughes's wife back in Washington, in care of the commodore. He knew that the Navy's casualty notification telegram would reach her long before this package did. He'd briefly explained what had happened and then expressed how much he, as the exec, had learned from Hughes and how everyone in the ship had respected and admired his professional expertise. The last bit was a stretch, of course, but one made with the best of intentions. It was Marsh's first command decision.

The next morning he expected a message from the task group commander announcing that they'd found a three-striper on the admiral's staff to send over to take command. Instead, the commodore sent them a message directing *Evans* to proceed in accordance with previous orders, namely, to detach from the *Enterprise* task group, proceed to a place called Leyte Gulf, and join Admiral Kinkaid's Seventh Fleet invasion forces there for duties as assigned. First they were told to go alongside the Big E and pick up an aviator who was being sent to one of the escort carriers. They dutifully made the transfer, with Marsh's letter going over and one lonely aviator coming back.

As they broke away from the carrier and headed south, Marsh was surprised to see whom they'd taken aboard. Mick McCarty, of all people. An image of a ravished Glory Hawthorne flashed through his mind, but he quickly smothered that and greeted Mick with as much civility as he could manage. Mick handed over a courier pouch containing the basic elements of the Leyte invasion operations order. They talked for a little while, and then Marsh turned him over to Lieutenant Hennessy to find him a bunk for the transit. Then Marsh retired to the captain's sea cabin to read the op order. He'd decided to use that smaller cabin for steaming operations and keep his XO's stateroom as his office until a new CO was ordered aboard. That left the captain's in-port cabin empty, a visible reminder for the crew that he was only the acting, or temporary, captain.

Two other destroyers were detached with *Evans*, and they officially became what was known in Navy jargon as a task element. The senior skipper of the three, which was most certainly not Marsh, took command of the three-ship unit and formed them up in a column for a twenty-knot dash to Leyte Gulf. The invasion fleet was some two hundred miles to the southwest of where the big-deck carrier groups were operating. Once they'd settled into transit formation, Marsh got on the ship's announcing system and formally declared to the crew that he had taken temporary command. He also laid out the details of what had happened to Captain Hughes, because he knew there had to be all sorts of rumors spreading below decks. He told them that they would be operating in support of a task group of escort carriers, who were in turn supporting General MacArthur's invasion of the Philippine Islands, beginning with Leyte Island.

Based on some of the things he'd read in the op order, he also briefed them on what to expect.

"Once American forces land on Leyte, the Japs are going to hit back and hit back hard," he said, pausing between sentences to let the echoes of his voice die down on the topside speakers. "If they lose the Philippines, we will be sitting on all their supply routes from Southeast Asia. That's where their oil comes from. If we can cut that off, they'll be finished. They have dozens of airfields and a large army on Luzon Island, and we're going to be hearing from them on a daily basis. They might even send out their battle fleet. The Philippines are that important." He finished up by announcing that they'd be refueling and rearming as soon as they joined the invasion task force.

The next morning they did just that, refueling from a fleet oiler and then going alongside an ammunition ship. It took most of the day to get their supplies topped up, and Marsh spent all of it on the bridge in the captain's chair or supervising the young officers who were conning alongside. They were still a hundred miles away from Leyte Gulf itself, which was probably why the Japs didn't come out to play. Yet. It would have been a tempting target, though—escort carriers, fleet oilers, transports, supply ships, some seven *hundred* ships in all, headed for Leyte Gulf, a narrow body of water between the Philippine islands of Leyte and Samar. Halsey's Third Fleet, back from a week of air strikes on Formosa, was operating to the north, conducting daily air raids on Jap air bases on Luzon and the primitive Jap airstrips on Leyte itself. That pressure may have accounted for the relative peace and quiet in the assembling invasion fleet.

The escort carriers were odd-looking ships. Some of them were converted merchant ships. The Navy designated these as CVLs, light carriers. The rest had been purpose-built and were designated as CVEs, escort carriers. They carried about two dozen aircraft, as compared with the ninety-plus carried aboard the much bigger Essex-class fleet carriers. They were unarmored and just about unarmed—one open five-inch mount on the stern was typical. They displaced eight to ten thousand tons, as compared with the thirty-six thousand tons of the fleet carriers. They made up for their light capabilities by their sheer numbers, though, and they'd been assigned to provide air support for the landing forces so that the soldiers didn't have to defend airfields ashore as they'd had to in Guadalcanal.

Evans was assigned to protect one of the three task units into which MacArthur's group of sixteen small carriers had been divided. The task unit into which *Evans* had been assigned was to be stationed closest to the actual invasion ships and the landing areas, and consisted of six of the small carriers and their escorting destroyers. The other two task units were to operate farther offshore as an air-support general reserve until the invasion revealed how much opposition was waiting for the landing forces. The task group's radio collective call sign was Taffy, and the three task units were Taffy One, Two, and Three. Everyone thought that it was a ridiculous call sign, but call signs were deliberately chosen so as not to suggest to a listening enemy what kind of ships were talking. By evening the three destroyers took up their assigned escort stations and began to settle in while getting used to the new, much smaller carriers. *Evans*'s first assignment was to transfer Mick McCarty to the USS *Madison Bay*.

The *Madison Bay* was not much of an aircraft carrier, Mick thought, as *Evans* sat astern, waiting to come alongside for the highline transfer. He'd read up on the class before he'd left the *Enterprise*. The *Madison Bay* was not quite five hundred feet long and barely displaced eight thousand tons. She carried a mixed bag of twenty-four aircraft, fighters and bombers, in a single so-called composite squadron. She had one catapult, and the island structure was almost all the way forward. Her smokestacks stuck out the side of the flight deck at an ungainly forty-five-degree angle to keep boiler exhaust gas turbulence away from landing planes. On a good day and going downhill, she could make a maximum speed of eighteen knots and still look pretty ugly doing it.

His departure from the Big E had been a quiet business. He'd said good-bye to his few friends in the ready room the morning of his departure. He'd actually gone to find Georgie until he remembered that he had not been recovered. The skipper had been "busy," but the exec had caught up with him in the passageway and wished him good luck. He'd stopped by sick bay and procured some more skin cream for his bad hand. Then he'd gone down to the hangar deck to the starboard side midships sponson for his transfer to *Evans*. He'd highlined over only to discover that his classmate was now the captain. After their quarrel back in Pearl almost nine months ago, Mick wasn't sure how he'd be received, but Marsh was courteous and reasonably friendly. By unspoken mutual agreement, neither of them mentioned Glory Lewis.

Now, one week later, they were bouncing around in a moderate sea behind his prospective new home, this ugly duckling of a carrier. He stood next to Marsh on the bridge, wedged between the captain's chair and the centerline pelorus station.

"So," Marsh asked. "Whaddaya think?"

"I think I've been well and truly shit-canned," Mick said. "Look at that thing. She's bouncing around as much as this tin can is."

"Yeah, but they see action damned near every

374

day," Marsh said. "The Big Blue Fleet does the grand-scale stuff once in a while, but these guys are smokin' Japs on a daily basis. There'll be sixteen of 'em out there when MacArthur's boys finally go ashore."

Sixteen? Mick thought. He did the math. Given the usual hangar queens, that was still more planes than they'd had at Midway. Too bad all they'd be dropping on was a bunch of pillboxes and trenched emplacements. The fighter guys might have some fun when the Japs came out in force from Luzon, but Halsey's big-deck carriers had been pasting their airfields for two weeks now. After the Philippine Sea, which the world of naval aviation was starting to call the Marianas Turkey Shoot, they couldn't have that many experienced pilots left. War birds without pilots weren't war birds.

Marsh had his binoculars up to his face. "There goes Roger," he called out. "Let's go."

The officer of the deck called the signal bridge and told them to two-block *Evans*'s *R* flag, indicating that the destroyer was commencing her approach. Mick said good-bye to Marsh and offered his left hand. Marsh took it absently, but he was already engrossed in supervising the dangerous maneuver coming up as *Evans* increased speed to twenty-two knots and aimed for a spot no more than a hundred feet off the carrier's starboard side.

Mick felt a bit dejected as he waited for the highline rig to go across. Ever since Midway he'd been bouncing around the Pacific from ship to ship, station to station. He was still a lieutenant, permanently so in all probability, while his classmate and roommate Marsh Vincent was a lieutenant commander with a destroyer command, however strangely he had come by it. The brass must think highly of him or they would have sent someone else aboard immediately.

Then there was Glory. That night in Pearl had not been about love and romance. His argument afterward with Marsh had probably damaged their friendship irretrievably, no matter how polite Marsh had been for the past week. Mick had brought up the argument only once since coming aboard. He'd apologized for calling Marsh a coward. Marsh had waved the whole incident away, citing the destructive power of too much booze in a hot climate.

"Lieutenant?" one of the sailors said. "We're ready if you are."

Mick tightened the strings on his kapok and climbed into the flimsy-looking highline chair. A minute later he was bobbing his way between the two ships, suspended in the chair from a rolling block on a two-inch-diameter manila line, getting splashed by the waves erupting between the steel sides of the ships and hoping like hell they didn't dunk him. Tin can sailors were known to enjoy giving the occasional flyboy a real scare with the chair. Finally he came bouncing over the folded-down lifelines of the CVE, where six strong hands grabbed the chair and invited him out. His damp seabag was already sitting on one corner of the after sponson platform. As he got out of his life jacket, a large officer in an oil-stained flight suit came across the deck to greet him.

"Beast McCarty, as I live and breathe," he said. "Welcome to the Untouchables."

Mick recognized him at once. He'd been the offensive fullback for Navy when Mick had played his first season as a youngster back at Annapolis. His name was Maximo Campofino, and he'd been two classes ahead of Mick. He was wearing a lieutenant commander's oak leaves.

"Mad Max, how the hell are you? You the skipper here?"

"For my sins. What'd you do—punch out the admiral's aide or something? C'mon, get your bag, and let's get inside the house before these deck-apes start throwing bananas at us."

Mick expected to step through the sponson hatch into the hangar bay, but instead it was just a passageway. Max took him to the ready room and introduced him as the latest exile from the big-deck Navy. Everyone seemed friendly enough, and they even had a flight suit already hanging for him.

"Where the hell's the hangar bay?" Mick asked after he'd shifted into more familiar working attire.

"We only have half a hangar on this boat," Max said. "Half an island, half a flight deck, one slingshot, two 'vators, and thass it, partner. Supposed to have twenty-four planes, but usually we have eighteen, nineteen, and maybe twelve of those reporting full up on any given day. The doughboys love us just the same, though."

"Missions?"

"We launch, we loiter, get a call from a FAC, go down to treetop level, and shoot the place up. Great fun, most of the time."

"I did some of that on the 'Canal," Mick said. "It wasn't like Midway, but you're right. The guys on the ground loved our asses."

"They still do, man. You were at Midway? Bag anything big?"

Mick told them of his experiences and then described the Philippine Sea engagement. He kept it fairly low-key, not wanting to sound like too much of a braggart his first day. The pilots around him were pretty junior, though, and several looked like downright nuggets.

"Are you an ace?" one of them asked.

"I'm a bomber guy, but I have shot down some Jap aircraft. That whole ace business is more of a fighter thing, you know?"

"Well, we're by God happy to have you with

us," Max said. "C'mon, lemme show you around the boat. Won't take five minutes, actually."

Mick found that it took longer, but not much longer. Max explained that the CVEs were being mass-produced as cheaply and quickly as possible. "They're not very capable, but there's lots of them. All together this formation can put up an aluminum overcast if we have to. It ain't glorious, but it's ordnance in the air that counts with the ground-pounders. So: What's with the glove on your right hand?"

Mick hadn't been aware that he was favoring his hand again, but it did hurt, and the color sometimes went very dark, especially at night. He explained how he'd been injured and that the choice had been to go back to the States to see a specialist or quit flying.

"Good choice," Max said. "Let our flight surgeon take a look-see. He's pretty good."

"This thing rates a flight surgeon?"

"Yeah, there's one for every three jeeps. This one happens to be embarked here for the moment, but they rotate 'em. Lemme show you the planes."

Max took him through the hangar bay and then up to the flight deck to see all the planes. Mick noticed that some of them had distinctive decorations—teeth on the nose, funny names on the cockpit side panels, or decorative decals. He asked if he could put his white horse emblem on one of the barges. Max told him to talk to one of the aviation bosuns, who did all the artwork. Mick noticed that Max didn't bother to ask about the significance of the white horse. Mick told himself that it was as much for Jimmy Sykes as for his own fleet reputation.

After the noon meal, Mick went to sick bay and met with the flight surgeon, a weary-looking, middle-aged lieutenant commander with really thick glasses named Lowenstein. Mick explained how his hand had been damaged.

"Wow," the doc said. "I'da been out of my ever-lovin' mind, buried like that."

"I was getting there. So, what do you think?"

"You're gonna lose it, is what I think. Not right away, but the circulation system has been badly compromised. One fine day you'll have to have it amputated. I'm surprised you can grip a stick."

"You shitting me?"

"Not a pound, Lieutenant. How bad's it hurt?"

"Sometimes it's really painful, especially when it goes dark on me. Other times it just aches."

"Well, if we were back stateside, I'd have to med-down you right here and now. But we're not. The invasion starts sometime in the next ten days, and as long as you can grip the stick and fly your barge, I'll clear you. But be prepared, young man."

"Jesus."

"Not like you did this in a bar fight, Lieutenant.

You've been wounded, like a million other guys in this goddamned war. How's the rest of you?"

The doc gave him a quick physical and then put him on a light aspirin regimen. He gave him some massage techniques to use on his hand and told him to sleep with it elevated as much as he could.

"How will I know when it's time to, uh—"

"You'll smell it."

Mick blinked at that. "Terrific," he said.

"You asked, Lieutenant. Like I said, they should have downed you right there on the island."

"They were busy, Doc. You have no idea what a horror show the 'Canal was."

The doctor gave him a lopsided grin and then raised his shirt, displaying two deeply dimpled bullet wound scars on his chest. "Yeah, I do, Lieutenant. I went in with the Breed in August 'forty-two. I was doing surgery in a bomb crater, water up to my knees, body parts floating around, when a sniper got me. Shot me right through my red cross, the little fuck."

"A flight surgeon, sent to Guadalcanal?"

"I was just a journeyman cutter then. Did aeromedical cert while recuperating in Oakland. The regular ones are all out on the big-decks. Oh, almost forgot. How's about you drop your skivs and we'll do the finger-wave, shall we?"

A-day was scheduled for October 20, with preliminary landings to be conducted by Army

Rangers to sanitize some vital islands on the flanks of the entrance to Leyte Gulf. *Evans* had arrived on the twelfth, and Marsh and all the other officers were immediately immersed in reviewing new operation orders, because the original invasion target had been Mindanao, not Leyte Island.

They also ground through the paperwork of the JAG-manual investigation into Captain Hughes's death. The facts, of course, were pretty straightforward. The background leading up to the incident was a more delicate matter, and Marsh took that part of it for action. They sent the package off via one of the jeeps to their distant commodore, who was still out there in the Philippine Sea with Halsey and the big-deck carriers. If it was anything like every other JAG-manual investigation report, it would come back with questions, procedural corrections, and directions to change wording, etc. Such an investigation would have been done regardless of who or how senior the person was who managed to kill himself accidentally. Since it was the CO in this case, the nuances of the wording would receive much more attention from the senior officers reviewing it. Marsh was just glad to have it off his back for a while.

One day he received a personal-for message from the commodore, informing him that a commander by the name of L. J. Benson, from

CincPacFleet's staff, was making his way across the Pacific logistics chain to take command of *Evans*. Marsh felt a momentary pang of disappointment, but then reality reasserted itself. He was a junior lieutenant commander. Even in wartime, he was probably two, maybe three years from a command of his own, assuming that the Navy Department wanted him in command at all. The message, however, set in motion preparations for yet another change of command. This time the poor navigation officer, John Hennessy, became the stuckee who had to honcho the paperwork, with Marsh's help, of course.

Marsh found it interesting to watch the crew try to decide what to call him—XO or Captain. With Commander Benson officially designated as the next commanding officer, he told them all to keep calling him XO. Some of them managed it, some of them did not. Anyone who approached him with business when he was sitting in the captain's chair called him Captain. If he was just walking about deck, they called him XO.

The *Evans* spent two days before A-day supporting the frogmen units that were doing clearance operations along the two main objective beaches. Jap snipers harassed the UDT boats but were quickly driven off by *Evans*'s five-inch gunfire. They couldn't actually see the snipers, so they simply clear-cut the jungle. They also had some fun blowing up mines that had been swept from the entrance to Leyte Gulf itself. They were large round black casings complete with contact horns, and their thousand pounds of explosives made for some spectacular explosions and pictures. They had help spotting the mines from the jeeps' aircraft, and one day an SBD with a rearing white horse painted on the side came by for a low pass. The canopy was back, and the bomber came down close and bridge-wing low. Marsh saw that it was Beast, waving casually as the noisy barge grumbled by. His goggles were up on the back of his head, and he had a big cigar sticking out of the side of his mouth. The crew loved it. Beast in his element at last, Marsh thought.

The actual A-day invasion was somewhat anticlimactic. It began with a thunderous predawn bombardment by a line of elderly battleships, a few of which had been raised from the ignominious mud of Pearl Harbor. It was satisfying to see them hurling their fourteen- and sixteen-inch shells into the jungles near and then beyond the beaches, although a bit unnerving when said shells came rumbling over *Evans*'s gunfire support position further inshore. The sixteen-inchers in particular, weighing nearly three thousand pounds each, made a deep wa-wa-wa sound as they sailed overhead in search of Jap pillboxes, spider holes, and hardened gun emplacements. Once the troops swept ashore, they encountered very light and disorganized resistance. Apparently the Japs had withdrawn their main army forces, estimated at twenty thousand, from the likely invasion beach areas up into a long, densely forested ridgeline that defined the geographical spine of Leyte Island. The inshore fire support destroyers were jumped by a few Jap planes that appeared out of nowhere. They were driven off by the ships' AA fire and the quick response of some fighters from the Taffy carriers offshore. Marsh recalled Mick's comments about the Turkey Shoot: These Japs weren't very aggressive.

On the twenty-fourth, all the gunline battleships and most of the destroyers assigned to the invasion turned south, heading down the east coast of Leyte for the Surigao Strait, a passage of water between Leyte and the next big island, Mindanao. Initially none of the other ships were told why, but later in the evening they learned from listening to the TBS radio that a Jap battleship force was headed their way to attack the invasion logistics shipping. Obviously no one wanted that, although by that time, and probably unknown to the Japanese, almost all the supplies had been landed ashore and most of the invasion transports were sitting there empty. Three other tin cans and *Evans* were left behind to protect the close-in Taffy Three escort carriers. Marsh suspected *Evans* was chosen to stay behind because she had an acting CO. Listening to the tactical radios as the hastily formed battle force went over the horizon, it sounded more like a hunting party than any kind of emergency to the south. As usual, they were mostly in the dark about the tactical situation beyond their own line of sight.

That night they secured from evening general quarters and prepared to go alongside one of the jeeps for fuel. At the last minute the refueling was canceled because of a steering problem aboard the escort carrier. That made Marsh a little bit nervous. One thing every destroyer captain monitors constantly is his ship's fuel state. The twenty-two-hundred-tonners were not exactly fuel efficient, which was not helped by the fact that their commanders expected them to execute every signal at top speed with as much seagoing verve and dash as they could muster. *Evans* was approaching the magic number of 50 percent, below which it was mandatory fleet policy that the ship refuel. The escort carrier, USS *Gambier Bay*, told them to come back tomorrow. They sheered off and headed back to their fire support station off a tiny village called Palo, where the army was encountering stiffening resistance as they moved inland.

Once on station in their fire support area, Marsh took a cup of coffee up to the signal bridge, where there was a little bit of a breeze on an otherwise stultifying evening. The rabbi joined him. Morgenstern had become a welcome addition to the ship's company. He made friends easily, liked people, and was always willing to lend a hand with paperwork or other admin matters if an officer needed some relief. He told corny jokes constantly, and the men always listened and laughed dutifully even if they'd heard it a hundred times. He also managed to find his way to the captain once a day to report on the pulse of the crew and any problems that had become ensnared in the chain of command.

"Rabbi, how's it going today?" Marsh asked, glad to see him.

"Suspiciously well," Morgenstern said, stirring his coffee with a pocketknife. "Seems quiet for a major invasion."

"We'll get some fire missions tonight," Marsh said. "The army likes us to shoot some H and I rounds at night forward of the front lines."

"H and I?"

"Harassment and interdiction. We shoot randomly into the jungle in a specified area. Japs never know where it's gonna land, so they worry and dig all night while our guys get some shut-eye."

"Lovely. Where'd the battlewagons all go?"

"Southwest. There's a rumor the Jap fleet is coming through Surigao Strait, and there's gonna be an ambush."

They talked about a few personnel issues, but tonight the rabbi had no major brushfires from belowdecks. They mostly watched the sun set behind the ridges and pretended that it wasn't all that hot.

"How are you enjoying command?" Morgenstern asked.

"Enjoying is not the right word, I'm afraid," Marsh said.

Morgenstern smiled. "I watch all these guys on the make struggling to get command," he said, "and then I watch them all turn gray over the next six months."

"I've spent my entire career thinking about how I would do everything differently. Not be so afraid to try something new. Now I'm just like all my bosses before me—very careful."

"Because your decisions affect us all, and if you screw up, we face calamity."

"Exactly. That was a personal surprise."

"At least you're aware of it," Morgenstern said. "I've seen some who haven't the sense to recognize the dangers of command at sea."

"Well, I'm trying. We have a real CO inbound, and as each day goes by, I'm getting increasingly anxious for him to get here."

"For what it's worth, I think the crew would be happy for you to keep her," the chaplain said.

"That's nice to hear," Marsh said. "Let's see what they say if we have to really get into it one day. The Japs will send their first team out to keep the Philippines, and I've met those boys."

At close to midnight they were released from naval gunfire support duties and ordered back out into Leyte Gulf to rejoin the gaggle of Taffys. The senior destroyer captain became the anti-submarine screen commander and sent *Evans* to a station on the northwest side of the escort carriers' circular formation. Three other tin cans rounded out the screen formation, which was a compromise between the best antisubmarine defense and the best antiair setup. When there were more "heavies" than escorts, neither formation offered very much defense at all. The other two escort carrier groups were even farther out, beyond *Evans*'s radar range to the southeast.

It was October, typhoon season, and the night air was heavy, hot, and very humid, with frequent squall lines sweeping across the outer edges of Leyte Gulf toward the island of Samar to their north. From time to time they would maneuver the ship into one of those rainsquall lines just to get the caked-on salt washed off the topside areas. If it looked substantial enough they'd pass the word and the off-watch crewmen would rush topside, wrapped in towels, and grab an impromptu freshwater shower.

At around one in the morning Marsh was called by the CIC watch officer. It seemed that the atmosphere was heavy enough that they could listen in to the radio transmissions coming from what sounded like a major sea battle going on to the south. TBS was usually good for talk only out as far as the visible horizon, but on this night the signals were being ducted by the atmosphere and thus reaching out over a hundred miles. Marsh couldn't sleep because of the intense heat, so he went to CIC and then out to the bridge, where they patched the southern battle force's tactical frequency into one of the bridge speakers. The rabbi showed up to listen in, and Marsh explained to him what they were hearing over the radio.

It was axiomatic in the Navy that the smaller the unit, the more it tended to talk on the radio. What was going on in Surigao Strait that night was no exception. The PT boats were apparently the first to attack, and they gabbed away nearly as much as pilots do, with excited claims about direct hits followed by high-pitched warnings to avoid collision in the pandemonium they had created. They were followed by the destroyer squadrons, which roared down the flanks of the strait firing swarms of torpedoes into a Japanese battleship and cruiser formation. Waiting patiently at the top, or northeastern, exit from the strait were the six old American battleships. Because they had been doing shore bombardment, they were not loaded with their full allowance of the armor-piercing ammunition needed for a battleship fight, so they held fire and waited for the Japanese to run the lethal torpedo gauntlet. Once the Japanese capital ships got within eleven to twelve miles, they opened up with a sixteen- and fourteen-inch gun version of Remember Pearl Harbor.

Sometimes the signals would fade away into static and garble but then return with such clarity and volume that men on the bridge jumped to answer the radio. It was exciting stuff, and pretty obvious that the Japs were taking a pasting few would survive. Around three or so, Marsh fell asleep in the captain's chair. Tomorrow would be another day, he remembered thinking, and then realized that tomorrow was already here. Dawn GQ, sunrise, breakfast, and then back to the gunline to tear up some more jungle.

THIRTEEN

The officer of the deck considerately woke Marsh at 0515, a half hour before they were scheduled to set the usual dawn GQ. This allowed Marsh time to get below to his cabin, grab a quick Navy shower, shave, change out of his sweat-stained khakis into a clean set, and be back on the bridge just as the GQ alarm sounded. They then test-fired all the guns, as did the other destroyers. The first time they'd done that, the jeep carriers had gone to GQ, thinking the formation was under attack, but by now they were used to it. After forty minutes of waiting around, CIC reported no contacts. Marsh noticed that a large rainsquall was bearing down on the ship, which would end up soaking all the topside small-caliber gun crews.

"Secure from GQ," he told the officer of the deck and ordered him to slow down to give the men topside time to shake off their kapoks and helmets and throw canvas covers over the exposed twenties and forties. Then they dived inside for breakfast just as a wall of rain hit the ship, completely obscuring the jeep formation. It also made the surface search radar useless, as sea-return static clobbered the entire scope in a large green swath of video noise. Marsh went below to the wardroom to get his daily ration of scrambled powdered eggs, liberally doused in ketchup, with cold toast and hot coffee. The docs had put away all their medical gear, and the rabbi, who mustered in the wardroom with the medical team at GQ, was already having breakfast.

"We going back in for fire support today, XO?" he asked.

"Don't know, Rabbi," Marsh said. "With all the big-gun ships down south, we probably will. Depends on what the Japs do ashore, I guess."

The sound-powered phone squealed next to Marsh's place at the head of the table. He reached under and grabbed the headset.

"XO."

"Captain, this is Ensign Cauley in Combat. We just heard a voice report from a black-cat saying he'd sighted three, possibly four battleships headed our way."

Marsh put down his coffee mug, making a mental note to tell Cauley not to call him Captain. "Where are these battleships?"

"The PBY's reporting they're coming around Samar, but Taffy went back to him and told him to verify that they're not our own ships coming back from Surigao. We're waiting for the answer."

Ensigns could be frustrating. "*Where* off Samar, please?"

"Stand by," he said. A moment later he was back. "Northwest of us."

"Surigao Strait is *south*west of us," Marsh said. The other officers had heard the word "battleships" and now detected the change in Marsh's tone of voice. Everyone stopped eating.

"Yes, sir," Cauley said. "I know that. I'm assuming the admiral meant Halsey's battleships."

"Don't assume, Jerry," Marsh snapped. Commander Hughes would have been proud of him, he thought. "Find out."

"Wait one, XO."

Marsh could hear Combat's watch standers' voices rising in the background. In his excitement Ensign Cauley was still holding the sound-powered phone's talk button down. Why on earth would Halsey's battleships be coming down to Leyte Gulf? Marsh wondered. Maybe to cover for the fact that the old-timers were still mopping up down south at Surigao?

Then Cauley was back. "Sir," he said, the pitch of his voice definitely rising. "The PBY says these ships are *Japs*—black ships, pagoda masts, and one of them is the biggest battleship he's ever seen. He says there's a bunch of cruisers with them, too."

"Sound GQ," Marsh ordered and then hung up the phone. The other officers at the table grabbed a last bite of breakfast and then pushed back their chairs to head for their general quarters stations. Marsh followed them out of the wardroom as the alarm began to ring. He could hear some complaining voices outside in the passageway from men obviously thinking this was another damned drill, but that stopped when they saw Marsh running up the ladder to the bridge.

By the time he got to the sea cabin he could hear the voice of the task unit commander calling an emergency order over the TBS for the destroyers to start making smoke. He grabbed his kapok and battle helmet out of the sea cabin and then hurried out to the bridge as *Evans* heeled over in a tight right turn to head across the prevailing wind.

"Where are they?" he called out over the rising noise of the relative wind rushing through the bridge wing doors.

"Three three zero, range sixteen miles," called the officer of the deck from the port bridge wing. "I can't see the ships, but they're shooting at our Catalina and I can see the ack-ack."

A flat silver sea was littered with rainsqualls. They were still low enough to clobber *Evans*'s radar display with thin, cottony green lines. The task unit commander issued maneuvering orders for all the jeeps to turn southeast at maximum speed. He also told them to launch every available aircraft. Because the *Evans* was behind the carrier formation, she didn't have to worry about being run over as six junior bird farms tried to turn together without colliding. Then Marsh realized that they were probably the closest American ship to whatever was pockmarking the skies to the northwest with tiny black puffs of antiaircraft fire.

Even with only two boilers lit off, *Evans* could make twenty-seven knots with ease. The jeeps, however, would be straining to make eighteen knots.

"Do we *know* they're Japs?" John Hennessy asked. "Big Eyes still don't hold them visually."

At that moment six enormous shell splashes rose almost casually all around the nearest jeep carrier, the *Gambier Bay*, which was already belching black smoke out of her angled stacks as her snipes poured on the oil.

"Now we do," Marsh said softly. "That has to be a battleship, firing at that range."

"And straddling," John said. "God, those are big rounds!"

"Bridge, Combat, radar contact intermittent due to weather," came over the bitch-box. "But it looks like two groups of contacts, range now fifteen miles and closing."

Son of a bitch, Marsh thought, his guts closing up. Fifteen miles? Jap *battleships?* Where the hell are our battlewagons?

"The jeeps are launching, Captain," a lookout called in from the starboard bridge wing.

Marsh looked out over the starboard bow and saw the first plane lumber awkwardly off the bow of *Gambier Bay* just as another six-pack of shell splashes rose up out of the sea, seeming to reach for the struggling airplane. The shell splashes were taller than the plane's altitude, which was not reassuring at all. A second plane flew off, a single large bomb visible under its belly.

The admiral's order for all the jeeps to turn southeast accomplished two things: It reduced the relative speed of approach of the Jap ships, and it was right into the wind, which the baby flattops needed to get their planes off. By now *Evans*'s smoke generators were going full blast, laying down huge clouds of grayish smoke that hung over the sea as they strove to shield the little carriers from the still-invisible battleships' optical range finders. The other destroyers were racing back through the formation of jeeps to get between them and the approaching enemy, laying down smoke clouds of their own. Between the smoke lines and the rainsqualls, Marsh thought, it was getting positively foggy out there. He ordered the engineers to make smoke with the boilers, too, and soon their stacks were belching out thick black clouds of soot.

Another salvo came in, and this time the pattern obscured *Gambier Bay*'s after flight deck. Marsh saw a piece of the jeep's flight deck go flying off her starboard side, followed by a gout of flame and smoke. She'd been hit, but she was still launching her planes. Some of them appeared to be taking off without bombs, but there were lots more of them in the sky now as all the fleeing jeeps began to spit planes off in every direction. If each one got off ten planes, there'd be fifty angry hornets to send against the Jap formation from just their piece of the Taffy task force. John Hennessy came back up on the bitch-box from inside CIC.

"Bridge, Combat, radar indicates the enemy has split his forces. The biggest contacts are closing from our west/northwest. It looks like the others are headed for the northeast side of the carrier formation."

Cruisers, Marsh thought, even though they were still too far away to be seen. Jap heavy cruisers. Those big black predators with their Long Lance torpedoes and eight-inch guns. Even as he thought it, smaller but still impressive shell splashes started landing in the neighborhood of *Gambier Bay* and just behind the other five jeeps. They're just at the edge of their range band, he thought. We're going to have to do more than lay down a smoke screen. Sure enough, the order came across TBS. It sounded like Admiral Sprague himself.

"Small boys conduct torpedo attack, I say again, conduct urgent torpedo attack!"

"Holy shit," muttered the officer of the deck.

Holy shit, indeed, Marsh thought. He told John Hennessy to come out to the bridge to take over as the officer of the deck and to take them in a sweeping turn to head toward the incoming cruisers, which were still invisible behind the Americans' own smoke screen. Amidships, the torpedomen trained out the two quintuple torpedo mounts and made ready to launch. The torpedo officer out on the bridge wing was ready to start taking sights and get a firing solution going. Marsh took a quick look around with his binocs to make sure the other three destroyers were coming along. They were, still making smoke and pouring on the fuel oil. Behind them it appeared that *Gambier Bay* was starting to fall behind the other jeeps. Hopefully the other two groups of Taffys were launching, too, but Marsh didn't really know where they were or how far away. Distance might save them, while their aircraft could get here pretty quick. They were going to need all the help they could get.

As the ship steadied up in the direction of the approaching cruisers, Marsh waited for the senior destroyer skipper to take charge of the rest of them, but the orders never came. In a way, that made sense: Their only hope of doing anything constructive lay in a melee, and for that, they all knew what had to be done. Pick out a Jap and start shooting. Lord Nelson rules.

Evans finally punched through the wall of smoke and beheld a fearsome sight. Ten miles to the northeast of them a line of heavy cruisers was boring in on the jeeps' flank, and to the left, much farther out than the cruisers, were the squat shapes of battleships, one *much* bigger than the others. Studying those ominous black pyramids through his binoculars, Marsh saw ripples of yellow-red fire bloom from them as they sent more six-gun salvos at the jeeps. A few moments later everyone could hear that menacing, rolling rumble of slowly rotating ton-and-a-half projectiles going overhead, followed by mountainous shell splashes all around the rearmost jeeps. Some of the splashes were brightly colored with dye, so that individual battleships could see where their own projectiles were landing.

Marsh knew there was nothing the destroyers could do about battleships, so the cruiser line became *Evans*'s objective. A gunfight between a Jap heavy cruiser and an American destroyer was a very uneven match. Their cruisers were armed to the teeth, with ten eight-inchers and more five-inchers than the American tin cans had. Coming right at each other, the Japs could swerve left or right and still fire six eight-inch guns against the two forward five-inch guns *Evans* could bring to bear. Now that they were approaching each other at a combined speed of nearly sixty knots, they could be alongside and duking it out, sailing-ship style, in only nine minutes. The problem was that they would have shot the American destroyers to pieces before they ever met, because, at the moment, the eight-inchers could hit the tin cans before the tin cans could reach the cruisers. Marsh realized they needed to disrupt the approaching formation somehow.

He ordered the torpedo officer out on the bridge wing to set up on the lead cruiser and told him they'd be shooting a four-fish salvo to starboard from a firing course of due north. The first cruiser in the Jap formation opened fire on one of the other destroyers racing in with *Evans* but overshot badly. The tin can fired back impudently with her forward five-inchers, although the cruiser remained out of five-inch range.

"Torpedo plot set," came from the talker.

Marsh told the OOD to steady up on 000. He held up one hand.

The ship curved left handsomely at twenty-seven knots, steadied up, and then Marsh dropped his hand. He heard the whoosh from amidships as four of their ten fish slapped into the water and headed for the lead cruiser. The Japs were paying attention, because the entire cruiser line immediately turned together to the east to avoid what was coming at them. Marsh realized too late he should have faked the shot, but at least the Japs' evasive turn would reduce their relative rate of approach on the carriers. That was the good news. The bad news was that it opened a firing arc for all of their eight-inch guns, not just their forward turrets. Every one of them began firing on *Evans* and her partners in crime. The seas around the ship erupted in a grand display of brightly colored shell splashes, some of them boomingly close. Marsh couldn't see them, but they'd probably also launched a spread of those Long Lance torpedoes in *Evans*'s direction.

Marsh stepped back into the pilothouse, personally took the conn, made a bold course change to avoid torpedoes, and began to chase the shell splashes. The theory was that, having missed, the Japs would adjust their gunnery solution. That should make the last spot they shot at reasonably safe, for the moment anyway. They must have realized that by tacking away they were giving the carriers a chance to escape, so back they came onto their original course, still firing at *Evans* but also at the nearest jeeps with their other guns. They were getting two salvos away for every one the distant battleships were firing, but the waters around the carrier formation looked like a cotillion of waterspouts.

Marsh told the gun boss to engage whatever was in range, and the five-inchers opened on the lead cruiser at a range of seventeen thousand yards, the extreme outer end of *Evans*'s effective reach. *Evans* was firing the five-inch version of armor-piercing rounds. Even so, if they hit the cruisers' armored sides, the projectiles would probably just bounce off. Marsh was hoping they'd get lucky and put a few into their upper works, which typically were not heavily armored.

A near miss went off right at the surface and blasted a spray of shrapnel through *Evans*'s bridge portholes. Something hit Marsh's steel helmet and spun it sideways on his head. The 1JV sound-phone talker grabbed his throat and slowly knelt down, spurting arterial blood everywhere. The wide-eyed lee helmsman bent down to help him, but there was nothing he could do for a severed artery. Marsh yelled at him to pick up the sound-powered headphones and take over as 1JV talker, just as another eight-inch round landed close aboard, showering the main deck with a combination of seawater and whining hot steel fragments. The lee helmsman slid the bloody phones on and tried a voice check with the other stations, but first he had to empty the mouthpiece of about a cup of blood. Marsh thought the man was going to puke, but then he buckled down. His own head hurt, and he wasn't thinking as clearly as he had been. He put his hand up to his neck and felt blood. His helmet didn't seem to fit anymore, so he took it off. It had a ragged dent the size of a tennis ball in it. Did its job, he thought, as he tried to clear his ringing ears.

He decided to keep chasing shell splashes while trying to get in position for another torpedo attack. Every time he turned *Evans*'s side toward them, they would zig or zag just enough to spoil the firing solution. Getting a hit on a cruiser going by at thirty-five knots was just about impossible, even though they were close enough now that the Japs' secondary batteries, four- and five-inchers, were joining the fight. It had turned into a melee, sure enough, and now it was pretty much time for Marsh to let the gun boss and director crews do their job. Everything out there was a viable target, and there were plenty of them. Marsh's job was to keep the ship from getting hit, and the secret to that was constant maneuvering. Like the fighter pilots said—never straighten up in a dogfight.

Suddenly the lead cruiser's forward section disappeared in an explosion of water and fire as one of the other tin cans managed the impossible and got a torpedo hit. She slowed down perceptibly but didn't stop shooting. The cruisers behind her, also blazing away with all guns, slipped around her, barely avoiding a collision, and kept coming, getting bigger and bigger. As the two cruisers overlapped, *Evans* got an opportunity, and two more of her torpedoes leapt into the ocean. One porpoised immediately and went skipping across the sea, utterly useless. At least it didn't circle back at *Evans*, for which Marsh was truly grateful. The other went true and banged into the side of the third cruiser in line right amidships, raising a satisfactory plume. To Marsh's dismay, she kept right on going, as if nothing had happened, and fired a full broadside at *Evans* as she went by. All ten shells went howling overhead.

Marsh heard a few cheers from amidships over the whistling wind when their torpedo hit, but then *Evans* took a partial salvo of eight-inch shells close aboard and all along her starboard side. The cheering turned to screaming as the forty- and twenty-millimeter gun crews were decimated. One round came through the chartroom, punching clean through because the armor-piercing shell's fuze hadn't even noticed *Evans*'s thin steel superstructure. A radioman in the chartroom did notice when the round drilled right through him, cutting him in half. Up forward, mount fifty-one blew a huge cloud of dirty gray smoke from both hatches and stopped firing. Fifty-two kept going, as did the after mounts. The salvo had missed the bridge, but one round had removed their bedspring-sized radar antenna from the foremast.

Then Marsh noticed that they were slowing down. He looked aft and saw that the forward funnel had two large holes and was leaning askew. As he was reaching for the bitch-box talk button, yet another salvo landed short, with one round hitting so flat that it skipped across the water and slammed into their starboard anchor without going off. The rest of the rounds did go off, throwing up an amazing amount of water on *Evans*'s decks. The chief engineer, Lieutenant Carson, came up on the bitch-box.

"Bridge, main control, we've lost one-Able boiler. I think the uptakes are damaged. We'll bring one-Baker on the line as soon as we can."

"Bridge, aye," Marsh answered. "It's getting pretty hot up here."

"So we're hearing, Cap'n."

Of course they were—any shells exploding underwater would sound like depth charges sounded to a submarine.

Marsh ordered another wide turn to get out of the kill zone, but not in time. As the helmsman spun the wheel, another salvo came in, and this time they took a solid hit or possibly two on the starboard side, right at the waterline. One went off right in the forward fireroom, where they'd been struggling to bring the stand-by boiler on the line.

Heavy black smoke came pouring out of the tilted forward stack, followed by the roar of escaping steam.

Marsh had heard that sound before, on *Winston*, and he knew what it meant. Everyone down there was probably dead, and *Evans* was now down to a single boiler back aft. The cloud of black oil-fired smoke coming out of the ruptured stack was enormous. The only good news was that the Japs were calling it a kill and had shifted targets.

He changed course again, but the ship was not responding as handily as she had been. The Jap cruisers were now mostly concentrating their guns on the two stragglers at the rear of the jeep formations. Both were smoking badly. Mount fifty-two stopped firing, as the gun crew had to let the ammo handlers down below catch up to their furious rate of fire. Mount fifty-one had gone silent on the sound-powered phone circuits and was still leaking smoke from every seam. It was then Marsh saw the through-and-through hole in the mount's side plating caused by an eight-inch round. If that one had exploded, it would likely have blown the ship's whole bow off. As it was, everyone in the mount was probably done for. *Evans* was running on borrowed time, and that thought made him sick. He realized that he was gripping his binoculars so hard that his hands hurt.

Then American planes began to show up as

Evans staggered away from her lopsided tête-à-tête with the cruiser line. He queried all stations to report damage while he watched a succession of planes roll in on the cruisers, dropping everything from bombs to what looked like depth charges. He didn't see much in the way of heavy damage, but the cruisers went into all sorts of evasive maneuvers trying to avoid getting hit, and two of them nearly collided. Marsh wondered where the planes had been all this time. Looking at his watch, he realized it had only been fifteen minutes since the action began. Time passes fast when you're having fun, he thought. At least the cruisers seemed more interested in the jeeps than in the tin cans, but then he remembered the battleships. He did a quick scan of the northwest horizon, and his heart sank. Not two battleships—three, still hull down on the horizon, but here they came, their forward turrets disappearing behind the fireballs of sixteen-inch salvos. He watched in horror as an entire salvo landed on one of the nearby American destroyers, obliterating it and seemingly everyone on board in a blinding second.

Time to find a rainsquall.

FOURTEEN

For the past ten days Mick and the other pilots in VC-Eleven had done some training missions, followed by the first softening-up raids behind the two main target beachheads on Leyte. They encountered no aerial resistance, and only sporadic flak from the Japanese army, which seemed to be melting into the jungles and leaving the beaches wide open for the anticipated landings.

Mick had just about gotten used to landing on the half-carrier deck. As Max had pointed out, the landing area was really no smaller than a fleet carrier's; it just ended at the bow instead of halfway up as it did on the big ones. A fleet carrier gave you the illusion that you had some margin for error, Max pointed out. The jeep made it clear you better know what you're doing. So far, the weather had been flat and calm. Mick wasn't looking forward to trying any of this in a real seaway.

In the wardroom that night there was lots of talk about a series of strikes carried out that day by the fast carrier striking forces up north of Leyte. Apparently the Japs had sortied from Borneo with some of their battleships but had been badly battered in the Sibuyan Sea west of Leyte. According to the radio scuttlebutt, the Helldivers had managed to sink the biggest battleship they'd ever seen. Now the big-decks were hauling ass up north chasing reports that the Nips' carrier fleet had come out to fight again. Halsey was apparently ready to make up for Spruance's much talked-about "failure" to get all the Jap carriers during the Philippine Sea battle. The pilots were all talking about it over coffee in the small wardroom.

"Seems to me," Max said, "if Spruance shot down all their carrier aircraft at the Turkey Shoot, who cares about their carriers?"

"What if they reloaded?" one of the other bomber guys asked.

"With what?" commented a fighter pilot. "More teenagers? Last Zero I went up against, the pilot looked twelve years old."

"You *saw* the pilot?"

"I T-boned his ass," the fighter jock said. "Saw his face just as his tail broke off. Looking at me in total shock. Then I killed him."

"There you go," Max said. "That's the important part."

"Halsey take the whole fleet with him?"

"Supposedly left the battleships behind, in case the Japs decided to make another try at Leyte."

The fighter pilot seemed surprised to hear that. "I was hanging on a CAP station this morning, northwest of here, up by Bernardino Strait? I didn't see any battleships."

"Probably out east, refueling. It makes sense that the Bull would leave them behind—battlewagons aren't much use when you're going after carriers."

"Hate to see one of theirs coming over the horizon," Mick said. "I've been on the receiving end of that shit. Really noisy."

They all laughed, then drifted off to their cabins. They would launch for the 0545 dawn GQ, then come back aboard for breakfast before heading over to the amphibious objective area gulf and their daily Army missions.

The next morning Mick went up to the flight deck from the wardroom for a cup of coffee and a cigarette topside after breakfast. The day was already warming up, with calm seas and scattered line squalls sweeping in toward distant Samar Island. There were five jeep carriers in their formation, scattered haphazardly with about five miles distance between ships to allow for unrestricted air traffic. Three destroyers and a lone destroyer escort were prowling around their stations outside of the carrier formation. The other thirteen escort carriers were out of sight to the southeast somewhere. *Madison Bay*'s group, known as Taffy Three, had the frontline support mission for the day. Taffy One and Two were offline, for the morning, anyway, but supposedly ready to launch whatever support might be needed ashore, be it fighters or bombers.

The Army had advanced inland from Leyte Gulf and finally run into real opposition in the hills behind the beaches. Mick anticipated a long day of dropping relatively small bombs on bunkers, while *Madison Bay*'s fighter guys would be loading up with rockets for essentially the same mission. The other CVEs would have already put up the CAP stations between the amphibious area and the main island of Luzon, from which land-based Jap air had been coming out in dribs and drabs to harass the invasion shipping.

Mick was settling into the routine and beginning to like his job again. The composite squadron was a mixed bag of nuggets and experienced fleet pilots who, for a variety of mostly unspoken reasons, had been eased out of their squadrons. Max, the skipper, called the gang the Untouchables, but that was a bit of an exaggeration. Everyone pretty much knew that the glory days with the big-decks were coming to a close; after Midway, the long, grinding, Solomons campaign, and then the recent Marianas Turkey Shoot, the big-decks were running out of worthy opponents. The real job from here on out was what Mick's squadron was doing, close air support of Army and Marine divisions ashore as they chewed up the islands in search of prospective long-range bomber bases close enough to start working over the Japanese homeland. For that, they needed numbers, and the shipyards at home had quit building big-decks and were now churning out dozens of the little carriers. As the crew said, the letters *CVE* stood for combustible, vulnerable, and expendable, but in a war of attrition, numbers counted.

Mick's plane was being refueled and armed up for the day's work. It was second in line for the lone catapult, and he watched as the shirts humped the small bombs onto their racks and fed shiny belts of fifty-cal into the wing guns. The rear gunner seat had been taken out to trade weight for ammo. His hand was throbbing a little this morning, and he'd already removed the glove to give it the ghoulish smell test. He'd taken to wearing the glove constantly to conceal the dark red skin; everyone knew about the problem, but no one said anything. As long as he could grab the stick and fly the plane, it was an entirely private matter. This morning the Hand, as he'd begun to call it in his mind, felt swollen, and the skin was tighter than usual. Some of the other pilots had some physical problems as well, and strangely, that seemed to cement the bonds within the Untouchables. One thing was obvious: There was none of the hypersensitivity to screwups that he had experienced on the big-decks. These little carriers were more like the tin can Navy.

Skinny Graham walked up, his face practically obscured by a big fat cigar.

" 'Nother fine Navy day," he commented.

"Yeah, buddy," Mick said. Skinny was overweight, which was hard to do on wartime chow. He had a big round face and a pleasantly hearty outlook on life. His fighter, an early model Hellcat, was the plane on the cat in front of Mick's barge.

"Ain't much wind," he noted. "Gonna shoot and droop this morning. Hear about the big fight down south last night?"

"Heard some guys talking in the wardroom about the Japs running into a buzz saw," Mick said. "What'd you hear?"

"Battleship fight," Skinny said. "Japs lost big."

"So our battleships *are* around," Mick said.

"These weren't Halsey's," Skinny said. "These were the old guard ships, the ones who got hit in Pearl. They raised some of 'em and put 'em back in service as shore-bomb platforms. They're too slow to run with the big-decks, but good enough to set up an ambush. It must have been a truly satisfying night's work."

"Isn't that something," Mick said. "I used to watch newsreels of the so-called battle line. Looked like a parade of dinosaurs. I guess Pearl was the end of an era for those things."

"You know what really hurt?" Skinny said. "The Japs used modified battleship shells to bomb those guys. Put fins on fourteen- and sixteen-inch armor-piercing shells, because that's what it took to get through their armor. In a way, they got sunk by their own kind."

Mick watched the red and white Fox flag travel halfway up the signal halyards atop the island, signaling that the ship was preparing to launch airplanes. The shirts had most of the planes' wings down and locked. The plane captains were walking around their grimy charges, making last-minute checks and wiping oil off the engine cowls, pulling tags, and cleaning windscreens. *Madison Bay* hadn't turned into what little wind there was yet, so Mick and Skinny walked over to one of the catwalk piss-tubes and anointed the deep blue sea one last time before strapping in for a three-hour close air support mission.

"What the hell's that?" Skinny asked as he was zipping up his flight suit.

Mick heard it, too, his brain telling him he'd heard that sound before but not yet being able to place it. In the next instant, three smallish splashes rose off the carrier's port side, which then turned into thundering eruptions of smoke and water, the edges of which were bright yellow.

"Holy *shit!*" Skinny said, as they stared at the enormous columns of water that were cascading back down to the surface a mere five hundred yards away. Mick was dimly aware that the ship's engines were turning up, and then the call for pilots to man their planes blasted over the topside speakers, followed by the GQ alarm. *All* pilots. On the double. Emergency launch.

Mick dropped his coffee mug into the catwalk and ran up three steps to the actual flight deck, sprinting for his Dauntless. The all-hands pipe was blaring again over the topside speakers, followed by the announcement that this was no drill. As Mick reached his plane, six more huge shell splashes erupted, this time in front of the little carrier, blasting red-dyed water a hundred feet into the air, close enough that Mick could feel the explosions through the wooden flight deck. Definitely no damned drill.

Skinny lumbered by him and was helped into his cockpit by three shirts. The carrier leaned over to starboard as she turned southeast into the prevailing wind, and Skinny, cussing a blue streak, almost tumbled out the other side of his cockpit.

By this time Mick was strapping in and starting up the engine. His brain had finally classified what he was seeing: battleship rounds. He'd done a quick horizon scan as the engine was turning up but could see nothing except distant rainsqualls. Then he remembered that the battleships could shoot from nearly eighteen miles away, and the visible horizon from a ship was only about eleven or twelve. He looked ahead as Skinny's fighter turned up, blowing clouds of blue and white smoke down the flight deck. Other planes behind him were also cranking up, and the carrier's slanted smokestacks were beginning to pour out thick coils of black smoke. The Fox flag snapped up into the two-block position, and the carrier leveled up as she came onto flight course. She was shaking. Mick realized he was, too.

Then Skinny was launching, accelerating in a ribbon of hydraulic mist down the cat track, disappearing for a few moments below the bow and then angling off to starboard at max power, his prop cutting visible spirals of moisture in the heavy tropical air. Just then three more shells came in. Two hit close aboard the port side, raising more of the towering shell splashes. Mick felt a double-thump through the landing gear. He looked over his shoulder and saw a commotion back on the flight deck. There was smoke starting to rise from the starboard side, but it was dirty brown, not oily black like the stuff coiling out of the stacks. He saw the flight deck medic crew racing aft, pushing their wheeled litters in front of them through the cluster of spinning propellers. Then the shirts were waving at him to mount the cat. He released the brakes and gunned the engine to move the Dauntless into position.

Battleships. *Jap* battleships. Right here?

Where in the hell had they come from? And where the hell were *our* battleships? Or, for that matter, Halsey's? If the jeeps were being chased by Jap battleships, there was going to be a real slaughter out here.

He snapped his chin strap and pulled the radio mike in front of his lips as the shirts hooked him up. There was already pandemonium on the land-launch circuit. Jap battleships approaching from the northwest. A line of Jap cruisers closing in from the northeast. The escorting tin cans had been ordered to make smoke and attack with torpedoes. The jeeps were getting rid of all their aircraft as fast they could, armed or not.

He checked in with PriFly. The air boss told him to switch to Tactical Four as soon as he'd launched, gaggle up with the rest of the squadron once they got off, and then go out there and get those bastards. Sounds like a worried man, Mick thought. With good reason. *Madison Bay* was in the back of the pack, along with *Gambier Bay*. More shell splashes erupted out of the flat gray sea, clawing ever closer to the fleeing carriers.

The cat officer was signaling him to run it up. He checked his straps, did a quick scan of the gauges, made sure his flaps were set, pressed hard on the brakes, and ran the mill up to full power. Another gauge scan, everything at twelve o'clock. He grabbed the stick, sending an unusual lance of pain up his right wrist. He cycled the stick, looking left and right to confirm that the control surfaces were responding, then centered it. He looked right to the cat officer, saluted him,

417

grabbed the stick again, took a deep breath, and held it. An instant later he was hurtling over the bow at just over a hundred knots. His head and body jerked forward in the harness as the g's came off, and then he nursed the Dauntless into a gentle climb after his airspeed built up.

Go get the bastards? With what, two hundred-pound bombs and fifty-cal? He switched to Tactical Four and found Skinny already up.

"Where are they?" he asked.

"Three one zero," Skinny said. "There's a whole shitpot full of 'em, too, and one of 'em's a real monster. Form on me until Max gets up. Angels eight."

As he gained altitude he could begin to see the big picture. Below him the little carriers were running for their lives, spitting off airplanes as fast as they could while dodging salvos from the distant battleships. His own carrier was leaving two trails of smoke, one on purpose, to obscure themselves from distant range finders, and one that indicated she'd been hit. As he watched *Madison Bay* weaving through the white circles of previous shell splashes, nine shells erupted around her, two close enough to obscure the flight deck in cascading sheets of water. She turned slightly in the direction of the center of the pattern, desperately trying to avoid the next salvo.

From a mile and a half in the air, he could

clearly make out two groups of enemy ships. One line of several medium-sized warships was steaming to the east by southeast, as if trying to get ahead of the fleeing Kaiser Coffins and box them in. They were all leaving broad white wakes behind them and firing their forward turrets as they came. If those were heavy cruisers, Mick thought, they'd catch the jeeps in about twenty, maybe thirty minutes, close in to point-blank range, and tear them apart with eight-inch.

Some distance behind the cruiser line there were two, no, three very large ships, whose features were indistinguishable in the hazy air. Then he saw what looked like a few dozen destroyers trailing behind them. Those had to be battleships, Mick thought, as he saw the red winks of their muzzle blasts envelop them in smoke. He also saw the American escorting destroyers, each streaming heavy smoke to further obscure the jeeps, heading in all directions but mostly northerly, running at high speed. Mick shook his head in wonder: What were they going to do when they got there?

The skipper finally came up on Tactical Four.

"Okay, you guys, we can't wait for the whole gang. Forget the battlewagons—we can't hurt them with these popcorn bombs. We might be able to give those cruisers a bloody nose, though. Any more bombers up?"

Two more Dauntless pilots checked in. Max,

who was flying a fighter armed with rockets, told Mick to take charge of the bombers and to roll in on the lead cruiser. He'd take the fighters to the rear of the cruiser column and make a rocket attack.

"Drop your whole load, guys, and then make one more pass with fifties. Aim for those pagoda structures. Kill the bridge officers, maybe we can slow 'em up."

"Roger that, Skipper," Mick said. "But these little bombs aren't going to do shit."

"We're buyin' time here, Mick. *They* don't know you've got little bombs."

"Wilco," Mick said and then shifted his three-pack of Dauntless dive bombers onto Tactical Two. He gave a quick briefing for the two nuggets who were flying against the Jap varsity for the very first time.

"They've covered their topside decks with twenty-five-millimeter guns for AA work," he told them. "That's like a fifty-cal times two. We'll roll in from ahead. Try to pull out directly on top—don't get out on either side, because that's where the teeth are."

"Pickle when?"

"Angels three," Mick said. "If your guns bear, shoot while you're pulling out. It keeps the AA crews occupied. Arm your toys."

Four minutes later they arrived within gun range of the lead heavy cruiser, whose forward turrets were firing perfectly timed salvos at the distant CVE formation. They knew they were in AA gun range because tracers began reaching for them through the patchy clouds below. As they circled into attack position, Mick switched back to Tactical Four and told Max they were rolling in on the lead cruiser.

"Roger that," Max called. "Boss says they've been hit three times and are losing way. She may not be there when we get back, so we may have to go find Taffy Two."

"You got pigeons?"

"Boss says pigeons to Taffy Two are one three zero for forty miles," Max said. "He *thinks,* anyway. We're right behind you, going for tail-end Charlie."

"Roger, roger, here we go," Mick said and switched back to Tactical Two. "Okay, Breakfast Clubbers, on your backs, on your bellies, aiming for the anchors."

Mick rolled inverted and began pulling on the stick as the horizon spun in his windshield. Sky-sea horizon line, then all sea, then black dashes with white wakes, each dash getting bigger as the altimeter unwound. When his nose was settled on the bow of the lead ship, now easily defined as a heavy cruiser busy shooting at his carrier, he split his flaps to steady the dive and concentrated on the pointy end. No circling carriers here, just a sleek-looking cruiser focused on carrier-killing while sending streams of hot red and white tracers up in his direction.

At five thousand feet he dropped the nose sharply and then at three thousand pickled his load of baby bombs. He had to pull hard to avoid driving his Dauntless through their bridge windows. As the g's built up he struggled to keep his injured hand tight on the stick, and then he felt a popping under his glove and a sensation of wetness that hadn't been there when he started down. For a brief instant the pagoda bridge structure had been visible, and he'd fired a burst from his fifties for as long as he could see it. His eyeballs were dragging under the g-load, so he couldn't tell if he'd hit anything.

He pulled out no more than five hundred feet over the cruiser. He couldn't see what if any effect his bombs had had, but it hardly mattered. Even if he had hit her, they'd mostly bounce off, with maybe a few topside AA gunners out of action if one dropped directly on a gun tub. He flew a jinking pattern straight out the cruiser's wake and then realized he was headed right for the next one. He saw a fighter drop out of the sky and unleash a barrage of five-inch rockets at the back of the cruiser line before pulling left out of his dive and right into the cruiser's full starboard-side AA barrage. An instant later he went into the sea in a ball of fire.

Mick had one split second to decide: Strafe

number two or pull out? He jinked right and pulled up, not knowing whether or not there were more fighters rolling in on the column. One of the nuggets came up on Tac Four.

"You hit him and I hit him, Mick," he said, "but he's still crankin'."

"Follow me back up," Mick said. "Angels eight. Where's Benny?"

"Right here, Mick. You guys started a fire, but she's still bangin' away down there. We gonna hit her again?"

"You bet," Mick said. "Same deal—come in from dead ahead, strafe her ass down the whole length. Then we'll go find us some real bombs."

They regrouped at eight thousand feet, out of range of most of the twenty-five-millimeter AA that was still streaming off the two cruisers. The lead cruiser had a fire going amidships, but it didn't look too serious. The second cruiser had fallen out of line for some reason and was no longer firing at the jeeps, but the next three in the line were blazing away. Mick could still see those much larger ships in the distance to the northwest, black blobs that flashed yellow and red once a minute like some lethal clockwork.

It took three minutes to get back into position to reattack the lead cruiser. Mick examined his right hand. There was watery-looking blood leaking out of his glove and down his right forearm. He considered taking the glove off but then thought better of it. Strangely, now it didn't hurt very much.

"Okay, boys," he said. "Roll in, steady up as soon as you can, and start shooting at three thousand feet. Short bursts until you're on target, then give it to 'em. Pull out on the deck and fly a snake dance straight down the wake. Gaggle-up at angels eight."

Mick put his right hand back on the stick. It felt spongy now, but at least it gripped the stick when he told it to. He slipped his oxygen mask aside for a moment and took a sniff. For the first time, he detected the odor of rot. He'd never smelled gangrene before, but, as in one's first encounter with a rattlesnake, he recognized it when he smelled it.

That's not good, he thought, but then had to start jinking hard to avoid a barrage of banging AA shells.

He went back on the mask and rolled in again. It seemed a little easier this time, and from ahead, anyway, there also seemed to be less AA fire. He could see smoke arising from amidships on his target, but it was white, not black. Something combustible but not vital. Or maybe steam?

He took it down to two thousand instead of three. He'd told the nuggets to start shooting at three to give them time to get their lineup right. He had done this before. He waited until he was about a mile and a half in front of the cruiser and

424

then opened up full throttle, walking the short-burst shell splashes from his fifties from the water directly in front of her bow and then across her foredeck and into that weird, castle-like structure of her forward superstructure. He held the stream of tracers for a dangerous few seconds right at the level of the bridge windows, watching the rounds pummel the glass and seeing ricochets flashing out the bridge wings from inside. At the last possible moment he flipped the Dauntless on her side and flew past the bridge of the ship in a full left-ninety bank to avoid collision. He blasted out from behind the cruiser and then dropped down to the deck, jinking hard right and then left to avoid the sudden stream of AA tracers. He heard a couple of pings on the hull of the aircraft and actually felt something hit the armored seat back, but then he was clear and climbing back for altitude.

While he waited for the nuggets, he switched frequencies and called Max. There was no answer. He tried the other fighters, but they weren't up, either. He checked the radio dial to make sure he'd picked the right freq and then went back to his nuggets. They were still with him.

"I can't raise the skipper," Mick said. "So let's go back to mother and see if she's still floating. If not, we'll go find Taffy Two and rearm."

They rogered as they formed up on him. Both

declared that they were out of gun ammo. Down below the first cruiser was still going, but her guns had, for now anyway, fallen silent. The tail-end cruiser, which Max and his fighters had rocketed, was headed northeast, apparently out of the fight for the moment. Mick couldn't see any smoke or fires, but she was definitely leaving the party. He looked for the *Madison Bay* up ahead but was unable to pick her out among the jeeps, who were still going as fast as they could to the east-southeast, pursued by shell splashes and clouds of funnel smoke. Mick switched to *Madison Bay*'s land-launch and called the tower.

Nothing.

Then he saw her, way behind the other CVEs. She was aflame from one end to the other and rolling over on her beam ends. He could see her hull number, emblazoned on the flight deck, through all the smoke. Two cruisers had closed into close range and were sportingly firing into the hulk as little black dots dropped into the sea from her side. He looked for *Gambier Bay*, the other jeep at the back of the formation, but couldn't find her.

The three other carriers were still steaming south of east, out of the wind now, trying to put as much distance as they could between themselves and the wolves pursuing them. Mick realized there'd be no landing on any of them, and he still didn't know exactly where the other Taffys were, or if they even knew what was going on back near Leyte Gulf. If he and his two nuggets took off on an Easter egg hunt, they could be out of the game for more than an hour.

"You guys know how to get to Tacloban?" Mick asked. They both rogered in the affirmative. The Army had captured that airfield a day after the initial landings. It was tiny, but they could get fuel and fifty-cal there, if nothing else.

"I've still got plenty of guns left. You guys head to Tacloban, get what you can, and get back out here."

"Where you goin'?" Benny asked.

"Back down to break some more windows."

Mick bent the Dauntless back down toward the Jap ships. His two wingmen rolled southwest to head for the Army airfield, which was actually inside Leyte Gulf. Mick saw the lead Jap cruisers leave *Madison Bay* to her fate and train their guns on the next nearest CVE, which was already making smoke from places other than her stacks. To the northwest he saw the battleships coming on through the line of squalls, getting bigger and bigger. Seeing that no one was shooting at him, Mick began a slow climb to get some more diving room and to take another look at his right hand.

Holding his stick with his knees as the Dauntless went up, he gingerly removed the sopping wet leather glove and sighed. The skin on the back of his hand had split like an overripe tomato, with deep cracks running all the way out to his knuckles. He could actually see tendons and the big vein that snaked across the back. Strangely, he felt no pain other than a general soreness, but then he saw what looked like a jagged red tattoo running up the underside of his forearm. He cracked his mask and then slid it right back on his face. No doubt about it—the gangrene monster had him by the arm, and that red snake progressing up his arm was not his friend.

He tried to get the glove back on, but that was hopeless. He scanned the instruments. Fuel, good enough. All the other dials were still standing at twelve o'clock, indicating ops normal. He knew the plane had been hit, but the nuggets hadn't warned him of a fuel or oil stream, so he didn't think he was leaking anything volatile, and the controls still worked. He had himself, probably one-third of his fifty-cal left, a working barge, and the world's supply of fat targets.

What more could I want? he asked himself with a grin. Pick one, go get it.

Piece'a cake, he thought, remembering the major. He would have loved this shit. His right hand felt like a warm sponge. He decided to ignore it.

FIFTEEN

A really dark rainsquall was blowing across the sea to their west, and Marsh turned *Evans* toward it to try to hide for a few minutes. They slipped into the welcome obscurity of tropical rain, although the ship was making so much black smoke he wondered if the Japs couldn't still see them. Apparently they could. Another salvo of eight-inch came howling through the rainsquall and thankfully went long. The steam leak from the forward fireroom was diminishing as the boiler emptied itself. Marsh prayed that all that steam was coming up through the stack; otherwise, his whole forward fireroom crew had been roasted at six hundred degrees. A shell would have been kinder.

Reports came in from the gunnery department. They'd lost mounts fifty-one and fifty-three. All the topside AA gun stations on the starboard side were reporting heavy casualties. Marsh knew that the forward fireroom had to be permanently out of commission. Damage control central reported that a DC team was still trying to get down into the space to determine how bad the situation was. Main control had cross-connected the forward engine room with the after fireroom, so they still had two engines, but no longer twenty-seven knots' worth until they could get a second boiler going in the after fireroom. From the feel of the ship, any fires still burning in the forward boiler room were being smothered by inrushing seawater. Marsh called main control and reminded them to shore up their forward bulkhead. They said they were already doing it.

The rabbi came into the pilothouse with a preliminary casualty report. His uniform was blood-spattered, not from injuries but from assisting in the wardroom, which was now the ship's principal casualty station. Twenty-seven known dead, that many again wounded seriously enough to be out of action. For once he was not smiling, and neither was Marsh. He said he was going back down the starboard side to tend to the wounded still in their gun tubs. Marsh told him to keep undercover as best he could, because *Evans* wasn't done with this fight yet. He nodded somberly, handed Marsh the blood-spattered casualty list, and then tried to get off the bridge without slipping on all the blood on deck.

Evans had expended six of her ten torpedoes and still had three five-inch guns out of five operational, although with an as yet unknown number of personnel casualties. Marsh was sorely tempted to just hide in the rainsquall for a while until they could get themselves back together.

Then he remembered the battleships.

He brought the ship about, slowing down to fifteen knots to ease the pressure on the snipes, who were trying desperately to get the remains of the steam plant stable again. They emerged from the rainsquall to a depressing tableau. Another of their tin cans was in the process of capsizing about five miles away. The Jap cruiser line was still pressing in on the fleeing jeep carrier formation, although they were now being swarmed by aircraft who were doing everything from dropping tiny foxhole busters to making strafing runs. The jeeps, like the old battleships, had been loaded out for close air support work at Leyte, not a fleet action, so the planes were reduced to doing whatever they could. Marsh didn't see any sign of the other destroyers, but much of the sea area was obscured by the remains of chemical smoke clouds and rainsqualls.

One of the jeeps, probably *Gambier Bay*, was burning from midships to stern and dead in the water some ten miles distant. Another ship, whose identity he couldn't make out, was also stopped and completely afire. Then he swung the binoculars around to the northwest to see where the battleships had gone.

Unfortunately, nowhere.

He lowered his binoculars to see two behemoths, followed distantly by their own pack of destroyers, lumbering in his direction while still lofting booming salvos at the jeeps. The only good news was that they, too, were being swarmed by naval aircraft. Marsh thought he'd seen three, maybe four battleships originally, but now he wasn't sure how many there were. Two were bad enough.

"Time to get the hell out of here, XO," a voice at his elbow said quietly. Marsh turned around. It was John Hennessy, staring at the oncoming battleships through his binoculars.

Just then, as if to make his point, three enormous explosions shook the ship as one of the battleships dropped a salvo two hundred yards short and directly abeam. The water columns from the shell splashes were higher than *Evans*'s masthead. The Japs were ranging on the ship with one turret. Once they got a hit, they'd let fly with all six guns and obliterate *Evans* and all her works. Marsh immediately ordered a left standard rudder to put the ship in a turn away from the enemy and back into the rainsquall.

"Think we can outrun *that* with only one boiler and a fireroom full of water?" he asked.

"We can try," Hennessy said. He wasn't kidding. He was pleading.

Marsh was certainly tempted. They'd done what the admiral had told them to do. They'd run straight in against outrageous odds, conducted a torpedo attack that had momentarily disrupted the Jap attack, and actually hit one cruiser. *Evans* was down to half propulsion power and two-thirds of her gun capability. The starboard-side main deck was awash in body parts among the forty- and twenty-millimeter ranks. The cruisers had beaten the hell out of them and sunk at least two brother destroyers, and now there were two battleships coming, one of which was taking an unholy interest in *Evans.*

Marsh looked around the pilothouse. The door to the chartroom was wedged open, and the deck inside the tiny passageway was covered in gore. The bridge 1JV talker's body had been wedged between the helm and lee helm, and the looks on his remaining bridge crew's faces clearly indicated their votes.

Unfortunately, at that precise moment, he could visualize Beast McCarty, sitting there on the O-club steps. *You're scared, aren't you? You've always been scared. This war is man's work. Warrior's work. One day you'll meet the elephant, and personally I think you'll fuck it up.*

He now fully understood what the Civil War soldiers had been talking about when they talked about facing battle, the elephant of the expression: certain death in the form of two black castles of steel, whose hulls were beginning to fill the view from what was left of their bridge windows. Mick hadn't mentioned that they might come in herds.

Hennessy saw that Marsh was thinking about

433

it. The torpedo officer stuck his head into the pilothouse, waiting for orders.

"XO, we *gotta* get out of here," Hennessy said.

Marsh bit his lip. God knows, he thought—I want to escape, too.

You're scared, aren't you? Scared every day you're out there with the Big Blue Fleet. Been scared since you first went to sea.

Yes, I am, he thought. Scared shitless. He took a deep breath.

"We have four fish left?" he asked, after giving the helmsman another course change. Never fly straight in a dogfight. Keep her weaving.

Hennessy's eyes widened, and he swallowed hard. "Um, yes, sir."

"Go into Combat, get us in position for a torpedo attack."

"Attack?" he said, his voice rising to a squeak.

"This is why we're out here, John," Marsh said as gently as he could, trying to keep the fear out of his own voice. "I don't know what that real big one out there is, but it's our duty to at least give him a bloody nose."

Hennessy gave him an agonized look. "Captain, that's fucking suicide," he whispered.

Now it was Captain, no longer XO, Marsh noticed. "No, John," he said. "It's our *duty.* Coming down here in the first place—that was suicide."

He turned to the men in the pilothouse, who'd been listening to all this and were white-faced with fear. Marsh suspected he was white-faced, too, but this wasn't the time to acknowledge it, not to all these terrified kids in front of him. "This is the captain," he announced, "and I have the deck and the conn. Helmsman, left standard rudder."

He looked back at Hennessy. "Get back down there. We'll shoot to port."

Hennessy backed away from him as if Marsh were truly insane, but then discipline asserted itself and he went back down to Combat, tiptoeing across the mess in the charthouse passageway. Marsh told the helmsman to steady up while he studied the relative motion of the two battlewagons, which were getting bigger by the moment. The leader was a type he'd never seen in their enemy warship recognition charts. The second in line was one of their older battle cruisers, modified to become a battleship, a Kongo class, with fourteen-inch guns. She was the one interested in *Evans*, and he saw her forward turret flash again in their direction. He put the rudder over, in the opposite direction this time, and hoped their maneuvers, lame as they were, were confounding the Jap's firing solution. *Evans* felt even heavier in her guts now. He had to assume the forward fireroom was almost fully flooded. The DC teams still hadn't managed to get into the wrecked compartment, and the black smoke rolling out of the bent-over number one stack was getting thicker. He visualized burning fuel oil floating on the rising waters in the fireroom.

Three more shell splashes, this time long. As a gunnery officer, he knew what they were doing. Shoot deliberately long in range, then short, cut the difference between the two range settings in half, and fire again. Do that often enough, you'll walk your shell pattern right onto the target.

He turned *Evans* again, and this time steadied up on his best guess for an intercept course on the lead battleship. He went out onto the port bridge wing and swept the sea with his binoculars. He couldn't see any of the other destroyers or the jeeps.

Evans was all alone. He felt his guts clench. Alone and taking on a battleship. He did see two of the distant heavy cruisers coming about in their direction. The admiral on the lead Jap battleship must have called for reinforcements when he saw *Evans* make that turn toward them, because, for some strange reason, he'd left all his own screening destroyers way behind him.

Marsh called down to Combat, telling them again they'd be firing torpedoes to port and asking them to compute an intercept course on the lead battleship, which was still lobbing main battery salvos at the jeeps.

"*Intercept,* Captain?" Hennessy called back. Marsh wondered if he was losing it.

"Yes—I want to lay her right alongside the big guy. It's the only safe place out here."

That provoked a stunned silence in Combat and also out on the bridge. One of the bosuns was calmly swabbing the deck where the phone talker had exsanguinated. They'd moved his body now to the back wall of the pilothouse. It was one more surreal sight that morning, a nineteen-year-old sailor in his battle helmet and kapok with swab in hand, mopping up the slippery blood, while outside another salvo of fourteen-inch shells walked even closer to the ship, this time shaking *Evans* from stem to stern. The shell splashes were so enormous that a fine rain seemed to be falling. Marsh made another course change, doing it randomly now, hoping the probabilities would work in their favor for a little while longer, long enough for them to get the last of their torpedoes away.

Marsh called the chief engineer, Kit Carson, down in main control. "Tell DC central to forget number one fireroom," he ordered. "I need all the turns you can give me, and I want a full team stationed in after steering, right now."

"Aye, Cap'n," Carson called back. "We're shoring both bulkheads, fore and aft of one-fireroom. I think she's flooded to the waterline—we're starting to get water through some of the overhead cableways."

"All right. I can feel it up here, too. We're

going in on a torpedo attack against a Jap heavy, so it's gonna get noisy again."

"Give 'em hell, Cap'n," he called back. No more XO, Marsh noticed again. When you're putting everyone's life on the line, they don't call you XO. Even the snipes knew what was coming. He could just imagine the chatter going on through the ship's many sound-powered phone circuits.

At that moment an entire line of relatively smaller shell splashes erupted around them. Marsh looked over the bow to see that the two heavy cruisers, closing in echelon formation to clear their firing arcs, were inbound with visible white bones in their teeth as they increased speed. Apparently the Jap battleship admiral had figured out what *Evans* intended by turning toward his column.

Marsh brought the ship farther to the right to keep a steady bearing, decreasing range on the lead battleship, which appeared to be doing close to thirty knots. With their limited speed he had to take a broad angle of approach to intercept, and this exposed more and more of *Evans* to more and more heavy guns. He saw the massive after turret of the monster swinging to face the *Evans* as she closed in. He called out to the torpedo officer that he wanted to fire torpedoes at four thousand yards, assuming they made it in that close. The remaining five-inch guns opened up at about that time and began firing at the lead battleship. The second battlewagon, the Kongo class who'd been ranging on at *Evans*, was still just beyond their effective five-inch range. His guns did not have a range problem, and at that moment the ship managed to drive right into the Kongo's range notch.

One fourteen-inch shell took care of the leaning forward smokestack by smacking it right over the side with a loud clang. A second punched into the hull just above the waterline, going right through the already wrecked forward fireroom and out the other side without exploding. Battleship projectiles were designed with fuzes that delayed the explosion until the shell had penetrated the target battleship's armor. *Evans* didn't have any armor.

A third round came through the portside wall of the pilothouse, obliterated the torpedo officer and both his enlisted men, wrecked the steering and engine-order telegraph, and amputated Marsh's right foot before smashing out the starboard side, taking most of the starboard bridge wing with it. Just as Marsh had predicted to the chief engineer, it was really noisy.

He had been sitting in his chair, leaning over the bitch-box to hear above the wind noise coming across the bridge and the sudden racket from their one operational forward mount, which was only fifteen feet away. His right foot had been pointed back behind the footrest so he could reach the face of the bitch-box. He never felt a thing, other than just a sudden pressure on his foot. He was as stunned by the sight of the two torpedomen literally exploding into a bloody blur as he was by the fact that he'd been hit, too. He turned in his chair, pulled up his right leg, and saw that everything below the ankle was gone, with only the top part of his black uniform sock still hanging on to his shin over a bright white bone. It was bleeding, but not as much as he would have expected.

"Six thousand yards, Cap'n," John Hennessy called from Combat. "Still want to wait?"

"Not anymore," Marsh called back, his voice suddenly weaker than before. "Tell the torpedo mount captain he has control. Let 'em go as soon as he's on solution. Fire two, wait thirty seconds, and then recompute if the target turns before shooting the other two. Set 'em deep, now—twenty feet."

The ship's junior pharmacist's mate came out of the haze of smoke and dust swirling about the pilothouse and knelt down by the captain's chair, his hands full of bandages. He ignored the human debris in which he was kneeling. Before Marsh could say anything, the corpsman jabbed a morphine syringe into his right thigh, applied a tourniquet below his knee, and then started wrapping the stump. Marsh still had experienced no pain from getting hit, but the moment the corpsman touched it he surely did.

He looked back through the bridge window openings while the GQ bridge team tried to reconstitute itself. They could no longer steer from the bridge so he shifted steering control back to the after steering compartment, relaying his conning orders through a sound-powered phone. Marsh knew he wasn't going to send any more engine orders other than what he'd already told the snipes: Crank the throttles open and leave 'em there. He tried to gather his wits and absorb the tactical situation, but it was hard. They were, despite the massive hits, still closing on that lead battlewagon, and she was getting bigger by the moment. The cruisers were firing at them again, but in a few minutes they'd have to stop or risk hitting their own flagship, assuming *Evans* stayed afloat long enough to get to the launch point.

Marsh heard the reassuring sound of two torpedoes going over the side above the banging of mount fifty-two, which was now landing hits on the big guy's towering pagoda superstructure. The after mounts were working him over, too, pelting the huge black mass of armored steel with their peashooters. Marsh thought he saw a couple of planes swooping down on him, but the battleship's AA fire was going like gangbusters, keeping most of the planes at bay. Where oh where was Halsey with all those brand-new Iowa-class battleships?

Another salvo of fourteen-inchers came howling in all around them, with one hitting the forecastle. The shock detached their remaining anchor, which went over the side in a rattling cloud of dust and perhaps ten shots of chain before the detachable links broke. The only thing keeping them alive was that these huge shells, designed for long-range artillery duels with another battleship, were still punching through *Evans*'s thin skin without going off. Marsh could barely see the Kongo, though, because his line of sight was being obscured by the fact that *Evans* was getting very close to the lead battleship, so close that his secondary batteries, five- and six-inchers, were opening up on *Evans* even as the monster began to turn away from their torpedoes.

Turning.

His mind was getting a little fuzzy not to have noticed that, probably from the morphine.

The battleship was turning away, and he'd stopped firing on the jeeps out on the horizon. Okay, Marsh thought. That's what they sent us out to do. He yelled into the bitch-box to tell CIC that the target was coming to port.

"We see it on the track, Captain," Hennessy called back.

Two eight-inch rounds hit forward, punching yet another hole in poor old mount fifty-one. The

442

second round hit somewhere underneath the bridge, probably in the in-port cabin, and this one did go off, with enough force to hump the bridge's deck up a foot or so, knock everyone off his feet, and shake Marsh's chair into a momentary spin.

He called back a new course to after steering, aiming to cut across the turning battleship's wake and then come around to match his course and get as close to him as they could, forcing the other enemy ships to stop firing at them for fear of hitting what had to be their flagship. Though making more knots than *Evans* was, his speed of advance slowed markedly when he went into his turn as that huge multileveled pagoda superstructure began to lean out over the water. Marsh could actually see the battle-wagon's enormous optical range finder way up on the tower, turning to stay on whatever target his main battery guns were working.

Their first two torpedoes had gone past him by a wide margin, as Marsh halfway expected, but they got the opportunity of a lifetime when he made that turn. Marsh heard their last two fish go off the starboard side at about two thousand yards range. As *Evans* closed in on his mile-wide wake, Marsh waited with his heart in his throat to see if they hit him. Then he saw the first fish broach as it encountered the huge ship's underwater pressure wave. It literally leaped out

443

of the water and went off on the side armor belt, making a big bang but not doing any visible damage. The second one hit him farther aft on the starboard side and produced a satisfying, thumping waterspout.

Ninety seconds later *Evans* cut across the battlewagon's wake. Marsh ordered hard right rudder to take station on the battleship's port quarter, where he then maneuvered to match the giant's wide, sweeping left turn back to the northeast. There now erupted a hot duel between every gun they had and every gun the Japs could point down, which thankfully did not include his after main battery turret, whose muzzles had appeared to be as big as the Lincoln Tunnel.

Marsh knew that once *Evans* steadied up on whatever course the looming battleship was coming to, he would soon draw away from them, and then they'd pop out from the big ship's shadow and become easy meat for the waiting Kongo. For an exhilarating few minutes, though, the tattered remains of their starboard-side twenties and forties fired round after round into his top hampers and his deck-mounted AA gun mounts. The *Evans* gunners could shoot up, but the Japanese could not shoot down. Even his bigger, six-inch secondary guns, designed mainly for antiaircraft work, could not depress low enough to get at *Evans*, although they tried plenty hard. There was an infernal blizzard of white-hot steel sizzling through the air above *Evans*, while her AA crews blasted away at his lightly armored AA gun mounts. Mount fifty-two, firing in local control now, took it as a personal mission to shoot up the towering heights of the pagoda structure. Marsh had visions of their bridge and staff people all lying flat on the deck from the hail of steel, and then a Jap twenty-five-millimeter managed to rake *Evans*'s bridge, and Marsh joined what was left of *his* bridge team on the deck until one of *Evans*'s forty-millimeters silenced the offending fire.

Marsh clawed his way back up into the captain's chair, which seemed the best place for him to be with one foot gone. The Kongo was visible about five miles behind them on *Evans*'s port quarter, coming to his left. Marsh told the torpedo mounts to train out in his direction. The Kongo must have been watching, because he put his rudder over at once and came back right, disappearing out of Marsh's sight behind the blocky stern cranes of their new formation partner. *Evans*'s five-inch guns had started a big fire on the battleship's fantail with a hit among his scout planes and catapults, although Marsh knew that wouldn't pose any real danger to this giant. Their lone torpedo hit hadn't even slowed him down. Then he felt a large thump way back near the stern, followed by another and another.

It took him a minute to figure it out: The gunners on the fantail were rolling depth charges, set at fifty feet, alongside the battleship. It was the equivalent of a five-hundred-pound bomb achieving a near miss deep along his port side. The charges were, however, also banging the hell out of the emergency steering team, so Marsh ordered them to knock it off.

At that moment one of the jeep carrier planes came out of the morning sun from low ahead and strafed the pagoda structure of the battleship. Some of the ricochets hit *Evans*'s own superstructure, but Marsh didn't mind too much. He could see their guy's shells and tracers slashing into the battleship's upper command and control levels. Definitely some Jap-burger being made up there, he thought. The plane shot overhead and banked hard, obviously intending to do it again, this time from the big guy's port side. Marsh weakly cheered him on, and then he disappeared behind that pagoda tower. Marsh caught a brief glimpse of something white painted on his fuselage, something besides the white star emblem. He wondered if it could be Beast. Machine-gunning a battleship would be right up Mick's alley.

As Marsh had anticipated, the battleship was steadying up now and beginning to pull ahead. This meant that those two cruisers would soon get a clear shot and be on them like a tiger.

Marsh wished they had more torpedoes, more ammo, more speed, but the truth was that *Evans*'s time on this earth was about up. Along with his own, he realized. As the battleship's massive stern pulled ahead up their starboard side, mount fifty-two finally ran out of ammunition with one last hit up on the battleship's searchlight platforms. The moment *Evans* emerged from her protective shadow, Marsh could see the two heavy cruisers dead astern coming on like black panthers, their forward eight-inch turrets training out over their starboard bows to begin the end of *Evans* as he watched.

Then another Jap cruiser came sailing in from the monster's *starboard* side. Marsh hadn't even seen her coming, but her intent was pretty clear: Cross perpendicular to the battleship's wake and then open an enfilading fire on *Evans* with every one of her eight-inchers. Now Marsh knew what the French admiral Villeneuve must have been thinking when he saw Lord Nelson's massive *Victory* sliding past, perpendicular to his flagship's stern, preparing to rake him from one end to the other.

Lie down, he thought. Lie down. But he was too tired now to get out of his chair.

Mick overshot the clutch of cruisers and was closing in on what he now confirmed as two battleships, followed by some destroyers with maybe a couple of cruisers in that mix, too. He fastened his attention on the biggest battlewagon, which looked to be nearly a thousand feet long. At the very least she was longer than one of the American big-deck carriers, and her forward turrets were belching out flame and smoke in the general direction of the jeep formation way off to the southeast. So far, however, Mick wasn't seeing any flak. Maybe they hadn't spotted his lone Dauntless approaching their formation. I'd give my right hand for a thousand-pounder about now, he thought. Or maybe my left—nobody'd want my right paw just now. Then he laughed and rolled in on the big bastard from ten thousand feet.

As he began his dive, he noticed something strange: The battleship seemed to have another ship close aboard on her port side. Dropping through the layers of light cloud, he could see his target and then he couldn't, but he would have sworn the little ship was firing at the big ship, reminiscent of the days when sailing ships went muzzle to muzzle at a hundred yards. Was that an American tin can? He focused on the big boy. He began to see some tracers coming his way from encased AA guns mounted right under that huge pagoda structure, but they had miscalculated his dive speed. He was flying with his left hand now. He'd balled what was left of his right hand around the sodden glove, holding the mess in his lap.

Finally he began the pullout, and started shooting when his gun sight crossed that enormous gilded chrysanthemum sculpture welded across the battleship's bullnose. He saw his own tracers ricocheting off the slabbed steel sides of the forward gun turrets, then the base of the pagoda, and then, as he pulled harder, into the lower-level bridge windows and then on up toward the director before he busted the stick hard left and slid by the towering pagoda, going so fast that he nearly rolled a three-sixty.

Two guns, shooting seven hundred and fifty rounds per minute, two dozen rounds per second, and he'd probably been on target for three, maybe four seconds. So, what did that make it: seventy rounds of fifty-caliber armor-piercing incendiary tracer blasting around the confines of the bridge levels. Had to have scared 'em at the very least, he thought.

He zoomed out behind the battleship far enough to get away from the stern twenty-five-millimeter mounts and then was surprised to see three enormous explosions blossom about two miles in front of him, low over the water, sending a forest of shell splashes rising through the smoke cloud.

My God, he thought, they're shooting some kind of AA ammo out of their main battery. He jinked hard right and began to climb. He hadn't seen the telltale you're-almost-empty solid stream of tracers coming out of his own guns, which meant he still had some rounds left. As he turned to the right he was able to make out the American ship that was still alongside the battlewagon, close enough to refuel, both of them going full bore across the rain-flattened sea in a broad left turn. It was definitely an American destroyer, its topsides shot all to hell, one stack gone, the radar antenna hanging off the yardarm, but most of its guns pointed up at the superstructure of the black giant and blasting away, tearing pieces of steel out of the pagoda and shredding whole AA gun mounts along the edge of the main deck.

"Get 'em, tiger!" he yelled, watching all the Jap's portside AA gunners clawing steel for cover what with all that five-inch going off up and down the decks from point-blank range. He turned hard, dropped back down to two hundred feet, and came in from the battlewagon's port side, leveling off at about the height of the navigation bridge. He bore in to just over a mile and began shooting, this time putting the tracer stream through the bridge compartments. He was actually able to see the tracer rounds ricocheting around inside the pagoda as they hit the centerline armored tower and bounced off. As he blew past the face of the pagoda, he felt multiple hammers on his right wing; a twenty-five AA gun had found his range on the way out. Something bumped his right leg, hard, twice.

It wasn't coming from the battleship, though. There was a heavy cruiser racing in as if to intercept the big ship's wake. Mick realized that the little destroyer was about to have company in the form of ten eight-inch guns that would be able to shoot parallel to the battleship's side and absolutely rake the tin can. As he turned again, weaving in and out of intensifying AA fire, he felt a strange heaviness in his right side and looked down for a moment. He could not quite comprehend what he was seeing.

His right leg was lying on the floor of the cockpit, severed at the knee by a twenty-five-millimeter shell. There were four large holes in the fuselage on the right side and three more exit holes on the left. The blood was coming out of his right femoral artery in small buckets. He realized he'd be unconscious in a minute and dead in two. Then the engine went unstable, coughing twice, quitting, then restarting, but with a violent vibration.

Well, God damn, he thought. Little bastards finally got my ass.

He turned hard again, fighting the wave of unconsciousness that was quietly enveloping his brain as his blood pressure fell toward zero over zero. At least it doesn't hurt, he mumbled to himself. There was a lot more AA fire now from that cruiser, as well as from a couple of quad batteries on the stern of the big guy.

Doesn't matter anymore, Mick kept telling himself. Nothing matters anymore.

He felt the right side of his face sagging as he gripped the stick as hard as he could with his good left hand, tugging his wrecked barge through one last turn as his vision tunneled down into a reddish haze.

Maybe I can help that tin can.

More flack hit the Dauntless as he steadied into a shallow dive on the cruiser. The canopy disintegrated in a blizzard of Plexiglas, slashing bits off his helmet. Then the engine positively seized, snapping the prop right off and jerking the nose sideways.

Doesn't matter. Doesn't matter. Got you now, grape.

He smelled smoke and saw flames rising along the aircraft's side as more rounds hit.

Bastards, he thought. Tore off my leg and now they want to cook it?

Well, God damn your eyes, eat *this*.

An instant later he flew eight tons of Dauntless dive bomber into the cruiser's midships Long Lance torpedo magazine and took them both to glory.

Marsh couldn't do anything but watch as *Evans*'s nemesis emerged from behind the battleship, every one of her guns trained their way. He yelled for everybody else to get down, get down, and was beginning to extricate himself from the captain's chair when that lone Dauntless dive bomber that had strafed the big guy from ahead appeared out of nowhere, trailing two streams of white smoke, banked clumsily right and down, and flew straight into the approaching cruiser. He hit her just forward of amidships, causing a massive explosion out of all proportion to one eight-ton airplane hitting a thirteen-thousand-ton armored cruiser. Bright white steam immediately erupted out of the cruiser's stack, and she staggered off to the east, her hull apparently so badly damaged amidships that her masts appeared to be sagging in toward one another. For a moment, anyway, she masked the fire of the other two wolves on *Evans*'s port quarter. Marsh gasped in relief.

Marsh had forgotten about the Kongo-class battleship, but he hadn't forgotten about *Evans*, whose world finally ended as a full salvo of fourteen-inch landed all around and aboard. The ship was whipsawed as the air was filled with an overwhelming roar of fire, smoke, and crashing metal. *Evans* went way over onto her beam ends with the impacts, coming back upright most reluctantly. To Marsh she felt an awful lot like *Winston* when she'd decided to give up the ghost. Then something heavy hit him from above and he blacked out.

He awoke to find himself on the buckled deck of the pilothouse, where it was raining. His whole body hurt, and both his eyes were swelling up. He tried hard to figure out this raining-inside-the-pilothouse business, until he realized that the pilothouse overhead was gone, along with Sky One, the primary gun director, the mast, and all the remaining bridge personnel. He tried to get up and then felt a lance of pain flash up his right arm.

Right *arm?* Can't be right—it was his foot, not his arm. He spat out a mouthful of saltwater and other things too terrible to comprehend, blinked stinging saltwater out of his eyes several times in order to focus, and realized the deck was no longer level. He looked down at his arm, or what was left of it.

His right hand was gone at the wrist, clipped as clean off as his right foot. This time there was no pharmacist's mate coming to his aid, and there was plenty of bleeding. His brain told him to tie it off, but, still fuzzy from the shock of the final hits and the morphine, he felt like he was living through a slow-motion nightmare. He finally struggled semiupright and managed to get his web belt off and make a tourniquet. He quickly found out that a tourniquet is really hard to do with one hand. The bleeding slowed, but he could barely pull the belt tight enough. He wondered how long he'd been out. Then he wondered if it even mattered.

Sitting up now on the battered steel deck of the pilothouse, he could feel the ship getting heavier and heavier. Although she was still on a relatively even keel, she definitely was starting to settle by the stern, and she'd lost most of her forward way. There were no more shells coming in, so he could hear shouts from out on the weather decks. He hadn't given the order to abandon ship, but apparently someone had, because those who could were going over the side. The sea was probably already lapping at the lifelines.

The interior of the pilothouse was a shambles of bodies, parts of bodies, wrecked steering equipment, fallen cables, steel helmets, and bloody insulation, which the sudden rainsquall was turning into a hideous soup on the deck. Only two men were left standing. Then he looked again. They only appeared to be standing up. They'd both been impaled on the steel ribs of the bridge structure where a big shell had left its entrance hole.

Of all things, his captain's chair was unscathed, so he pulled himself over, grabbed the footrest with his remaining good hand, and somehow clambered into it. Staring through the gaping row of half-rounds where the bridge windows had been, he could now see the forward part of the ship. "Their" battleship was steaming majestically away, stern pointed at them as her huge guns lofted more monster shells downrange toward the now invisible jeeps. She was still afire aft, though, which gave Marsh some small measure of comfort.

Mount fifty-one, the forward-most five-inch mount, was completely gone, leaving only a round hole where the stump of her barbette protruded a few inches above the forecastle deck. Mount fifty-two was trained almost back at the bridge, with her right side peeled back like a sardine can and her blackened barrel pointing almost straight up. Marsh flinched when he saw the burned, gory wreckage inside the mount. They'd reported running out of ammo as *Evans* fell out of the shadow of the big battleship, which probably explained why the ship hadn't been already obliterated by a magazine explosion. Looking at all the damage, Marsh realized that that was a distinction without a difference.

He felt himself leaning back in his chair and then realized that he wasn't leaning back—the ship was. She was definitely settling by the stern and also beginning to list to port. He took a few deep breaths, rubbed his swollen eyes, and undid the snap on his borrowed battle helmet. He thought about getting out of the chair to see the damage back aft but then asked himself: What did it really matter? In a few minutes *Evans* and her crew would all be a memory.

He'd felt the hits. Fourteen-inch armor-piercing rounds, they'd gone right through, coming in from astern and some of them ripping their way completely through the ship. They'd torn the life out of *Evans*. He knew she was a goner. He was very, very tired. With two amputations, there was little point in his going into the water with the remnants of the crew who were going overboard. The ones who did manage to get away wouldn't need any more bleeding shark bait.

The familiar roar of a boiler's safety valve opened up as the snipes in two-fireroom dumped steam so that the boilers wouldn't explode when she went down. Marsh wondered if John Hennessy was still alive. Maybe *he'd* given the order to abandon ship once he got a look at the pilothouse. I would have, he thought. He no longer had the strength to turn around to see if the passageway down to CIC was still even there. He looked at his remaining hand. Who's going to take my academy ring back to Sally? he wondered.

The bellow of the dying boiler drowned out whatever noises the men were making now in getting off the ship. He closed his eyes. His right foot throbbed, even though it wasn't there anymore. His right forearm hurt like hell. He wondered idly if he shouldn't just relax the tourniquet and be done with this mess. Then he fished out a relatively clean handkerchief from his pocket and wrapped the stump, tying it off with his watchband. The warm rain pelting down on his face felt good, and for the moment it was probably hiding them from those two heavy cruisers. The handkerchief quickly turned bright red.

Part of his exhausted brain was chiding him to do something.

You're the captain.

No, I'm not. I'm the XO.

You're supposed to be giving orders and telling people what to do next.

Like what? Come back aboard and keep her afloat?

The simple truth was that there was no need for further orders. Much as in battle itself, if the officers and men had been properly trained, they would know what to do. A loss of communications between the Sky One director and a gun mount didn't mean the gun mount stopped shooting. Can you see a Jap ship? Shoot at it.

What was it Nelson said back in 1805? No captain can do very wrong if he places his ship alongside that of the enemy. Something like that. Lord Nelson would have approved of *Evans* this morning. Now that it was over, though, nobody needed captaining.

Suddenly he sensed a shadow to his left. He opened his eyes. The rainsquall was lifting south. One of the Jap heavy cruisers was sliding by, close aboard to port, her alien-looking pagoda superstructure momentarily blotting out the sudden sun.

She was really close, and she was rolling slowly in the underlying deep Pacific swell. One moment he could see her starboard side, the next he could see all the way across her decks. Her topside AA gun crews in their bulky battle dress were pointing at *Evans* and at the men in the water, now sandwiched between the two ships. Some of them were cheering and probably shouting banzais, although the steam plume was still drowning out all sound. Every one of her eight-inch guns was pointed right at *Evans.* Marsh winced when he visualized what was about to happen. He could see several of his people down in the water between the two ships trying to get out of the way of the salvo that had to be coming.

Then he noticed something else. Way up on the multilevel pagoda, a single officer was standing out on his starboard bridge wing. He had a battle helmet on and binoculars hanging from his neck, and, of all things, he was wearing white gloves. Marsh tried to sit up in his chair and almost rolled out of it. With *Evans*'s pilothouse roof ripped completely off, they could look right at each other.

To his amazement, the Japanese officer lifted one of those gloved hands in a formal salute and held it. After a few seconds, Marsh lifted the stump of his right arm and tried to return his salute. A pulse of pain made him drop his arm almost immediately, but Marsh was pretty sure the Japanese officer had seen that bloody handkerchief. The officer followed suit, dropping his hand, nodded or maybe even bowed once, turned around, and went back into his own pilothouse. Then that big black beast settled by the stern and accelerated away, a bright white foaming wake enveloping her fantail as her eight-inch turrets lifted their barrels in perfect unison southeast in search of more promising meat.

Marsh sank back in his chair and wondered if they would move off and then send one of those terrible Long Lance torpedoes into *Evans*, just to make sure—but as he watched, the cruiser's side decks erupted into a barrage of antiaircraft gunfire. A flight of planes from one of the jeeps fell out of the sun and swooped down on her. The flow of steam from the after fireroom ebbed suddenly and then stopped with a wet gasp. Marsh could now hear the racket of the Jap cruiser's secondary battery, thumping away and filling the sky overhead with black puffs, out of which more and more planes seemed to be descending. She was a few thousand yards away and starting to twist and turn as the attack strengthened. He watched in fascination as she went off toward the horizon, trailing some black smoke now and still enveloped in a swarm of attacking planes.

The other Taffy groups must have joined the fight, he thought. Twelve jeep carriers could field over a hundred aircraft of all types. Hopefully the Japs would think Halsey's big-decks had gotten into the game, not that it was going to make any difference to *Evans.*

The list to port was increasing. Once again he felt he should be doing something, but he could not focus his brain through the fog of pain. He looked out over the port side again, where he could see men in the water, gray life jackets concealing their faces in many cases. Most were upright and swimming away from the ship; some were dragging buddies, and some were motionless. A lot of them were clustered around life rafts, which meant that the abandon-ship order had been given in time. A sudden stink of bunker oil invaded the wreckage of the pilothouse. Marsh remembered that smell. A warship, bleeding to death. He hoped the depth charges had been safed.

The depth charges.

Now *that* was something he could do.

He slid out of the chair and tried to lower himself gently onto the torn deckplates. He didn't do very well, ending up on his belly, trying to get his breath back and blink the tears out of his eyes after whacking his right arm stump on the footrest. It took him another few minutes to clamber through all the wreckage in the pilothouse and out to what was left of the port bridge wing. He went to port because it was downhill, and that was when he finally got a good look at the rest of the ship. There wasn't much left to see. There was a single, ominous hole in the port bulkhead down where Combat had been. The lifelines stanchions along the port quarter were already getting their feet wet, so if he was going to do any good, he had to hurry. Now he wished he'd let the gunners back aft have their fun, but *Evans* would have lost her rudders, too.

There was no way he could manage that steep steel ladder from the bridge wing to the next level down. He lay there for another minute, trying to gather his wits while he watched what was left of his right forearm drip into the sea below. He was exhausted. It would have been wonderful to just put his head down in that soft rain. The ship wasn't moving forward at all. She, too, was rolling in that deep swell, but not coming back very much after each roll to port. Pretty soon she'd take one last roll and keep right on going.

Get a move on.
Why?
The depth charges.
Right.

Then he noticed that what was left of the bridge wing no longer had any sides. He was lying on a diving board. A moment later he just slid into the sea from about fifteen feet up. As he fell, he remembered the big day back at the academy swimming pool when the entire class had to do the dreaded platform jump as they trained for what it would be like to abandon ship. He managed to do a complete somersault on the way down but failed to take that big breath. Submerging to what seemed like a hundred feet, he woke back up and scrambled hard for the surface, which was maybe two feet away. Fortunately the sea was still calm, and, after the initial stinging shock, the warm saltwater actually felt good on his two stumps. He tried to eke out a clumsy sidestroke along the battered hull, very conscious of all the bloody arms and legs hanging through the lifelines. The torpedo mounts were both gone, as were mount fifty-three and most of the after superstructure, courtesy of probably just one of those fourteen-inch shells. He looked around to see if there were any more Japs inbound, but the rain obscured the surrounding sea. If there was a Jap destroyer coming to machine-gun the survivors, it was probably better not to know.

After two hundred feet of grunting and splashing, he slithered back aboard, rolling over rather than through the fantail lifelines as *Evans* leaned way over, as if to see where she was going. Mount fifty-five was still trained out to starboard, its blackened gun barrel still searching for another battleship to annoy. Fifty-four had been split clean in two, as if by a giant hatchet. The barrel was missing. He could see some arms and legs in the mess, where glinting brass hydraulic lines contrasted brightly with the burned wreckage inside.

The fantail was intact, but the deck was already under about six inches of water. There were a half-dozen bodies piled up around the after windlass, their faces covered in black oil like some ghastly caricature of a vaudeville crew. Marsh flopped across the deck like a seal, pulling with his one good hand and pushing with his remaining foot to get back to the depth charge racks. Captain Hughes's policy had been to keep the fuze pistols set on one hundred feet as long as they were in enemy waters. What he had to do now was apply the settings wrench to each depth bomb and spin the dial over to the safe position. Otherwise, once the ship sank below one hundred feet, the depth bombs would all go off, crushing the guts out of any man still floating nearby.

He found it difficult to concentrate. Small waves were obscuring the settings dials and momentarily blinding him each time he tried to set the wrench. That morphine injection was working too well, damping the pain at the cost of dulling his brain. He was also running out of strength. It was difficult to do the simplest things, especially without his right hand, and each time he tried to brace his body with his right leg, he came up short. Literally.

He thought he heard someone shouting.

Sorry, bud, he thought. I'm busy here. Couldn't help you even if I wanted to.

Put the wrench on the tabs. Turn it counter-clockwise, all the way through the detent to SAFE.

More shouting, excited voices. His vision was beginning to tunnel up again, but he was determined to get this final thing done.

Ignore the noise. Move to the next one. Clear your eyes. Find the dial. Take the wrench out of your teeth, fit it on the dial. Counterclockwise. Lefty-loosey. Feel the detent. Push through it. SAFE.

Put the wrench back in your teeth. Move to the next one. Clear your eyes. Find the dial. Spit out the wrench and fit it on the dial.

The water was getting deeper as *Evans* gave in to her fate. It felt so strange to feel his knees on steel while the sea was enveloping the collar of his life jacket. The kapok was actually making it hard to stay next to the racks.

One rack done. Now to the other side. Have to get them all, he thought, before my brain swirls into a salty, purple haze. Fifty percent isn't good enough.

Blink away the salt and oil. Find the dial. Spit out the wrench. Five hundred pounds of TNT. Good stuff. Kill a sub quick. Kill the swimmers even quicker.

More voices, close aboard now. Don't bother me. Gotta do this, see? Five hundred pounds, turn your leg bones into broken glass and your pipes into applesauce. And I even like applesauce.

Then strong arms. One of the voices sounded like Chief Marty Gorman. Pulling him away from his duty.

He tried to protest, got a mouthful of seawater. Three guys yelling: It's okay, it's okay, you got 'em all. Come on, now. She's going down.

Going down. That's what the captain is supposed to do, isn't it? Go down with his ship? But you're the XO, not the captain. The ghost of Beast McCarty's face swam into his vision. "Congratulations, classmate," the ghost said with that irascible grin. "You met the elephant today. You did good."

You, too, Beast, he thought.

Okay, then.

For the first time in the war, he was no longer afraid of anything, and on that happy note, he let them pull him off the fantail and into the welcoming sea. From behind them he thought he heard a loud, ship-sized groan.

Good night, sweetheart. Good night.

· · ·

Water, water, everywhere,
  and all the boards did shrink
Water, water, everywhere,
  nor any drop to drink.

He mentally recited Coleridge's agonized words as the life raft bounced around in what looked like calm waters, under a blazing tropical sun. He dimly remembered last night, after the ship went down and they found themselves alone on the Philippine Sea. He kept trying to get his mind back to the surface to reassume command, but their sole surviving pharmacist's mate had given him one more jab of morphine, reducing him to a relatively comfortable zombie. When dawn broke, the mate prepared to do it again, but Marsh told him not to. He was sure they were going to be rescued soon and didn't want to be completely out of it. That was at dawn.

By midafternoon, it was becoming clear that they were *not* going to be rescued anytime soon. They'd seen distant aircraft, and even a PBY, flying low over the waters to their south, but no one came for them. It was as if the battle had never happened. No Japs, no jeeps, nobody at all except a hundred or so survivors from *Evans*, clutching to life rafts or floating nearby, while the Philippine sun slowly roasted them. He'd never heard such silence, but it was broken soon enough when the sharks moved in.

There were four rafts. The most seriously injured were in the rafts. The rest of the survivors were clinging to them as their kapoks tried to soak up the entire ocean, rendering them useless. Marsh's right forearm throbbed, and his right foot was positively on fire. They periodically dipped each severed appendage into the sea on the theory that the saltwater would keep infection at bay. It seemed like a good idea at the time, but his bleeding stumps were not impressed. The pain became his all-consuming focus, and then the waiting pharmacist's mate gave him another stick.

Marsh was only peripherally aware of what happened next, when the sharks came in force. The first man taken made not a sound, but the two men next to him certainly did. There was nothing any of them could do. There was nowhere to go, and no way to drive them off. If a man kicked at them, he simply confirmed he was live prey. They would circle the rafts and all the floating men, then submerge. Men would look down into the water, waiting, ready to kick or thrash or do anything that might prevent what was rising from the deep to take them, but the ones taken never had a chance to do anything but open their mouths and then disappear in a bloody swirl. It was horrible, and their helplessness made it even worse. Marsh eventually felt guilty being in the raft and thought about ordering men to take turns, in the rafts and then alongside, to give everyone an equal chance at survival. Deep down, though, he knew that was nonsense: No one already in the raft would have budged.

Where were the rescue forces? There should have been planes combing the sea, looking for survivors from the tin cans who'd gone north to die under the guns of battleships. Then a thought occurred to him: Maybe the Japs had won and wiped them all out. Maybe there was no one left out there on the horizon—three, maybe four battleships against even eighteen jeeps was no contest at all. Maybe they'd sunk them all and then gone back to wherever they'd come from. Maybe the planes they'd seen had been Japs, looking for stragglers to machine-gun. His brain whirled with the effort of the what-ifs and the maybes. Once every four hours, someone gave him a couple of sips of water. They had to wrest the cup away from him each time they did. Marsh knew better, that the water had to go a long away with all these men, but his thirst was urgent. He automatically reached for the cup with his missing right hand, which they gently pushed aside.

When night fell on the second day, he let them give him another morphine jab. He remembered telling the pharmacist's mate, "No more water for me. I'm not gonna make it anyway." The badly sunburned young man grinned in the darkness.

"Yeah, you will, Skipper," he said. "They'll figure it out. Tomorrow for sure."

They did come. The young pharmacist's mate had been right. A Black Cat PBY seaplane showed up one hour after sunrise, circled them twice, dropped some water supplies and four more rafts, and then flew off. A small herd of Army Higgins boats arrived four hours later to begin the rescue, while the seaplane flew overhead, making sure no one was left behind.

They were much diminished. Marsh wasn't sure how many of them had made it into the sea as *Evans* went down, but there were fewer of them than that waiting to be picked up. John Hennessy was in another raft, and Swede Bolser was alive but badly burned. Marsh's second night had been one of violent dreams as he relived taking his ship alongside that battleship, her towering steel sides rising in front of his face like a moving black mountain, looming ever closer until he was smothered by her sheer size.

As the captain, he felt he had failed the survival experience entirely. Once a day, someone jabbed him in the thigh with a syringe, and all became better. He was actually *in* the raft, while most of the survivors were hanging on to the sides. Even so, he was often out of his head, which was a mercy when the pharmacist's mate dunked his severed limbs into the saltwater. Every time they relaxed one of the tourniquets he bled like a stuck pig. They gave him precious water and salt tablets, while making a paste of seawater and sulfa powder as a poultice for his open wounds. There were times when he thought the crew ought to just pitch his useless ass over the side to make room for men with better chances. He was pretty sure he'd babbled on in this vein, because one of the gunners finally put a wet cloth over his mouth and told him to "hesh up," as he was encouraging the sharks.

There were moments of lucidity. He remembered that fateful decision to go back and expend their remaining torpedoes. *What price had we all paid for that decision?* he thought sadly. The look in John Hennessy's eyes, the terrified faces of the bridge watch, the false bravado of the chief engineer—*Give 'em hell, Cap'n*—they'd trusted in him and he'd killed many of them in the next half hour, while doing next to nothing to the Japanese. He himself had been reduced to a one-legged, one-armed impostor. If this was what command was about, he wanted no further part of it. These were good men, brave and true, and he'd selfishly led them to slaughter, egged on by a memory of being called a coward by a man who'd taken a woman with whom he was still in love. Because he could, and Marsh couldn't.

He was in tears when they passed him over the

471

gunwales of the Higgins boat. The Army medic on board took one look at his injuries, thought Marsh was weeping because of unbearable pain, and gave him yet another jab of morphine. By now Marsh welcomed it, but not because of the physical pain.

SIXTEEN

Glory Lewis felt despondent and didn't know why. Her confinement and delivery had gone as well as any other, as the attending midwives so amiably put it. No infections, normal baby. They had let her nurse the baby, a boy, for three weeks before switching him over to a bottle. After that she was permitted to feed him once a day, while one of the nuns took care of the rest. "We have to wean both of you, don't we," Mother Superior had reminded her, "since you are giving him up for adoption." Glory had wanted to name him, but they wouldn't allow it, entering the words "unnamed baby boy" on the birth certificate along with her name. When he was placed, his new family would name him, they told her; that was how it worked. The sisters, for the most part Hawaiian women, had been universally kind.

Increasingly Glory had wanted to keep the baby, but the logistical difficulties would have been overwhelming. She had no husband and no place to live where she could care for an infant. This war seemed endless, grinding up lives, families, and all the normal functions of what used to be everyday life. There were even more casualties now that the Japanese were fighting a Pacific-wide rearguard action. On every island the Allies invaded, Japanese in their thousands fought to the last man, each determined to take at least one Allied soldier with him. Far too many of them were succeeding in that.

Sally Adkins had shipped out to Guam with one of the augmentation units under Stembridge's command, leaving Glory without her closest friend in Hawaii for the last three months of her pregnancy. She'd been transferred to administrative duties in the hospital's main office as her third trimester began. There she endured real and imagined slights from the nonmedical people around her. As she had predicted, no one except the hospital commanding officer had directly addressed the socially charged issue of her being an unwed mother. The captain, however, had been surprisingly supportive: Work the OR for as long as you're able, then we'll put you in the office. You can have the baby here, if you'd like, as long as we have facilities open. You're doing the right thing, and once you've gotten through it, we want you back here. Business is, unfortunately, booming. And don't let all those gossiping bastards get you down.

The first time she'd had to acquire a larger uniform, she'd sat down with Stembridge before he left and told him what was going on. He had begun to fold her back into the expansion planning, and she knew that the project would be disrupted if she had to leave it, as she certainly would. He reacted with uncharacteristic silence and then surprised her. "I wish it were mine," he'd said. She had been too astonished to respond. He'd asked her who else knew, and she told him. Then he'd surprised her again. "If you'd like, I'd be more than happy to tell everybody it's my child and that we've been secretly married since last year. That'll wipe away the social stigma. Accidents and unplanned pregnancies happen. I'm sure we could find quarters in town. I'm sure we—"

She'd raised her hand and told him that everything was going to be okay, and thank you so much for your kind and generous offer. She was not going to marry anyone just because she was pregnant, and if there was stigma attached, so be it. He'd protested, saying he didn't mean they'd actually have to get married, just pretend they were. He'd be shipping out to the western Pacific any day now, the war couldn't go on forever, and . . . then he'd run out of words as he saw the impossibility of it. She'd squeezed his hand and apologized for the way she'd behaved that night at the New Year's party. That was their last personal conversation before he'd gone off to Guam to the same new hospital as Sally.

So now she was alone, really alone. There'd been major personnel upheavals as both the Navy and the Army established forward base hospitals, saving the Pearl Harbor facilities for the long-term repair of the most grievously wounded men. Of the original team of post–December 7 OR supervisors, she was the only one left, and she felt much older than the women who were coming in now, even though she was only thirty-four. She'd moved into a different room once Sally left and now lived by herself. It had been two weeks since she'd seen her baby. She knew without asking that the next time she visited the convent they were going to tell her the baby was somewhere else. It had seemed like such a logical and appropriate thing to do when she'd discovered that she was pregnant, but now she knew she'd given away something very special.

The only times she felt at peace were when she made her nocturnal visits out to the *Arizona*. A cottage industry had sprung up in and around Pearl Harbor during 1943, one that the harbor authorities knew about but chose officially to ignore. More and more of the Americans coming to and through Pearl wanted to see where the battleships had been sunk. Locals with small boats would show up at fishing piers outside the base after hours and off the Hospital Point seawall at night. They would offer to take people out to Ford Island so they could get a close-up look at *Arizona* and *Utah*. They would accept either the military scrip or a carton of cigarettes in payment.

Glory had befriended one of these boatmen, Manoea by name. Because she could buy more cigarettes with her ration book than she could ever smoke, she paid him in cigarettes to take her out to what remained of Battleship Row. The boatmen were careful not to get too close to Ford Island, which was still in use as an auxiliary air station. They carried a single candlelit lamp in the bow of the boat, and the Ford Island sentries all knew who they were, what they were doing out there, and that it was harmless.

Manoea liked to talk, and Glory had been on the island long enough that she could understand most of the pidgin dialect the locals used when they spoke to haoles, as all white foreigners were called. When he'd learned that her husband was entombed in the battleship he stopped charging her, although she still made sure she left some cigarettes in the boat when he brought her back to Hospital Point. Now when he took her out there, he would simply let the boat drift near the *Arizona* and smoke while she let her mind drift along with the boat. The Navy had removed all of the remaining superstructure by then, so the only prominent features visible were the after turret foundations and the large centerline hole that had been the belowdecks base of the armored conning tower. A sheen of bunker oil surrounded the wreck. Schools of small fish swam between what had been the front face of the bridge superstructure and the forward part of the ship where the fourteen-inch ammunition magazines had exploded.

As the boat drifted with the eddies and currents coiling around Ford Island, she would reminisce about her life together with Tommy and the all too many what-might-have-beens. She knew it was an unhealthy exercise, but life's prospects seemed to be flowing around her while she stood still or even slipped backward in time. Pearl Harbor had been the center of the world's attention right after December 7, but now everyone stationed here was definitely classified as being in-the-rear-with-the-gear. The naval base was vital, but the real war was moving west and north thousands of miles away as the Allies closed in on Japan itself.

She kept telling herself that giving up the baby was for the best, certainly for the baby, but her heart ached as if he had died at birthing. Even Hawaii, with its never-changing weather, was depressing. She hadn't seen Marsh or Mick since New Year's, Stembridge had gone west, as had Sally, and her dear Tommy lay moldering out in the harbor with over eleven hundred of his shipmates. Nothing in those gay weekends at Annapolis had prepared her for any of this.

"Ready, Ensign Lewis?"

Glory looked up from the lunch table at the new OR general supervisor, Carolyn McPeak. She was a full lieutenant in the Nurse Corps and at least forty-five years old. Positively ancient.

"Yes, ma'am," she said. Time to get back to work.

She walked behind the small group of nurses headed back to the hospital, no longer interested in their gossipy chatter. Lieutenant McPeak dropped back to talk to her.

"You seem to be in the dumps these days, Ensign Lewis. You know that's normal, don't you? After having a baby?"

"No, I didn't," Glory said. She wasn't sure what the lieutenant thought of her personal situation, but these days she didn't much care.

"Well, it is. I've had three kids, and each time I felt like a lost soul after the baby was born. Then one morning you wake up and feel just fine, and then it's over."

"I suppose that's true," Glory said.

"Suppose?"

"If you get to keep your baby, I mean."

The older woman gave her a sympathetic look and then nodded. "Ah," she said. "I hadn't thought about that. Well, listen, you want to talk, you feel free to come see me. I know this has been very difficult for you, but, as they say, there's a war on, and we need everybody operating at full power."

"Yes, ma'am," Glory said wearily, as they climbed the steps to the hospital entrance. She wondered if she would ever be at full power again. There were nights when she wished she simply wouldn't wake up.

After a day of frustrating surgeries, including three consecutive deaths on the table, Glory went to dinner at the O-club. It was late, and the dining room was not very full. She sat by herself in one corner and had a salad and some rubbery baked chicken with a glass of white wine. She found herself much more interested in the wine than in the chicken. Five surgeries, three deaths, one doubtful, and one obvious success. Where oh where was Superman? she wondered. These new cutters weren't very good at this.

At around nine a group of staff officers from Makalapa came in, carrying drinks they'd brought from the bar. They sat not very far away and continued an animated conversation about what was going on out in the Philippines. Glory could usually tell the staff officers from the shipboard personnel. The fleet headquarters "staffies" always managed to talk about the so-called big picture, as if to make sure that any other officers in the room knew that they were exceedingly important. They'd throw last names around as if they knew all the three- and four-star admirals personally: Chester said this, and John Towers was against that. She tuned them out as she asked the waiter for another glass of wine, then changed it to coffee.

I've been here too long, she thought, and not for the first time. It was plain food, much better than the soldiers out in the Philippines were getting as they slogged through jungle, heat, mud, venomous insects, and the even more venomous Japanese army. Maybe I should volunteer to go west into one of the new base hospitals, Guam maybe, where Sally was—but Stembridge was there, too, and that would make things too complicated.

Then she heard one of the staff officers mention a ship's name: the *Evans*. She refocused on what they were saying. She was pretty sure that Beauty Vincent was still the XO on the *Evans*.

"Pretty amazing stuff," one four-striper was saying. "Picture it: Jap battleships and heavy cruisers showing up out of nowhere in the Leyte AOA. Halsey's Iowa class are off chasing empty Jap carriers above northern Luzon, and Jesse Oldendorf's antiques are still down in Surigao Strait. Ziggy Sprague is going out of his mind, so he sends these three tin cans to go after the Japs all by themselves. Talk about David and Goliath— one of the BBs apparently was *Yamato*, the biggest battlewagon ever built, with eighteen-inch guns."

"*Eighteen*-inch?!" a commander exclaimed. "Jesus. How long did they last?"

"Not very," the captain said. "All three were lost with all hands. The jeeps lost most of their planes. But the amazing thing? Right in the middle of it, the Japs turned away. They'd already sunk a couple Jeep carriers and all the poor bastard destroyers, so there was nothing between the amphib force and a massacre except some planes from the jeeps. Ziggy couldn't believe it when the Japs turned away and ran back for San Bernardino Strait."

"Which jeeps were lost?"

"*Madison Bay*, *Gambier Bay*, and possibly one more. The details are still filtering in. After Surigao Strait, we thought they'd all withdrawn or been sunk, but apparently this one Jap admiral didn't get the word and kept coming. Shame about the tin cans, though. Can you imagine— seeing Jap battleships on the horizon and turning *toward* them? Man!"

Three tables away, Glory sat there in shock.

Evans? Lost with all hands?

That certainly would make sense, she thought. A destroyer going up against a battleship? She'd seen the new Iowa-class battleships in Pearl Harbor after the attack, and they were enormous. Why would any destroyer captain do that? What kind of admiral would *order* such a thing? And where were the aircraft carriers? Halsey had, what—*twenty* aircraft carriers? Thirty? How could this have happened?

She realized she was holding her coffee cup in

midair. She put it down gently as she absorbed the terrible knowledge. The other name she'd recognized was *Madison Bay.* She was pretty sure that was Mick's ship. She tried to imagine one of those slow, flat-topped ugly ducklings, merchant ships disguised as aircraft carriers, trying to get away from Japanese battleships. Kaiser Coffins, their crews called them. Any planes that did get off would have had nowhere to land when they ran out of fuel. It would have been a slaughter.

No, it *had* been a slaughter.

Lost with all hands? The way these officers were talking, they hadn't even bothered to go out to look for survivors.

"Will that be all, miss?" the waiter asked. Startled, she nodded numbly and handed him her chit book. He tore out two coupons and handed it back to her. She sat there, trying to absorb the enormity of what she'd just overheard. The staff officers had moved on to even weightier matters, like their next assignments.

"They're all gone," she said softly.

The waiter turned around. "What, miss?"

She shook her head and tried to hold back the tears.

Tommy. Beast. Beauty.

All gone. Her whole world, all gone.

Her child, too, gone.

She felt as if the world were falling in on her. She could barely breathe. Her cheeks were hot, and her ears were humming. She'd suddenly become a ghost, walking, talking, working, but devoid of any human extension.

All gone.

Where? Out there in the vast western Pacific Ocean, thousands of miles away and probably miles deep, too. Where thousands of Americans had already gone, never to come back, drowned in the sea or buried in shallow graves on no-name atolls. Or, worst of all, simply "missing."

Sally and Superman were the only people she knew still alive out there, and they were so far away that only mail could reach them.

A decision coalesced in her mind.

Enough of this, she thought. Everyone's gone. I might as well be gone, too.

She gathered up her purse and her nurse officer's cap. She got up and walked past the table of staff officers, aware that they were staring at her covertly. She even thought she heard one of them give a low whistle. She kept going, her back rigid as she tried to control her emotions.

Talking casually about ships being lost with all hands while leering at her body. Incredible. Here they were, safe and sound in the gentlemanly ambience of the officers' club, anticipating a cognac and a cigar, while out *there,* way out there, whole ships were being eaten alive by monstrous Japanese battleships. She wanted to whirl and scream at them, but instead, she just fled.

· · ·

Mano showed up at his usual time, a little after ten thirty. Glory was waiting for him, two cartons of cigarettes in hand this time, her whole hoard. The night was dark because of a waning moon and a high overcast. Glory stepped into the little boat and sat down, smiled at her boatman, and put the two cartons of cigarettes on the midships thwart. He dutifully picked them up and put them behind his seat, near the engine, bobbing his head in thanks.

"Missy okay?" he called from the back of the boat.

"Missy's just fine, Mano," she said. "Let's go see the big black ship."

"Okay, missy," he said, in the familiar formula. "We go."

The engine was a single-cylinder putt-putt number. From the smell of the exhaust it was running on something truly obnoxious, such as used fish-fry oil. Mano used his usual indirect approach, going across the harbor toward the west side of Ford Island before making a gentle turn to head for Battleship Row. She could just barely see the white concrete moorings in the dim light, two by two, protruding along the edge of Ford Island, each with its own clutch of sleeping pelicans.

Glory could hear her heart beating, almost in time with the rackety little engine. She felt the slippery wooden sides of the boat as she gripped with white-knuckled hands.

All gone. Everyone dear to her, or close to her, or both, permanently extinguished by this eternal war. They hadn't even let her name her baby.

Gone. Now that would be an appropriate name, she thought: Baby Boy Gone.

Mano slowed the little engine to a bare crawl as they came abreast of the rusted buoy marking *Arizona*'s submerged port bow.

"Closer," she told Mano in a firm voice.

"Oh, no can do, missy," he said. "Navy say, no touch."

"No, Mano," she said. "Navy say, no *take*. Closer okay."

"Oh, missy," Mano said. "Mano get in trouble, Mano touch ghost ship. Ghost ship big kapu."

"The ghosts are all inside, big steel ship," she said. "Ghosts can't swim."

"No?"

"No, ghosts can't swim. I'll show you."

With the little boat barely gliding ahead, she put her hand in the water on the port side and began to gently back-paddle. They went past the rusted round barbette of a turret. She flattened her hand deeper, forcing the boat's bow to the left and right over the middle section of the ship, which was perhaps three feet under the surface.

"See, Mano? No ghosts. Just the big black ship."

"Oh, missy," Mano complained, anxiously searching the seawall for Ford Island sentries.

"Mano," she said. "The cigarettes—look, they're getting wet."

Mano turned on his thwart to see what she was talking about. When he looked back, Glory was standing up in the boat. Before he could open his mouth to protest, she stepped out of the boat and into the water, directly over that big black hole in the middle of the hulk, and quickly went out of sight.

Mano gasped but then had to lean right quickly to keep the little boat from capsizing. Even so, a small wave of oily harbor water slopped over the port gunwale and nearly swamped the boat. He grabbed the dipper and frantically started bailing. Then he remembered the crazy haole woman. He looked around, but she was nowhere to be seen.

He peered over the side and thought he saw a pale, fluttering thing deep down in that big square hole.

Ghost! Coming for *him*.

Even with the boat partially flooded, he turned the throttle hard and got out of there.

"*Goddamned* stupid haole woman," he muttered. "They never listen, these white people. Don't believe in ghosts. Don't they ever look in a mirror?"

He looked back in the direction of the *Arizona*,

the big kapu. He shivered in the warm, wet air and made a beeline for the back of the Pearl lagoon as fast as he could make the little engine go, resolved to tell no one about what had just happened. *Big* kapu alla way around.

Stupid damned haole.

SEVENTEEN

Sally sat by the bedside of a badly burned sailor, writing a letter to his wife for him. The man had been blinded by a flare-back while he was lighting off a boiler. His face was burned dark red, and his eyes were padded with ointment-soaked gauze circles. Both his hands were lumps of gauze.

"Don't tell her I'm blind," he said through crusty lips. "She might Dear-John me if she finds out. "

"Well, based on your chart, that blindness may only be temporary," Sally lied. The chart did in fact say that, although she knew his chances of regaining his sight were slim, given the third-degree burns on the rest of his face.

"Yeah, they told me that, but, man, when I blink under these bandages? All I see is that fire."

"Ensign Adkins?"

Sally looked up and saw the orderly standing at the entrance to the barrackslike ward. She raised her hand.

"Admissions needs help with a big intake," he said.

"Okay, be right there."

Sally had been out in Guam for six months, and the "intakes" were getting more frequent now that the invasion of the Philippines was fully under way. This was one of two wards under her direct supervision, and both were nearly full. The Pacific aeromedical evacuation operation was getting bigger by the day as new and improved planes were added to the system. Guam was considered 99 percent secure now, with only an occasional rumble of artillery or crack of small-arms fire drifting down to the base from the northern heights. Dr. Stembridge, who was now the CO of the hospital, told them the troops were just mopping up a few Jap stragglers.

She finished the letter, signed it for the sailor, and promised to mail it that very day. Then she went down to the admissions and triage area, dropping the letter off at the censor's office.

"Who are they?" was always the first question any of the staff asked. The hospital people often knew more about what was happening to fleet units than many of the staffies back in Pearl.

"A tin can called the *Evans*," one of the triage docs told her. "Went down somewhere in the Philippines. These guys are all that's left, and there aren't that many of them. Ship sank, and then they spent the next two days and nights adrift with the sharks."

"Oh, no!" Sally cried, her hand going to her mouth. Sharks scared her to death. But had he said *Evans*?

"You know someone?"

"Yes, yes, the exec."

The doctor looked at the flight manifest. "I'm sorry, Sally. The CO's listed, but not the XO."

Sally bit her lower lip as tears formed in her eyes. "Damn, damn, *damn!*" she said. "We'd been—pen pals."

"Yeah, well, shit. Sorry again. But right now, grab your chart pad, please. We need to get them sorted out."

She went to work, trying to hold back her tears and not succeeding very well. She'd had such dreams for their future that she felt as if she'd lost her spouse.

The survivors, some ninety-six men, were laid out on olive drab canvas stretchers down both sides of the admissions hallway. One triage team went down one side while Sally and her doc went down the other. Injuries ranged from dehydration, exhaustion, and serious sunburns to thermal burns, broken limbs, amputations, and shrapnel wounds. Two men had died en route, and their remains had been sent to the morgue. The surgical suite orderlies had gurneys standing by to take the most urgent cases in right away. Sally ended up escorting one of those, holding his IV bottle while the gurney was pushed into an elevator. The man was semiconscious and mumbling something about a battleship. Much of his right hip had been savaged by a shark, and the bandages had been on far too long, based on what she could smell. The orderly, recognizing the dreaded gangrene, was wrinkling his nose and shaking his head as they went up.

The rest of her day consisted of being one of five nurses completing the admissions, starting charts, and reassuring the men she could talk to that everything was going to be okay. One of the younger sailors told her that *Evans* had torpedoed three battleships before one of them finally put her down. He said it had been a hellacious fight and that the Jap shells that went right through the ship were big as refrigerators. Sally kept up a brave face, but her heart remained heavy. Her letters back and forth with Marsh had been increasingly intimate, especially after the lovely time they'd had at Pearl after the New Year's party. She had begun to dream about their getting married after the war, even while being very aware of the fragility of such dreams. Destroyers, as he had told her often, went in harm's way, on purpose. She'd thought he was being just a bit melodramatic, but not anymore.

Her shift ended at 1800. She went down to the hospital canteen for something to eat and then returned to the wards to help the oncoming shift with all the new patients. While she was working she noticed that one of the four private rooms, down at the end of the ward, was occupied. She asked the nurse next to her who was in there.

"The skipper of the *Evans*," she said. "Kinda iffy right now. Double amp, some second-degree sunburn, still somewhat shocky. They've had him back to surgery and recovery twice, but now I think they're gonna just wait and see."

"Wow," Sally said. "I wish I could talk to him, ask him about my guy."

"Not tonight, Josephine," the nurse said. "Maybe tomorrow, if he's still with us. Ooops, there goes a bottle."

They went back to work.

The next morning she came on at the regular time, 0700, after an uncomfortable and depressing night. She'd seen some surgeons going into *Evans*'s skipper's room just before she checked out for the evening. That doesn't look good, she'd thought. Damn. She'd cried herself to sleep for the first time in the war.

The next day's duty roster had her assigned back to her regular ward, where she spent the morning assisting rounds, bringing charts up to date, and dealing with one young Marine who'd decided to get back up to the front line with his buddies, the major problem being that he did not have legs anymore. Three orderlies and a dose of tranquilizer solved the problem. It was hard to be gentle while doing forcible restraint. The rest of the day passed in a sorrowful haze.

The following day there was a buzz in the canteen line at breakfast. An admiral had landed the night before with some staff officers from Admiral Nimitz's headquarters. Supposedly they were going to conduct some kind of inquiry into the *Evans* sinking and the battle surrounding it. They rarely saw admirals at the naval hospital, although there were also rumors that Nimitz himself was going to move his headquarters to Guam sometime early next year. The orderlies in front of her were scanning the plan of the day, a mimeographed paper put out by admin each day, laying out the day's scheduled events.

"Can I see that when you're done?" she asked.

They handed it back to her and waited for the line to shuffle forward. Apparently the cooks had temporarily run out of scrambled eggs.

Sally scanned the front page and then turned it over. On the back was a list of the recent admissions by name, rank, and assigned command. Toward the end of the list she saw the name Vincent, M., LCDR, USS *Evans*, and an asterisk, indicating a commanding officer.

"Oh, thank *God!*" she blurted, startling the two men in front of her. She handed one of them her tray and ran upstairs.

As she hurried down the ward aisle she saw that

the door to the private room was closed. She stopped short. At this time of day, that usually meant the patient inside had died and staff was waiting for the morgue to come get the remains. Then to her vast relief the door opened and two doctors stepped out, conferring over their notes. One of them saw Sally, standing there with a hand to her mouth.

"Yes, Nurse?" he asked.

"Is he—"

"I think he's gonna make it now," the doctor said. Sally recognized him as one of the senior internists.

"Can I speak to him?" she asked.

"Keep it short, Sally," the other doc said. "He's pretty weak. You know this guy?"

She nodded, not trusting her voice anymore.

They said okay, stuffed their notes into the chart box on the door, and left. She went in.

She hardly recognized him. His face was in the peeling stage of a serious sunburn. His head had been shaved to allow his scalp to be stitched up, and his lips looked like a miniature red and black picket fence from all the cracking. The stump of his right arm was suspended in a tri-wire, and his right lower leg, or what was left of it, was elevated on some pillows. For some reason, both of his eyes were black and blue, but they were open. His left hand rested on his chest. His big academy ring was missing.

"Well, aren't you a regular beauty," she said.

He tried to smile, but all the cracks in his lips immediately bled. She pulled up a metal chair and sat down next to the bed. She took some tissues out of a box and dabbed his lips as gently as she could.

"I'd have been here sooner, but they told me the XO didn't make it," she said, no longer trying to hold back tears of relief.

He nodded but didn't say anything. She reached across his chest and took his left hand. His chest felt bony underneath her wrist, all his ribs tangible, and his remaining hand had the strength of a damp rag.

"I am *so* glad to see you here," she said. "I was—" Then she stopped.

He'd gone back to sleep. She slipped a finger under his wrist and felt the pulse. Thready, weak, but there. His breathing was okay, but just barely. She examined the stump of his right arm, made sure his eyes were still closed, and then leaned forward to take a sniff. It smelled of bandages, iodine, sulfa powder, but not of gangrene. His right leg had gone septic and had been amputated just below the knee. That dressing looked all right, too. She began to take away her right hand, but his fingers pressed against hers.

She left her hand right there and began to rub his forehead as gently as she could. She saw tears at the corner of his eyes, and, strangely, this made everything all right. She cried with him, soundlessly, not wanting to upset him.

When she came out a half hour later, she closed the door and then hung a MEDICAL STAFF ONLY sign on the door handle. At the other end of the ward she saw a small group of khaki-clad officers sitting next to one of the beds. She went down there to see what they were doing. The nurse in charge of the ward intercepted her.

"That's an *admiral*," she said breathlessly. "Stars and everything. The other three are all *captains*."

"Wow," Sally said. "That's a lot of brass for this place. What's going on?"

"Some kind of big-deal investigation. They want to talk to everybody as soon as they can. Especially the captain."

"That'll be a while," Sally said. "Maybe a coupla days. He's pretty beat up."

"I'll tell them that. I'd heard you lost someone on the *Evans*?"

"Found him," Sally said, beaming, wiping fresh tears from her eyes. The other nurse squeezed her hand.

Over the next few days some facts of the battle began to leak out within the hospital gossip networks. The presence of the high-level team from Pearl, of course, had everyone talking. Sally thought that the rumors were pretty wild, considering that they were talking about a lone destroyer, but one of the doctors said they had other people in the hospital who'd been there on one of the escort carriers and were corroborating the rumors. The story was that they'd been attacked by Japanese battleships, that the Japs had been driven off by three or four destroyers. Everything Sally knew about actual naval warfare she'd learned at the O-club, but that didn't seem plausible. She'd seen some American battleships in Pearl, the new ones, not the sunken ones, and they looked like they'd just run smack over any destroyer that was pestering them.

She saw Marsh at least three times a day when she could sneak away from her regular duties, which she increasingly managed with the covert cooperation of the other nurses. He was making steady but slow progress, but she still had to dab his lips with an anesthetic ointment before he could speak coherently. She did not ask about the battle, but on the third day she did tell him about the delegation from Pearl.

"Have some questions for them, too," he said.

She blinked in surprise. "You do?"

"Like why they didn't come looking for us. The guys saw Catalinas picking up aviators, but no one came for us."

"My God, are you serious?"

"How many here now from *Evans*?"

"I think ninety-some."

"Had more than that get off the ship," he said.

"But where—"

"Sharks got the rest. We got to watch."

She gasped. How could the Navy *not* have been looking for them?

"We've been putting them off," she said, "but they really want to talk to you."

He nodded. "I'm ready," he whispered. "Just keep that goop handy."

They came into his room, the three of them—a two-star aviator and two captains. Each of them was carrying a metal chair. They must have gotten used to looking at the blasted human wreckage from the battle off Samar, because none of them flinched when they saw his face. Even Sally, a wartime nurse, had flinched. Hell, he had flinched when Sally brought him a shaving mirror. He felt like he should be sporting a bell and a candle to warn people off. Between the stubble, the red sutures, raccoon eyes, and the peeling skin, he looked like a candidate for the leper colony at Molokai.

The admiral introduced himself as Bill Devereaux, deputy chief of staff for operations at the Pacific Fleet headquarters. Marsh thought he looked too young to be an admiral, but he guessed being an aviator accounted for that. The two captains were probably five years older than the admiral was. They looked like seamen.

"Captain, I'm honored to meet you," Devereaux said.

"Why?" Marsh croaked, which took Devereaux aback for a moment.

"Well," he said, "you and your crew drove off the Jap battle fleet at Leyte. They had the destruction of MacArthur's whole invasion fleet in their grasp, and yet they turned around and ran."

"We had lots of help," Marsh said. "Planes from the jeeps. The other tin cans. Hornets' nest around each Jap."

"Yes, we're finding that out," Devereaux said. "Let me explain why we're here and what we need from you. First let me emphasize that you talk only as long as you're able. We'll quit whenever you say so. Okay?"

"Yes, sir," Marsh said. His mouth was hurting already.

The admiral explained that they had the preliminary operational reports from the task force and task group commanders and from the COs of the Taffy Three light carriers who had survived the attack. All three of Taffy Three's destroyers who'd gone out to attack the battleships had been lost, and only one other CO had survived. Navigation, engineering, and damage control logs and records had, of course, all gone down with the ships, so for right now, the Navy was dependent upon individual testimony from survivors to reconstruct what had happened. He acknowledged that a lot of the information would be unreliable—sailors always exaggerated, and the stories got bigger the more often they told them. The horrors men had witnessed were in many cases erased in their minds by the brain's survival mechanism.

"So the idea is to move quickly, take everything said as the gospel truth, and then go back to Pearl and try to put it together."

"How did it happen?" Marsh asked.

"How did *what* happen?"

"Jap battleships in the amphibious objective area? And none of ours?"

"That's the supreme question, Captain," Devereaux said with a wry smile, "but that is handsomely above your pay grade and mine. For what it's worth, that question is a matter of intense discussion between Admirals Nimitz and Halsey. I won't be invited to those talks, and neither will you."

He smiled again to make sure Marsh knew that he wasn't admonishing him. Marsh liked the guy, actually. No stuffiness or superior airs. Sally sat on the other side of the bed, periodically dabbing the ointment on his lips with a cotton stick so he could keep talking.

"What we need to know from you, and others, is how the small forces there managed to drive off three, maybe four battleships, not to mention all those cruisers. So to start with, why don't you tell me what happened from the very beginning, when the first reports came in that there were Jap battleships approaching Leyte Gulf."

So he did. It took the next three days, with morning and afternoon sessions each day. Marsh was good for about an hour before his energy would run out. The first day he actually went to sleep on them in the middle of a sentence. They were patient, polite, and very thorough. He had been afraid that talking about it would bring back all the bad dreams he'd been having since being picked up, but the reverse was true. It was cathartic, even though at the time he didn't know that word. He wept a couple of times, such as when he described his last sight of the rabbi, kneeling on the port side in waist-high water, burned blind and bleeding from both eyes, holding a dying sailor's head above the water as long as he could. Marsh could not judge their reaction at moments like that, because he was no longer with them in that room when those memories surfaced. There were some long silences, which they respected.

One of the captains was particularly interested in his decision to turn around and go back in after the first torpedo attack. "Why didn't y'all just git while the gittin' was good?" he asked. He was a Southerner.

"Still had torpedoes and targets," Marsh said.

He nodded and wrote something down in his notebook. "And why did you lay *Evans* alongside the *Yamato*?"

"Is that what she's called? I'd never seen anything like her."

"No one had until Halsey sank her sister ship, the *Musashi*, in the Sibuyan Sea."

"Big bastard. Actually, big doesn't describe it. But I put *Evans* alongside because there were two, maybe three heavy cruisers and a Kongo class shooting at us. I figured if we closed in on the big guy, they'd have to stop firing, and they did."

"How long were you alongside?"

"A year?"

They smiled at that. Sally smiled, too, probably because Marsh was starting to show some signs of life.

"We were hurt pretty bad by then, so we could only stay in her lee while she was making a wide turn. As soon as she steadied up, she drew ahead, and then we were back in hot water, with one cruiser in particular. He'd set up to enfilade us with his eight-inch. One of the bombers from the jeeps saved us."

"Yes, I wanted to ask directly about that," Admiral Devereaux said. "We've been told by one of your chiefs that a Dauntless purposefully dived into a cruiser and blew her up."

"Certainly what it looked like," Marsh said. "He was smoking pretty bad, and I'm guessing the pilot was already wounded, because he was doing everything too slow."

"Deliberate or just how it came out due to his damage?"

"Deliberate, I think. One moment he was climbing out of the AA fire, the next he rolled over like they do when they're going to dive on something and then flew straight into that cruiser's side. Huge explosion."

"Could you see a bomb?"

"No, sir. None of them flying around us had bombs, or if they did, they were little-bitties. Most of them were strafing the bridge levels. Some of them couldn't even do that, so they made fake torpedo runs, which made the Japs turn and evade."

"Why do you think the cruiser exploded, then?" one of the captains asked.

"Couldn't tell you, sir, but she surely did. I could see the masts tipping into each other after the blast. Had to have broken her back."

"And you say *Evans* got two torpedo hits on the *Yamato*?"

"Such as they were, Admiral. One fish porpoised, hit the side. It did go off, but it mostly scratched the paint. The other one hit farther aft, went off high order, but didn't seem to faze him."

"Gentlemen," Sally said, pointing at her watch.

"Right, of course," the admiral said. "Thank you very much. We'll probably be back."

"One question for you, Admiral, when you do come back."

"Yes?"

"Why did we have to spend three days and two nights drifting at sea before they came looking for us?"

The admiral gave Marsh a stern look, suddenly less nice guy and more admiral. Then his face softened, and he nodded. "Fair enough," he said. "I don't actually have the answer to that question now, Captain, but I will. Will you entertain my best guess?"

"Certainly, sir."

"My best guess is that Admiral Sprague saw all of you disappear into the smoke screens, headed for a force of battleships and heavy cruisers, and nobody returned. I think he simply assumed no one could have survived an engagement like that."

"Assumed," Marsh said.

"Yes, exactly," he said. He paused for a moment. "Assumptions in wartime," he said. "They'll bite you in the ass every time."

"Every time, Admiral. I lost a lot of men out there, and the ones who did make it want to know why nobody came."

"I understand, Captain. For starters, you can tell them the fault was all ours."

It was a gracious reply to a question the admiral did not have to answer. Marsh had one further question.

"You've been calling me Captain," he said. "I was only acting commanding officer. The real captain was killed in an accident. I—"

"Were *you* in command when you put your ship alongside an enemy battleship?"

Marsh took a deep breath. "Yes, sir, I guess I was."

"Then you were the captain. Besides, there's another reason we're calling you Captain."

Marsh waited.

"Someone has to be responsible for the loss of the *Evans*. Captain."

"Right," Marsh said. "Of course."

Then Deveraux grinned. "I'm kidding. Mostly. Get well. We'll talk some more."

On that happy note, they left.

Marsh was exhausted. Talking was physical torture. His cracked lips stung. His missing limbs also hurt. Not the stumps but the limbs themselves. He couldn't understand that. It hurt to breathe, and he wondered if he'd lost a lung or something. After this long session, he asked Sally for some morphine.

"Let me see what I can do," she said. He later learned that what she brought him was a Coke laced with some codeine. "Drink this," she said, "while they rustle up some morphine for you."

Ten minutes later he was long gone.

The admiral and his team went on to pick on someone else. Marsh spent the next few days sweating through the hours between pain medications. The docs told him that this was a good sign, that the tissues were trying to heal. He told them to bring the tissues some morphine, they apparently had developed a taste for it in the life raft.

At night he dreamed that he could hear the shrieks of men being hit by sharks in the darkness. He recalled the excitement when the Black Cat flew close overhead, the noise of its engines hurting his head, the hoarse cries of the guys in the rafts, followed by the smoky roar of the landing craft who had come way out to sea from the beaches of Leyte to pick them up, the Sixth Army boat crews throwing up when they saw some of the wounded. He could still hear the rattle of small-arms fire as they shot at the sharks that had become their constant companions. In his dreams they became Japs, doing what they did best, reveling in death and feasting on helpless sailors.

In the days following the interviews they fed him mush. Baby food, as Sally called it. For some reason all his teeth hurt. Hell, everything hurt, even his hair. Several times he went right out of his head as passing fevers took a bite. He didn't know how Sally managed to be with him, but she did. Other nurses came and went, but each time the door opened he'd say, "Sally?" They finally got the idea, and then all of them conspired to let her care for him. At night sometimes he would lie there in a cold sweat, breathing in and breathing out, wondering if his heart was going to stop. Each night she would slip into the room and sit down next to him and rub his arms. Then and only then would he fall asleep.

As he submerged, he thought that it might not be such a bad thing if he did die. So many of his people had been lost because of him and his "glorious" decision to turn around and go back against those big black ships. The admiral and the captains had been "honored." Marsh wished they could have met those of his people who were now no more than tattered phantoms in the dark deeps of the Philippine Sea. The feel of her hand on his arm in the darkness was a potent barrier against his personal despair, but it didn't assuage his growing sense of guilt.

He was convinced *he* had killed them, every one. One night he told Sally why he'd really turned around and gone back into the fight. He told her that he was pretty ashamed of his secret reason for making that decision. He'd killed half his crew because of an insult.

"Nonsense," she'd said. "The Japs killed them. You said it yourself: You had torpedoes left. You just did your duty. They sent you and those other ships out there to break up their attack, and it worked, didn't it?"

His heart was not so sure.

· · ·

When the doctors came in on morning rounds one day, there was a new face in the group. Dr. Stembridge, now Captain Stembridge, CO of the hospital. Marsh recognized him from the New Year's party, when Glory had paraded herself in front of him with Beast. He remembered the shocked look on Stembridge's face that night and thinking, *I know just how you feel, pal.*

"Good morning, Captain," Stembridge said brightly. "Ready to get up and move around?"

"Absolutely not," Marsh said.

"Super," Stembridge replied, ignoring Marsh's reply. "It's time, you know. You're going to get bedsores just vegetating like that. Need to get your muscles working again, get vertical, maybe even get some fresh air."

Marsh looked at him as if he were nuts. His arm stump still leaked, and he hadn't even been able to see what horrors were going on with his leg. He looked at his regular docs for moral support.

"We, ah, need the room," one of them said quietly.

"Oh," Marsh said. "That's more like it. But how?"

As if on cue, one of the nurses rolled in a wheelchair. It took ten minutes to get him into it. Marsh didn't help much by fainting in the middle of the evolution. Stembridge, however, was nothing if not determined, and when Marsh came to he found out that wheelchairs have both seat belts and chest straps. He felt like a jellyfish in that chair and was nauseous the moment the nurse started pushing him out of the room and into the ward. Then he heard voices.

"Hey," someone called out. "It's the skipper."

The nurse slowed his procession between the rows of beds, and for the first time since coming into the hospital, Marsh started thinking about someone other than his piteous self. Still fighting nausea, he greeted the guys, trying not to stare at their bandages, eye patches, burns glistening with ointment, plastered fractures suspended in various slings of torture, or the uneven shapes of legs and arms hidden beneath blankets. They in turn were not so circumspect as they stared at his own amputations, and then some of them began to applaud his appearance.

As guilty as he had been feeling about them, they seemed glad to see him and almost eager to remember the pasting they'd given that Jap battlewagon and the way their guns had blown all the glass out of the giant's bridge windows, or knocked his scout planes out of the hangar and into the fiery sea.

For the first time Marsh felt the gulf between captain and crew to be filled with something besides official decorum. In their young eyes, and with carefully filtered hindsight, they'd whupped the bastards, and Marsh had led them to it and through it. Marsh knew better, having been out of his head for the three days in the water. They weren't having it—the captain was back. They were a crew again, albeit one without a ship anymore. Details.

That was when he finally realized that it was time to pull himself together and get back to work. He needed to know who'd made it and who had not. There were condolence letters to be written, medal citations and commendations to be crafted. He needed to reconstitute his chain of command, however slender it might turn out to be. He found himself grinning as he realized what he really needed: He needed an XO.

All of that occupied the next three weeks. The hospital people were extremely helpful, given the fact that every day more wounded were being flown in. Most of the *Evans* survivors were moved to satellite wards to make room for the never-ending river of broken bodies. Marsh saw less of Sally because she was main hospital staff and he was no longer physically there. She got over to their building as much as she could, but there were days when he didn't see her at all, and he missed her smiling face. Wisely, he told her that every time he saw her.

Seeing Stembridge had surfaced memories of Glory, and one night he gathered up the courage to ask Sally what she'd heard from Pearl, carefully not mentioning Glory by name.

"Not a thing, actually," she said, not fooled for a moment. "We exchanged some letters early on when I came out here, but then we sort of lost touch. You know how it is, new assignment here, one emergency after another. We all just put our heads down and hit the deck running. I haven't even been able to keep up with my regular pen pals. You're looking so much better these days."

Marsh understood all that while at the same time wondering if she wasn't being a tiny bit evasive, as if maybe she and Glory had had a spat before she left for Guam. He could still remember the expression on Sally's face when Glory had stood up in all her drunken splendor. It had not been one of admiration. God only knew what expression had been on his face seeing Glory half naked, but for weeks afterward, he realized that his romantic image of Glory Hawthorne had been badly damaged that night.

Had Sally just changed the subject?

The next morning, he had a visitor: Chief Marty Gorman. He was virtually unscratched, looking healthier than anyone out in the wards. His Irish good luck charms were still working. He told Marsh that his raft had become separated from the rest of the cluster and that he'd been in transit from one ship to the next, trying to get back to Guam to rejoin the crew. It had been a struggle because he was not injured, and no one went to Guam unless he was hospital bound.

"You indulged in some serious sweet-talking, I'm guessing," Marsh told him.

"I surely did, Cap'n," he said. "A little bribery, the promise of unnatural acts to come, the occasional sideways step at muster. I've had experience, you'll recall."

"Haven't we all, Marty," Marsh said. "It's been a long, wet road since that night in *Winston*."

"Wet being the operative word there, Skipper. I've taken to introducing myself as Chief Jonah."

"That's my line," Marsh said. "Except I'm waiting for the Court of Inquiry to decide on my punishment for losing yet another ship."

Gorman laughed. "I'm hearing that admirals will be talking to other admirals about all that," he said. "Us chickens just happened to be on the wrong ships at the wrong time."

"What else you hearing?"

"That there's a commander wandering the halls here, looking for his crew."

"Benson? He's here? He kept coming?"

"I am told that command of a destroyer being the Holy Grail for you officers, he did indeed keep coming, and now is ready to meet you."

Marsh felt a pang of disappointment. Of course he was. He had a future to attend to. Marsh did not. The chief saw his face.

"He looks like a good guy," he said. "Not a

screamer like that Hughes fella, God rest his soul. May I bring him in, Captain?"

Marsh nodded wordlessly. He'd forgotten all about the new, real replacement for Commander Hughes.

Gorman brought in Commander L. J. Benson, prospective commanding officer of USS *Evans*, or *former* prospective commanding officer of the *former* USS *Evans*. Marsh offered his functioning left hand to Benson's proffered right hand, and they both grinned at the awkwardness. He was tall, over six feet, and extremely thin, unlike many of the staffies Marsh had seen around Pearl. He had blond, graying hair, piercing blue eyes, and a genuine smile. Marsh sensed that Chief Gorman was right: The crew would like this guy. He already did.

Chief Gorman excused himself. "Still learning how to do all this," Marsh said. "Sorry about losing your ship, Commander."

"It's Larry, and if half the stories I've been hearing about that are true, I'm honored to meet you. You getting fixed up?"

"They're talking prostheses, but for that I have to go back to Pearl. Don't know when or how that's all going to work. I'm surprised they didn't turn you around."

"Me, too," Benson said, dropping into a metal chair that was too small for his lanky frame, "but then I got new orders. In Bureau-speak, I'm supposed to take inventory of the surviving crew members, separate the long-term disability cases from the guys who can come back to duty, and then take them back to Boston as the nucleus crew for the new USS *Evans*. There's a fresh-caught lieutenant commander already back at the shipyard standing up the rest of the precom crew."

Marsh nodded. He'd been expecting something like this. "They broke up the crew in *Winston* when she went down," he said. "I wasn't sure what they'd do with my guys. Your guys, I guess."

"The theory is if they can salt the greenies with some veterans, the postconstruction workup goes twice as fast, and the ship gets into service that much sooner. I'm going to need your input on this little project. Who the experienced guys are, who if anyone should *not* be part of a pre-commissioning crew, like that."

Marsh realized that Benson was already speaking like a commanding officer. "A lot of the experienced guys went to Davy Jones," he said.

"I understand," Benson replied. "That must be painful for you."

Marsh sighed. "There are times I'm sick at heart for what happened. Then I get out in the ward with the crew, and they make it better. Don't need an XO, do you?"

He smiled. "I wish I could," he said, "but your Navy career is over. You know that, don't you?"

"I hadn't considered it that way," Marsh said, a little surprised by Benson's bluntness. "Avoiding the obvious, I guess. One leg, one arm. One claw, one peg leg pretty soon. I guess that would scare the shit out of a bunch of boot recruits."

Benson laughed. "Yes, I think it would. On the other hand, no one would screw around with the XO, would they?"

"Everybody who survived and who isn't still hard-down is out in this ward," Marsh said. "Let's go meet them, tell 'em what's going on, and then we can get started." He paused. "They're all going to want to go, you know."

"I was hoping they would," Benson said.

He helped Marsh climb into his chariot and then wheeled him out into the ward. Their joint appearance got everyone's attention, and Marsh gave them the skinny. He could see them sizing up the new guy, who was sizing them up right back. When he'd finished, Marsh nodded at Commander Benson to see if he had anything to say. He did.

"Gents," he said, "the Japs killed the *Evans*, but there's a brand-new one almost finished up in Beantown, and I'm going to be the captain. I'm hoping to take many of you back there with me. I need experienced hands who can teach all the boots what to do and how to act, me included. You've been through things I've only read about, but I'll do my best to keep you safe while we go out there and kill more Japs. How's that sound?"

There was a quiet but sincere rumble of approval from the guys. His guys now, Marsh reminded himself. Then Commander Benson turned around, put on his gold-braided cap, drew himself to attention, and saluted Marsh in his wheelchair.

"Captain Vincent, I'm ready to relieve you, sir."

Marsh was stunned. It was truly a class act. He tried to stand, but he couldn't. He tried to return Benson's salute, but as he raised his stump he realized he couldn't do that, either. Ordinarily the departing CO would make a short speech to thank his crew for their service. Marsh could not find the words for a speech, so he just looked around at all his people, mouthed the words "thank you" several times, and then spoke aloud the words expected of him to Commander Benson: "I stand relieved, sir."

All he could do then was sit in his chair and try to keep the tears back. The crew clapping and cheering like a bunch of high schoolers from their beds didn't help.

The moment Sally saw the Guam-to-Pearl med flight patient manifest with Marsh's name on it, she knew she'd have to sit down and finally tell him about Glory's pregnancy. She had ducked his oblique questions about Glory, how she was doing, do you ever hear from her, should I write her a letter, and she was pretty sure Marsh had picked up on her evasions. Almost like an old married couple, she thought wistfully.

They'd become so much closer through their letters, which had been necessarily cryptic about operational matters as the censors demanded. Technically neither of them could talk about what they were doing or where Marsh was, so the only subjects left were personal—feelings, likes, dislikes, plans for the future. Now that they were here, together, those spidery lines on crinkly airmail paper were coming to life. Sally had been much freer with such sentiments than Marsh, but over time she'd gotten him to open up, with the result being that they'd drawn together, as friendship morphed into something else, something more substantial. Her being able to care for him directly when he and the remains of his crew hit Guam had only reinforced their bond—but how strong a bond? she wondered. Telling him about Glory might be the first real test.

She went to see him one evening and wheeled him out onto one of the ward's porches to watch the sunset. Most of the hospital buildings were up on Agana Heights, overlooking the harbors and facing generally north and west, as if to remind the patients of where their duty still lay.

"Got something to tell you," she said, even then not sure of how to say all this.

He looked over at her with interest. "That sounds a little ominous," he said.

"Serious, not ominous," she replied. "It concerns Glory Lewis."

He sat up in the chair and immediately winced as his phantom lower leg yelled at him. "Is she okay?"

Sally nodded and then told him the story. As she'd expected, he was stunned. She understood, however reluctantly, that an unreasonably idealized image was dissolving with every word she spoke.

"You asked about her the other day, and I avoided your question," she said. "I apologize for that, but since you're going back to Pearl in two days, I thought you should know."

He took her hand. "Don't apologize. I fully understand. Do we know, um—"

"She never so much as said," Sally replied. "All she told me was that *she* knew who the father was and that that was all anyone else needed to know."

"Wow," he said after a minute's reflection. "How did the hospital staff people treat her?" he asked. "A commissioned officer, an unwed mother, an unknown daddy—I can just hear the alley cats singing."

"There was some of that," Sally said, "but most of the nurses who'd been there for a while treated her with sympathy and, as her term approached, with care. An armchair at meetings instead of one of those folding metal chairs. Subtle changes in her work assignments that didn't involve heavy lifting. One of the OR supes gave her a wedding ring, so that the men out in the wards didn't crack wise. She wore it, too."

"The doctors?"

"They were too busy to be catty. Stembridge was knocked for a loop, as you might imagine, but the hospital CO was very supportive and told her that she could even have the baby at the hospital."

"Did she?"

"No, she went into a convent downtown in Honolulu for the last four weeks. I thought it was almost medieval, but she was healthy, strong, well nourished, and in the hands of a dozen or so midwives. It was probably a safer place than the hospital."

"And then?"

"The nuns took over. The baby was a boy, and she says they'll have no problems placing him, although I wondered about that, in Hawaii and in wartime. A haole boy? Another mouth to feed?"

"A boy," Marsh said wonderingly. "Wow."

She examined the expression on his face. He looked like a brand-new father himself. "Marsh Vincent," she said. "Is there something you haven't told me?"

He gaped at her and then turned red in the face. "Good Lord, no," he said. "I mean, all those years

I used to dream about her and what it would be like if we got married. Then Tommy's face would intrude, and I'd kick myself for being silly. So: You *have* heard from her?"

"No, actually," Sally said, trying to keep a pang of disappointment from showing in her voice. The love of his dreams still wielded her powers. "The last I heard she was back at work and everything was fine. I left for Guam before she delivered, but the girls back in Pearl wrote. Have you heard from Mick McCarty, by the way?"

He shook his head. "He was on one of the jeep carriers, the *Madison Bay*. She was sunk that day off Samar, but I've heard they got all their planes off before she went down. The sky was full of planes from all over, so I'm guessing they found other decks. There were twelve more escort carriers farther out to sea, so there were places for the orphans to go."

"So he's still down in the Philippines somewhere?"

"I suppose so," he said. "There's so much scuttlebutt floating around here, who knows. Anyway, I guess it's no longer my concern."

"What? What are you saying?"

"I'm all done, Sally, dear," he said, squeezing her hand. "I'll be medically retired as soon as someone gets around to declaring me 'healed.' One-armed, one-legged lieutenant commanders are not in high demand."

"Gosh," she said. "I never thought of that."

"Me, neither," he said. "I was looking for orders. Now I've got to figure out where to go and what to do."

"I can't believe they'll just, what's the word, discard you like that. The Navy's been your whole adult life."

"I can't complain," he said. "I'd rather be a discard growing a victory garden somewhere than a drifting cloud of shark poop."

"Marsh!" she scolded.

"Those are the choices, my dear, when you lose a sea-fight." He took a deep breath. "Every time I feel sorry for myself, I think of the guys who're still out there. They may park me on a shore staff somewhere in Pearl. God knows there are plenty of staffs back there. How long will you be assigned here?"

She shrugged. "For the duration, I guess, or until we build another hospital even closer to the action."

"So," he said. "Back to letters again, hunh?"

"If you'd like," she said, looking away.

"If I'd *like?*" he said. "Where'd that come from?"

"You're going back to Pearl, back to *her,*" she blurted.

He let go of her hand and sank back into the wheelchair.

"Back to her," he said quietly. "Oh, my, Sally.

You've got that all wrong. I'll admit to having been besotted with Glory Lewis for many years, but that was all in *my* head. She made that very clear, even when I said some really juvenile things to her after Tommy was killed. I'll even bet it was Glory who suggested that you and I start up a correspondence."

She colored when he said that, then nodded.

"See? I've been a bachelor for a long time. Glory was a placeholder, a beautiful woman I could dream about, but I think that even before December seventh, I knew it was just that—a pipe dream, and a safe one to boot. There's probably a dozen men out there who've had the same dream, and they—we, I guess—all secretly knew it was just a figment of our imaginations. There are some teeth behind that gorgeous facade, too. Remember what she did to poor Stembridge?"

"I do," she said. "So where does all this leave *us?*"

"Right where we left off on New Year's Day of 1944," he said. "We court, that's all. By mail if we have to, but you're in my heart, Ensign, and that's no pipe dream. Although you may prefer a guy with all his parts."

She whirled on him and then saw that shy grin. "You better not turn into some kind of whiner," she said. "I'm bigger than you are now, and I'll hide your wooden leg if you're not good."

"What wooden leg?" he asked.

"The one I'm going to beat you with, Marshall Vincent."

"Can we hold hands until then?" he asked.

"I'll think about it," she said, as they reached for each other in the twilight.

EIGHTEEN

After a long and bumpy flight from Guam to Honolulu via Wake Island, Marsh was assigned to a rehab center on the naval base at Pearl Harbor. There he spent a day learning how to use a wheelchair by himself and was measured for some temporary prosthetic devices. These would be produced back in the States and sent out to Pearl, after which he would come back to the rehab center for more training. The next day he had to go through the sadly familiar routine of reacquiring personal effects, beginning with clothes that could accommodate his injuries. That meant long-sleeved khaki shirts to hide the arm stump and some khaki trousers altered to cover up the leg stump. The ships-service sales store was kind enough to sell him a couple of left shoes. Apparently that wasn't a unique request.

Once again he had to reconstitute his service, pay, and medical records. These all existed in permanent form back in Washington somewhere, but he needed local records to get things like a new ID card, a BOQ room, and a ration book. Naturally there was no single office on the base that could do all these things, so he spent a lot of time on shuttle buses, being helped on and off by willing sailors.

He was acutely aware of the fact that he had avoided calling Glory. If asked, he could have provided several excuses: He was very busy. He was in rehab. He'd lost enough parts to make him feel like less of a man. More importantly, if he went to see Glory, he'd have to tell Sally, and that would break her heart. Breaking Sally's heart was not an option.

Each night, however, he thought about it. Then he thought about how the light in Sally's eyes could be dimmed by just the suggestion that he was still interested in how Glory was doing. Sally was his future. Glory was, well, what? Tommy's widow, Beast's one-night stand?

No, that was too harsh. Glory was an intelligent and gorgeous woman. Just not in his league, at all. A future with her was a figment of his imagination, if he was to be truthful to himself. He wasn't in Sally's league, either, but she loved him and he loved her. That's all that mattered. The war would end some day, and he wanted to both survive it and spend the future with Sally.

So: Don't call. It was as simple as that.
Right.
On his third day back at Pearl he received a call

to report to the admin officer at base headquarters. He wheeled himself with his one good arm down the main hallway in a series of interrupted right turns and into the administrative office, where he was asked to wait. By then he was fully qualified to wait. His brand-new khakis felt stiff and itchy, and his missing right foot ached, as usual. Then he was surprised when the admin officer's batwing doors bumped open to reveal a commander in his own wheelchair. He saw Marsh and rolled his way over in his direction.

"Welcome aboard, Mister Vincent," he said. "In case they didn't tell you, you're my new assistant admin-O. I'm Hugo Oxerhaus."

"Commander, pleased to meet you, and, no, they didn't tell me."

"For what it's worth, you are now officially part of 'they,' " he said. Then he grinned. "And you're out of uniform, by the way."

"I am?" Marsh said. He immediately felt his shirt collars to see if he'd forgotten to put on his gold oak leaves.

"You definitely are," he replied. "Come with me, please, and we'll rectify that."

He spun his chair around with more ease than Marsh could manage—he still had both hands. He had two legs, too, but they didn't seem to move at all. It took Marsh a minute to get his own chair turned around, and one of the yeomen asked if he needed a hand.

"I need an arm if you've got one lying around," he said. "Otherwise, I've got to learn how to manage this. Thanks anyway."

He followed Oxerhaus down the hallway toward the front of the building, where they entered the naval base commander's office suite. Two pretty female yeomen stood up when they wheeled in. One went into the admiral's office through yet another set of batwing doors. A moment later she reappeared and ushered them in to meet the base commander, a rear admiral. He welcomed Marsh aboard and then picked up a piece of paper from his desk.

"Got something for you, Commander," he said. Marsh thought he was talking to Oxerhaus, but the admiral was looking at him. Then he read out a promotion order that apparently had Marsh's name on it. Oxerhaus produced a small box of silver oak leaves, and the admiral pinned them onto Marsh's shirt collar.

"Congratulations, *Commander* Vincent," he said.

"I don't know what to say, sir," Marsh said. "I thought the next official letter I'd get would be from a Court of Inquiry."

The admiral smiled. "That's been concluded, at least for the moment," he said. "You're a surviving commanding officer of one of the destroyers who went up against Jap battlewagons off Samar. If anything, you're something of a celebrity up at PacFleet. One of these days you're going to get to meet Admiral Nimitz."

"I'd be honored to meet Admiral Nimitz," Marsh said.

"Most people are," the admiral replied. "He's quite something in person. Anyway, you'll be assigned here for a while until the Navy decides what to do with you."

"I assumed medical retirement."

"Perhaps," he said. "Do you have somewhere to go urgently?"

"No, sir, unless you've got a seagoing XO job that needs filling."

He smiled. "I suspect the Bureau of Navigation will come up with something useful for you to do. In the meantime, this war is far from over."

"Don't I know it," Marsh said, not meaning to be funny. Oxerhaus and the admiral both laughed, and finally he did, too.

Oxerhaus rolled back to his office with Marsh in tow. He described Marsh's duties, which didn't sound a whole lot different from when he'd been an XO aboard ship. The whole idea of being promoted to full commander hadn't sunk in yet. He was still looking over his shoulder for some grim-faced captain to summon him in front of a board or a court of some kind for "losing" *Evans*. Commander Oxerhaus assured him that he would not be stuck doing make-work. The naval base at Pearl had become the collecting point for most of the Pacific Navy's wounded, creating a veritable mountain of paperwork, Marsh's included.

"At least I won't make you push my chair around like I did to one of your predecessors, that McCarty fella."

"Mick McCarty?" Marsh asked. "He's a classmate. In fact, he was at Leyte in one of the jeeps."

"Really," Oxerhaus said, frowning. "Every class has its share of jerks. I've had an informal query in to the Bureau of Personnel now for a month trying to locate him. Which ship?"

"*Madison Bay*. Actually, she was sunk, but I believe they got all their aircraft off before she went down. There's a possibility that he was shot down that day, but he's probably on one of the Taffys out there."

"What's a Taffy?" he asked, and Marsh explained the call signs of the escort carrier task groups. Then he asked why Oxerhaus needed to get hold of Beast.

"It involves one of the Navy nurses over at Hospital Point," he said.

It was Marsh's turn to take a breath. "Which nurse?" he asked. "Is her name Lewis?"

That surprised Oxerhaus. "Yes, it is. You know her?"

"Very well," Marsh said. "What's happened?"

Oxerhaus blew out a long breath and then suggested they go for a roll. It took Marsh a minute to figure that out, but then he did, and they went outside the building and into the morning sunlight. Marsh was a little surprised that two commanders in wheelchairs didn't seem to attract any special attention, but Pearl was full of wounded men.

"Ensign Lewis disappeared one night about three weeks ago," he said. "Nobody saw her go, and she didn't talk to anyone about going anywhere. She simply disappeared."

Marsh's blood ran cold. "Was there an investigation?" he asked.

"Oh, yes," Oxerhaus said. "We got the CID branch of the HASP into it right away; she was supposedly a beautiful woman, and everyone was thinking some kind of assault. Plus, there were special circumstances."

"Her recent pregnancy."

Again Marsh had surprised his new boss. He explained how he knew about that.

"Okay," Oxerhaus said. "I personally spoke to her supervisor at the hospital, a Lieutenant Somebody. She said she'd seen some signs of postpartum depression but nothing she would call out of the ordinary. Apparently all women go through it after having a baby."

Marsh had never heard of postpartum anything, but he accepted the conventional wisdom. "Her best buddy at the hospital was Ensign Adkins," Marsh said. "She was sent out to Guam to stand up the new hospital out there. That's where I ended up after Leyte, and she told me she hadn't heard from Ensign Lewis for some time."

"Well, the HASP came up empty-handed. They coordinated with the Honolulu police, but they usually don't get involved in military cases. Said they'd check their informants, see if anyone had heard about a haole being abducted or anything, but nothing came back."

"My God," Marsh said. "This is such a small place. How could she simply disappear?"

"Was she a swimmer, do you know?"

"She was not," Marsh said. "Avoided deep water entirely."

"We lose a surprising number of people to the sea around here," Oxerhaus said. "People forget that Oahu's a volcanic mountain, sticking up out of twelve thousand feet of water. Some of the beaches are superfine black volcanic sand. Underwater it acts like quicksand. Your feet get stuck, then your legs, then a big wave comes in and you can't move, so you drown. We warn everybody, put signs on the beach, but many don't pay any attention. All they want to do is go to the beach, drink beer, and meet women."

"She would *not* have gone into any kind of surf."

"Was she involved with anyone, romantically?"

Marsh elected to keep Glory's connection to Mick out of the conversation. If he even

529

mentioned Mick, Oxerhaus would make him suspect number one. He also knew that there was no way Mick could have been involved in Glory's disappearance. Besides, he was pretty sure now that had been Mick's Dauntless diving into that Jap cruiser. "Must have been, at least once" was all he could manage.

"Yeah, right," Oxerhaus nodded. "At least once. The other nurses mentioned McCarty as a possible, but he'd left Pearl long before this happened. Which was too bad, because he'd make a great suspect."

Suspicions confirmed, Marsh thought. "Why?"

"Your classmate, McCarty, was a big-time drunk. Started a fight with the HASP, with predictable results. He was miraculously the sole survivor off a med flight that ditched near Guadalcanal, and, speaking from personal experience, he pulled some seriously dangerous stunts back when I was air boss in *Yorktown*. I had him in hack at the BOQ after the HASP incident, and, frankly, I was looking for a way to yank his wings. Found out that, these days, anyway, a bar brawl with the shore patrol won't get you kicked out of naval aviation."

Marsh just shook his head and didn't say anything. They went back into the office, where Oxerhaus had a yeoman show Marsh to his first in-box.

That night Marsh had dinner at the O-club for

the first time since his last visit to Pearl. It hadn't changed much, except to become if anything even more crowded. The new hostess, a gorgeous young thing arrayed in Hawaiian costume, took Marsh back to a corner of the main dining room that he later learned was called Crip's Corner. The tables had been modified for wheelchairs, and there were four other officers in chairs already there. They'd been drinking awhile, based on the elevated noise level at their end of the table.

As a waiter rolled Marsh into an empty slot, he realized he was the senior officer there; the rest of them were lieutenants. The one seated next to him had lost his entire right leg at the hip, which might or might not have accounted for his unsteady condition. He was staring at Marsh's shiny new silver oak leaves and shaking his head. Marsh obviously looked too young to him to be a three-striper.

"A commander?" he began, slurring his syllables just a bit. The man next to him nudged him in the ribs, and the guy blinked, burped, and then closed his eyes.

"Sorry, sir," the other lieutenant said. "Harry's got kind of a load on."

"No problem," Marsh said. "Where you guys from?"

They were all aviators, including Sleeping Beauty. They told Marsh that Harry had brought his fighter back aboard his carrier, caught a wire, stopped, slid back his canopy, ducked down into the cockpit, and then thrown the remains of his leg onto the flight deck and asked for a medic before passing out. Harry was now, of course, rapidly passing into naval aviation legend.

The waiter brought Marsh a Scotch and a menu. One of the lieutenants worked up the nerve to ask what had happened to him. Marsh told them he'd lost an expensive sea-fight against a Jap battleship. "Expensive?" the young man asked. "Cost me an arm and a leg, didn't it?" Marsh replied. They laughed and promptly went back to drinking, probably thinking that Marsh was lying, nuts, or both. Harry continued his nap, which Marsh thought was probably a good thing.

As Marsh sipped his Scotch, he tried to get his mind around the idea of Glory disappearing. He simply couldn't comprehend it. He kept running through scenarios that could explain it. She'd been abducted, raped, strangled, and thrown into the sea. She'd gone into the city and stolen back her baby and was hiding out in the countryside somewhere with a Hawaiian family. She'd become fed up with all the backbiting about her unwed-mother status and stowed away on a troop transport or hospital ship headed stateside.

None of his theories seemed likely. As a commissioned officer who'd gotten herself knocked up, to put it in the vernacular, she must have been pretty humiliated. On the other hand, she'd had the personal courage to see the thing through. As an experienced operating room nurse, getting rid of her "problem" would not have been that difficult. Instead, according to Sally, she'd put her head down, ignored all the smug looks and snippy comments, and gone back to work. That was not the course of someone who would run away from Pearl.

Could she have committed suicide? That was always possible, but usually there was a note and a body. She'd been pining for her husband ever since December 1941, with her loss compounded by the fact that Tommy was entombed in a burned-out hulk no more than a half mile from where she worked and walked, every single day. If she could handle that, plus the enormous strains of a frontline wartime hospital, she was not a likely candidate for suicide.

So what the hell *had* happened?

He decided that for as long as he was stashed here in Pearl, he'd make it his mission to find out. Somebody over there in the nurses' quarters had to know something. In the meantime, he had to tell Sally. All things considered, he'd liked her recent surprise a lot better than the one he was going to drop on her.

For the next month he settled into the work of routine in the base headquarters, pushing more paper than he thought even existed. Oxerhaus had a formidable reputation in the headquarters building for an unstable temperament, but Marsh thought the fact that they were both wheelchair-bound kept his bile pointed elsewhere. He became more proficient at doing just about everything with one hand and one leg, including the basics of personal hygiene, printing legibly with his left hand, getting in and out of buildings that were never built with wheelchairs in mind, and gritting his way through the travail of a rehab program that was supposed to prepare him for the attachment of his prostheses. He never did get to go meet Admiral Nimitz, though.

In his spare time, he obtained a copy of the HASP investigation on Glory's disappearance and pored over their interview reports in the evenings. They'd done what looked like a thorough job, talking to everyone with whom Glory had come in contact, both on the base and even at the convent. They'd visually confirmed that her baby, who was still at the convent nursery, had not been kidnapped by his distraught mother. The conclusions section was succinct in the extreme: The case officially remained open. Given the fact that literally thousands of personnel were flowing through Hawaii on their way west, with a considerable number of them getting in some kind of shore patrol trouble downtown, "open" was tantamount to "closed."

Sally wrote constantly, especially after Marsh

told her about Glory's vanishing act. She was working on getting a transfer back to the hospital at Pearl so that they could be together, and he was hoping that she succeeded. On those nights when his stumps hurt and his future looked increasingly bleak, he often worried that Sally might back out of their budding romance in favor of another guy with all his pins still in place. When he listened to the other crips at the O-club, the Dear Johns were a frequent subject of conversation. At one point he talked himself into a guessing game: Was she still giving him the time of day simply out of sympathy or loyalty? Was he reading too much into their relationship, which, after all, was based more on letters than weeks of personal contact? Should he broach these thoughts in his letters to her?

Fortunately he kept in mind that old saw from the academy's little plebe-year book containing the so-called Laws of the Navy, and one rule in particular: They prosper who burn in the morning those letters they wrote overnight. Everything looked better against the backdrop of a Hawaiian sunrise and the first cup of Navy office coffee. Even Oxerhaus was reasonably nice for that first hour in the office until something set him off. It didn't take much, Marsh discovered.

One Monday the something was a report of the casualty lists from the Samar engagement. Under the *Madison Bay*'s embarked aviation squadron report was the name of Mick McCarty, who was now officially listed as missing in action. Marsh was taken aback when he showed the lists to Oxerhaus. He'd expected an oh-well-too-bad reaction. Instead Oxerhaus fulminated about not getting another chance to chew Mick's ass for something.

"He's listed as MIA," Marsh reminded him. "More than one MIA has popped back up when the paperwork got straightened out."

"Knowing him, he's on some island out there lollygagging with the bare-breasted natives," Oxerhaus grumped. "Find out who the skipper was of VC-Eleven; get official confirmation that professional fuckup isn't just laying low."

"Aye, aye, sir."

Marsh followed up on that order the next week. It turned out that the skipper of Composite Eleven was right there in Pearl, the newest orphan in the Aviation Motor Pool, awaiting orders to take what remained of his people on board a new CVE that was coming through Pearl in three weeks. Marsh invited him to come to the base headquarters building for a meeting. That afternoon, a yeoman stuck his head into his office and said there was a Commander Campofino to see him.

"Max Campofino," the commander said as he came through the batwing doors. Marsh recognized him as one of Navy's better-known varsity football players back in 1932. He introduced himself, and they did the usual do-you-know drill common to Naval Academy graduates.

Campofino confirmed that Mick had gone up with two nuggets, who'd quickly used up all their ammo, such as it was. Mick had detached them to fly to the Army airfield on Leyte to rearm. The last they saw of him, he was headed back to harass the Japs.

"Harass?"

"You gotta understand, Marsh, we were goin' up there with fifty-cals, trench-busters, eggs and potatoes. None of the ordnance Mother Madison was carrying would do much against a battleship, and, believe me, we had zero time to upload what they did carry. There were Jap cruisers punchin' holes right through her as we launched."

"And Mick never came back?"

"Nope. I landed on one of the Taffy One jeeps, rearmed, went back out, and then it was all over. Japs turned tail for Bernardino Strait. I spent the next five days trying to gather in all my chickens. Fifteen guys made it off the ship. I got nine back."

"Did all the squadrons experience such losses?"

"More than we would have expected, but, again, you gotta remember, we had lots of nuggets, guys who'd never been up against much more than Jap snipers in trees. A heavy cruiser throwin' directed ack-ack is something else again, especially when some of the guys were making fake bombing runs with empty racks. It was more than surreal. You should have seen it."

"Actually, I did," Marsh said.

"Yeah? You were there? At *Leyte?*" Then he registered that Marsh was in a chair.

"That's how I ended up short a wing and a wheel," Marsh said. "I was skipper of *Evans*."

"Holy *shit,* really? You *were* there."

"And then we weren't," Marsh said with a grin. "Pissing off a pair of battleships will do that."

Max sat back in his chair. "God *damn,*" he said. "We heard about the tin cans getting between the jeeps and the Japs, and how none of 'em came back. One of our guys told of seeing a tin can almost alongside one of the Jap heavies, blasting away while that big bastard tried to get away from him. Said they were pointing main battery at the destroyer, but she was too close."

"That was us," Marsh said. "I put us alongside because then the cruisers couldn't fire at us without hitting their flagship. That was the theory, at least. Didn't last long, but we were pretty much done by then anyway."

Max nodded, but his eyes were far away, remembering the chaos of that morning. Marsh recognized that look.

"Tell me something," Marsh said. "I saw a Dauntless crash into a heavy cruiser, just before the Kongo put us down for the count. Hit her amidships, and then there was a really big blast. Any chance that could have been Mick?"

"I heard that story," Max said. "That one of our planes did a suicide attack. I didn't believe it, mostly because I can't imagine doing such a thing. If I could fly it, I could ditch it."

"Maybe he couldn't," Marsh said. "I only had a few seconds to see it, but he didn't seem to be flying very well, like maybe he was wounded."

"Plane smoking? On fire?"

Marsh closed his eyes, trying to recapture the image. "No, he wasn't on fire, but there were streams of smoke," he said. "He was sluggish, like he was really working to get that plane to maneuver. Like everything was taking too long."

"Sounds like a guy who looked down after getting hit and found his guts in his lap. They say that when it's really, really bad, the body doesn't feel it for a minute or two. But the brain knows."

"I wonder," Marsh said.

"Coulda been," Max said. "Sounds like something Mick might do, if he thought he was gonna buy the farm. Funny thing is, the Japs did just that the very next day. Some Jap pilot came in on the *St. Lo* and blew her in half in what everybody who saw it agreed had to be a deliberate suicide attack. The difference is that he apparently came out *intending* to do that, based on the scuttlebutt. He didn't make any other bombing or torpedo runs, just appeared out of nowhere, nosed over, and took himself and his bomb through the flight deck and into the hangar bay. Big ball of fire, and she was gone."

Marsh nodded absently. Now it was his turn to be back there, watching fourteen-inch shells come through the tin-clad sides of the bridge to impale his watch standers on the edges of the hole.

"Marsh?"

He snapped back. "Sorry," he said. "Sometimes . . ."

"I understand. Truth is, I didn't know that any of the tin can guys made it back. Word was they all went to Davy Jones."

"A reasonable assumption," Marsh said. "At times I was more than ready."

Max nodded and stood up. "I'll ask around, see if anybody actually saw that guy dive in on purpose. Right now, it's rumor, but I'll shake some rumor trees, see what I can find out."

"One last question: Did Mick have something painted on the side of his plane? Something white?"

"Yeah, he did. He said he was naval aviation's version of the Lone Ranger, so he had one'a the shirts paint a white horse on the fuselage. Why?"

"The guy who flew into the Jap cruiser had something white, besides the star, on his side. I couldn't see what it was, other than it was white."

"Well, I'll be damned. Maybe you just answered your own question, and some of mine, too."

"Would you check anyway?" Marsh asked. "I'm hoping I'm wrong."

"Absolutely," he said.

"I'd appreciate it," Marsh said and offered his left hand.

"You're class of 'thirty-two and a commander already? Somebody thinks highly of you."

"I'm not sure why," Marsh said. "I keep waiting for a summons to a court of some kind. The funny thing is, *Evans* wasn't even my ship, really—I was just the acting CO until a new skipper got out there."

"Class act," Max said. "Honored to meet you, Skipper."

That evening Marsh wheeled himself out to the Hospital Point seawall from his BOQ room. It was another depressingly perfect Hawaiian sunset. He saw some nurses out behind the quarters but decided he wanted to be alone this evening. He went to the channel seawall at the end of the street where the nurses' quarters were located and set the brakes on the chair. There were more lights on in Pearl Harbor these days, reflecting the fact that the Allies were now bringing the war to the doorstep of the Japanese Home Islands. Streetlights were back on over on Ford Island, and the major base buildings were no longer blacked out. It was all very different from those dark days of early 1942 when he'd come through on *Winston* and everybody was searching the skies for round two and the beaches for signs of the expected invasion. He automatically looked for the *Arizona*, but now she lay invisible in the sparkling harbor waters, with only the top of one barbette and two lonely buoys marking her resting place.

He'd received a letter today from Sally saying that she was wrangling a leave back here to Pearl and still working on a permanent transfer. He'd not been surprised how happy that news had made him. He missed her very much and was finally accepting the fact that they'd managed to fall in love. That didn't dampen his determination to find out what had happened to Glory Lewis, but he knew he would have to tread carefully to make sure Sally didn't misinterpret that determination. He'd already made inquiries at the Hickam air base, reviewing passenger manifests for her name. He'd actually gone downtown to HASP headquarters to talk to their detectives. It wasn't that they didn't care—they did. Absent any evidence of foul play or knowledge of anyone who might have wanted to hurt her or abduct her, they simply had nothing to go on. She was there one day, gone the next. Many of the possibilities Marsh had been checking were already documented in their records of the case.

The lead detective was a local, as people born and raised on the island were called by the occupying military people. He was a giant Samoan who looked like Marsh's idea of a Japanese sumo wrestler. They'd had to put two desks together for him to be able to put both arms on the top. He'd introduced himself as George Kamehaohno; he told Marsh to call him Kam.

"Me, I'm thinkin' she's in the water," he said, closing the record binder. The word "water" came out as "wadduh." "People disappear like that here on the island, no jealous husband or boyfriend, no big money trouble? Usually the sea has 'em."

"But why no body?" Marsh asked and then remembered the obvious answer. Sharks. He didn't even have to say it. He nodded, having answered his own question.

"You gonna keep lookin'?" Kam asked.

"Yes, I am."

"Go talk to alla those women at the hospital, then. Women know things. Sometimes they know things they don't know they know. And they're all Navy people. Maybe don't wanna talk to the HASP, see?"

"Good idea," Marsh said and went back to the base.

The problem wasn't that the nurses had been unwilling to talk to the HASP. The real problem was that none of them assigned there now knew Glory all that well. Most of the first wave of nurses had been shipped out to the western

543

Pacific. Even so, he took to wheeling himself along the channel seawall in the evening with a glass of Scotch planted in a makeshift cup holder taped to his wheelchair. There were usually nurses out there every evening enjoying the breeze and getting the smell of a day's bloody work in the hospital out of their hair. They all looked so very young, even though he was perhaps not much more than twelve years their senior—in age. Most of them immediately retreated behind wide-eyed yes-sirs and no-sirs once they found out he was a commander. Whatever their experience in nursing, they were all ensigns, and full commanders were really important people. If they only knew, Marsh thought.

They'd heard about Glory's disappearance, and a very few knew about the pregnancy. None of them had any ideas on what might have happened, but the unspoken consensus was, surprisingly, that it had something to do with her having been an unwed mother. Marsh had to restrain himself from asking if they'd ever seen her wearing a scarlet letter on her uniform. He'd chat with them for a little while, enveloped in clouds of cigarette smoke, and then wheel himself down to the point to think about both Glory and Sally.

One night a voice interrupted his reverie. "Boat ride? Boss wanna boat ride?"

Marsh couldn't find the source of the voice until a head popped up over the lip of the seawall.

"Boat ride?" the man asked again, and then he saw the wheelchair. "Oh—oh, sorry, no can do, bro."

The man was a local, dressed in a faded Hawaiian shirt and khaki shorts. His boat looked like an overgrown sampan, complete with a badly rusted engine clamped to the transom.

"Boat ride?" Marsh said. "Where to?"

"Harbor side," he said. "Very pretty. Go see lotsa stuff. Five dollah, or you gimme cigarettes." Then he frowned, staring at the wheelchair again. "You can walk? Stand up to get in?"

"Afraid not," Marsh said. "Can't swim so good, either. The Navy lets you do this?"

He shrugged. "Navy fellas no care, long as we stay away from big kapu ship."

Kapu. That was the only Hawaiian word Marsh knew besides aloha. Americans would have said taboo. He had to be talking about the *Arizona*. Marsh asked him why that wreck was kapu.

"Ghosts," he said. "Lotsa gottem ghosts. You go too close, they get you, pull you down inside. You die then. Big kapu."

"That makes sense," Marsh said, fully believing that the wreck would be haunted, what with over a thousand still inside her.

"Well, I wish I could go with you," he said, "but . . ." He pointed at his leg and a half and shrugged.

"You got cigarette?" the boatman asked.

Marsh had been carrying cigarettes to use as an icebreaker when he rolled up, since most of the nurses smoked. He gave one to the boatman and lit it for him. The man smelled faintly of fish and charcoal. He thanked Marsh and sat back down in his little boat. "I go get Navy nurse," he said. "They like go boat ride. Lotsa Navy people go boat ride. See the lights?"

Marsh looked out over the harbor, and in fact he could see the dim stern lights on some small boats.

"The nurses are back over there," Marsh said, pointing over his shoulder at the seawall area behind the quarters. "They've got cigarettes, too."

A question occurred to him as the little man began to push the boat away from the seawall. "You say lots of nurses go boat ride with you?"

"Oh, yeah," he said. "We go 'em alla time. Alla Navy ladies wanna see da big kapu, but we no go dere. We go see da oddah one, backside Ford Island. Dey call it *Oo-tah*. No kapu dere. Not like *Ah-zona*. One Aiea guy, he go *Ah-zona* one night? Said crazy haole woman *make* him go. Plenty ghost come for him, but he get away. Next day, da guy? He break both da legs. *Ah-zona* big kapu. *Bad* kapu."

He waved and backed the boat around the corner of the seawall and went down to see if he could scare up some able-bodied passengers.

Marsh finished his Scotch and started back to the BOQ. Halfway there, he stopped.

Crazy haole woman *made* him go? To the *Arizona*?

He wheeled the chair around to go see if he could find the boatman, but it was now full dark. He wanted the name of "da guy" who took a crazy white woman out to the *Arizona*. He didn't want to think about what might have happened out there, but a little voice in his head told him he'd maybe solved the mystery. Especially when the boatman had called the woman crazy.

He realized he needed some local help. Big Kam came to mind.

Three days later the big Samoan appeared in Marsh's office in his HASP uniform. Beside him was a very frightened local, a scrawny old man who looked like a stick-figure doll next to the giant patrolman. He was dressed just like the other boatman—khaki shorts, flip-flops, and a faded Hawaiian shirt. He had dirty casts on both shins, and he was walking stiffly with two canes.

Marsh invited the old man to sit down. He dropped into the chair, licking his lips nervously, looking around at all the uniformed haoles. The Samoan stood behind the chair, baton in hand, slapping it quietly into his enormous palm. Before Marsh could say anything, Kam nudged the old man with the end of his baton.

"You tell'm now, alla same you tell me," he ordered.

The old man nodded, looked at Marsh, and then looked away, cleared his throat, and told the story. As soon as Marsh heard him say the haole woman got into the boat demanding to go to the *Arizona*, not the *Utah*, paying twice the fare in cigarettes, he knew.

Would if I could, she'd said. Glory had gone back to Tommy in the only way she could.

Marsh could not imagine *why* she would do such a thing. He had long thought that she'd come to grips with Tommy's passing and that the night of the New Year's party had marked a milestone of sorts, where she decided to come back to life.

As he sat there contemplating the enormity of what the old man had just told them, Marsh realized that he had finished talking. The Samoan detective was studying the floor. Big Kam obviously understood that he had stumbled onto what the haoles would call a very hot potato and was trying hard to become invisible. Me, too, thought Marsh.

"You want we take him in?" Kam asked.

"No," Marsh said. "He told the truth, I believe. You think this was *his* fault?"

Big Kam thought about that. He was HASP, and they only dealt with guilty bastards, but then he shook his head. "No."

"Then let him go," Marsh said. "I think the Lewis case is finally closed."

Kam nodded. "What *you* gonna do now?" he asked.

"Beats the shit out of me."

Kam gave a big grin, then prodded the old boatman none too gently with his baton. "You go now," he said, "and you keep mouth shut about haole woman."

The old man stared up at him blankly, as if he didn't understand. Big Kam launched into some high-speed Hawaiian dialect, which produced a series of urgent nods. As they prepared to leave, Marsh asked him what he'd said.

"I tell'm, ghost of haole woman know where he lives. I tell'm, he talk about haole woman, her ghost come to his house, eat all his children."

"That ought to do it," Marsh said.

Oxerhaus and Marsh went in to see the admiral that afternoon. Marsh told him the story and waited for some kind of tirade, but it didn't come.

"You think that's where she is? *Inside* the *Arizona*?"

"I don't think that old man was making this up," Marsh said. "I learned earlier that the nurses sometimes go out into the harbor with these guys, just as a lark. They pay in cigarettes, which sounds right. If she jumped over the side right above that hole, she'd have gone straight down into whatever remains of the boiler rooms."

"Jesus," the admiral said softly. "And she was not a swimmer?"

"No, sir," Marsh said. "Tommy Lewis, her husband, was the main propulsion assistant in *Arizona* on December seventh, and he was aboard that morning. He had the duty."

The admiral grimaced. "So the question now is, do we send divers down there to find her remains."

"I think we have to," Oxerhaus said. "Her body might not be, um, intact at this point in time, but there will be women's clothing, something . . ."

"I disagree," Marsh said. Both of them looked at him in surprise. "First, it would be a very dangerous dive. When that magazine blew, it sent a fireball all the way back through the ship, confined internally by the armored box section. That included the boiler and engine rooms. God only knows the condition of bulkheads and decks down there."

"Go on," the admiral said.

"Second, everyone's already talking about the *Arizona* as some kind of shrine, a monument to be dedicated to the memory of the Jap attack and the thousands who died that day. That's a noble prospect. Do we really want to contaminate that with a suicide?"

"But," Oxerhaus began. Marsh held up a finger to interrupt him, not something people ordinarily did to Hugo.

550

"If we really have to know what happened to Ensign Lewis, then we'd of course have to investigate the wreck. But here's the thing: This sounds like a reasonable explanation for her disappearance. She was depressed after having had an illegitimate child, probably still being semi-shunned in the hospital, and she had a breakdown. Suppose we send divers down there and something happens? A deck collapses, a boiler falls over on them while they're looking? If she did kill herself, is it worth losing more men in that ship just to prove that thesis beyond a reasonable doubt? Perhaps most importantly, is anyone besides us asking?"

The admiral swiveled around in his chair and looked out the big windows. From his office he could see the spot where the *Arizona* lay, still bleeding oil.

"All good points, Commander," he said softly. "You're recommending that we close this case with what we know and what we surmise?"

"Yes, sir, I am. The Navy does not need something like this coming out just now."

"Or ever," the admiral said. "Hugo?"

"I can live with that, Admiral."

The admiral nodded. "Make it so, gentlemen."

"Aye, aye, sir," they both said and left his office.

"This is personal, isn't it?" Oxerhaus asked as they rolled together down the hallway.

"Yes, it is," Marsh said. "Very."

551

"Okay, then. The Navy owes you one. I'll support it. Was she beautiful?"

Marsh was suddenly having a problem seeing as they approached their respective offices. Oxerhaus pretended not to notice.

"Beyond compare, Commander," Marsh said. "Beyond compare."

That night Marsh went to the O-club, rolled himself up to the main bar, and told the bartender he needed to get very drunk. The bartender took one look at his face, called over a waiter, and handed him a bottle of Scotch and a glass. He told the waiter to roll Marsh over to Crips Corner and make sure he ate something in the next hour. Marsh reached for his wallet, but the bartender waved him off. "Sometimes, Commander, we drop a bottle, it breaks, and we gotta write it off. I think I just broke one."

Sally arrived two weeks later, just in time for Marsh's first prosthesis, a cuffed clamping-hand replacement. The rehab plan was to get that attachment up and working to the point where he could operate crutches, and then proceed to the next step: an artificial lower leg. After all the operations, Marsh had about three inches of forearm left below the elbow, which was enough to support the cuff attachment. The clamping mechanism was operated two ways. To pick something up, he would wrap the clamps around the object, and then close them using his left hand. To let go of it, all he had to do was bump the button on the bottom of the cuff on any hard surface, and the spring-loaded device would open.

The whole contraption could come off for cleaning and for what the nurses euphemistically called stump hygiene. The first day he wore it, he managed to knock just about everything off his desk and break not one but two coffee mugs. Oxerhaus told him if he couldn't do any better than that he'd get him an eye patch because obviously he didn't have any depth perception.

Sally showed up at the base headquarters at 1600 and surprised Marsh in his office. She was in uniform, a lieutenant junior grade now, and she looked wonderful to him, albeit thinner than he remembered. He introduced her to Oxerhaus and all the yeomen, whom she charmed with her brilliant smile. She then insisted on pushing his chair all the way back to the BOQ. His room was on the ground floor because there were no elevators in the building. Once inside the room she pulled the shades, took off her cap, and sat down in his lap.

"Hey, sailor," she said, and then she kissed him. When they came up for air she began unbuttoning his shirt. Then she unbuttoned her blouse and took it off. She told him to remove her bra.

Marsh laughed. "One hook or two?" he asked her, waving the stainless steel prosthesis at her.

"*Left* hand, if you please."

"Not sure I know how to do that with one hand."

"Time to learn," she said, and so he did. She helped by pressing her front into his face.

"Can't breathe," he mumbled.

"Then die happy," she said. "But first? Get closer to the bed and then set the brakes on this thing. We're about to fall."

Marsh would never have thought of that. In fact, he wasn't doing that much thinking just then. After a little while, neither of them was.

Much later, they had dinner at the O-club. Sally rolled his chair to a regular table and asked the waiter to bring a cushion so he could get his one and a half arms up over the edge. He waved at the guys over in Crips Corner and then explained to Sally who they were.

"That's terrible," she protested. "Making you into lepers just because you're in a wheelchair."

"Seemed fine to us," Marsh said. "Better service, too. But it is kind of nice to be back with the whole folks."

"You going to turn martyr on me?" she asked.

"Every chance I get," he said.

The waiter brought their drinks and a menu. He toasted Sally, and then he asked her to marry him. She was in the middle of taking a sip of her drink when he dropped that little bomb. She put down her glass and cocked her head to one side.

"Seriously?"

"I love you dearly," Marsh said, marveling inside at how easily that came out. "I'm tired of living alone, and after Leyte I have a whole lot better appreciation for life. I'd like to share it with you."

She looked down at her left hand and then extended it to his hook. "On one condition," she said. "This horrible thing comes off at bedtime."

"Aw, I'm beginning to really like this hook."

"I do not love your hook, for reasons I should not have to go into."

"You want me to take it off right here?" he asked. "Maybe wave the bloody stump around? Probably get us a better table."

"Don't you *dare*," she giggled.

"So the answer is yes?"

"The answer is yes. I would be thrilled to marry you."

"How about tomorrow?"

"Fine."

"Oops," he said. "I forgot to get an engagement ring."

"I think I'll survive," she said.

"Maybe we can use this," he said and slipped off his naval academy ring. He put it on her ring finger. It promptly fell right off. She retrieved it, put it back on her finger, and held up her hand. "This works," she said. "But since it will just get lost, why don't you keep it warm for me."

· · ·

That night, as they lay in bed in his BOQ room, he told her about what they thought had happened to Glory. She went rigid for a moment, then sighed and wiped away some tears.

"I often wondered if it had been something like that. She seemed so sad when I left for Guam. I was worried about her."

"Beast McCarty is missing, too." He told her of Oxerhaus's vindictive determination to find him and take away his wings. "There's a story going around that he was the one who crashed into that cruiser. I think I told you about that. We don't know the truth, and I don't suppose we ever will unless a better witness comes forward."

"He was the father, don't you think?" she asked.

"Yes, of course," Marsh said after a moment. "I do."

She was silent for a few minutes. The subject of Glory was still a delicate one between them, something of a double-edged sword. He worried that she'd interpret his telling her about what had happened as a sign of some lingering love.

"What would you think," she said, "if, after we get married, we go find that baby."

"Wow," Marsh said. "That's an amazing idea. We could adopt him, raise him as if he were our own."

"Yes," she said. "We could."

"Then maybe add some brothers and sisters?"

"Count on it," she said.

He held her close that night. Taking Glory's foundling into their brand-new family was the one way they both could lay her ghost to rest, and Mick's, too.

A year and a half after the end of the war, Marsh was the admin officer at the naval base. Hugo Oxerhaus had managed to have one temper tantrum too many, stroking out in his office one day after a particularly violent episode. The new naval base commander asked Marsh if he could just step in and take over the whole office. With no other prospects for naval service, a postwar recession building back on the mainland, and a brand-new wife and baby, Marsh quickly said yes.

The Navy had come out with a notice that they would be offering early retirement at the fifteen-year point to officers in the grade of commander and above. They needed to cull the service of an unbalanced number of senior officers. Combined with a medical disability rating, his pension would be almost as much as if he had gone the full twenty, so he elected to get out before they changed their minds. Sally was enthusiastic about his decision. She wanted to go back to the World, as people who'd been in Hawaii for a long time often called the mainland. Hawaii was a nice place to visit as long as you knew you could leave whenever the urge struck. After four years of war, that urge was very much there, for both of them. Between his pension and her ability to earn as a nurse, they'd be all right until Marsh could find a gainful career.

The paperwork war continued unabated after the Japanese surrender in the fall of 1945. The fleet was demobilizing from ten thousand ships down to one-tenth that number, and, while the ships were being mothballed back on the mainland, much of the Pearl Harbor operational infrastructure was also being shut down. The other major effort was the repatriation of American remains from distant Pacific battlefield islands and atolls back to the brand-new National Memorial Cemetery of the Pacific. This was a cemetery located in Puowaina Crater, an extinct volcano referred to by the locals in Hawaii as Punchbowl because of its shape. The Army had begun something called a database project at Tripler Hospital, because the repatriation of remains offered an opportunity to conduct a final accounting of the missing and the dead. It was a somber project, done all by hand, and it was expected to go on for the next decade, if not longer.

The Punchbowl memorial wasn't scheduled to be dedicated formally until 1949. Sally and Marsh had settled in San Diego by then, so Marsh was surprised to receive a formal invitation in 1948 from the Navy Department for both of them to attend the first reinterments, which would be some seven hundred sets of remains from the Japanese attack on December 7.

Marsh wanted no part of a return to Pearl Harbor, with all its painful associations. He was still experiencing bouts of depression whenever he allowed himself to brood about everything that had happened. His physical disabilities were less onerous than he'd anticipated, but there were many times when memories ambushed him. It was difficult for some of his civilian friends to fully understand why he'd drift away from a conversation and stare out into that mental middle distance. He was getting around on a cane and a crude artificial leg, but the wheelchair had not yet been fully retired. That said, he knew that, as a disabled vet, some doors had opened to him in his new career as a law student that might not have opened to someone with both his wings and wheels. He decided to decline the government's invitation.

Sally seemed to accept his decision, but a week later, she apparently changed her mind. Now she said they had to go. She said that the best way to face down the ghosts of war was to commit them to consecrated ground. Besides, she argued, the president was going to be there. He apparently wanted to see Punchbowl before the formal opening next year. Mr. Truman was in the middle of his own presidential election campaign—his first, since he had become president upon the death of Roosevelt in 1945. Marsh was surprised he would take the time to go all the way out there to an American territory, where there were no votes to be had. Sally told him that he clearly didn't understand anything about civilian politics.

Marsh's real problem remained, however. He really didn't know if he could stand going back. He hadn't been there for Pearl Harbor, as the December 7 attack was universally called now, but he'd seen the wreckage of the Pacific Fleet soon after. More importantly, the association of Pearl with Mick and Glory was like one of those small red-hot coals that lurk in what appears to be a spent charcoal briquette that suddenly burns the hell out of you. He didn't want to relive any of that again, both for his sake and for Sally's, but of course he couldn't come out and just say that. After three years of marriage, though, with two kids, one adopted and a little girl of their own, Sally got her way. She told him he wasn't fooling anybody but himself by not talking about it. Finally he gave in and agreed to go.

Once he responded to the Navy Department, they received an official travel manifest to board one of the few remaining Army troop transports still operational for the five-day trip out to the islands. Sally's mother came out from St. Louis to take care of their little ones. The week before they embarked, Marsh learned that two hundred vets and their spouses had been invited. Sally said that would make it easier, since everyone on board would have experienced the same things.

Marsh didn't find that news comforting, either. He had already met some wounded vets who were obviously going to make a life's work of whining about their injuries. Just being at sea again, even on a converted ocean liner, he had to be careful to fully occupy his time and his mind, sometimes with inane activities or conversations, so as not to brood too much about all the friends, classmates, and shipmates who were still out there and who would never be coming back. Even as the transport plowed its way to Hawaii, he was aware that on another transport, at another time, they'd been burying shipmates at sea on this very route.

The day of the Punchbowl ceremony dawned bright and clear. They were all bused out from downtown Honolulu in those familiar gray Navy buses, and once there, the wheelchair brigade got front row seats. Because the president was going to be there, all of them had to be on deck one hour early. Nobody seemed to mind very much. The Punchbowl, which actually he'd never seen in all his years there in Hawaii, was gorgeous. The ancient Hawaiians had thought so, too, because the name of the crater translated roughly to "hill of honor or sacrifice." In many ways, some of them pretty old, it was already consecrated ground. He wondered as they waited if, by taking it over for a cemetery, the haoles weren't breaking some more big kapus.

Sally must have known that he would have a hard time with what was coming, because she held his hand from the moment they sat down to listen to the Pacific Fleet band play. Marsh kept his eyes straight ahead and tried to just listen to the music. A few minutes before the official party was scheduled to arrive, a Navy captain went up to the podium and explained the protocol for the presidential visit. The band would play ruffles and flourishes appropriate for the president and then "Hail to the Chief." Everyone would be requested to stand for the honors. Then he looked down at the line of wheelchairs. "If you can, that is," he said with a smile. "If not, I'm very sure the president will understand."

After the official party was seated there would be an invocation, followed by the president's remarks. Then, he said, there would be a brief awards ceremony.

That surprised Marsh. Most of the vets present were already wearing their medals and decorations, especially among the wheelchair-bound. Marsh hadn't brought any of his since he was going to be in civvies. He looked around at the battered crowd and wondered who was going to get a medal. Then the band sounded off, the guns banged out the salute to the head of state, and there he was, his back ramrod straight, wearing a white suit with his trademark bow tie and those round glasses twinkling in the sunlight. Behind him came Fleet Admiral Chester Nimitz himself. Marsh smiled. For the Navy people attending, it was an honor to be present at a ceremony that included the president of the United States, but Fleet Admiral Chester W. Nimitz? That was like a god stopping by.

Truman's speech was short and utterly to the point. If ever they had a president who did not indulge in BS, here he was, Marsh thought. When he was finished they all gave him a big hand, although some of them, like Marsh, had to settle for banging claws on their wheelchairs. He'd said the right things, and he'd obviously meant them. Marsh was proud of him.

Then Admiral Nimitz got up and took the podium. He looked unchanged since the war, at least from the pictures Marsh had seen of him both during and afterward. I never did get that personal audience with him, he reminded himself. A silence built as Nimitz stood there and rustled some papers on the podium as if he were waiting for something. Then he looked behind the audience and nodded. At what? Marsh wondered. Sally gripped his hand harder. Then two very large Marines appeared in front of Marsh, came to attention, saluted him, and asked if they could move his chair.

"Oh, of course," Marsh said, anxious to get out of the way of whoever was going center stage. He looked left to Sally, whose eyes were for some reason brimming. Then the Marines took charge, as is their wont, and now Marsh was being rolled across the front row and then up onto the stage itself, where the principals were all getting up. Even then, he had no idea of what was coming. He looked anxiously for Sally but couldn't see her, and suddenly he was afraid again. One of the Marines must have sensed it, because a big warm paw landed discreetly on his left shoulder and patted it twice.

They parked him in front of Mr. Truman, who was already standing. The stage and the audience became still. He could hear the flags fluttering and a tropic breeze swishing through the grass along the sides of the Punchbowl. Mr. Truman was looking down at him with a strangely sympathetic gaze. He had a black box in his hand, and finally Marsh understood what was coming. He felt the blood drain out of his face, and only that big warm hand on his shoulder kept him steady in the chair. Now he understood why Sally had insisted they come back to Hawaii. She'd been told.

"In the name of the Congress of the United States of America and a grateful nation," Truman began, "I hereby present the Congressional Medal of Honor to Commander Marshall Stearns

Vincent, United States Navy, Retired, for heroic service and personal valor above and beyond the call of duty as set forth in the following citation."

As he read out the citation Marsh's ears began to hum. He didn't hear a word of it. What he could hear was the cries of his sailors in the dark as the sharks bore in. Once again he saw the rabbi, kneeling on the 01 level on broken legs as the ship began her death roll, his eyes bleeding down his face like Indian war paint, ministering to a man who was already dead. Or the torpedo officer and his talker, who he had thought were still alive, when in fact they had been nailed to the pilothouse bulkhead by a fourteen-inch shell. Or Beast McCarty in his plane with the rearing white horse on the side, turning lazily, almost casually back toward that cruiser that was shooting his Dauntless to pieces and then swooping down like Nemesis herself to break that ship in half. Or Glory Lewis, the bright light of despair in those beautiful eyes, sitting on the front porch of the nurses' quarters, ashamed of herself as a woman could ever be.

Then Harry Truman was bending down, talking to him. Marsh shook his head, trying to silence all those ghosts and clear his eyes.

"I know exactly what you are seeing," he said, so quietly Marsh didn't think anyone but the two Marines holding him up could hear him.

"You're seeing everyone who never came back

and who will never come back," he said, "and that's what you *should* be seeing. You do not 'win' the Medal of Honor. You hold it, and you hold it sacred to the memory of everyone who was with you, the quick and the dead. If you did not weep, you would not be human. If it's any comfort, I still grieve, for all of them, and for all of you. From the United States Congress, and from a grateful nation, our profound thanks."

These kind words from a man who had implacably loosed the fires of the sun itself against two Japanese cities, and who reportedly did not agonize over making that decision for more than ten minutes.

"Yes, sir," Marsh whispered. "I understand. Thank you."

Truman nodded once, then draped the medal pendant over Marsh's head and down onto his chest. Then he stood back and held his hand over his heart as the Navy band broke into "My Country, 'Tis of Thee." The only thing Marsh was conscious of for the next few minutes was that Marine's strong hand, without which, he felt, he would have dissolved into thin air.

It was only much later he realized that he still never did get to meet Chester Nimitz. Sally told him that was all right. It had been Nimitz who'd put him up for the Medal of Honor, she said, and he was never one to intrude on someone else's moment in the limelight.

Nautical twilight was just ending when I finished my tale. My son who was not my son sat in his deck chair, his eyes owl-like and unfathomable. Over on the naval station, a destroyer tested its whistle in preparation for getting under way. The sound carried across the harbor, stirring the sleeping pelicans on their begrimed battleship moorings.

"Got any coffee in there?" I asked, mostly to break the silence.

He nodded absently, then realized that I wanted him to brew some.

"Right," he said. "Coming right up."

He stood up, stretched, and then looked back at me. "I don't know what to say," he said. "I feel like—oh, hell, I don't know what I feel like."

"You go make us some coffee," I said. "I'll get us under way. We have one last thing to do."

"What's that?"

"You'll see," I said. He frowned again.

"It'll be okay," I said.

I clumped up into the bridge area, air-purged the engine compartment, and then lit off the mains. Once they were rumbling happily, I began to bring up the anchor. The boat eased out in the direction of the hook. Across the harbor, that destroyer let out one long and then three short blasts on her whistle as she began to back away from the pier. There were a dozen gray shapes over there on the destroyer piers, all topped with red aviation warning lights, but one suddenly began to separate from the others.

After a few minutes my son brought up two mugs of coffee, one for me and one for himself.

"Where to?" he said.

"Over there," I said, pointing with my chin at the *Arizona* Memorial. "There's something I have to do. *We* have to do."

"I've brought countless visitors to that memorial," he said. "Everyone who comes out here wants to see it. Now you're telling me that my mother is buried there?"

I nodded. The anchor broke ground with a shudder in the chain, and I slipped the boat into forward drive. Since the sun had not yet risen, my son reached over and switched on the running lights.

We drove forward in silence at idle speed toward the white, bridge-like memorial. I could feel his apprehension, but I had none. I'd done my duty and told him the story. It was all so very long ago and well burned out of me, or so I told myself, anyway. Sally knew that my coming out here now, after all these years, to tell our son the truth was being done as much for my sake as his. I thanked God she had the strength to let me do this, even as I told myself that it was all for him.

We drew abreast of the landing on the harbor side of the memorial. The water still shone with the surrounding shore lights. There was nothing to be seen of the sleeping battleship. She'd settled over the years as her bones, both human and steel, disintegrated. I put the boat in neutral, and we coasted along what would have been her port side. The gates to the memorial were closed at the top of the pontoon ramp. The two obstruction buoys winked at us in their measured sequence: Something's here, something's here. Bear away.

I turned to face the memorial, took my son's hand, and recited the following words as we drifted by her tomb:

> *Full fathom five thy* mother *lies;*
> *Of her bones are coral made;*
> *Those are pearls that were her eyes;*
> *Nothing of her that doth fade*
> *But doth suffer a sea-change*
> *Into something rich and strange.*
> *Sea-nymphs hourly ring her knell.*

Our wake caught up to one of the buoys and set it in motion. Its bell complained, allowing me to finish.

> *Hark! now I hear them.*

I turned to him with brimming eyes and squeezed his hand.

"And her name was Glory," I said.

AUTHOR'S NOTES

I first heard the story of the destroyer fight at Leyte Gulf from my father, who was a destroyer division commander in Halsey's fast carrier task force when the battle occurred. He was Naval Academy class of 1927 and rose to the rank of vice admiral before retiring after forty-two years' service. Like many officers of his vintage, he had strong opinions about the battle, and the debates about Leyte probably go on until this day.

As a midshipman I studied the battle in my first-class (senior) year at the Naval Academy in 1963. I can remember voicing some of my father's opinions on what happened to our professor, E. B. Potter (professor emeritus of history at the academy and biographer of Nimitz, Halsey, and Burke) and being taken to task by him for uttering various heresies. The way I saw it, though, Pop had been out there when it happened, so I thought his version was more likely to be accurate.

When my first destroyer visited San Francisco in 1964, I learned that Fleet Admiral Chester Nimitz lived in the big quarters up on the hill on Treasure Island, where my ship was tied up. My dad had told me that if I ever got the chance to meet him, make sure I did. So I called the quarters and told his aide that I was Ensign Deutermann and that I'd like to make a formal five-minute call and that Admiral Nimitz might remember my father. The aide was probably so astonished by this request that he forgot to say no. An hour later I showed up in my best uniform, calling cards in hand, to pay my respects to the admiral who had overseen victory in the Pacific.

Nimitz looked just like every picture I'd ever seen of him except perhaps grayer: I didn't know the meaning of the word "gravitas" then, but afterward I did. He solemnly bade me sit down. A steward brought coffee, which I tried hard to keep from spilling. The admiral told me a story about my dad that I hadn't heard and then inquired if I had any questions for him. I asked him what had been the Navy's most glorious battle of the Pacific war.

Only an ensign would ask such a question, especially the "glorious" part, but he was nothing if not a kind man. He said there were two that came to mind: Midway and Samar, which is another name for what happened that day off Leyte when the destroyers took on the IJN *Yamato* and her consorts. Midway was almost a given, but I then asked how such a thing as Samar could have happened. His aide, aghast at my impertinence, stiffened in his chair, and I scrambled to take back my question, but Nimitz just waved me silent with an imperial hand.

"Don't ever make assumptions," he said,

somewhat sadly. "I made an assumption, and *that's* how Samar happened."

He didn't say: Bill Halsey screwed it up. He was saying: *I* screwed it up. Such was the moral serenity of C. W. Nimitz, and I never forgot it, or his advice about making assumptions.

I wrote this book because I've always wondered what it would have been like to do what they did that day. Having been a destroyer skipper and, later, a destroyer squadron commander, I've often wondered what *I* would have seen, heard, and, most importantly, done when the orders came to go drive off those approaching Japanese battleships, and eighteen-inch shells began to fall around my ship.

I chose in some cases to invent ships' names, such as *Winston*, so as not to tread on the ordeals of the real ships and their officers and enlisted men. Once I did that, I then had to take some liberties with the real history in terms of precisely when and where things happened. After refreshing my own knowledge from more recent works than were available in 1963, I concluded that the pilots from the little jeep carriers played just as important a role in making the Japanese admiral blink as the destroyers had. Some historians/authors take the position that the planes were actually *the* decisive element, leading Admiral Kurita to conclude that Halsey's fleet-carrier formations, by which his forces had already been savaged while approaching Leyte, were right over the horizon. That might be true, but it wasn't the airplanes that made Kurita turn his flagship away in the middle of the fight and effectively out of the action—it was the threat of the destroyers' torpedoes.

Kurita was embarked on the battleship *Yamato*, sister ship of *Musashi*. These two behemoths were the biggest battleships ever built. Admiral Kurita had been promised that he would be supported from airfields on Luzon. No such support ever materialized. Having watched American carrier pilots destroy *Musashi* a day before he came through the San Bernardino Strait to surprise the Taffys, I think he decided to get out of there while he still could once that increasingly hostile aluminum overcast began to form over his head. This persuaded me to write in the character of Mick "Beast" McCarty to tell the story of what the jeep aviators did on that terrifying morning. Beast ended up grabbing a bigger role in this book than I'd anticipated, but that's the nature of carrier aviators, God love 'em.

For a general appreciation of what happened at Leyte, I recommend four books, two of which are recent. *The Last Stand of the Tin Can Sailors*, by James D. Hornfischer, is an outstanding blow-by-blow description of what happened to the destroyers. *Sea of Thunder*, by Evan Thomas, expands on this story by folding in the Japanese view of the battle as well as Admiral Halsey's. Thomas Cutler's 1994 book, *The Battle of Leyte Gulf*, has an extensive bibliography if you want to gain an expert's understanding of the battle. And, of course, there's always Theodore Roscoe's 1953 classic, *United States Destroyer Operations in World War II*, a book I read and re-read a hundred times as a teenager in a Navy family.

All that said, I must beg the indulgence of both the professional and amateur historians who will undoubtedly harrumph when they see some of the historical distortions I've introduced in this story. For instance, in Pearl I've made it sound like the hospital, the base O-club, and the BOQ were all close together. In fact, Hospital Point is part of the Pearl Harbor Naval Shipyard and not really near the O-club or the BOQ. (The hospital is long gone.) I have the Punchbowl cemetery being finished in 1948—that actually happened in 1949. Marsh Vincent's ship, *Evans*, I named for the skipper of the USS *Johnston*, Commander E. E. Evans, USN. USS *Johnston* was one of the destroyers that went down off Samar after a gun duel with a battleship. Commander Evans was of Cherokee extraction, and he won the Medal of Honor for his gallantry that day. Posthumously. There was no USS *Evans* in those days, because the last U.S. Navy ship of that name had been "lent" to England at the start of the war under the Lend-Lease program.

It may also interest the reader to know that there are over two dozen Navy vets whose ashes have been interred within the hulk of *Arizona* since her destruction on December 7, 1941. The Navy has a policy that anyone who survived the attack on that ship may be interred inside her when the time comes. Men who were otherwise veterans of *Arizona* but not aboard that dreadful Sunday may have their ashes scattered over the sunken hulk.

Having finished the book, I still wonder if I would have had the guts to do what those captains did that day, especially Commander Evans, whose decision to turn again into the fight committed his already crippled ship, his battered crew, and himself to just about certain destruction. I've concluded, after twenty-six years in the Navy and three commands, that one simply cannot know until the time comes and the elephant rises over the horizon.

The skippers of those destroyers off Samar apparently had no doubts as to what had to be done. "Glory" is usually an inappropriate word when applied to war, man's most horrific endeavor, but what the planes and the destroyers did that day was surely a moment of glory and unsurpassed valor. To this day, I remain in awe of them.

Center Point Publishing
600 Brooks Road ● PO Box 1
Thorndike ME 04986-0001 USA

(207) 568-3717

US & Canada:
1 800 929-9108
www.centerpointlargeprint.com